ALSO BY JAMES IRWIN

Nina's Friends

LUCKY GUY

JAMES IRWIN

 Vague Apparatus Press

Vague Apparatus Press is the publishing imprint of Vague Apparatus LLC

E-book ISBN:978-1-967223-02-2

Paperback ISBN:978-1-967223-03-9

Cover image is Stiletto, from the Arms of All Nations series (N3) for Allen & Ginter Cigarettes Brands, 1887. The Jefferson R. Burdick Collection, Metropolitan Museum of Art. Image enhanced by Kevin David Pointon aka Firkin via OpenClipArt.

No artificial intelligence was used in the creation of this work. Human Authored™ certification 488392

“Violence is both unavoidable and unjustifiable.”
Albert Camus, The Plague

“When we attempt to exercise power or control over someone else, we cannot avoid giving that person the very same power or control over us.”
Alan Watts, The Way of Zen

“I am free because I know that I alone am morally responsible for everything I do.”
Robert A. Heinlein, The Moon is a Harsh Mistress

Part I

THE INCIDENT

one

Jesse interrupted her morning routine, toothbrush in hand and minty foam on lips, to give Matt grief about going down to Atlantic City for a weekend of poker.

"I expect better from you," she said, although given his commitment to becoming a professional gambler it was hard to understand how she could have expected anything different.

"It's sort of an add-on, after I see Apá," Matt explained. "After Sofia and I meet the social worker."

"Which should be over by noon," she said. "I'd rather you come home."

He couldn't meet her eyes. "Going to the casino is what I do now, like you going to work."

"I go to work to earn money, not to lose it." She shoved the toothbrush back in and retreated to the bathroom, closing the door with enough emphasis to make Matt wince.

When she came down the hallway, buttoning her coat, Matt was on the living room couch in the thin grey sweatpants and faded red Phillies tee shirt that served as his favorite pajamas. Coffee in his favorite old Crystal Cave souvenir mug was propped on his knee.

"I gotta go see my dad," he said, as if that was the controversy.

"Not relevant. I'm glad you're visiting him, though, it's the right thing to do."

"You're dressed nice."

"Thank you, also not relevant." She grabbed her bag from the kitchen table. "I'm worried about the money running out."

"I know. But I'm lucky about this stuff. Something will break my way, it always does."

"You persevere until something good happens, which is not the same as being lucky."

"Perseverance is an outstanding character trait."

She sighed. "The way it has to work, the rewards need to be a lot more than the time and effort invested."

"I can't win all the time," he said. "There's ups and downs, but my luck always comes through."

"Matt, if you were smarter about things, you wouldn't get into fixes in the first place," she said, hand tight on the banister. "Then you wouldn't need to be lucky."

"But I am lucky."

"You make a lot of poor decisions and hope it will work out."

"And it does work out," he said. "Usually."

"We can't stay here on my salary alone."

"I know."

"It's a pleasant apartment and I like it. I don't want to move."

"I enjoy living here too."

"We need to be responsible and think about the future."

"I know."

"You're nearly thirty years old; it's time you got your act together."

"And become like you?"

That startled her. "What's wrong with me?"

"You've changed with this job. Now you use words like *purview* and how you agree with something one hundred and ten percent."

"What's wrong with that?"

"You can't agree one hundred and ten percent, one hundred is the highest you can go."

"It's a phrase, Matt. You're being too literal again."

She left.

Her exit was abrupt, in his opinion. He stood in the empty living room, grateful for the quiet. Unclenching his hands, he focused on breathing, his eyes closed. These confrontations were stressful, exhausting, and made him feel a little outside of his body. He needed to drink a glass of water and have something to eat.

Jesse was a lovely person, and he appreciated that. She was smart, and fun when she wasn't so worried. Sometimes when he looked at her, he wanted to kiss her for hours, or eat her whole, or squeeze her in his arms forever under a starry summer night sky. But lately she was killing his vibe.

Keeping Jesse happy and their relationship intact was one of his two major life goals. She was the most important person in his life, more important than his sister. He felt tethered to her and should that line ever break he was afraid he'd spin out into space, never to find his way back. The other goal was to make a living playing poker. In his daydreams those goals dovetailed, he and Jesse traveling the country as he played high-stakes tournaments, meeting interesting people. It would be an ultra-cool existence.

Unfortunately, he had nearly burned through his gambling stake. He and Jesse had agreed that once it was gone, he would give up the poker career. Of course, when he made that deal, he didn't think he'd ever run out of cash. He anticipated a boulevard of green lights leading to consistent triumph at the tables.

That wasn't how things worked out.

Becoming a successful gambler was going to take longer than expected. Now his immediate need was to find enough funding to keep going. He had to stay in the game long enough for his luck to turn. Unless he had an exceptional idea, however, or the courage to openly betray his promise to Jesse, he would need to give up on his dream. He would have to admit he was a failure.

It was a source of considerable pain that his lack of accomplishment at the poker table threatened the sanctity of his relationship. He feared if he didn't start winning soon, she would be exasperated and throw him out. If he took money from the remaining inheritance, breaking his promise, she would be furious and throw him out. He wouldn't have enough time to turn his poker fortunes around unless he increased his stake, and the best way to increase his stake was the thing that would upset Jesse the most.

He quickly downed half a glass of water and thought about how badly he was in a bind.

He made himself toast with butter and jam, along with plain Greek yogurt topped with a little honey. Another cup of coffee. He showered and handpicked his clothing: jeans, black Nike Air Forces, a chocolate henley sweater over a performance tee. Topped by an olive field jacket, a denim ball cap, and sunglasses he liked, knockoffs of Ray-Ban Clubmasters. He thought of this look as his poker uniform: cool guy on the weekend with a touch of business casual, not intimidating, quite forgettable. The idea was to be unnoticeable until he stealthily emerged as the big winner.

Other players made a statement with their clothes. Some dressed with flair, such as sequined jackets and bold-colored cravats, to distract opponents. Some dressed like Latvian assassins in bad spy movies, all black leather and sunglasses, hoping to intimidate. Some looked like they were attending a Halloween party: the faux cowboy in the ten-gallon hat, the babe in the tight top and overstuffed bra, the bro in the hoodie and backward ballcap, the accountant in tie and glasses, the goofball in the sports jersey and earphones. That sort of thing wasn't for Matt. He didn't have the knack for performance, and he didn't like attention.

He packed his overnight bag, put on his hat and jacket, and looked at himself in the mirror. Not bad, he thought. He headed out to embrace his day.

On the agenda was a reluctant last visit with his dying father.

TWO

There were twenty or so miles between Tohickon in northern Bucks County, where he lived, and the town where he grew up, Norristown, the seat of Montgomery County, crouched on the eastern bank of the Schuylkill River. The landscape between those towns used to be an undulating plain of farms, mostly corn and dairy cows and horses out to pasture, with the occasional orchard. Now condos and apartment complexes much like his own cluttered the view, along with gas stations to feed the cars, fast-food chains to feed the people, and big box stores to feed the lifestyle.

He thought about the argument with Jesse all the way down, replaying it in his mind. Intimate conversations didn't come easy for him, especially if they involved conflict. He tended to overlook, or misunderstand, important moments. Particularly things that were assumed or left unsaid.

Matt entered Norristown at the northeast corner, made his way down Markley Street past his old neighborhood, past his grade school, and on to the river. The town looked shabby; it had been in disrepair for a long time. Even with the train and the nearby expressway for commuting into Philadelphia, and old mansions ripe for renovation that could be had for a song, it had resisted gentrification. Investors had gone elsewhere. A population of about thirty-six thousand people, with nearly twenty percent of them living below the poverty line.

He pulled into the three-story garage that bordered the northern edge of one of the few areas of redevelopment. It was a mix of new businesses and an apartment building, sitting on a long, narrow strip between the river and the railroad tracks. The land was once occupied by breweries, garment and cigar factories, and metal works, when Norristown and the much smaller Bridgeport across the river were thriving business centers. That was all long gone.

The sun was out and strong, and the day was quickly warming, so Matt left his jacket and cap in the car. He crossed the small plaza to Riverside Care, a new, sleek medical facility. His older sister Sofia put their father into palliative care there, after that last stroke sent him into a coma he never came out of. Since Apá still lived in Norristown she thought friends might visit. No one came, as far as Matt and Sofia could tell, and they concluded he no longer had friends, which was sad but not surprising considering the kind of man he had become at the end. He had a sister somewhere in New York State, but she couldn't be bothered to make the trip. When it was clear to everyone he was past the point of no return they moved him to hospice.

Matt did not want to be there. He would have preferred not seeing his father at all, and he found hospitals simultaneously chaotic and dreary. But Sofia said the appointment with the social worker was important, and he had to come.

A sign in the lobby stated the facility was part of the Schuylkill Health System Medical Group, whatever that was. The place appeared modern and clean, but visitors always saw the best sides of hospitals. When he entered the hospice wing, however, it was like stepping into a different world. Soft carpeting with a tasteful abstract design. Color-coordinated, cushioned furniture, and curtains framing the windows. It was quiet as an abandoned church. All of this was for the benefit of grieving relatives; the patients were beyond caring about carpet pile size.

The reception desk wasn't some dented steel thing, but a wooden structure the color of autumn. Behind the desk sat a young woman far prettier than necessary. She appeared calm and sympathetic, but Matt thought he saw lines around her eyes and mouth, a tenseness to her jaw. Maybe sharing space with those a step away from heaven wasn't such an easy gig. She warned him his father was unconscious, sedated, and wouldn't hear him or even know he visited.

He nodded with what he thought was appropriate deferential sadness, crossed the floor to the room, and hesitated a beat before entering. Enrique Martinez, known as Apá to Matt and Sofia as well as to some of his friends and most of his employees, was on his back, blanket to his chin. His eyes were closed, his lips parted. Tubes entered him in several places. He looked thinner and frailer than the last time Matt had seen him. An old man in a coma waiting for his body to completely give out.

"Hi, asshole," said Matt.

For a few minutes Matt sat in a chair and looked at his father. There was a period when Matt had loved and idolized him, Apá the restaurant owner and family man who had space for Matt, had taught him golf and stole time from the restaurant to attend all the games when Matt played pee-wee football. Those early years were the good ones.

Enrique had always been a heavy smoker. While Matt never witnessed it as a kid there was also a lot of drinking. In later years, when people told him the stories they kept from him when he was younger, Matt heard about his father getting drunk at the restaurant, his philandering, his scuffles with men who got on his nerves. But that was his outside life, away from home.

When Matt's mother passed away, however, his father let the demons take control. There were a few periods of tentative sobriety, when Apá was in and out of Alcoholics Anonymous. Other than that, the tobacco and bourbon carved a convenient path for the diseases that put him down, rendering him the quietly wheezing, shrunken simulacrum in the bed.

"I arrived early," said Matt. "Sofia will be here soon. I wanted to spend a little alone time with you. For a proper goodbye."

He closed the door to the room. He paused and sighed. He took out a folded piece of paper on which he had written notes about what he wanted to say, so he didn't forget anything.

"Do you remember the last big fight we had?" Matt asked. "You accused me of trying to sabotage your business, though you couldn't say sabotage, you were too drunk, I thought you were saying 'cabbage.' I laughed at you, which was mean, I admit. You slapped me. Then you threw me out of the house, but I was already on my way because that slap was the final insult I was going to tolerate."

Matt put his right hand on his left forearm and squeezed. Physical repetition calmed him. He referred to his notepaper and started again.

"So I left. Then I found out you told everyone I was a terrible son, a backstabber. You said I was the reason your restaurant was failing after all those successful years. Not your lousy attitude, not your drinking, not your abuse of the staff. Somehow it was my fault. You thought I wouldn't know, but I heard."

Matt paused and looked at the floor, then back at his father.

"All this time has gone, and we've never talked about it. Now we never will. All I can do is tell you what a piece of shit you became, and how disappointed I am in you."

He watched the old man's face, his closed eyelids, and the fingers of his exposed hand, for some gesture, some sign that he was conscious enough to have heard, but there was nothing.

The receptionist knocked on the door, and stuck her head in. "Your sister is here. She asked me to let you know."

THree

M att and his sister sat in the small conference room, walls painted a calming slate blue, waiting for the social worker. Sofia's eyes looked down at the table, her shoulders tense and her skin pale. Her cotton blouse was neatly ironed, her hair carefully pulled back, and the nails on her hands, clasped on the table in front of her, were immaculately manicured.

"You couldn't come into the room yourself?" Matt asked her. "You had to send the girl? You don't want to see him?"

"I spent half yesterday with him," she said without looking up. "I don't think he has anything new to tell me. Were you saying goodbye to him?"

"I said goodbye to him a decade ago."

She nodded. Sofia was fourteen years older, a product of their father's first marriage, and her memories were different. Yes, she could talk of their father's infidelities, and his temper. How he mistreated Sofia's mother until the desperate woman ran away with the soft-spoken man they hired to repair their porch. Nonetheless, Sofia was more attached to their father than Matt was, and more distraught over the old man's condition.

"I talked to a friend who went through this," said Sofia. "She told me the social worker will discuss end-of-life care, make sure there is a plan, guide us through the steps, and offer tips for our own well-being, too."

"I assumed something like that. You going to post about it?"

"I'm a dating influencer, Matty. Why would I post about this?"

"I don't know. Relatability? Sad stories are good for engagement."

Her eyes widened and her entire face seemed to pull back. "No, I will not do that."

He shrugged. "You're more a blogger than an influencer."

"Bloggers are influencers, too. Besides, I'm on Instagram."

"How's it going?"

"There aren't many of us giving dating advice for older single women, so I've attracted a strong following."

"What are your numbers?"

"It's about more than numbers."

"That's what I thought, your numbers are crap."

"They're not crap. Better than your numbers."

"I don't have numbers." He grunted. "Why do the ones giving dating advice stay single? All they do is go out on dates with a parade of new people."

"Uhmmm... That would be the job description."

"Is that true, though? Isn't the idea of dating to meet someone you like well enough to have a relationship? If these so-called experts never go beyond a few dates with anyone, I don't know, it seems like they're not doing it right."

"Well, aren't you being a judgy little boy? You know, women entering the dating pool in their forties or fifties can use advice on how to meet people. What's normal protocol these days, that sort of thing. What I do has value for them."

"I get it. But if I was in that situation, I think the real value would be in helping me avoid the losers. Tell me how to narrow in on people I could fall in love with, possibly marry. If all I want to do is go out indiscriminately, and sleep with a bunch of people, I can get online and do that on my own. I don't need a dating guru for that."

He stood up to make them both a cup of coffee at the pod machine on the credenza. As he added cream to the cups the receptionist stepped in. The person they were meeting was stuck in traffic, the young woman explained, and would be there soon. Matt placed a cup in front of his sister and sat down with his own.

"There's no reason for you to criticize me or make me feel bad," said Sofia. "It's not fair. The dating thing brings in some money, which I need after the divorce. I didn't get an inheritance like some people."

"Oh boy," said Matt, rolling his eyes.

"Well, it's true."

"Sorry we had different mothers and grandparents, Fifi. Not my fault. And I did give you a piece."

She reddened and lowered her eyes. "Yes, you did."

"And you got some coming from Apá, right? You'll be the executor, that comes with payment too, I think." He looked at the coffee in his cup and asked, "Think dad's leaving me anything in the will?"

"I doubt there's anything left for either of us."

He nodded. "The only thing I want is that pair of bronze elephant bookends. They remind me of the good times, way back when I was a kid. They fascinated me, like they were exotic sculptures."

"They're not valuable, you know. You could get something similar at HomeGoods for under fifty bucks."

"I know. It's the one thing I can keep and enjoy. Anything else from him I'd want to take outside and burn."

She finished her coffee and leaned forward. "Speaking of money, is your back still against the wall with this gambling thing?"

He grimaced. "Not been good for a while. I'm thinking about dipping into the primary account."

"No, Matty, bad idea. You promised Jesse you wouldn't. She know about this?"

"God no. She turned pale the first time I told her I played a tournament for a one-fifty buy-in. Like we couldn't afford it."

"I don't think it was the specific amount that bothered her."

"She said, you pay a few hundred to play every time, it won't take long to burn through the money."

"She had a point. I mean, that's what happened, right?"

He waved it away. "I made a little profit that trip, though. That won the argument for me, in my opinion."

"How you did in one tournament didn't address her concerns, and you know that."

"She asked, and not nicely, if I thought it's not gambling if I win once in a while."

"Legit question." Sofia stared at her brother, knowing it would make him uncomfortable. It was a small act of hostility. "You know, taking more from your savings wouldn't only be stealing from yourself, but also the future you and Jesse could have together."

He looked away from her gaze.

"It would be a betrayal of her and of you," she added.

He pursed his lips and put both hands around his empty cup. He said, "When Jesse finds out how little is left of my stash I'll be hearing I-told-you-so's from here to the end of time."

Four

After the depressing conversation with the social worker, Matt left the Riverside Care building and instead of going to the parking garage he crossed the tracks and walked up the hill on Warren Street. He wasn't even sure why; perhaps seeking communion with a painful part of his life.

Matt ended up in that neighborhood when his father slapped him and threw him out of the house. Before Matt walked out the door that night, he saw the shame and guilt on his father's face. He saw the weakness, the lack of consideration for anyone other than himself. He recognized his father as a bully who never grew up, and who was increasingly turning his rage toward his son.

Well, all that was in the past. Matt was confident he had moved on.

He took his time strolling past the brick duplexes. He walked a lot back in that dark period, too, with little money and nothing to do. He'd trek down to the river, where the hospice was now, back when the site was just brush and a couple of abandoned industrial buildings. Occasionally he'd think about drowning himself.

Warren Street had a few curbside trees in those days, but no more. Long ago, he knew, the street had been lined its entire length with sycamores on either side, he had seen old photos. Many of the remaining sections of brick sidewalk were still warped by the roots of those trees, weeds peeking through the joints. He assumed they all died, which saddened him. The absence of trees made the neighborhood appear depressingly bare, less safe, uninviting. In Matt's opinion, trees made everything look better. They kept the neighborhood cooler, held off wind and rain. Sitting on the porch felt a little more private with trees between you and the passing cars. Any block in town looked more civilized with a canopy of trees.

He came upon a dry cleaner at the corner, across from a convenience store with signs promoting snacks, cigarettes, lottery tickets, and Pepsi. He remembered both places from before. He walked by a hairstylist, a hand-written card in the window proclaiming it was a Dominican-style unisex salon. Matt couldn't remember what a Dominican-style haircut was.

He reached the top of Warren where it ended at Church Street. With nowhere else to go that ugly night, Matt had rented a room in a cheap motel at the corner of Warren and Church. Called the Colonial or Valley Forge something at the time, it was a dive, dirty and unsafe, a haven for hookers and druggies and transients. Housekeeping was an older woman and her silent, slow-moving husband, and they did the bare minimum, if that. The room had smelled of dust, bleach, and cigarettes even though you weren't supposed to smoke in the rooms. He stayed there until his money ran out and a friend let him crash on the couch.

The motel was still there, now called the Blue Blanket Inn. It aspired for legitimacy. The sign, emblazoned with a regal serif on a rich cerulean field, was the most elegant thing about the place. There was new paint on the trim and an updated roof, but fundamentally it was the same unhappy, two-story brick structure with external stairs and walkways. Perhaps it had become cleaner and safer since the last time he was there.

He stood at the corner and considered the neighborhood. Grand old homes around him, remnants from the town's best eras, all now chopped up into apartments, some with first-floor businesses. Across Church was a large brick and wood house with an expansive porch missing balusters in the railing, its façade marred by an array of mailboxes. Across Warren was a stone mansion with a round turret that rose above the trees, as if Rapunzel would be at the top. A handful of others, equally large, dotted Church up and down the block, rich people homes from a century before, faded survivors of the prosperous community Norristown had once been.

The motel still featured a boxy detached wing, linked to the main building by a trellised roof over a driveway connecting the front and back parking lots. The wing still held a bar & grill, just as it did a decade earlier. Emphasis on bar, little more than a shot and a beer place that served burgers and sandwiches and grilled chicken, everything with a side of fries. A place populated by neighborhood characters who were too broke or too lazy to go anywhere else.

Out of curiosity, or perverse desire to revisit one of the worst times of his life, he thought maybe he would stop in, have a beer before heading down to Atlantic City. See if the place had changed.

Once inside he saw immediately it hadn't changed, not in any way that mattered; it was the same room he used to hang in. It still smelled of beer and grease. The new wall color had the old lack of personality. The furniture was no more inviting than before. He recognized the pool table and shuffleboard as the same, remembered the bits of graffiti scratched into the wood. The customers, too, appeared unchanged; if they weren't the identical people he saw in the neighborhood back then, it was a distinction without a difference, their lives still in a loop, without progress, unplayable characters in the video game of modern existence. The dim lighting was a blessing.

He scanned the bar. There was a plump older woman in baggy jeans and a loose red blouse with puffed balloon sleeves, a denim jacket draped on her lap, eyeing him sideways. Two older men in flannel and ball caps watched a game show on the television. At the far end was a woman about Matt's age with red hair and round wire-rim glasses, wearing a cable knit sweater over yoga pants. A scrawny young Mexican or Peruvian stared at his phone, in boots and a dirty tee like he recently got off a shift. The same kind of mix that filled any down-market saloon in late morning.

He sat on a stool with an empty spot on either side, to give him a little breathing space. Nobody wants to be crowded in a place like that. He ordered a Yuengling from the hawk-faced, tattooed woman behind the bar.

A voice to his right said, "How you doing, hon?"

It was the older woman in the puffy sleeves, a couple seats to his right. *Oh no*, he thought, *she's going to chat me up, pestering until I buy her a drink. Then in gratitude she'll yak even more.* Not what he planned. He didn't like small talk and was in no mood to pretend he did. What do you say to old people anyway?

But she surprised him by asking, "You look sad, you okay?"

Sad? He didn't think so. Maybe. "I'm fine," he said. "Long day and it's only half over. You know those kinds?"

"I do, hon, I do. Had more than my share. My name's Janice, if you're asking."

"Nice to meet you." He reached across and shook the hand she had stretched out. Then on impulse he lied. "My name's Alan."

Why did he lie? He wasn't sure. It was something he sometimes did with strangers, though. He didn't much like talking with them, and they never seemed genuinely interested in him, so he avoided sharing anything personal. Including his name. What was it to her if he said Alan or Jeff or Matthew? It was all the same to a stranger. Better to err on the side of caution and stay under cover. The woman went back to her drink and the television.

Matt scanned the room and noticed the redhead glancing his way. There was something familiar about her.

He turned to avoid eye contact and contemplated the pageant of old Valley Forge Beer cans lined up on the shelf high above the bar. That brewery had closed decades ago, and dust coated the cans. He remembered staring at the same cans back when he stayed at the motel. There was the white can with the red shield label, the blue can with the red shield label, and the gold can with the white shield label. He started counting how many of each variety there was. He noticed the white cans repeated every nine spots; someone had taken the time to make patterns. Deep into it, he didn't notice the young redhead slide onto the stool next to him on the left, until he felt her knee brush against his leg.

"We're the only ones here under sixty," she said with a chuckle.

Close up, she still seemed familiar.

"Except for that guy," said Matt, gesturing with his chin toward the scrawny worker in the dirty tee staring at his phone.

"Yeah, except for him," she said. "I thought maybe you and me could talk, I'm tired of the grandpas complaining about the price of gas."

Her eyes were a luminous green, peering at him through round wire rims. He remembered the eyes, and similar glasses, from somewhere before.

He asked, "Do I know you?"

"Maybe," she said, her eyes darting around. "You come here a lot?"

That implied she was a regular, which surprised him. She didn't seem like she belonged in that place. But one thing he had learned working in restaurants, hanging out in dodgy bars, and sitting around poker tables, was that most of the time if a person was someplace, they belonged there, even if they didn't appear the type.

"No," he said. "I haven't been in here for years."

"Okay." She did a tilt with her head, like a compulsive thing. He thought she seemed a little buzzy, like a wall outlet spilling electricity onto the floor. She rotated the empty tumbler in front of her, spinning the melting ice at the bottom. She said, "I guess you don't know me, then."

Then it hit him. This was Debra Maines. She was now a little fuller in the face and the waist than she was in high school, and she seemed a bit worn compared to the chatty young woman of a dozen years ago, but it was her. She still had appealing, delicate features and skin the color of peaches. He recalled how she would bounce down the hall, her long copper hair parted in the middle, emerald eyes flashing, vibrant and casually sexy. He assumed the years may not have been kind to her, if she was spending her days in that dump. Was she down on her luck, living a marginal life?

"I guess I don't," he agreed, choosing not to tell her.

"But who knows?" she added. "I meet a lot of people."

How could she not recognize him from high school? They didn't have classes together, but there was a small overlap of friends. They sat next to each other at graduation. He was insulted; was he that forgettable?

She used to have a slutty reputation, the reasons for which he witnessed first-hand during a weekend at the shore. Several of them were crashing on the floor of a rental held by the family of a mutual friend. Matt and his girlfriend at the time, a little miss bossy boots named Rachel, were on cushions, and Debra was in a sleeping bag near their heads. In the group was a football running back named Lenny Stevenson who Matt knew a little from when they were kids. Debra didn't seem to know Lenny at all until meeting him that afternoon, but that night he crawled in with her and they went at it.

Rachel griped about it the next morning, saying that if anyone should do that it should be her and Matt, since they were the only official couple in the crowd. This was mostly a position on principle, since she and Matt weren't having sex at the time, nor would they ever it turned out, since they broke up two weeks later. Not to mention, doing it in front of other people was not something Rachel would have been on board with. His relationship with her was less about romance and hormones, and more about Rachel wanting a boy she could tell what to do, and where to go, and to take her places, like shopping at the mall.

Matt, meanwhile, marveled at how the hook-up between Debra and Lenny the football player had come together, since he had seen no exchange between them, no signals for what was going to happen that night. He could never accomplish that sort of seduction, not only because he was insecure and shy, but also because he was incapable of navigating the complexities of non-verbal communication it must have required.

"My name's Debbie," she said.

Now he was obligated to respond. But he had already told the woman, Janice, on his other side, that his name was Alan, and she was straining her earflaps to listen in on what he and Debra were talking about.

Plus, somewhere deep in the back of his brain, fighting to be heard while the rest of him was so distracted by those eyes and pouty, pink lips, a tiny voice asked: *If she didn't know who I am, why did she come over to talk with me?*

"Alan," he said, raising his glass to her.

Then he noticed her glass was empty, and he gestured to the bartender. The hawk-faced woman and Debra shared glances and a new glass of clear liquid with ice and a slice of lime appeared on the bar.

When Debra reached for the glass to bring it closer, Matt noticed her hands with their long fingers and a way of touching the bar surface that reminded him, for some reason, of a creature exploring the bottom of a lake. Her nails were pink, almost the exact shade of her lips, all of them severely chewed, with little skin tears around the nail.

Poor Debra is anxious or a little obsessive-compulsive, thought Matt.

Her skin tone complemented the deep walnut of the bar in a manner he found aesthetically compelling and sexually attractive. He felt the urge to touch her but didn't dare. She was the hottie teenager that football players had at will, apparently, which meant she was out of his league. Yet now she was flirting with him.

She asked what he was up to that day, what brought him to the motel bar?

"I came down to see my dad," he said, pointing in the river's direction. "He's in hospice care over there in the medical center."

"Sorry to hear that," she said, not convincingly.

"It's okay. He's in a coma, drugged up."

She turned to appraise him through the wire rims. Her pupils were large, and she didn't seem to focus on his face but on something beyond, something through him.

"So, what do you do for a living, Alan?" She leaned in.

He wasn't sure how to answer. What's the right thing to say, when it's complicated? He was never good at boiling the pieces down into a simple statement. "My skills profile is a little erratic," he said. "I'm great at some things, not good at others."

He could tell that was an awkward answer because her face went blank. So he quickly added, "I used to work in restaurants, now I'm a professional gambler."

That got her attention. It got the attention of good old Janice on the other side of him as well; he heard her make a little squeaky noise.

"Wow," said Debra. "I didn't ask about your skills profile, honestly... but professional gambler, that sounds cool."

He shrugged. "After I leave here I'll be down in Atlantic City, playing a little poker."

"Ooooh..." Debra made a fetching round shape with her mouth. "I always wanted to do that, except that I don't know how to play poker. How does it work? You go down and sit at a table?"

"You can, but many of us go down for a tournament."

"I didn't know they did that."

"Yeah they do, in most casinos," said Matt. "The games are serious, but it's affordable down there."

"What do you mean, affordable?"

He gestured for another Yuengling. "You have to register for the tournament before it starts, in person, and you pay your buy-in, to get your stake for the games."

"What's a buy-in?"

He smiled. Most people he talked to were already familiar with this stuff. It was fun explaining it to a newbie, and it let him show off a little. "Like an initial payment. It includes the fee for the house and gives you a certain number of chips. In a tournament it also includes an amount for the prize pool."

"How much is the buy-in?"

"For the tourneys I'll be playing, a few hundred. And it has to be cash."

Her eyes brightened and widened. "That's all you're allowed to play with, then?" she asked, frowning in a way that, if they weren't in a poorly lighted dive bar, might be coquettish. "If it's all gone, is the game over for you?"

"In a tournament yeah. In a regular game no, you can buy more chips if you run out, as long as you have the cash to pay for them. Players bring a lot more than a buy-in." He felt like someone of stature and mystery, talking about this. "Plus, there's more than one tournament per day, so over a weekend you can play several."

Debbie had been leaning in toward him, and they were now touching arms. "Wow. And you need cash for all of them?"

"Yeah. I mean, you can always get the cash out of an ATM down there, but I worry the ones in the casinos tack on a big service fee. So, I come prepared for the weekend."

"That seems like a lot to carry around!" She was so close he could smell her, a combination of inexpensive perfume and vodka and a hint of cannabis.

"Well, that's the rules."

"That is so interesting." She pulled her phone out of her purse. "Sorry, got a text," she explained. She made a show of checking her phone, and said, "I gotta call my friend, she's in Germantown somewhere lost, hold on." She stepped away and went to the other side of the room where she made a call, speaking softly, while monitoring Matt.

"I heard you talking about casinos," said Janice leaning over.

"I thought you might," said Matt. "Do you play poker?"

"No. Used to go down for the slots, though. You ever play the slots?"

"Not my game."

"Mine neither!" She laughed. "No luck at all, that's me. You lucky?"

He smiled. "Yeah, I think I am."

"Yeah, I'll bet. Some people are." Janice was about to say something else but saw Debra returning, narrowed her eyes, and pulled back.

"Sorry about that," said Debra, plopping back onto her seat. "We were talking about your exciting life as a professional gambler!"

"Not so exciting," he said, blushing a little. She was interested in him. He was flattered. A girl who never noticed him when they were teenagers, now fawning over him. Imagine that.

She leaned close and whispered, her hot breath on his cheek, "You must be carrying thousands in cash, right?" He nodded. "Aren't you afraid, walking around with that on you?"

"Nah," he said quietly. Confiding in her was okay, but no reason to tell everyone else in the place. "Who's going to know? I don't appear to be a guy with a lot of money on him, right?"

"No, you don't!" she said, laughing, a trickling schoolgirl laugh. She gave him a little shove on the shoulder, and when she dropped her hand it caressed his thigh, for a moment, just long enough.

In high school, when he was what his mother described as a social late bloomer, the popular girls weren't much interested. To his surprise, when he grew older an attractive woman like Jesse chose him. He wasn't rich, not a movie star, he carried a little excess weight he couldn't seem to drop, and he never figured out how to manage his curly hair, yet there she was. He asked Jesse once, why him? She said he focused on who women were and listened to what they said, and not a lot of men did that. He was honest, and dependable, and said what was on his mind. He had clear moral beliefs, which she considered important.

Was it possible Debra, an object of lust from the past, after all these years saw the same things? Maybe even things Jesse had taken for granted or never understood? Was it possible that all along he only needed to stay the same, waiting for the girls to mature and recognize what he offered? What if—and he smiled to himself at how brazen a thought it was—what if his natural luck created a special aura around him, and some women sensed it and were eager to nourish themselves a little? Even thinking like that was exciting.

He wouldn't figure it out sitting in a Norristown dive bar nursing a midday beer, that was for sure. He'd mull it over later.

Debra leaned closer, her warm breath tickling his neck, and her hand fell onto his thigh and lingered. "I have some coke if you'd like," she said. "We could get a room, have some fun."

FIVE

M att was normally a restrained young man, conservative in his personal habits, and not one to do drugs or pick up women in bars. However, given his belief in luck and his own mystical connection to it, he was capable of recognizing the opportunities luck brought his way. Also, he rationalized, after the morning he had, he could benefit from a little letting go. A little naughtiness. No one would ever know if he indulged in a side festa.

He glanced into Debra's eyes and found them bright and inviting. Two beers in, hormones kicking in, he saw her attractive in the same way she was back in the day, a little trampy but not quite sleazy. In fact, her being trampy was a significant part of the appeal. He nodded his head yes, trying to hide his enthusiasm.

"I know the clerk at the front desk, I'll get a key for us," she said. "But we should be cool about it, this is kind of like my home base, so I got a reputation to worry about."

Matt didn't understand what she meant by "home base," and it also seemed unlikely that her reputation was crucial to her if the home base was this bar. But he nodded in agreement anyway. Sure, it was all fine with him.

"You leave first," she told him, her fingers on his forearm. "Kill a little time. Then go up the stairs to the second floor, wait for me near the rear part of the building."

Nodding, he downed the last of his beer.

"Bye hon," said Janice with a weak smile as he passed her.

Outside, he walked around the motel, lingered on the corner of Church and Warren, checked his phone for messages. Then he went back to the motel stairs, climbed to the second floor, and ambled along the walkway to the rear, where he leaned against the iron railing and waited. He noticed the motel had planted a row of little evergreens in the ribbon of grass between the parking lot and the street, an attempt at improving the property. He counted the evergreens. He counted the few cars in the lot. People living in the motel might be at work, he thought, if they have jobs. The ones using the motel for private time, seeking a location for an affair or a little partying, wouldn't be coming for at least a few hours.

Debra came down the walkway. "No one was in the office," she said, "so I helped myself to the key. We're in two twenty-eight." She nodded toward the door behind Matt.

"They don't mind?" he asked.

"Like they would notice."

"Is it a good room?"

She laughed. "You think there's a difference between rooms in this place?" She smiled and touched his cheek. "I'll settle up with the manager later. He's a nice guy, he knows me."

The room décor wasn't exactly as it was when Matt had resided in the motel years ago, but it didn't seem any different either. The short-napped gray carpet would be rough on bare feet. Pale yellow walls surrounded a queen bed, which was topped by a cover sporting a motif of plant designs in rows, all terracotta and olive green and dark burgundy.

Why name a motel the Blue Blanket Inn, he wondered, *and not put blue blankets on the beds?*

On the nightstand sat a lamp roughly the shape of a rotting tree trunk and the color of the moss growing on one, along with a cheap alarm clock, both bolted down. An air conditioning unit jutted into the room under the window, which was covered by closed drapes in an abstract pattern of colors similar to, but not quite the same as, those on the bedcover. There was a floor lamp, an old wood cabinet with the television and a few drawers, and a shallow side table with a single wooden chair. Matt smiled at the small refrigerator capped by a tiny microwave, remembering how those appliances enabled him to live in the motel back then, when he was desperate and all but broke.

It was like any of the dreary, inexpensive motels dotting the country coast to coast.

"I stayed in this place for a couple of weeks," he confessed to Debra as he inspected details. "It was long ago. Bad time in my life."

"Oh yeah?" She didn't seem all that interested, staring at her phone. "I heard it was pretty crappy back then. It's not so bad now, I guess."

"I found a syringe under the bed once."

"Eewww!" She didn't raise her head. Nor was she making any moves to get cocaine out of her purse or take off her clothes. He wondered what they were doing there.

He asked, "Should I check under this bed, see what we get?"

"If it's a syringe don't tell me about it."

He got down on his knees, lifted the cover where it touched the floor, and examined under the bed.

"Holy crap," he mumbled to himself.

Lying near the wall, nearly hidden by shadow, was a long knife. Matt perceived it as well-made, dangerous. Who would put a knife like that under the bed and why? Someone who wanted a weapon close by, obviously. Maybe a druggie worried about his real or imagined enemies, or a prostitute uncertain about her customer. Whoever it was, how could they forget something both dangerous and valuable? Someone who had to flee the room, perhaps, or died of an overdose, or needed to hide it from the police. Matt imagined how it would have been, the knife closer to the edge of the bed where it would be handy for its owner to reach down and grab when the time came. Later, when its owner left, it could have been pushed further under the bed by a vacuum.

He retrieved it. In his hand it was even more impressive. The blade was at least nine inches long, frighteningly sharp, tapering to a point that threatened to pierce armor. The handle was black metal with a dark wood grip, a dramatic and likely high-cost design. The lack of dust and the sheen of the blade suggested it hadn't been there long, maybe week or so at most. Beautiful and scary.

Someone knocked on the door.

Still on the floor, Matt heard Debra curse and say, "Too early, asshole." At first, he assumed she was talking to him, and was confused. Why would she say that? What had he done? He pushed himself up and stood, holding the knife in his right hand along his leg.

She opened the door, and a man walked in. Matt recognized this person from high school, too. His name was Anthony Ciccone. They had been in the same peewee football camp when they were kids, though Anthony was two years older, and almost certainly wouldn't remember Matt. What upper classman paid attention to anyone younger?

Matt remembered Anthony as uncoordinated but big, one of those boys who grew faster and larger than his peers, and thus imagined themselves as athletically gifted because, for a few early years, they could hit or throw a ball farther or block any shot. Until, of course, their classmates caught up and put the lie to that. High school exposed Anthony as mean, lumbering, and not smart. Now he was gym-muscled, thick with a layer of fat, his face flush from steroids or amphetamines or alcohol, the scarlet showing through several days of beard growth. He wore a greenish-gold hoodie sweatshirt the color of sick baby puke.

Anthony closed the door behind him and scowled at Debra, who didn't show any concern. "What the hell is going on here?" he asked.

"Nothing, babe," she said.

"Don't nothing me." His teeth were gritted, his eyes bloodshot, and he put a lot more energy into the performance than she did. He turned to Matt. "This the guy you've been fucking?"

Matt took a step back. Anthony stripped off his sweatshirt and tossed it on the bed; it had a huge American eagle design on the back, in front of one of those blue and black American flags that means either police solidarity or white supremacy, depending on who you asked.

It was one of the ugliest sweatshirts Matt had ever seen.

Under the hoodie Anthony wore a black tee with "Hatebreed" on it in flaming blackletter type, hovering over a skull wearing sunglasses;

Matt assumed it was a band. He found Anthony's entire presentation ridiculous.

"No babe, he didn't mean anything!" said Debra, with not much conviction. "Don't hurt him."

Matt was confused. There was a lot of intense emotion from Anthony, but it wasn't being matched by Debra, who seemed annoyed. Matt often had trouble with the complexities of social interactions, but this was on a different level. How was he supposed to respond?

"Sure, I won't hurt him, much," said Anthony, taking a small step toward Matt, who retreated a little more, his butt hitting the wooden chair. He was running out of space.

"He's got cash," said Debra. "He can pay his way out of this. Can't you Alan?"

"Pay my way out of what?" asked Matt. "I didn't do anything."

"Maybe I'll mess him up and take his cash anyway," said Anthony, eyes darting toward Debra. "Then I'll smack your lying ass, bitch."

"Leave her alone," said Matt. Both Debra and Anthony turned their heads in surprise at his bold, gallant, foolish response.

Anthony said, "I think first I should shut his fucking mouth."

Something is wrong about this, thought Matt, trying to parse it out. The entire scenario was out of whack.

Anthony stomped forward, his large hands tight fists, the muscles in his forearms tense, his face a red mask of rage. At the last moment he dropped his arms, leaned forward aggressively, and stuck out his chest to bump against Matt's, clearly intending to make contact strong enough to send Matt backwards against the wall.

Matt, however, without thinking about it, brought his hands up in defense. His right hand still held the nine-inch knife, the tip pointed out. Anthony didn't notice because he was focused on Matt's face, which was turned away in fear. Anthony stepped into the blade, hard and urgent, and it entered his chest through the blackletter R on the tee shirt, and into his heart.

Matt felt the initial resistance, felt the knife enter Anthony's chest. He glanced down, saw the blade was in nearly to the hilt. Alarmed, he pulled it out, frictionless, as the blade was sharp as a razor. He saw the shock in Anthony's eyes, which dimmed. The angry, muscled bully lost consciousness.

"Tony!" squawked Debra in a choked, shaken voice.

Anthony crumpled to the floor.

Debra growled, bounded over the bed, and jumpcd on Matt's back, trying to pull him away from her dying boyfriend. She reached around and grabbed his nose, and his chin. Thrashing left and right, like a punker in a mosh pit, Matt tried to toss her off, but she was manic and shockingly strong. Desperate, Matt reached back with the knife, jabbing. The blade hit her skull, slicing a strip of skin on the top of her head like an orange peel, then taking part of her ear. Another jab pierced her eye and penetrated the socket. She screamed, most of it muffled against his shoulders. He slammed his head back, breaking her nose, but she wouldn't release her grip on his chin and her left hand had moved to his throat, tight, cutting off his oxygen and strangling him. One more frenetic backwards jab with the knife entered through her temple and penetrated deep into her brain. She grunted three times and slipped off him, leaving Matt standing, trembling and astonished, in the middle of the motel room, knife in his hand, his shoulders covered in blood.

"Oh my god," said Matt. "This is not good."

SIX

A part of Matt's mind separated from his body and looked down. *Is this real? Or just a daydream, a bit of delirium?* It was certainly a spectacular capper to what had already been a wretched morning: Jesse criticizing him, the sniping with Sofia, sitting reluctantly with what was left of his father. Now this.

He caught himself turning woozy and took stock. There were no shouts from outside, no hurried footfalls on the walkway, no sirens approaching. The room was silent, other than his labored breathing. The air was still dense with the electric tension of violence, and the room smelled dreadful. Blood stained Matt's hands and sleeves. The back of his head and neck were wet. Two people lay dying on the floor.

He didn't panic, didn't cry. *Why am I so calm?* He dropped the knife, then ran to the bathroom and vomited in the toilet. When he finished, he rinsed off his hands and splashed water on his face. The mirror assured him, to his relief, that Debra hadn't marked him. Thank goodness for her compulsive nail-biting. That was a bit of luck.

He felt dizzy and wandered back to prop himself against the side table. Debra was on her back a foot away, a pool of blood beneath her head, her right eye socket a dark, destroyed mess, and he avoided looking at her. Anthony's tee was turning darker on the front, the white blackletter type now burgundy.

How did I miss the danger flags? Same as he always missed the subtle stuff, he decided. *How did I think she was interested in me?* Because she said she was, she touched him, and he took her at face value.

Badger game. An outdated term, he learned it from old movies. Would other people have picked up on that? They were running a badger game on him, although at the end it was turning into straight-up robbery. *Should I call for an ambulance? Are they still alive? Can they be saved? Should I turn myself in?*

"Self-defense," he said aloud, trying it out, feeling the weight of it in his mouth, assessing plausibility. He repeated it half a dozen more times.

The police wouldn't believe him. He was the only one with a weapon. They would never accept such an expensive, formidable knife would be lying under the bed, where and when he would need it. He barely believed it himself. Matt imagined telling them the knife was there simply because he was a lucky guy and of course it would be. He imagined how that would go over.

The stress was rising. He was not yet disturbed by his actions, but he was concerned about the consequences.

Why wasn't he covered in Anthony's blood? Why did the man collapse like that? Matt searched the Web on his phone. He learned that a stab wound to the heart, which he believed had happened, would cause significant blood loss, resulting in cardiac arrest. The knife was so sharp and thin, blood seeped through the wound rather than spurted, the rest contained within the chest cavity. The drop in blood pressure was severe and quick, so Anthony collapsed and lost consciousness. He would be brain-dead inside of ten minutes, and dead-dead soon enough. It was already over for Anthony.

What about Debra? He didn't even want to think about piercing her eye socket, that was disturbing. What about the side of her head? The stab through Debra's temple would have caused a lot of bleeding, explaining the back of his head, and at least some brain injury, though how much was down to whether the knife moved around when insert-ed. Matt didn't know about that, things were frenetic at that point. Did he jam it right in and right out again, or when he was thrashing about, trying to get rid of her, did he scramble her brains like an immersion blender? *Jesus, what a disgusting thought.* What he read online said she could still be alive, despite how she seemed. It took minutes to summon the courage to touch her. He didn't feel a pulse.

Okay, then. They were both dead. Now what was he going to do?

He spontaneously rehearsed plausible explanations. "I didn't expect this," he said to the room. "I didn't expect this, didn't see it coming. It wasn't in my plan for the day. I was unprepared. They kidnapped me. They were running a badger game. It was self-defense. It was an accident."

He sounded desperate.

Even worse: "I found the knife when I checked for syringes under the bed."

His brain felt cloudy. His vision was like viewing everything through a gauze curtain. Muffled car noises from outside. Revolting smells thickening the air. His head hurt. His insides were like a tangle of bungee cords.

A few minutes later he went to the bathroom and retrieved a wad of toilet paper. With it, he lifted the knife off the floor and smeared the blood where his fingerprints would be. He rubbed the knife into Debra's blood and tried, as best he could, to put her fingerprints on it. Clotting had already begun, and it was sticky. Careful to avoid stepping into any blood pools on the carpet, he did the same with Anthony, then dropped the knife between the two of them. He flushed the toilet paper.

With a new wad of toilet paper he went through Anthony's pockets, finding two condoms and a wallet with over three hundred and fifty dollars. He put the wallet on the nightstand, crushed thirty-two dollars, which felt like a plausible amount, into a wad and placed it next to the wallet. The rest of the money he shoved into his pocket.

Pulling down the bed cover exposed the ghosts of old stains. He put the pillows in a couple of places on the bed and tossed the condoms into the middle, then tore one of the condom packages half open and tossed a pillow onto the floor at the far corner of the room.

Debra's small sling purse was a bonanza. In it were twenty-six little baggies—Matt counted—almost certainly crack cocaine. Also, a baggie of what appeared to be regular cocaine, so Debra actually did have some. He dumped a teaspoon of the white powder onto the top of the nightstand, getting some on the wallet. He snorted a bit of it off his finger, not too much, to help him focus. There was a clear, unmarked vial with pills Matt didn't recognize. Maybe opiates? He opened it and put it on the nightstand, on its side, pills artfully spilling out. There were several flat little blue and white envelopes labeled as Suboxone; he didn't know what that was so he left them in the purse. Debra also had over a thousand in cash shoved in an envelope with scribbles on the front. He counted out nine hundred and sixty dollars and put it in his pocket with the rest of the cash, then tossed the envelope onto the bed by the condoms.

He stepped back and surveyed his handiwork. It wasn't a Macy's window at Christmastime, but it would do. It was a complicated and sordid tableau filled with significant but contradictory and meaningless clues. He hoped it would keep the Norristown police busy running into each other.

"I can't believe you didn't know who I was," he told Debra on the floor in front of him. "You fucked Lenny Stevenson two feet from the top of my head. We sat next to each other during graduation, for chrissake."

In the bathroom he removed the plastic bag lining the small trash bin and was happy to find two replacement bags underneath. He stuffed his blood-soaked henley and performance tee into one of the bags. He soaped up the washcloth from the wire shelf on the wall and washed off the blood from his neck and head as best he could. He washed his hands, and wiped off the sink and the faucet handles and the toilet flush lever. When he was finished, he dried off. His pants and shoes would need to be replaced but they were okay for now. He put the soap bar, washcloth, and towel into a second plastic bag, and tied both bags.

He retrieved Anthony's green-gold hoodie and put it on. It stank of sweat and strong cologne. He zipped it all the way up and pulled the hood as far forward over his head as he could. Cradling the two packed plastic bags under his arm he stepped over the bodies, opened the door, and dared a glimpse outside. There was no one on the second-floor walkway, and he didn't hear voices below. He hurried toward the stairs.

Out of the corner of his eye he saw movement below. Janice, the older woman in the puffed sleeves who chatted him up, was walking away from the bar & grill toward the back of the motel, to the other side. He couldn't stop now, and quickened his pace. She half-turned and watched him descend the stairs, his back to her. He walked up to Church and turned right, heading around the block to his car in the parking garage near the medical center. Janice watched the man in the ridiculous sweatshirt disappear behind a building near the corner, then continued to her room.

***

Matt didn't stop driving until he pulled off into a shopping mall near Deptford in New Jersey, where he visited several stores and purchased a set of new clothes from underwear to shoes, a box of heavy-duty black plastic trash bags, and a jumbo shopping tote. He paid with some of the cash stolen from Debra and Anthony. He changed in a restroom stall. Pants, shoes and underwear went into a black trash bag, with Anthony's hoodie into a separate bag. He put the two black trash bags into the shopping tote, and left the mall. Back out at his car, the two bags filled with bloody clothes and linens from the motel went into a third black trash bag.

He blasted rock all the way. People tended to be surprised that a guy who disliked noise, who found even a television on low volume across the room an annoying distraction, would listen to such intense music. But that was the point. If Matt was trying to read or write or do something personal, the chatter from a TV was an intrusion, demanding attention from him. But aggressive music wasn't intruding in his space, it *was* the space, creating an aural cocoon that protected him. Nothing could get in. And at moments such as these, "Black Tongue" by the Yeah Yeah Yeahs filling the cabin of the car like carbon monoxide from a loose hose, what it was protecting him from the most was his own distressed thoughts.

He pulled off the Atlantic City Expressway by the Gloucester Premium Outlets where he parked in the rear and placed the bag with the bloody items into a dumpster behind the Reebok store. A little later he pulled into the transportation center in Sicklerville where he disposed of the bag with Anthony's hoodie. Further down the Expressway, at the Frank S. Farley Service Plaza, he paid cash to gas up his car and disposed of the third trash bag in a large bin by the pumps.

In his room at the Ventura Hotel Casino in Atlantic City, he took a shower and fell back on the bed. He stood again, raced to the bathroom and vomited; brushed his teeth, stumbled back to the bed and lay on it, his head on the pillow, staring at the ceiling.

The truth was, he still didn't feel horror at the violence he committed. The nausea was from stress, not guilt. He shouldn't feel remorse, he told himself. Those people intended to rob him, perhaps worse. They were criminals. Drug dealers, likely addicts themselves. Bad people. It was something that happened to him, and he responded. It wasn't personal and could have happened to anyone who entered that bar. He would bet those two had pulled that sort of thing multiple times before.

He wondered if Debra would have left Matt alone if he immediately told her they went to school together. What if he waited until the motel room, would they have let him go because he could identify them, or would they have killed him for the same reason?

He felt a little pride in being able to defend himself in a tough moment, and gratitude for the outrageous good luck in finding that knife. He was a lucky guy. It wasn't limited to the knife, either. It was giving a false name to that lady in the bar. It was Anthony taking off his sweatshirt and tossing it where it wouldn't get bloody. It was no one hearing Debra's shouts. It was the extra plastic trash bags in the bathroom. Luck, luck, luck, all the way down. Matt felt invincible.

Good luck, bad luck, consequences. Thinking about it made Matt dizzy. He stressed about it all until, exhausted, he dropped off into sleep.

The day was far from over, however.

seven

Earlier that day, while Matt and Sofia critiqued each other in the conference room of the hospice wing at Riverside Care, Jesse was at her job as a benefits analyst in human resources for a tech company, where she was overworked and undercompensated. She should have been drafting a travel reimbursement update memo, which her boss wanted to see and approve by end of day. Instead, she stared out the window thinking about the situation with Matt.

Contrary to what her boyfriend assumed, she had an excellent idea of how little was left in his gambling stash, because she had been paying attention all along. It was why she was spending so much time that morning worried about their finances, stressed over their fight, and anxious about their future together.

Things did not look good from her point of view. Oh joy.

***

She and Matt first talked about poker while they were walking on a trail through woods in the northern part of Valley Forge Park. They had paused at the edge of a meadow to watch a large herd of white-tailed deer emerging from the trees.

"I can't do the restaurant thing any longer," he said, without any context. "Out on my own, away from Apá, having management responsibility, it was exciting at first. Back then I thought, look at me, I'm an adult. Now I hate it."

"Okay," she said. "You should look around for something else. There's always opportunities for good restaurant managers."

"It's the business I hate not the job," he said. "I've been pretending for a while I was fine, but I haven't been fine at all."

Jesse had noticed he wasn't fine. As he put extra effort into his work, he became increasingly miserable. "I understand being a manager can be too much work and stress," she said. "Go back to being a server, or a bartender. You'll probably make more money anyway, if it's a good place."

Matt shook his head. "I don't know..."

"I don't want to bring up a touchy subject," she said, "but does this have anything to do with your father, that he ruined the business for you?"

"Some of it is that, maybe. But the problem is the environment. I'm overwhelmed by the noise and the people. There are constant changes: daily specials to be memorized, different sizes of dining groups, kitchen personnel that come and go. It all makes me uncomfortable. I tried convincing myself that I needed to work through it. I told myself everyone else seemed okay with the business. If not, why would they work there? If they can do it, why can't I?"

"You should have told me about this earlier. We could have talked it through."

"Yeah, I know. Isolating made it worse, honestly."

"So what would you rather do instead?"

"Play poker."

That brought her up short. She turned away from him, so he wouldn't see the surprise on her face and take it for judgement. Her eyes rested on a doe, about twenty yards away, leading her two fawns toward the trees. The doe paused and looked into Jesse's eyes as Jesse looked into hers.

There was no context for this poker idea that Jesse knew of. Where was this coming from? Playing online? She assumed he was half-joking, and that it was a pipe dream, the fanciful hope of a frustrated young man. In keeping with that, he didn't talk about it after that walk, other than a passing comment or two on bad days at work.

Then his maternal grandfather died.

After debt resolution, and a sum for the grandfather's church, the inheritance was substantial, in the low six figures. Not life-changing but enough to prompt soul-searching on the part of both of them. Enough for Jesse to think about putting a down payment on a house, though she acknowledged it wasn't her money, and they weren't married.

Enough for Matt, on the other hand, to see it as an opportunity for an entirely new career. Soon enough, being a professional gambler was all he thought about. In Matt's mind, playing poker for a living was a sensible choice. He loved playing cards and always thought of himself as a lucky person. He believed he was good enough to pull it off, despite (or perhaps because of) his limited experience.

Jesse was horrified. Disregarding her anxiety, he quit his job and took sixty grand as his gambling startup fund. To compensate for the loss of his income, before he started generating positive cash flow from the tables, Matt proposed he take a portion of their living expenses out of the inheritance funds. Jesse was expected to cover the rest of the bills through her income.

"Short-term, babe," he assured her.

She saw the sixty grand as too little for what he wanted to do and too much for what they could afford. The risk seemed monumental. Household expenses would be too much burden on her shoulders. She thought the entire project was a waste of money and opportunity. She believed it should be invested, and told Matt as much.

"It is being invested," he said. "It's an investment in me!"

"I feel like I'm subsidizing our slow collapse," she responded.

He said that kind of attitude didn't do a lot for his confidence. He also pointed out it was his money to do with as he wished. In response, she pointed out while that was true, he was also quitting his job, reducing their joint income, so his poker obsession directly impacted her.

And so, with fundamental conflicts unresolved, Matt started off on his absurd pursuit. All Jesse could do was stand off to the side and wait for the inevitable crash and hope the damage to their finances and their relationship wasn't insurmountable.

***

Later in the day, as her boyfriend was cleaning the blood off his hands in the motel, Jesse had a small salad for lunch in her cubicle. As he was disposing of evidence in New Jersey she worked on that reimbursement memo, trying to ignore the anxious thoughts that intruded. She still didn't understand what Matt was doing, nor why he was doing it. Wouldn't it be better to have a comfortable, modest life, one that was well-managed? She was risk-averse, didn't like major changes in her life, and had long thought he was much the same way. Now she wasn't sure. He was the same, but not. Who was this new Matt?

Her cell chimed and it was Sofia, Matt's sister, suggesting they meet for a drink after Jesse ended work. This sort of thing was not typical of Sofia, who led a dense social life and preferred her calendar organized well in advance. She was not prone to spontaneous invitations, nor was Jesse prone to accept them.

"Okay," said Jesse, naming a place. "Are you in the car?"

"Yup," agreed Sofia. "I'm heading out for a day date with a man I met online. In New Hope. Maybe a walk, stick my head in a few shops."

"Good enough weather for it."

"I have high hopes," said Sofia. "He owns a coffee shop, used to have some management role in the insurance industry, seems smart and financially savvy, and I like coffee. Wish me luck."

"Wished. In the meantime, how concerned should I be about this conversation you want to have? It sounds like bad news is coming." Her voice was shaky.

"Nothing bad, only some info to share," said Sofia.

Jesse could immediately tell Sofia was, if not lying, at least misleading. More bad news was incoming, she was sure of it.

EIGHT

A few hours later Sofia sat in her car in the restaurant parking lot, worried about her brother. By the time Matt and Apá began fighting Sofia been out of the house and married. She understood the arguments were ostensibly about whether Matt was going to take over the restaurant. But as an occasional first-hand witness, and knowing the two of them as she did, she understood the actual conflict was Matt's dislike of the man his father had become. Enrique once confided to Sofia, in a rare moment of insight, that he suspected Matt blamed him for the death of Matt's mother. This was true, though Sofia did not confirm it, sparing him that. The fights between father and son continued for years of swallowed resentment and stubbornness on both sides, until the bond between them permanently broke. And now here was Matt going through some sort of existential crisis around his professional and personal lives, and she wondered if she should have done more to help him.

Well, no one intervened before I married my idiot ex-husband, she thought as she got out of the car, so we all have things we would change, if we could.

The Stone Tavern was a sprawling suburban eatery covered in faux-stone facing, with an attached event space, serving elevated pub food and a vast array of craft beers. It was a couple of miles outside of Colmar, where Jesse worked. Sofia made a quick stop at the central bar in the wood-paneled main space, then continued into one of the smaller rooms toward the back, where she found Jesse, an Aperol spritz on the table in front of her, near a window offering a view of the dollar store across the street.

"I thought I'd pick something up at the bar on the way in," said Sofia, holding up a glass. "I knew you'd already be started!" There were air kisses and a hug.

"I'm thrilled to see you," said Jesse. "What do you got there?"

"It's a Paloma. Think Mexico in the fifties. The bartender was too young, didn't know how to make it, I had to tell her. Try it."

Jesse took a sip. "Oooh."

"Yeah. Tequila, lime juice, and grapefruit soda. Like a margarita but more snooty."

"I hope meeting here wasn't out of your way. You are something, the things you cram into your schedule."

"It's planning, Jesse. Your calendar is your friend. Plus being efficient."

Jesse responded with a shrug and a head tilt; it was easy for Sofia to talk like that, but not everyone was wired the same way. "How did your date go, then?"

"Was it a date?" Sofia frowned. "I'm not sure. A meet-up, certainly. He was nice enough, though not the most talkative man I've ever met. I made the mistake of telling him I'm a dating influencer. He pulled up my account on his phone, right there as we were walking over the bridge."

"Oh dear."

"That was the end of that. He didn't like I told everyone I was seeing him."

"You mentioned him by name?"

"No! But he said, since I wrote he owned a café in New Hope, used to work in insurance, and owned a Schnauzer, it would make him easy to identify."

"To be fair, he had a point."

"What he really didn't like was how I talked about my dating strategy, and where I placed him in it. Said it was demeaning."

"He ended it right there?"

"He didn't jump over the railing into the water, if that's what you mean. He was polite enough about it."

"Sorry that happened. A lot of people will find the situation uncomfortable, I guess."

Sofia waved it off. "I'm not changing my social media approach to make some man more comfortable. There wasn't a spark, anyway. I did get some charming photos of myself and a few good anecdotes for the blog, before he bailed."

"Well, there you go." They clinked glasses and drank.

"How are you doing?" asked Sofia.

"We're overworked and understaffed, and my boss is terrible."

"At least the benefits are lousy."

"She's not the worst boss I've ever had," said Jesse. "She's not evil or malicious. It's that she has the worst personnel management skills in the history of the universe, and it causes nothing but stress."

"I love when you talk like this, it makes me feel better about my career choices."

The waitress came by to check on them. Sofia spoke with her in Spanish.

"They have some zucchini bite things that sound good," she said to Jesse as the waitress left. "We can share an order."

"How did you know she spoke Spanish?"

Sofia laughed. "I heard her and the bartender talking."

"I wish Matt could speak it. There's lots of times where it would come in handy."

"Different mothers," said Sofia. "My mom was Columbian and they spoke Spanish all the time in the house when I was growing up. Matt's mom was German-Irish and she never learned it, so neither did Matt. Our dad couldn't be bothered to teach him."

"That's too bad."

"No, it's for the best. Toward the end dad used to insult Matt in Spanish and Matt assumed it was the usual complaining. If he knew what Apá was saying he would've been super angry." Leaning forward, she asked, "So how's things with my brother, then?"

"He's down in Atlantic City for the weekend again, but I imagine you know that," said Jesse. "I wish he'd give this poker thing up and get his career back on track."

"It doesn't seem to make him happy."

"Which one? The career or the poker?"

"Both, from what I can tell."

"He thinks he's good at gambling," said Jesse, "but I can tell he's not."

"The bank account tells you that. He's deluded."

"The way he talks about it, like it's his job."

"He assures me he's lucky, that's how he knows he'll be successful," said Sofia with a sad shake of her head. "Honey, let me assure you that boy's never been lucky."

Jesse nodded. "I can see it for what it is, the rationalization, the delusion. But he can't."

"He can lose five hundred bucks, but then if he wins fifty he thinks he's a hero."

"His idea of good luck is wearing down the bad luck."

Sofia laughed. "Like a boxer who lets himself get beat up, until the other guy collapses from exhaustion. Not a sustainable strategy."

Jesse nodded, laughed, and wiped a small tear from her eye. "We had another fight this morning."

"He seemed crabby."

"I insulted him again, said he makes too many bad choices."

"Truth there. Sometimes I think he's incapable of making a smart decision. Except for dating you, of course."

"Well, yes of course," said Jesse with a small, wry smile. "He's not that bad, though. It's the gambling."

"That's why I called you, so we could meet up," said Sofia, becoming a little more serious. "He told me something today I think you should know."

"You said it wouldn't be bad."

"It isn't... not yet anyway. At this point it's information. Please, see if you can keep it to yourself, if he finds out you already know before he tells you he'll figure it came from me and we're barely getting along as it is, with the pressure from dad and all."

"Okay. I don't think I'm going to like this."

"He's burned through his gambling stake."

"That I know."

"He's thinking about dipping further into his core savings."

Jesse sighed. "Which is what I've been afraid of. Which he said he wouldn't do. That promise was the reason I was okay about the stupid poker experiment. I figured he would last a while with the stake he had — a lot longer than he has, actually — and get the gambling thing out of his system."

"I know."

"I expected he would learn a few lessons. Be inspired to grow up."

"Reasonable assumption," said Sofia. The waitress brought the appetizer, then left. Sofia reached around the plate and took Jesse's hand in hers. "Guys get the motorcycle they always imagined they wanted, then six months later they admit they didn't know what they were thinking, and they sell it. Should have been the same for him and cards."

"But that's not what happened," said Jesse, her eyes moist. "Now I don't know what to do. It's like he's destroying our relationship over this."

"Don't despair yet. He'll figure things out."

Jesse began tearing up again. "As long as I've known him, he's always had a plan, always tried to work things out in advance."

"To control things."

"Yes. But now he seems to be making it up as he goes. Trying this gambling thing on a whim, jumping around to casinos, being impulsive about the inheritance."

"You're worried that's out of character?"

"No, the opposite. I worry this *is* the plan, that he's not being impulsive. That he never intended to quit no matter how poorly he did."

Sofia didn't know what to say to that.

Jesse rolled her eyes. "This is not a one-sided situation," she said, a little fire in her voice. "I'm not sitting and waiting for him to make the right decision. I have a life I want to live, and I make my own choices too."

"Yes."

"I have a stressful job and a lousy boss, and a car I need to replace soon before it strands me in the middle of nowhere. But at least all those things are mine."

"You're in a tough situation," said Sofia. "But you're holding up well."

"I'm not just a bystander in this, I'm capable of fighting for my relationship," said told Sofia sharply. "But if it comes to it I'll fight harder to protect my own well-being."

"I know, I didn't mean..."

"I proved this to myself soon after Matt started playing poker. This is a secret, Sofia, the biggest secret I ever kept, and you can't tell anyone, but I want you to understand who I am. I got pregnant, and didn't want the baby. I didn't think our life could handle it, I wasn't ready, Matt certainly wasn't ready. So I never told him about it; I never told anyone. When he went on one of his multi-day trips to play a poker tournament down the shore, I terminated it. I expected to carry that secret to the grave but here I am telling you."

Sofia was stunned. "*Hijole*, I had no idea. I'm sorry you had to go through..."

"That told me a few things about myself. I was overwhelmed with sadness at the loss, and all the what-ifs. There was also the pervasive guilt about keeping it from Matt. But I did it, dammit, on my own, without anyone's help or interference."

They sat in silence for a minute or two. "That was an important moment in your life," Sofia said eventually.

"Hell yeah."

Sofia nodded, and said, "I don't blame you if you kick him out." She took up one of the zucchini bites. "I'll let him crash at my place, but not for any longer than a month." She bit into the appetizer.

THE CASINO

NINE

M att opened his eyes, disoriented. He'd been having some kind of nightmare, about which he remembered nothing, and was relieved to find himself in the room at the Ventura Hotel Casino. The shades were drawn, the room dark. His watch told him it was after five. *In the morning? I couldn't have been asleep that long!* But no, it was five in the afternoon.

He turned on the bedside lamp, sat up, and inspected the room. The walls were a grayish beige, the bedspread a creamy beige, the carpet a brownish beige, the abstract art on the wall was three shades of beige with bits of turquoise and scarlet and emerald. The furniture was also beige, but not as grayish as the walls, nor as creamy as the bedspread.

Unpleasant memories surged: the incident in the Norristown motel had been real, not a nightmare. He hoped he covered his tracks, and that he would never have to answer for what he did. There was a life to live and he deserved to live it. His luck would hold out, he assured himself.

"Go about your business," he said out loud, but his hands were trembling, and his stomach was in a knot.

He made himself a cup of coffee in the little pot in his room. He needed to eat something, play a little poker. His plan was for a two-fifty buy-in tournament the next day, and he didn't want to hit the tables cold.

He checked online news in and around Norristown, including the Philly area feeds, for items about killings in a motel. He couldn't find anything. Too early? Debra said the manager wasn't there when she took the key, so it was possible no one would know she and Anthony were in there. No one would search for them. Housekeeping wouldn't even check a room that wasn't supposed to be occupied, so it could be days before the bodies were found. If Matt was lucky, it could be longer than that. Somewhere in the back of his mind he knew the smell would demand attention, but he didn't want to think about that.

He could feel the anxiety building. Managing his fear was going to be the hardest part of all of this. He had to stay calm. Stay chill. Act like nothing bad had happened at all, other than the tragedy of seeing his father in hospice. If he was going to put the Blue Blanket Inn behind him, he needed to move forward.

He could do that. Especially at the poker table. He loved the insularity there, the lack of windows and clocks, the diversity of people, the restrained hum of hands dealt and bets made. Slots were sensory overload; they made him jumpy, and he never played them. Poker rooms, however, at a distance from the slots, offered a welcoming environment. They were his office. He would be fine as long as he could focus on the hand in front of him. One step at a time, one ante at a time, one foot in front of the other. He dressed in a dark red polo shirt and black Carhartt work pants and headed downstairs to the casino.

***

There were three poker rooms in Atlantic City. The one in the Orchard Green Casino had thirty tables, buy-ins as low as sixty bucks, which was affordable. It was adequate and where Matt first started playing, but he came to think of it as suited to amateurs: he grew past it. The Galeria Casino had less than twenty tables, but games ran around the clock, with bonus points for being the one remaining Atlantic City casino on the boardwalk. There was something beautiful in being able to walk through the doors after a long night, onto the boardwalk as dawn broke and high tide sent waves up to greet you. Matt used to try convincing Jesse to come down to the Galeria with him so they could experience that moment together. But he knew he was kidding himself; she had no interest in coming down, and if she did, she would be asleep at dawn. It wasn't likely he could drag her out of bed to walk out onto an empty boardwalk. It's the same sunrise we have at home, she would say.

The poker room in the Ventura Hotel Casino was the best, and any genuine poker player on the East Coast knew Ventura was the place to play. A fixture in Atlantic City for half a century, it offered sixty tables available twenty-four hours a day, seven days a week. Once he became serious about poker, Matt honed his play at the cheaper Ventura tables, two-dollar small blind and four-dollar big in Hold'em, sometimes pot limit Omaha or old-style stud for variety. It was where he built up his confidence. He started playing tournaments there, with buy-ins starting around a hundred-fifty but going up to four times as much.

When the elevator opened and he walked through the lobby and into the casino, he felt like he had come home. His sunglasses were on; the bright lights and constant noise of the casino made him uncomfortable, and while there wasn't much he could do about the sound as he skirted the slots area, sunglasses helped him stay calm until he reached the relative quiet and more subdued lighting of the poker room. He registered with the Ventura poker staff, told them he wanted Texas Hold'em with low stakes, no limit. All the ongoing games were full at the moment, he was told, and they would alert him when he could join. He sat on the cushioned bench near the poker room entrance and tried to relax, but that was impossible given the stress from the morning. Images of Debra and Anthony crept into his consciousness. That was no good. He stood and surveyed the tables and his potential opponents.

It was counter-intuitive how much he enjoyed assessing who he was up against. Normally he was poor at interpreting people. He could be oblivious to the nuances of social interaction. That didn't happen in poker rooms, however. There, Matt could break down situations by focusing on an opponent's mechanics. Minor details of their hands, their eyebrows, a thing they did with their shoulders. The smell of anxious sweat emerging through cologne. Whether their tapping on the table was done with the tips of the fingers or the pads. These Matt could notice and interpret, even as he struggled to understand their jokes and to differentiate sincerity from sarcasm. In this way his poker play wasn't about reading the emotions of competitors, it was more like reading a dial on a machine. He maintained complete confidence in his ability to succeed in this way, despite his abysmal results so far.

An attendant told him a seat was available. He followed her to a table filled with people indistinguishable from the ones at other tables, in other poker rooms, in other cities. These were the card players: college students, retired business executives, musicians, salespeople, priests, stay-at-home moms, postal workers on their day off, anyone and everyone with the necessary card savvy and extra cash. They would bring a predictable mix of playing styles, and he had pet names for most of them.

In-&-Outers, for example, called on nearly every hand, occasionally raised, and dropped quickly. Safe, and boring, they rarely won, almost never won big, and took a long time to lose their pile, like party guests who refused to leave.

Dropsies were those who folded most hands but the best ones. This type rarely bluffed, so if you had a mediocre hand and they bet or raised, you knew to get out.

The worst to play against were the Chatterboxes, the ones who wouldn't shut up, whether because of nerves or some misguided distraction tactic. They were annoying and could take all the fun out of a game.

Matt considered himself ready for all of them.

He made it through two hands. On the third he felt faint and folded after the flop, took his chips and excused himself. Stress, he told himself as he walked along the perimeter of the casino, letting his hand caress the wall when possible. It had to be the stress from the incident that morning. It felt like his nerves were beginning to poke out of his skin. When he first came down from his room he expected to have a great time and forget about what happened. Now he wanted to go home.

He needed to eat something, to calm down.

At the Japanese restaurant in a far corner, away from the slots, he bought tekka maki, two pieces of salmon nigiri, sunomono, and spicy gyoza, along with a Sapporo beer. He sat on a stool at a long communal table. It was tall enough that someone could stand on it to watch a distraught player on the other side of the room scream at a dealer eighty-sixing them, but not so tall they would hurt themself if they jumped off it in bankrupt despair.

Matt removed his sunglasses, slid onto the stool, and glanced up in time to see a portly man with hair like he stepped out of a wind tunnel walk by, wearing a cape. *Where does one even buy a cape?* wondered Matt. People who have never been to a casino envision James Bond movies, wealthy people in formal outfits playing baccarat. In real life it was a diverse crowd of regular schmoes, screwballs like cape guy, and retirees. Matt saw this as a good thing, since he didn't want to play poker against James Bond, he wanted to play against screwballs and retirees; he assumed the odds were more in his favor that way.

A Chinese-American couple sat down across from him, placing their beef and rice plates on the table. He recognized the woman, he saw her earlier playing blackjack; pretty, in her fifties he guessed. She gave off a nice vibe, like the mother of a school friend. Her thin-faced husband was older, with a scowl. To Matt he seemed like a slots player and a smoker.

Matt went for the gyoza while they were hot. He picked one up with chopsticks and dipped it in the spicy sauce. The woman across the table watched.

"You're good with those, almost better than me," she said, smiling.

Is she sincere, or condescending and making fun of me? He couldn't be sure. He most certainly was not that adept with chopsticks. Perhaps it was polite flattery designed to make small talk, and he disliked small talk.

"Someone taught you?" she asked.

"Yes, a long time ago." Matt smiled, polite. He wanted to say something about not signing up for the group conversation but knew enough to keep his mouth shut. He was still out of sorts. Why create conflict?

A man, alone, sat in the stool next to Matt. He was in his sixties, at least, bald with a silver beard, a style so many old guys adopt. He was wearing an unstructured blazer and faded jeans. The old guy was working hard to come off as cool.

The man felt Matt watching him, turned and said, "Hey champ, how's it going?" He smiled with the bottom half of his face, while his eyes remained watchful, distant. It immediately made Matt uncomfortable.

Ten

"Oh, that looks delicious," said the woman, eyeing the old man's poke bowl.

"Doesn't it?" agreed the man, in a voice like someone on the radio who reads the news. A great voice like that was another reason for Matt to dislike him. "My name's Aaron." He reached his right hand across the table to her, to shake. "Aaron Stoltzfus." With his left he offered her a business card.

"I'm Ruby," she said, shaking with one hand, taking the card with the other. "This is my husband Jon." Jon raised his eyes from his Kindle, nodded, and gave a cursory wiggle with three fingers. Ruby and her husband and the new guy Aaron all turned to Matt. Whatever was going on here among these strangers, they were hellbent on including him.

"I'm Matthew Martinez," he said, in response to the peer pressure.

"Aaron Stoltzfus," the man said again, shaking Matt's hand as he gave him a card. "I paid for these, got hundreds of them, might as well use them. You never know who you're going to meet, right?"

The card had Aaron's name, profession, a phone number, an email, and a post office box. "Where the heck is Larnersville?" asked Matt.

"Off eighty, west of Stroudsburg, up there in the Poconos."

"Says you're a communication consultant."

"Used to be a newspaper reporter before that line dried up. Got into corporate comms but tired of the long commute, driving into North Jersey. Now I freelance."

"We're from Jersey City," Ruby said brightly. "My husband's retired, he's on disability with his leg, but I still do real estate half-time."

"I'm sure you are terrific at it," said Aaron, giving her another beaming smile. "You have the right kind of positive energy."

She liked that.

Aaron turned to Matt. "Where you from, young Matthew?"

"I grew up in Norristown."

"I've been there. Up the Schuylkill River from Philly. Saw Joe Frazier coming out of the courthouse once."

"I don't live there anymore. I'm in a town called Tohickon, northern Bucks County."

"Nice area."

"It's okay."

Aaron nodded in agreement. "What's Norristown like these days? Last time I was there, it seemed like a place that couldn't figure out what it wanted to be."

"I wouldn't call it booming," said Matt. "Was there this morning to visit my dad in the hospital."

"Sorry about your dad," said Ruby. "What's wrong with him?"

"He got old," said Matt. "Then tried to hurry his way out through cigarettes and booze."

"Oh! Sad to hear that!"

"It's alright. We haven't had a relationship for a long time."

Ruby raised her eyebrows at his candor. Matt realized he was over-sharing.

Aaron appraised Matt, and asked, "So what do you do in Tohickon? You're not a farmer."

"I used to be in the restaurant business. Now I play poker."

Aaron's eyes lit up.

Ruby said, "Two New Jersey people, two Pennsylvania people!" She seemed delighted by this. She turned back to Aaron and asked, "What are you playing?"

Am I picking up a flirting vibe? thought Matt.

"I used to play poker," said Aaron. "Not any longer. I'm here tonight for the concert." He pointed across the room, where big wooden doors led to the theatre. Matt had seen the posters around the place earlier, some unfamiliar band from the nineties reunited for a tour.

"Why did you quit poker?" asked Ruby.

"A few reasons," said Aaron with a half-smile. "Though I miss the dopamine."

That was greeted with blank faces.

"What does that mean?" asked Matt.

"People like you and me, poker players that is, we have too much dopamine in our systems, and we want more," said Aaron. "That's what gambling's all about, not the money."

"You mean the thrill?" asked Ruby.

"Sure. Not so much excitement, though, more about regular pleasure, shot into your system." Aaron added spicy chili oil to his poke. "Some think it has to do with stories. Everyone recognizes patterns, turns them into stories, and gets pleasure from that. Stories are hard-wired in humans, it helped cave people survive. It's why we love books and movies."

"What does this have to do with gambling?" Ruby was perplexed.

Aaron saw Matt frowning, and turned to speak directly to him. "People like us, poker players, we get more dopamine boosts from stories than most people. We live for that stuff."

"What stuff?"

"We love activities with a lot of pattern recognition that we can turn into little stories."

"Activities like poker?" Matt was struggling to follow.

"Yeah. Roulette is a mechanical wheel, blackjack is percentages. Poker is about the people. Human drama. It's storytelling."

"And that's why we like it?" asked Matt, with a dab of hostility.

"Has a downside, though," said Aaron, holding up an index finger. "The more we turn patterns into stories, we become less cautious, and more arrogant about our interpretations. We see patterns in random events where there are no patterns. It can make us overconfident. Then mistakes follow."

Matt was turned off by Aaron's little classroom lecture. "I don't think that's it," he said.

"No, it's true," said Aaron, putting salmon and rice into his mouth. A minute later: "Some people who have this extra dopamine thing might become storytellers, like writers and filmmakers, or business analysts, or psychologists. We—you and me—gravitated toward the gambling table."

"I'm not sure..." started Matt.

"I don't even have to ask, I know you create stories in your head about the people and the hands you've played. I know you've done it, we all have. It gives us a false sense of security."

"How is that?"

"Makes us think we understand gambling, and by extension understand life in general. It helps us pretend things are predictable, but they aren't predictable at all. Stuff happens out of the blue all the time, things you can't expect."

Matt smiled slightly. *You have no idea, old man.* He said, "You're trying to tell me everyone here is like that?" Matt swung his arm around, taking in the entire casino floor.

"Not everyone," said Aaron. "Mostly the poker players." He turned to Ruby. "What's your favorite game?"

"Blackjack," said Matt, before Ruby could answer. She raised her eyebrows. "Sorry," he said, "I saw you playing earlier."

"Okay," said Aaron. "Blackjack. Before you sold real estate part time, what did you do?" he asked Ruby. "What was your training?"

"Accounting," she said.

"There you go," said Aaron. "A number cruncher, not a pattern seeker. Blackjack is a numbers game. You count cards a little, I'll bet."

Ruby pouted, and shook her head no.

"I don't mean so much they flag you," said Aaron with a small laugh. "But enough to track your odds, right?"

She nodded oh so slightly.

"How about your husband?"

"Slots," said Ruby.

I knew it! thought Matt.

"Well, that's pure mysticism," said Aaron, and he and Ruby laughed. Her husband Jon laughed too, without lifting his eyes off his Kindle. Jon was listening to all of this, even though he pretended he wasn't.

Matt found all this annoying. He said, "That's fine about why people enjoy poker, but it's luck actually determines who wins, not the best storyteller."

Aaron glanced at him. He said, "Explain."

"Poker players don't play against the house, they play against people, like you said. In other games, the casino's slight edge ensures the house will win, that's just math. But in poker somebody wins that pot, right?"

"Yeah," said Aaron. "It takes discipline and being observant, not luck."

"They only take you so far, it's luck separates winners from the pack." Matt knew this was true because he was lucky, despite his long dry streak. He understood the magical forces.

"You think so?"

"Patience and bankroll management will let you sit at a table for a long time, but they won't win you the big hand. That always comes down to luck."

"Luck?" Aaron was amused.

"The key indicator of success in the long run," confirmed Matt, with an emphatic nod.

"I see your point, somewhat," said Aaron, his voice tentative, shifting on his stool. "But you know, Jack London is supposed to have said that life is not always about holding good cards, sometimes it's about playing a poor hand well. That sounds more like being smart and tactical, not lucky."

"That's half right," said Matt, not sure he remembered who Jack London was. "Good cards or not, what matters in the end is whether you beat the guy across from you, right? A lot of that comes down to luck, and to which player has the guts to lean into that luck, sort of molding it to his will." His hands formed an invisible object in the air. "A cautious player will see a risky deal and fold quick, so he's a loser. What I try to do, if I have any chance with a hand, is bend luck my way."

"How do you do that?"

"Through my connection to the energies present in the moment." As soon as it came out of his mouth Matt regretted saying it. It was the stress from the morning, he wasn't self-regulating his public face. *Now they're going to laugh at me.*

"Energies?" asked Aaron, eyes wide. "In the moment?"

"Yup," said Matt, soldiering on. "Then I can pull a winning hand out of my butt. To be lucky, stay in the game. Most people don't have the courage."

Matt said this like it was his mission statement. Maybe he believed it, maybe he didn't, but it what he was going with at the moment.

Matt's phone buzzed. He answered without excusing himself.

"I wanted to see how it's going, babe," Jesse said on the other end. "Find out when you're coming home."

"I'm comped for the weekend," Matt told her. "I'll be home Sunday."

He noticed Aaron watching, side-eye, and that Ruby and Jon were listening, too.

"Don't go too deep tonight." Her voice sounded stressed. She was worried, maybe a holdover from the morning argument. Matt understood. She was good-natured and generally supportive, but she had limits.

He said, "I'll be fine."

"I know you're running out of money, Matt. I'm not keeping a rolling total, but I know you have to be near the end."

"I have stash left."

"Not much, I know. I'm worried you're going to dive into the savings."

"I haven't done that."

"I'm worried that you will."

"It's my inheritance, Jesse, you need to remember that."

"So, you are going to do it."

"No... not yet."

"You promised."

"I gotta go, my food is getting cold and there's too much noise in here. Let's talk about this later. I'll call you in a little while."

Matt hung up. *That didn't go well.* He felt a flush of anger at himself for not handling it better. Now he would be on the defensive when he returned home. He recognized someone talking, outside the periphery of his attention, then he heard his name.

Aaron was staring at him. "Everything okay?" Aaron asked, again.

That's bold, considering it's none of your business. Aaron was holding a Sapporo which he got from somewhere. There was also a new one in front of Matt. Ruby and Jon pretended to not be eavesdropping, and they had beers in front of them, too. Aaron must have bought a round when Matt was on the phone.

"My girlfriend's a little antsy about me being here," Matt said. "She wants me to go back to managing restaurants."

Aaron raised an eyebrow. "But you don't want to do that?"

"I have a plan," said Matt, putting his elbows on the table, "and I want to see it through."

"A plan?" asked Ruby, perking up. She seemed to like the idea of plans.

"Nothing complicated," said Matt with a shrug. He explained his decision to play poker, how he set up his fund, and that any money he won went right back into the stash. "I continue this until the stake becomes large enough, I can make poker an actual career."

"Good plan!" said Ruby.

"Or until the stash runs out," said Aaron. "How much was your original stake, if I may be so bold?"

"Sixty grand." He had never told anyone other than Jesse or Sofia how much he carved out for cards. Now that he said it aloud, he didn't know if people like them would think it too large an amount, or too small.

Aaron asked, "Where did your seed money come from?"

"Part of an inheritance, from when my grandfather died. I was fortunate."

"So sad about the grandfather!" Ruby seemed upset.

"Fortunate?" asked Aaron.

"Yeah," said Matt. "The gods sent a message at a crucial moment, and I listened."

Surprise crossed Aaron's face.

Matt realized he might appear callous. "What I mean is, I was sad about my grandfather, but the inheritance gave me the resources to do the thing I wanted to do. That was the message—telling me to do it. So I quit my job. That was me listening to the message, and then making my own luck. See what I mean?"

Aaron frowned and nodded. "The girlfriend's not on board with this plan, is she?"

"Not so much. But... if I could get the poker thing going, win a few tournaments, she could join me. We'd travel together and see the country and have a blast."

Matt glanced across the table at Ruby and Jon. They were a couple who liked to gamble together, they should understand. Instead, Ruby seemed concerned, and asked, "She doesn't like you coming here?"

Here we go, advice coming in, thought Matt. Everybody's a therapist. "It's not her favorite thing. She'll come around, when I get things on track."

"And you'll start winning because poker is a skill game and you're superb at it?" asked Aaron.

Matt glared at him. *We spent all that time talking about luck and he's bringing up skill like he misunderstood everything I said? Is he goading me?*

"No," said Matt. "Because I'm a lucky guy, and my luck will come back."

"His shirt," said Ruby, pointing to Matt's knit pullover. "Red with turtle. Both good luck!" She smiled.

Matt turned to Aaron, took a pinch of his shirt near the turtle logo, and pulled it forward like he was proving Ruby's point. Aaron had that odd smile on his face again, the one Matt didn't like.

ELEVEN

"**Y**ou've been talking about luck all this time," said Aaron. "What do you mean by that word?"

Matt sighed. "If I need a hundred dollars to buy a thing, and I come across an envelope on the street that has a hundred dollars in it, that's luck. Obviously."

"Okay. But how long was the envelope sitting there? Two minutes? Two hours? Two days, maybe. How many people walked past it and never noticed it lying there? Or saw it and didn't stop to inspect it? From that perspective, it's not luck at all. You were observant, and curious. So you got the reward."

Ruby gave out a little "Ooooh." Her husband nodded.

Aaron said, "The veil between luck and causality is often an illusion."

"What?" Matt screwed up his face. *Who talks like that?* "But I said I needed a hundred dollars, then there it was," said Matt.

"Everybody always needs a hundred dollars, for something."

"If some drunk guy comes out of nowhere and crashes into my car," argued Matt, becoming annoyed, "that's bad luck, man, not a result of anything I did."

Aaron gave a tilt of his head, then said, "An accident like that is unfortunate, yes. However, that crash is on you as much as on the other person. Why were you driving? Maybe you should have been walking, it was such a short distance. Did you have your turn signal on? Were you so lost in thought that you didn't see the car coming in time to brake and avoid the crash? Maybe the color of your car is the hardest to see at dusk."

Matt believed Aaron was being perverse. "That's bullshit."

"Think of it this way. In every scenario that guy was going to be drunk and run through that intersection. It was up to you if you put yourself in his path, or not."

"Still not my fault."

"You're thinking in terms of blame, I'm talking about causality. A guy mugs you. You're right, he's at fault—that's a criminal act. But you were the one walking alone in that neighborhood late at night. It doesn't change his responsibility for what happened, he's still a criminal, but there were things you did that contributed to make it happen."

Ruby and Jon moved their attention from Matt to Aaron and back again.

"What's the point of all this?" asked Matt.

"Choices have consequences," said Aaron. "All throughout our lives. And nothing happens in a vacuum. For example, from the sound of it, you're making choices, big and small, that affect your relationship. If I were you, I'd think about going back and being with your girl, not here."

Matt felt queasy. Nobody told him there would be amateur counseling that evening. The nerve of the guy, pretending to be some sort of analyst, some sort of philosophy professor giving out unwanted advice. After the morning Matt had, his father in a coma, the horror in the motel room, he was in no mood for that. He wasn't anyone to mess with, there were two dead people who could attest to that.

"So you don't play cards anymore, ever?" Ruby asked Aaron, attempting to redirect the conversation.

"I used to play a lot, like this young man," said Aaron, "but no more."

Matt considered this, and decided Aaron quitting poker was the key to the conversation. He met plenty of these types, players who lost their nerve, who dreamed big but couldn't follow through. *Losers.*

"At least I don't play in casinos," Aaron added. He turned to Ruby and said, with a wink, "You have a penny-ante game in your dining room I'll be happy to join in."

Jesus, is Aaron flirting with Ruby now? Matt couldn't keep up with the layers of interaction. He rested his arms on the table and asked, "What happened?"

Aaron heard an edge, a derisive tone, in the question. He turned, but didn't answer.

Matt pressed it. "Why did you quit? Your luck run out?"

Aaron put on a crooked smile. He asked, "You want to hear my little poker story?"

Matt, Ruby, and Jon all nodded.

"This was in San Francisco, years and years back," he said. "I was in graduate school, and we didn't have much money, but I liked to play poker with friends, and friends of friends. They all had better jobs and could afford their losses a lot better than I could. But I was a pretty skillful player and held my own, although it made my wife nervous."

Aaron gave Matt a meaningful glance.

"One night we were playing seven-card stud—Texas Hold'em wasn't a thing then—at an apartment South of Market, before the neighborhood scaled up, and I was having a good run. I nursed a beer or two, but most of the others were getting drunk on tequila, and the more they drank the more they lost. I benefited from their lack of discipline, and so did another player. He was an analyst for Arthur Andersen when that company was still around, to tell you how long ago this happened. Not my favorite guy, the kind of prick who would work at Andersen."

"What was Arthur Andersen?" asked Matt.

"Long gone. Don't worry about it. That guy was staying sober too, and his pile got bigger at a faster rate than mine. He was smug, taunting me with comments about how the pots were getting over my head and that sort of thing."

"Mind games," said Matt in recognition.

"At the end of the night, there was one of those weird hands where everyone thinks they have a winner," said Aaron. "The pot grew, all these drunks raising. They couldn't sustain it, though, and by the fourth up card most of them had dropped, leaving a huge chunk of their cash in the middle of the table. I was showing a pair of tens and a queen. The Andersen analyst was showing an ace and junk."

"He had more than an ace high or he wouldn't be staying in while everyone else was being reckless," Matt said, unable to resist adding commentary.

"Exactly. I figured he was trying to scare me away with a pair of aces, but I had a queen in the hole giving me two pair. We raised twice, driving away the last straggler who had been too drunk to know he had nothing. There were the two of us left. With the last card down I had, miracle of miracles, a ten for a full house."

"Damn!"

"Like you said earlier, I pulled it out of my butt. I bet aggressively, of course, hoping to put the hand to bed, but to my surprise so did he. Which made me nervous. Here was my secret: the man was right, I was in over my head. I brought too much money thinking I would break even, not lose it all. I couldn't afford that. My wife wouldn't tolerate it. My mind was racing; if he wasn't bluffing, what could he have in the hole that made him confident? I was so nervous I was having trouble thinking right. I thought I saw one of the aces disappear in a folded hand, but now at that point, in the crisis moment, anxious, that pile of money on the table, I couldn't trust my memory. If he had an aces-over full house, I was gonna be sucked down into the vortex of doom and my life would be screwed. And good god, I'm thinking, could the guy have four of a kind? My palms were moist from nerves. I was in too deep, there was no point in folding, not then, not with that hand."

"You were panicking," said Matt.

"This is exciting!" said Ruby. Even Jon was paying attention.

"I went all in with what little I had left and he matched it. The poor bastard had two aces in the hole for three of a kind. Must have had them the entire time."

Matt laughed with delight. "He was pissed off!"

"He was right to bet the house," said Aaron with a shrug. "His aces would have won over my possible three tens, and any two pair. He couldn't have seen a full house coming. He made the smart play. If that final ten hadn't come my way, I would have lost everything."

"Good story," said Ruby. She suddenly brightened. "Oh! A poker story, like you said!"

"And you were right, Matt. I panicked and it clouded my brain. It shook me up. I won huge that night, but if things had gone a little differently, I would have lost huge. I broke one of the most important rules, which is to never risk more than you can afford to waste. It was a sign that I needed to stop playing."

Matt was quiet. In his mind, the story was evidence of Aaron being a loser. "So that's it?" he asked. "Your big explanation about why you quit cards?"

Aaron gave Matt a sharp look. "What's that?"

"You buckled," Matt told him. "You stopped playing because you got scared, right? That's what you said."

Aaron pursed his lips and said, "It's common sense to avoid things that harm you."

"We impose our own limits," said Matt, waving away Aaron's comment. Two beers in, still on edge after that morning, he was being what Jesse would call a little extra, but didn't care. Earlier in the day he had faced death and came out the victor, so the evening belonged to him. "If you want to succeed, you have to show up. You no longer showed up."

Aaron was pensive.

He's both insulted and angry, Matt assumed, *but he should also be ashamed if he had any pride left at all.* Old guys like that, in Matt's view, expect to tell their stories to friendly audiences that never challenge the assumptions. Maybe Aaron needed a wake-up call. Matt could live with Aaron's resentment if it kept the old man's defeatist attitude at a distance. Matt wasn't about to fall for negative thinking. You get on the pessimism slide and you can kiss your poker career goodbye.

Matt knew being so aggressive and mean-spirited was not normal for him. It was almost certainly due to shockwaves from the day's events. But he couldn't stop. He was angry at the world in general and, right then, specifically at Aaron. The emotion was twisting his rational function. He saw Ruby's face, however, with her judgmentally tightened lips and evasive eyes, and felt a tug of guilt. Perhaps he had gone too far. Perhaps he should have read the room better. Maybe. *Take a breath. Think it through.* All he could do at that point was scramble and attempt to smooth things over.

"It takes commitment, is all I'm saying," Matt explained, backtracking. He felt the need to be heard, to be understood. "The hard part is knowing what you want. You can't have everything. You need to decide."

Aaron and Ruby glanced at each other, the condescending exchange older people give each other when faced with a younger person who thinks they have all the answers. Matt realized he had left the path somewhere and was lost in the reeds.

"Are you talking to us, or to yourself?" Aaron asked him. "Because you sound like you're trying to justify something."

Everyone waited, but Matt said nothing.

"Not much of that stash left, is there?" asked Aaron. "That's what you and your girlfriend were arguing about on the phone." The old man had some dangerous insight. It made Matt uncomfortable. Aaron was getting on his nerves.

"It's been a tough run," said Matt. "They happen sometimes."

"Yes, they do. How much do you have left from that original sixty?"

"None of your business."

"Ten grand?"

"None of your business."

"I'll take that as a no. I'll take that as admitting you have a lot less than ten."

"I have four." It popped out of Matt. The situation was humiliating.

The old guy moved a bit closer. "I'll bet you're considering breaking your own rules about that stash and tapping more of your inheritance."

Matt regretted telling them about it.

"That doesn't sound like a good idea," said Ruby.

Matt stared at her. Great, another chef in the kitchen. It's a goddam intervention in the middle of the Ventura.

Aaron asked, "Does your girlfriend know you're planning to do this?"

Matt shook his head no.

"You're out of money and you're thinking of tapping your security buffer," Aaron said. "Son, this is not how you want to do things."

"It's my life."

"And your girlfriend's too, based on what you've told us."

Matt rubbed his temples. Could this old guy be any more condescending? Things were a bit tense; Ruby, in another attempt to lighten things up, started chatting with Matt about her life, living in Jersey City. Matt was not paying attention.

"You say you think this is all about luck?" Aaron asked.

"The important stuff, yeah."

"You think luck is more than a heads or tails of a coin toss? That's the way you talk, like you think it's something spiritual."

"Yeah, I guess so." Matt thought, *How could I describe the experience of the motel room in any other way?* He wanted to shout out loud, *What were the odds of finding a knife under the bed at the exact right moment I needed to find a knife under the bed? Astronomical!*

"Some kind of mystical accounting process?" asked Aaron. "You're rewarded by the universe?"

"Something like that."

"Then there's punishment in there, too? Carrot and stick? I mean, if you get rewarded in poker, the other players are being penalized, right?"

"I guess... Collateral damage." Matt had never considered it that way. He was embarrassed to realize that.

"In other words, sometimes even when you have good luck, it's not about you at all," said Aaron, his hands moving left and right, making a show of following the logic out to its conclusion. "Sometimes the gods want to slap the other person."

Matt wasn't having fun with this Socratic dialogue bullshit. "If you mean some people need to be taught a lesson, then sure, I guess that's part of it."

Four more Sapporos appeared, along with four shots of whiskey. Somehow, Aaron again ordered a round without Matt noticing. Aaron proposed a toast to new friends. Matt, wanting to calm down, tossed back the whiskey. Ruby said she didn't drink the hard stuff, and Aaron told her to give it to Matt, who didn't waste too much time before he had that one, too, chasing the two shots with beer. Aaron watched intently.

"Let me show you something," said Aaron. The other three ogled what he had in his hand.

TWELVE

"I have a random number generator app on my phone," said Aaron. "I'll set it for between one and one hundred."

He handed the phone to Ruby. Jon glanced up from his Kindle, sipped from his shot glass. Matt grimaced; he didn't like it when someone told him the rules for a new game he didn't know.

"When I say go, push that button there," Aaron told Ruby. She nodded.

Aaron took out a dollar and told Matt to do the same. They put their dollars on the table between them.

Aaron said, "She'll push the button and generate a number between one and a hundred. I'll guess a number first, then you. Whoever comes closest to the number on the phone wins the pot."

"For a big two-dollar pot?" asked Matt. "Sure."

Aaron told Ruby to push the button. She said she had a number.

"Sixty-one," said Aaron.

"Forty-three," said Matt. The woman turned the phone around. Twenty-two, it said.

"See?" said Matt, feeling good about himself. "I'm lucky. It's how it is."

"Now double or nothing," said Aaron, smiling a little. He pulled two dollars out of his pocket and put them on top of the first two. He took the phone from Ruby, set the app up again, and gave it back to her. "You first this time."

Matt didn't want to overthink it, but his gut said to go high on the second round. But how high? "Seventy," he said.

"Thirty," said Aaron.

Ruby turned the phone around, smiling at Matt. Thirty-seven.

"So maybe I'm more lucky than you," said Aaron, sipping his Sapporo while keeping eyes sideways on Matt.

"One round doesn't determine that," said Matt, his face flush from the alcohol. "Again."

Aaron nodded. He left the four dollars on the table, then counted out forty-six dollars to make it an even fifty and said, "Let's do it for real, then."

Matt didn't know what the old man was up to. He wasn't even sure if little private games for cash were allowed in casinos. *But okay, let's play*. This was going to be fun. Even three beers and two whiskeys in, Matt had enough presence of mind to recognize the simple game was a joke. It was simple percentages. The player going second had a huge advantage: if winning was coming closest, all the second player had to do was bid one or two higher when the first player bid below fifty, and one or two lower when the first player bid above fifty, so he controlled the majority of the numbers. When he went first, Matt needed to choose close to fifty, so the split of numbers was even. Since Aaron, the old nitwit, seemed unaware of this strategy, the longer they played the greater the advantage to Matt.

Matt was delighted. Since he was playing second, he put a fifty on the table, then another one. Aaron glanced at the raise, then at Matt, and smiled. He added a fifty and set up the app again.

Aaron bid first with forty-six. Matt said forty-seven. The app said sixty-two. Matt won.

They went again, and even playing first Matt won. And won again. The game moved quickly. Aaron won a couple, Matt won more than a couple, and in a short time Matt was three hundred dollars ahead.

Aaron is soft, Matt told himself. With his strategy, and all that luck on his side, it was too easy for Matt to win. He almost felt sorry for the bald old man.

"You're the big winner, so you should buy this round," Aaron said, gesturing for the waitress. Ruby and Jon both brightened up at that; they were the bystanders swept up into a crazy party. Gambling protocol being what it was, Matt couldn't refuse. So a round of beer and a shot of whiskey for all of them.

"Make it doubles," Aaron said to the waitress as she turned to leave. She was gone before Matt could stop her.

They started playing again, the rhythm of Aaron resetting the app, Ruby examining the screen like she was overseeing a moon launch, her finger ready to push that button, with Aaron and Matt taking turns choosing the first number. Matt won again. Then Matt won again.

The waitress came back. Matt savored the smooth, full-bodied, complex flavor of the whiskey, but it burned a little going down. It felt like victory. Like vindication. He was in the groove and his momentum was controlling it all.

Ruby was happy to have the beer, but not the whiskey. She moved it in front of Aaron; he moved it in front of Matt, who was ruminating and not paying attention. Aaron lifted his whiskey, paused before sipping it, and instead watched Matt take a big taste and chase it with a gulp of beer.

"You're up half a grand," said Aaron, the whiskey still poised in the air. "Let's go one more time, for five hundred each. Your five hundred is my money anyway, you got it off me. I'm taking all the risk. The worse that could happen for you is you'll be right where you started safe and sound, no harm no foul."

Ruby and Jon watched. Whatever their gambling plans for the evening, they had discarded them for the drama at the table.

Matt thought, *The old man is desperate to get his money back. Maybe at his age he can't afford to lose that much, maybe he needs it to buy adult diapers.* He took another large sip of whiskey. *Hey, Aaron's the one risking a grand.* A gulp of beer to chase it. *What the man said, sometimes people need a lesson.* The person getting a lesson would be Aaron, and Matt would be glad to deliver it. He finished the remaining whiskey and was delighted to discover another full glass in front of him. *Where did that come from? No matter, don't question a gift horse.* Or whatever the phrase was.

"Okay," said Matt. Even that single word was a little mushy, coming out of his mouth.

Aaron, with professional care, reset the app on his phone, handed it to Ruby. "I'll go first, I don't mind," he said.

Matt nodded. The old man was a fool.

"Seventy-two," said Aaron.

Matt couldn't believe it, the man bidding so high. "Seventy-one," said Matt. Aaron owned twenty-nine percent of the numbers, while Matt had all the rest. It was highway robbery.

"What did you say?" Ruby couldn't make out Matt's number, it was so slurred.

"Seventy-one." Said slow and careful this time.

"Seventy-nine," she said, showing the two men. Matt snarled, and she frowned.

As soon as Aaron took the money into his hand, Matt, wobbling a bit on his seat, said, "Again."

Aaron frowned. "Are you sure? We're even now, it's all cool. We could end it."

"Again."

Aaron hesitated, exchanged looks with Ruby, then pocketed five hundred and put the other five hundred back down. Matt considered the money, then Aaron. He drank more of his beer.

"I can't let this loser get the better of me, he's soft," Matt said to Ruby in a stage whisper that Jon and Aaron easily heard. "The gods have already spoken to me."

"They said he's soft?" she asked with a quick glance at Aaron.

"Yeah. They told me to punish this condescending jerk."

Aaron put an elaborate frown on his face. "I'm condescending, am I?"

Matt wanted to punch the man. "You talk like you're the master of things." Matt pointed his finger at Aaron's chest. "You need to be taken down."

Matt slipped five hundred on top and Aaron reset the app.

Matt said, "Fifty."

"Thirty," said Aaron, never taking his eyes off Matt.

"Thirty-three," said Ruby.

"Again," Matt said, almost without thinking, refusing defeat. He saw the concern on Ruby's face. "Commitment, right?" he asked of her. Embarrassed, she turned away.

Aaron bid thirty again. When Jon, who had been listening to everything, heard that, he looked up at Aaron with narrowed eyes. Matt bid thirty one. The app said twenty-four, Ruby told them. Matt was down a thousand and it took only a few minutes.

This isn't the civilized rhythm of poker, Matt said to himself, fighting the haze in his mind from the alcohol. He didn't want to lose to Aaron, not to that old man who presumed to talk to Matt that way, thinking his stupid advice was worth listening to. Fuck that. Matt had a point to make. Like he told Jesse, he would keep playing until his luck turned, which it would, it always did, and he would show Aaron and that nosy Chinese couple what luck was about, what a cosmic connection to the forces of nature was all about. Fuck them and this game.

They went again. Then again. Two more losses, five hundred a go. Matt was down two thousand. Ruby and Jon were staring at him, concerned, waiting to see what he would do. Aaron looked off into space, biding his time, the picture of professional calm, holding his full Sapporo bottle like he was about to drink from it, though he never actually did.

"I'm not giving in to you, not tonight," Matt said, but it sounded mumbled even to himself. He was drunk, he damn well knew it, as did the other three. More than drunk, he was angry, drunk angry, his mind still screaming from the events of the morning, searching for trouble, the alcohol unleashing a barely suppressed desire for annihilation. A moment, a pause. Re-orienting. Matt said," Again."

"No," said Aaron, shaking his head. "That's enough."

"Fuck you," said Matt, "I wanna go again."

"You lost half of your remaining stash," said Aaron. "I've been keeping track, even if you haven't. Isn't that enough?"

This was not true, though Aaron didn't know that. Matt had lied about how much money he had. Even with the cash stolen from Debra and Anthony, he only had about three thousand when he sat at the table. There was under a thousand left. He had to get some of that money back.

"Eight hundred, almost everything I have, one shot," said Matt, his eyes bleary, his words mumbled, his heart full of the conviction of the true believer. "The gods will not betray me."

THIRTEEN

Aaron scratched his nose and considered it. He shared glances with Ruby and Jon, then turned back to Matt. He shrugged. "I don't know which gods you're talking about, but okay," he said, putting money on the table. He reset the app and handed it to Ruby.

"Your turn to go first," said Aaron.

"No. I want you to go." Matt's eyes were red.

"That's not the rules."

"Sure it is. Called loser request."

"You made that up," said Aaron, with a mild chuckle.

"Try and prove it, asshole."

Aaron smiled in that unnerving way of his, nodded, and said, "Ninety-six."

Matt seemed a little stunned by the ridiculously high bid, hesitating, thinking such a stupid bid might be a trap.

Aaron glanced at Jon, who was staring at him. Aaron turned away.

"Ninety-five," said Matt, thinking: *A straight up ninety-five percent chance of winning!*

"Is that your call, then?" Aaron asked. "Ninety-five?"

It suddenly occurred to Matt that Aaron was probably giving him the win, being all magnanimous and letting Matt walk away with some cash and a little pride. It made him dislike the old man even more, giving Matt charity and expecting gratitude back. *Fuck him*, thought Matt, *but I'll still take the money.* "Yeah," he said, "ninety-five."

Ruby held up the phone. In bold numerals on a deep green field, it said ninety-eight. Aaron gathered up the money, peeled off three hundred dollars and held it in his palm, then put most of the rest in a clip he stuffed into his jeans while some went into a shirt pocket. He took his phone back, closed the apps, and slipped it into his jacket. He gave the three hundred to Ruby.

"For staying here and helping us play our amusing little game," he explained.

Ruby eyed Matt with sympathy. His eyes were watering, his dignity in tatters.

Aaron turned to Matt. "After that poker game in San Francisco, I told my wife what happened," he said. "She was furious at the risks I took. Sure, I won a bucket of cash, but I might have lost an amount we couldn't afford. She pointed out that the smart thing to do was quit several hands earlier, when I was ahead. Say I was tired, had early work in the morning, whatever it took to gracefully bow out. But I stayed and risked it all. It was the foolish choice. That it worked out for me that night didn't make it any less foolish in her eyes, and she was right. She told me I had to stop gambling. It was the message I needed to hear at that time, from the person best positioned to deliver it. The gods talking, as you say. The key is to recognize it and listen. I should have listened. But I didn't. I continued to gamble, for years. It was an unhealthy lifestyle, and it took its toll. It cost me my savings and my marriage. Apparently, I needed to get beaten up a lot more before I understood."

"Oh my," said Ruby.

Matt saw that Aaron's second Sapporo was down a finger at most. *But wait*, Matt said to himself, *I watched the old man drink it. Or I thought he drank it*. One of Aaron's whiskey glasses, the one in front of him, was full, while the double sat off to his right, untouched, half-hidden behind the condiment basket. Yet Matt could have sworn he saw Aaron sipping it as they played.

Aaron followed Matt's eyes. He picked up the glass.

"I guess it's okay to have this now," Aaron said with a grin, and downed the whiskey. "I saw a video by a mathematician, and he shuffled a deck of cards and announced, with all confidence, that no one else in the history of mankind had ever shuffled a deck of cards in exactly the same order. Then he shuffled them again, and again said no one in history had done it the same way. That every shuffle is unique, because the number of possible shuffles is roughly the same as the number of atoms in our galaxy. That's poker. The limitations are severe: fifty-two cards, strict rules of the game, the same ritual of dealing and betting over and over. But every hand is different from every other hand before and every other hand to come. Infinite orders of cards. Infinite games. Infinite stories. That's why people play poker, because it's always the same, yet every time it's unique."

"I never thought about it that way," said Ruby. Jon nodded in agreement.

Aaron continued talking to Matt. "Here's the thing, kid. Poker is chaos. Every deal is a thin slice of that chaos you hold in your hand. You convince yourself you see patterns, but you don't, because there's no patterns. Just chaos. If you were a card player you would know that, instead of talking mumbo jumbo about luck. You're not a card player, you're a gambler. I can tell, you're addicted. I think you need to ratchet it back, for your own good."

But Matt hardly heard what Aaron said through the stress and alcohol fog in his mind. Realizations started to form regarding what had happened.

"I'm not an addict," said Matt, his eyes moist, his speech sloppy. "That was my father. He was a drunk."

"There's all kinds of addictions, kid. Gambling's one of the most common." Aaron slid off his stool and stood. "Plus, you don't seem all that sober yourself right now."

"I'm a professional." Matt was ready to throw hands.

"No, you're not."

"Fuck you," Matt said, so quietly that the other three didn't hear it over the white noise of the room.

"You don't want things to get worse," Aaron said. "There's always more to lose, and you need to avoid that. You had a good run. You have cool stories to tell at parties. Go home to your girlfriend and take it as a second chance." He had a slug of beer. "Now I have to see that concert."

He moved the double whiskey into the center of the table, letting Matt and Jon decide who got it. He walked off.

"His eyes are pretty," said Ruby.

Matt watched Aaron cross to the entry area and walk up to a casino host, a thin young blonde man in the standard black suit. They talked, and Aaron made a waving gesture. Matt caught the blonde host glance in his direction then walk away with Aaron.

Matt turned back to the table. Ruby and Jon wouldn't acknowledge him, in consideration of his embarrassment and shame.

"It was his phone, and his app," said Jon in a smoker's growl.

Matt was startled to hear Jon speak. Then what he said sank in. "You think he cheated?" asked Matt, putting it together, his brain a little slow on the uptake.

"He said one to one hundred and we believe him," said Jon. "Could've changed it any time."

Could have changed it any time is right. Matt looked at Ruby, and she anticipated the accusations welling up in Matt's throat.

"All I saw was a screen with a button," she said, alarm in her eyes. "I push the button and a number came up. Only that."

"Too late to know now," said her husband. "Phone is locked and in his pocket. He's in the concert. Nothing to do."

Nothing to do. Maybe Aaron cheated with the app, maybe he didn't, but Matt would never know. He should have seen the possibility, at least. He was so focused on beating Aaron, thinking he was a loser, Matt didn't pay attention to what was happening, in plain sight no less. Manipulating Matt into drinking while Aaron stayed sober, like in his story.

Exactly like his story. He told Matt what he was going to do, then did it. Working Matt, distracting him.

"He suckered me in," Matt said, anger rising.

"He gave you chances to stop," said Ruby, sadness in her eyes.

"What?"

"In the beginning, when he played double or nothing. Then later when he got the five hundred back. You were both even. You could have stopped. He waited to see what you wanted to do. You were the one who said to go on, not him."

She no longer sounded so supportive. She sounded disappointed, in fact. Matt considered the strong possibility that she was right. Was this about his vanity and greed? *Damn it.*

The blonde casino host stepped over, and begged pardon for the interruption.

"Are you Mr. Martinez?"

Matt nodded.

"The gentleman asked me to give you this," he said, handing Matt an envelope.

The envelope had the Ventura logo and address on the upper left, and in the center of the envelope was written "Matthew Martinez, Tohickon PA" in a showy script with oversized capital letters and much smaller lowercase letters.

Matt asked the casino host, "Did you write this or did he?"

"He did sir." The host waited. Matt wondered why.

"He's waiting for a tip," said Ruby, as quietly as she could, which wasn't so quiet at all. Matt stuffed a few bills into the host's hand and opened the envelope. In it was five hundred dollars and a note in the same handwriting as on the envelope, on Ventura Hotel Casino stationery.

"I cleaned you out, kid, and I'm sorry about that," the note said. "You needed a lesson. You also need enough money to get something to eat and get back to your girl, so here's some pocket money. If you squander it at the poker tables and are stranded down here, that's on you. I hope it hurt when I took your stash. It was ridiculously easy. I'm surprised you've lasted this long. You're addicted. Like all addicts you think you're in control but you're not. You should join Gambler Anonymous. There's a meeting in Doylestown, less than half an hour away from your house. You have my card. Give me a call when you're ready to get your life back on track again. I sponsor a few people but have room for one more. In the meantime, consider all the great things in your life. Good luck."

Matt reddened as he stared at the paper. Ruby and Jon pretended curiosity in everything else besides Matt, but he could feel their attention. The slots noise became louder, the lights brighter. He felt the urge to run, somewhere, anywhere. He put his sunglasses on. His muscles felt tense, his vision cloudy, and he wanted to cry.

"Why are you pacing?" asked Ruby.

He hadn't been aware of getting out of his seat. He felt energized. Was it resentment? Anger? Self-loathing? How do you deal with emotions when you don't know what to call them?

"Nice meeting you," he told Ruby and Jon, and they nodded in response as he staggered away from the table and moved unsteadily through the aisles, trying not to bump into anyone.

The smart thing, of course, would be to go back to his room, lick his wounds, crawl back to the woman who loved him, and throw himself into building a good life. But that wasn't what he was going to do. Not today. Today the booze and his own distorted worldview guided Matt elsewhere. He was a criminal, a dangerous man, with the Norristown motel to prove it.

He was going to rob Aaron and get his money back.

Fourteen

Matt went upstairs to his room and took a cold shower in a futile attempt to sober up. He was about to commit a crime, on top of already committing a doozy of a crime that morning. He wasn't going to back out. The morning was self-defense; what he was about to do was protecting his livelihood. A person should have a right to do so.

He went back downstairs and lingered at the edge of the poker room, near where it connected with the blackjack tables, where there were a few high tables that gave him a view of the theatre doors. The liquor was dying inside him so he sipped beer, keeping himself at a low level of intoxication.

People trickled out as the concert neared the end, then it was a full crowd and he had to concentrate. Aaron might be hard to spot. Matt was afraid he missed him, but then caught sight of him as he ambled out, the sole male in a clutch of suburban women.

Matt stayed with Aaron as he left the casino, then worried he wouldn't have a chance for a confrontation if Aaron used valet parking. Luck was on his side, though, as Aaron headed down the hallway to the parking garage elevator.

At that moment Matt recognized he had no actual plan. He was driven there by his pride and what he convinced himself was a strong sense of justice—along with being drunk—and his normal attention to detail and thorough planning had been absent. Well, he was there now, and the best strategy available was to follow Aaron to his car and face him there.

Aaron stopped by the elevator and pushed the button.

There was no way for Matt to follow him without being seen, but neither was there time to reconsider. It was then or never. Aaron stepped into the elevator, followed by two couples. Matt hesitated, but since there was no other way to learn what floor Aaron parked on, he entered before the doors began to close. Matt allowed himself a glance over at Aaron, who was staring at him. They nodded to each other without smiling.

They were the only two left in the elevator as it made its final stop on the top floor of the garage, neither speaking, the silence tense and awkward. Aaron walked out first. Matt followed a moment later. A few steps in Aaron stopped and turned.

"You parked on this floor, too?" asked Aaron. "Imagine that. Most people park lower, it's closer to the exit. But it's emptier up here, less chance of your car being dinged."

When he got no answer he continued on. Matt followed, eyes down, mustering his courage and focusing his anger.

"There's an old proverb, it's Chinese so our friends Ruby and Jon back there would have known it," said Aaron over his shoulder as he walked. "Wealth doesn't last more than three generations."

"What the hell is that supposed to mean?"

"The first generation builds the wealth, the second manages it, the third squanders it. Had your mother lived she would have managed that money from her father, probably for your benefit. Instead, it skipped that generation and went straight to you wasting it. Oh, this is me." Aaron stopped by his Toyota SUV. He turned to watch Matt, who stood a few feet away. "I take it you don't have your car this level. What's on your mind, kid?"

Matt couldn't meet the other man's eyes. His hands clenched at his sides, his face flushed from alcohol and anger, he said, "I want my money back."

"That's not going to happen."

"You cheated me."

Aaron laughed. "For all the millennia since the invention of gambling, losers claimed they were cheated. No, I didn't cheat you."

"You cheated me," Matt shouted. A couple walking to their car at the other end of the level turned.

"There's people around," said Aaron. "This is embarrassing. For you."

"I don't care. I'll beat you if I have too."

"You got guts, give you that much. You're a lot younger than me, and you're bigger. But you're drunk, and I've been in more bar fights than you, guaranteed. You start something it won't turn out the way you think."

"I already killed two people today," said Matt. "What's one more?"

Matt felt power in saying that, putting the full psychological weight of it behind his threats. He was now a man who could utter such a thing. He was different from others around him. He was an alpha and had the receipts to prove it.

Then he immediately felt regret and nausea at having brought that shameful secret out into the glare of this parking garage, with this stranger. Maybe not so alpha. Maybe just insanely stupid. *Why did I say that?*

Aaron, at first, was astonished by what Matt said. Then he laughed at what he realized must be a ridiculous claim, a drunk kid trying to scare him. "When were you supposed to have done this?" he asked. "Up there in the farmlands, while you were having your cereal with marshmallows? Or at the hospital visiting your dad? All this time telling us you were Mister Lucky Guy, now you're Mister Dangerous Guy..." He turned to enter his car and laughed again, shaking his head.

The garage closed in around Matt and the air grew thick. How could he have given away so much? Then to have the man laugh at Matt's darkest secret was too much. While Aaron laughed, distracted and his head turned, Matt struck out with a fist, a sucker punch. But he was no fighter, and still drunk. He hit Aaron's head at an angle, doing no damage, but it was enough to cause Aaron to lose his balance, stumble back against the car, and slide down onto the floor. Matt stepped forward and leaned over, his fist raised, ready to strike again.

"Listen old man, I've had enough of you," roared Matt, his breath like a distillery. "I'll pound your face until you give me my money back."

"You're going to do that for a couple thousand dollars?" asked Aaron. "You're a cheap thug."

"It's all I got left, and I need it. And you cheated me out of it."

"Prove it."

"How about we get security involved, and they force you to show them that app, and how it works?" asked Matt. "How about they conduct a review, knowing you cheated? Maybe we could even find the Chinese couple, see what they say about it."

Aaron thought about it. He also considered the big, drunk young man holding up a fist and ready to use it. "I'll give you fifteen hundred back."

"Four thousand."

"Then you'd be dipping into my money. Right now we have a dispute over a game, and whether I should give you back the money I fairly won. But if you take some of my money, that pushes it into first degree robbery, meaning prison time. You want to risk that? I'll offer everything you lost, less the five hundred I already gave you, and your half of what I gave Miss Ruby back there."

Matt considered it. He nodded. Aaron counted out the money and handed it over.

"Thanks, old man," said Matt as he put the money in his pocket. He started walking off, but turned abruptly and came right back. "You could've use valet parking, or parked on the lower floors where there would've been a lot of people, and I couldn't have done this. But you parked up here. That's luck. See how it works?"

"Like you said, I chose to park up here, and put myself in harm's way. Causality. That's how it works."

"I got luck, racing through me," said Matt, sneering, jabbing his finger at Aaron.

"You're a delusional moron," said Aaron. "This moment is only dressed up as good luck. Maybe that will change, soon."

"I'll be fine." As emphasis, he shoved the palm of his hand into Aaron's forehead, banging his skull against the fender. "I don't want to see you again, here or anywhere else."

Matt walked away. He passed the elevator and entered the stairs. At the first landing he paused, stood facing the wall, closed his eyes, and focused his breathing. In, out. People were making noise, but they were far below. *Ignore them*, he told himself, *concentrate on breathing*. In, out, down the stairs and on to his floor. He entered his room. *Don't forget to drink water*. He flopped into the chair and stared at the painting above the bed.

He closed his eyes and envisioned the two bodies in the Blue Blanket Inn room; with a spasm he opened his eyes and thought he saw the bodies there with him, in the Ventura, but it was a shadow on the carpet. *Is this what it's going to be from now on? Seeing them everywhere?*

He felt overwhelmed. The adrenaline from arguing with Aaron was sobering him, smacking him across the face with reality. The enormity of the day, and what he'd done, fell upon him.

Damn, all that terrible stuff happened in one day. How could that be? How crazy and awful can one day be?

There may be severe consequences; he needed to be alert, watch out for cops. He broke down and again cried, for himself, for Debra and her boyfriend Anthony, for his father, for Sofia and Jesse. What had he become?

He crawled into bed. As he dropped off his phone vibrated.

"Hey," he said, when he answered.

"Hey," said Jesse. "I thought you were going to call back."

"I should have."

"You didn't."

"No."

"You sound funny. Are you alright?"

"No. Been a long day."

She was quiet, waiting for an explanation, but none came. She said, "Do you want to come home?"

"Yes, I want to, but not now. I can't now."

"Are you drunk?"

"A little, maybe. I'm not feeling like myself."

"Are you sick?"

"I don't think so."

"Did something happen today?"

"A few things. Visit with dad was weird. Then some old guy harassed me down here."

"What do you mean, harassed you?"

"You know..."

"No, I don't know."

"Anyway, I took care of it."

She was quiet on the other end. She said, "I'm sorry all that happened." She didn't mention the conversation with Sofia.

"Sometimes I feel like I'm in over my head." He said it more to himself than to her.

"Maybe you need to take a break from the casino thing."

"Maybe."

"You're out of money, anyway."

"I'm not out of money yet. Mostly I feel like I'm out of time."

"You have the rest of your life."

In prison, maybe. "I haven't been at my best."

"You going to tell me about it?"

"Probably." Matt sighed. There was no way he would ever tell her about the Blue Blanket Inn.

"You're human," she said. "You're allowed to make mistakes. As long as you learn from them."

"I'm sleepy... I need to go..."

"You coming home tomorrow?"

"Not sure, Jess. Probably not."

"Matt, I don't..."

"It's fine, I'll talk to you soon."

Matt put his head on the pillow. He needed to buy himself some time. Enough time to figure out how to continue his path without alienating her. Which meant finding a way to shut her up for a while, appease her for a few months. There was no freaking way he was giving up playing poker and going back to his old, dull, doomed way of life. He had a mission and a vision.

He'd go back and try to make her a little happier. Try to avoid the arguments. Yes her to death for a while. First, though, there was a tournament, and now that he had the money back from Aaron he could enter. If things went well it would be the first step on his way back up the ladder. Focus on the future. Forget about the motel.

"What a hell of a day," he said out loud to the dark hotel room.

Sleep came fast.

FIFTeen

No one was around when Aaron picked himself up off the floor of the parking garage, no one to see his humiliation. He couldn't believe he let that big, doltish, drunken kid surprise him like that. Well, that's what underestimating an opponent will get you. The back of his head was sore where Matt shoved him against the car.

He was angry about the assault, and about having to give up that cash, but he wasn't thinking about that. His mind was on that threat of Matt's, the boast of killing two people earlier in the day. It intrigued him, as he reflected on it. He first took it as an absurd claim, something said to intimidate, from someone weak, scared, and in over their head. And yet... Matt didn't exhibit exaggeration or falsehoods during the conversations in the Japanese restaurant. The opposite, in fact, he seemed compelled to tell the truth even when it reflected poorly on him.

Wow, thought Aaron, *what if that kid was telling the truth about the murders? Wouldn't that be interesting?*

In Aaron's point of view, if a person killed two people, they would be an emotional mess, but Matt was comparatively calm and collected. Maybe the full weight of what happened hadn't hit him yet. Thinking back, it was true the kid did seem high-strung. Hostile and resentful. Snappish. Which could be from the stress of a traumatic event earlier in the day.

Or maybe he was simply an asshole.

It was worth checking. Aaron entered his car, locked the doors, but didn't start the ignition. Instead, he sat quietly, contemplating. He was not a man who let small insults upset him. When you spend a lot of time with addicts and drunks, you know they say and do things under the influence, and under duress, that are more aggressive than normal. As a substance abuse recovery sponsor, Aaron let most of it slide in pursuit of helping them change their lives.

However, it was axiomatic that while being drunk might explain why someone acted badly, it didn't excuse it. They were still responsible for their behavior, and there were still consequences. Therefore, when someone, under the influence or not, did something through word or deed against Aaron that crossed the line he had drawn regarding such matters, there was no longer willingness to let it pass.

Aaron might not have been able to identify where that line sat at any given moment, but he knew when someone stepped over it. And young Matthew Martinez had, by any measure, crossed that line and romped far into the other side. It was an offense requiring punishment.

Aaron pulled out his phone and found a Holiday Inn in Kulpsville, under ten miles from Tohickon. He booked a room and headed out. This time of night he could be there in about an hour and a half, if they weren't doing nighttime construction, and if there weren't a bunch of troopers out for speeders. He would use the time to consider his response. He was confident that Matt was in no condition to leave the Ventura that night nor early the next morning. For that matter, if Aaron was any judge of character, Matt would take the money he stole and spend Saturday at the tables. So Aaron could take his time. Which was important. Whatever he decided to do, it would require patience and craftsmanship.

***

The next morning Aaron showered and dressed and had breakfast in the hotel's restaurant. On his phone he searched on Matt's name and found his current home address through a white pages site. It also identified a woman named Jesse Blaese as a co-resident.

He then searched news feeds and social media platforms for any information related to a double homicide in Norristown, but nothing showed up. Most likely the kid was lying, though it was possible the bodies were still undiscovered. Or the police hadn't released information for some reason. He'd continue monitoring. When he checked out he asked the desk clerk where he could find a florist.

The place where Matt and Jesse lived was part of a development on the outskirts of Tohickon, carved out of the farmland. Condominiums, many of them likely investments that were rented as apartments. Identical two-story buildings, patio for the first floor, balcony for the second. Each apartment had its own private entrance from the outside. No amenities like a pool or tennis courts that Aaron could see, but that would make the place more affordable. Most of the residents, Aaron assumed, worked in the area; there were corporate offices littered about within a half-hour drive. A little too far to work in Philadelphia, though, it was well over an hour to get there by car in the middle of the night without traffic. Rush hour on a workday forget it, you were talking at least two hours each way. But never underestimate how far people will move from their job to live where they want. Aaron knew from experience; he used to drive three days a week from his little mountain retreat into an office in Rutherford, New Jersey, which would take at least ninety minutes and, on bad traffic days, as much as an hour longer. Well, no more of that sort of thing for him.

Aaron found the right address, and rang the bell, a small bouquet of flowers in his hand. He heard a woman call, and he stepped to the right, peered around the corner of the building, and saw Jesse on the balcony wearing sweatpants and a tee shirt.

"Can I help you?" she asked.

"I'm searching for Matthew," said Aaron with a smile. "He asked me over for coffee."

She hesitated, tilted her head, trying to sort this out. "He's not here right now."

Aaron made a show of being perplexed. "You must be Jesse," he said. "Hi, I'm Aaron Stoltzfus. Are you saying he didn't come back from Atlantic City last night?"

This also took Jesse by surprise. "No, was he supposed to?"

"Yes. I'm his..." Aaron trailed off. His face showed concern, and he took a step further toward the balcony in a gesture of greater confidentiality. It was performative since they still needed to shout. "I don't want to be rude and invite myself in, but this is rather personal. Plus I'm concerned to hear that he didn't come back." He held up the flowers. "At least I need to drop these off so they can be put into water."

Jesse wouldn't normally be a woman who would fall for that sort of thing. But she was curious about what he could tell her about her boyfriend and why he was supposed to be home. She sized Aaron up as a sincere, cordial older man. Criminals don't bring flowers, usually. She came down the stairs to the front door.

"We could talk here, if that makes you more comfortable," offered Aaron, in considerate gentleman mode.

"Are you a process server or a bill collector?"

"Good grief no... do they still send bill collectors around?"

"I don't know," she said with a laugh.

"I'm Matthew's sponsor," he said, in a low, conspiratorial voice. Then, in barely a whisper, "Gambler's Anonymous."

"Oh." She gasped. She was uncertain what to do next. "It's silly to have this conversation here, come on up."

Aaron stepped into an orderly second-floor apartment. On his left a small dining area and efficient kitchen with good quality appliances, on his right a living area with a built-in fireplace and sliding doors out to the balcony. Ahead was a short hallway with two bedrooms and a bathroom. Not palatial, but well-made, plenty of room for a couple. She took the flowers and laid them on the kitchen counter. She offered coffee and he accepted. She set up the drip coffeemaker and joined him in the living room, sitting on the compact armchair while Aaron sat on the couch facing the fireplace.

"These are nice apartments," said Aaron. "Close to your job?"

"Thank you," she said, distanced but polite. "I work for a tech company in Colmar, about fifteen minutes."

"Matthew told me he doesn't have a day job any longer."

"No. Before he quit to play cards, he worked in the other direction, near Perkasie, managing a restaurant on the ground floor of what used to be a pretty nice old hotel. It was a cool place, with a big bar and plenty of marble. If you had to earn your living running a restaurant it was a good option."

"But that wasn't what he wanted to do."

"No. He used to complain the job was pressure and solving problems."

Aaron chuckled in an amiable, non-judgmental way. "That's most jobs, isn't it?"

"I suppose." She twisted her hair into the shape of a braid, and when she lowered her hands it came undone and fell loose again. "Matt thought there was too much drinking and drugs, and no career path."

"Other than moving on to manage a bigger place, I imagine."

"With bigger problems and more substance abuse."

"I can see his point, to be honest."

"I can too. I worked in restaurants—that's how we met—and got out of it myself. But I'm not sure jumping into professional gambling is the answer."

Aaron nodded. He gestured with his chin across the room.

"Wood-burning fireplace?"

"Yes, it's great in the winter," she said, rising out of the chair. "I like the wood smell."

She brought their coffees. As she placed a cup on the low table in front of Aaron, she asked, "What's this about, Mister..."

"Stoltzfus. Doesn't get much more Pennsylvania Dutch than that, I know."

"No, I guess not."

Aaron gave out a polite little cough, suggesting a man reluctant to raise a sensitive topic, but bound to do so. "So yes, I'm Matthew's sponsor. From your reaction, I take it he hasn't mentioned me."

"No, not at all. I didn't know he was doing that."

Aaron gave a quick, sympathetic nod. "I'm not surprised. He's torn about his relationship with gambling. It's not uncommon, people keeping their membership in GA a secret even from those closest to them."

She concentrated, trying to digest everything. "I assume it's something like Alcoholics Anonymous?"

"A lot like AA, yes. We're a fellowship who share our experience, strength, and hope with each other so we can solve our common gambling problem and help others. Matthew is new. Acquiring a sponsor early is important."

"Does that mean you're a gambler, too? Not a professional counselor?"

"Sponsors are fellow members, yes, from all walks of life. I've been away from the tables for over twenty years, but it remains a day at a time for me, too. Sponsoring young people like Matthew is one of the best ways to help myself, to be honest."

"I can understand that." She folded her hands. "Are you permitted to talk about any of this? Tell me what's going on?"

"Of course. There's no client privilege if that's what you mean!" He laughed. She smiled.

"Does this mean he's giving up gambling?"

"Most of us are unwilling to admit we have a gambling problem," explained Aaron, in a deep, warm, kindly tone. "But Matthew told me he's been struggling with it for some time. We met at a meeting a couple months ago and we talked. I offered to be his sponsor and he accepted. We had a few good conversations on the phone, then I didn't hear from him until we ran into each other in Atlantic City yesterday, by coincidence. I was there for a concert, and he was both surprised and embarrassed for me to catch him there... gambling. But we went to a café in the hotel and got to talking, and he seemed to be relieved that I wasn't criticizing him, not passing judgement."

"Matt doesn't like being criticized."

"None of us do, do we? He opened up about his struggles. Which I took as a good sign. He said he was ready to stop. He was going to drive home, unburden himself to you. Asked me over for coffee this morning, to continue our conversation, and to tell you about GA and his commitment to getting his life back on track. That's why I brought the flowers, to mark the occasion."

"They're lovely."

"It's a silly gesture, sentimental, but I like the ritual. Some men I sponsor get a little weird when I do it, like I'm inviting them to the prom or something. The women appreciate it."

She cried. Aaron reached out and held her hand, letting her get it out. She squeezed his hand and pulled back, sniffling. She went to the tissue box on the end of the kitchen counter.

"I'm sorry," she said as she cleaned her face.

"Don't be embarrassed. An addiction takes its toll not only on the gambler, but their family as well. It's an emotional time, going into recovery."

"I'm happy to hear he's coming to his senses, and you're being kind." Wanting something to do, she clipped the stems of the flowers, and put them in a vase. "But then why isn't he here? Should I call him?"

"Maybe he stopped at the house of a friend, to talk it over with someone he trusts."

"Matt has no friends."

Aaron raised his eyebrows at that. "Well, I admit I'm a little concerned, too, as I said outside. But that comes with the sponsor role, unfortunately. We're always worried about our sponsees. He intended to be here this morning, I'm sure of it. But to be fair, he seemed exhausted when I left him, so it's not surprising if he wasn't up for the drive back. He might be on his way here right now, running late."

"Maybe you're right."

Neither of them believed he was actually on his way.

"I talked to him late last night and he said nothing about you, or about coming home." She put the vase on the coffee table in the living area. Her face was lined. "He sounded a little drunk. Or agitated. Maybe a bit of both."

"Gambling has been a big part of his life, and now he's considering giving it up. That can be stressful."

"He also said somebody was harassing him."

"He mentioned that to me, too. I think there was some kind of misunderstanding at the tables." He sipped his coffee. "What's happening is that he's recognizing more of the disagreeable parts of the gambling life, becoming disenchanted. When that happens, it makes people want to get out but they find it hard to quit, and they become impatient. Even irritable."

"He has been pre-occupied."

"I'm sure."

"He's almost run through his funds," she said, opening up, trying to explain to a stranger what it's like to be her. "He'll start using the savings we put aside for our future. We've already been drawing from it to help pay our bills."

Aaron frowned. "He told me some of that, about an inheritance. It was on his mind at the coffee shop. He was tempted to use those savings, but knew it was the wrong thing to do. And that it would break your heart."

"It would." She nodded.

"Money from a grandparent, I believe he told me."

"Matt's grandfather, on his mother's side. Had a farm out past Ephrata. Didn't do farm work, a corporation had bought the workable land, they just lived in the house and restored furniture in the barn. Matt and his mother would go out to visit sometimes."

"Not Matthew's father?"

"No, never, I think. The grandfather didn't approve of the marriage to Matt's dad. I think he offered her money to leave him, and when she said no he put a lot away for her, for when she left the marriage, which he was sure was coming. Put it in one of those trusts, where he gave it all to her and her son, but not her husband."

"To keep it from being community property."

"I imagine. That's the story I heard, anyway. She died before the grandfather did. Matt didn't know about the trust, until on one of the visits out there, a few years ago, his grandfather told him about it. The two of them were in a restaurant, what Matt described as a little family place in the middle of nowhere, with oldies from the seventies on an old jukebox. They both had broiled haddock and roasted potatoes, which Matt thought was funny for some reason, a private joke maybe, and his grandfather dropped the news right there. He explained the trust was to keep the money out of the greedy hands of Matt's father.

Matt said that was smart, that his father would have squandered it all in no time."

Aaron waited a beat, two beats, then said, "Which is what Matt's in danger of doing right now."

That prompted another brief period of crying from Jesse.

"He claimed the sequence of events was a message from the gods," she said, giving into her frustration and anger. "That his grandfather passed at the crucial moment, when Matt was hoping for a way to start playing poker full time, and that the money would open the gateway to his success. Can you believe that?"

"A message from the gods," repeated Aaron, shaking his head in dismay. "And he listened, obviously."

They sat in silence for a bit, thinking it over.

Jesse asked, "Would you like something to eat?"

"No, I'm fine."

"Are you sure? After taking the trip here for no reason? I have those big corn muffins from the Costco bakery. I could toast one for you."

Aaron smiled. "No, thank you. I should go. My work here is done."

Part III

THE POLICE

sixteen

Matt had a rough Saturday.

He woke up from an another disturbing nightmare before dawn, and lay in bed a long time thinking about the day before. What he had done. The sight of Debra and Anthony on the motel floor, the odors of the room, the terror at being caught. He had convinced himself he was being calm under stress, but it was likely shock. A delayed reaction, at least. His terrible behavior the night before, with that Chinese couple and annoying prick Aaron, was not like him. It was the trauma talking. He believed at the time he had put the events of Norristown in a mental locked box, safely stored. The truth was there was never a moment since the incident when he wasn't thinking about it, grief mixed with fear of consequences.

Compelled to do something, anything, he went for a walk along the surf as the sun rose. His shoes in his hand, his pants rolled up, he allowed himself to feel the edges of saltwater spreading along the sand. The water was choppy. Sandpipers eyed him uneasily as he stood facing the ocean, wishing the shame and self-blame could go out with the tide. He considered walking into the water and not stopping. His actions had violated his own sense of morals. It seemed like he had betrayed himself and everything he thought he stood for, and it caused him to question whether those really were his morals. If a person violates their sense of themselves, then what remains? Does a new person emerge from the rubble, with a raw identity to be molded? He felt genuine physical pain, and feared a lifetime of regret. He bought a bottle of whiskey, took it back to his room, and after two drinks he curled back up in the bed, arms wrapped around a pillow, and allowed himself to sink.

***

He woke up again in the early afternoon, disoriented, still in a cloud of grief and anxiety. He had one thought: *I need to do a reading*.

Matt had numerous secrets, but one of the most deeply held—because of the derision he would face had people known—was his reliance on cartomancy, the use of cards for divination. It developed during his teens hand in hand with his card-playing fascination, back when he had few friends and immersed himself in fantasy and science fiction books. He came to see all activity with cards as part of the same metaphysical phenomenon. Over the years he used cartomancy as underpinning for the confidence in his luck at the poker table.

He read up on the history, how as soon as playing cards were introduced into Europe in the fourteenth century they were used to reveal the shrouded, to illuminate the past and the future. For hundreds of years, long before the emergence of tarot, regular playing cards were employed in telling fortunes. Matt still did divination this way, using a regular deck with the twos removed. No one was aware he did this, not even Jesse or Sofia, and certainly not his father.

He had a peculiar, personal kind of faith in it.

He once heard divination explained as a snapshot. All human events moved forward in time, like through a giant pipe, with everything bouncing around and impacting everything else. All of life was connected, including the cards he used for a reading. An array of cards dealt on a table was like a super-thin slice of life, a moment in time captured so it could be inspected and understood at leisure. You could see where you came from, where you were, and where you were likely to go. Well, that was the idea, anyway. Cards, coins, dice, it didn't matter, they all worked. Which sounded a lot like what that guy Aaron said about a poker hand capturing a moment in the chaos of life. Sitting on the bed in his room at the Ventura, preparing for a reading, Matt considered how weird that coincidence was, he and Aaron saying the same thing differently.

He'd have to think about it later.

Matt had a deck of cards he used for divination, never for gaming. When he traveled he kept it hidden in a zippered side pocket of the lining in his overnight bag. It was a rare design, a little oversized, with eccentric illustrations inspired by nature and by the legends of the British Isles. It was from a limited run, reproducing a hand-illustrated deck found hidden in the wall of a bishop's private space in a cathedral in England. There were a couple hundred copies and he had one. Not especially valuable—worth about a hundred and a quarter—but an uncommon and cool possession, and a secret one.

Did he *believe* in divination through the cards? He couldn't answer that question. He didn't *not* believe in it. He viewed the concept of divination much like he viewed the concept of luck. He recognized luck when it happened, and if it happened it was real, therefore believing or not believing was irrelevant.

He shuffled the cards. The afternoon sun came through the curtains. A cup of coffee from the in-room drip maker sat next to him, residue from non-dairy creamer powder floating on top.

He turned over the queen of hearts, which he interpreted as confirming what he already knew, that Jesse, and his future with her, was on his mind.

The five of diamonds told him there would be changes to his financial situation. God, he hoped so. There was nowhere to go but up.

Finally, the ten of clubs told Matt he should complete his current tasks, then transition to a new path into the future. What new path? So ambiguous! That was the problem with divination, it wasn't specific enough. *Why was seeing the future so difficult?*

***

He skimmed the news feeds and social posts for anything related to the dead couple in the Blue Blanket Inn, and found nothing. It had been over twenty-four hours, but still possible they hadn't been discovered. He felt sure there would be coverage; a couple of bodies in a motel is irresistible clickbait for any news site.

He went downstairs to the tiny convenience market on the first floor of the hotel and got a cup of real coffee and a pre-packaged Taylor Ham, egg, and cheese sandwich on a roll. He briefly heated the sandwich in the microwave, and took his food out to the side patio. While he sat morosely chewing and wondering what to do next, his phone buzzed. It was Jesse. He sent it to voice mail.

He continued to ignore her calls all day. Twice he texted her he was involved in an intense game and would get back to her soon, though he never did. He knew it was what Jesse would call passive-aggressive behavior, but he did it anyway. He didn't want to shove her away, what he wanted was to stall for time. He had a natural aversion to being proactive after a card reading, preferring to interpret the guidance as how he should *react* when external things occur. In other words, during that entire Saturday, he was treading water, waiting for an important *something* to happen, something to embrace or push back against.

In an attempt to distract his mind from his situation he went down to the gaming floor, where he played poker with little enthusiasm and less skill. It would have been more efficient to stand in the middle of the tables and toss cash out of his pockets to everyone. He finished the day with a poor performance at a one hundred and forty buy-in tournament and walked away nearly broke. He was in terrible mental shape, barely keeping it together, and retreated to his room where there was the rest of a bottle and he could watch old movies half the night.

The next day was Sunday. Jesse might go to church, something she tended to do when she was worried or unhappy, then come home hell-bent on finding out where he was and what he was up to. He would deal with that when it happened. For the time being he wanted to get drunk and chill out.

After he kicked off his shoes and turned on the television, he poured a couple of fingers and checked the news feeds and social posts.

There it was.

"Man and woman found at Norristown motel believed dead two days," said the headline above a short news story.

Here we go, though Matt.

seventeen

It was a cloudless Sunday morning when Aaron Stoltzfus went to the driving range to hit a bucket of balls. It was a chore to get there, since the closest golf center was on the other side of the ski resort and there was no direct road. He had to drive down a few miles to Larnersville, then go up the road, wrapping around the mountain where the ski slopes were. There was a genuine country club a little nearer his home, but it was an expensive members-only kind of place, which Aaron couldn't afford, and filled with the type of people he didn't want to spend time with.

On the way home he stopped to get a couple bagels—not like Brooklyn or New Jersey bagels, but they did their best out there in the Pennsylvania Appalachians—along with cream cheese, some packaged smoked salmon, and a few oranges. Back at his house he made strong coffee and sat at the small table by the large window overlooking the woods.

He didn't mind living in the middle of nowhere in the Poconos, where he had to drive miles to do anything at all. He had experienced plenty of urban life, on both coasts, had enjoyed the base pleasures and spiritual deprivations of that world, and found the quiet of the mountain suited him better now, at his age. The house had been in the family for a long time, built more than a hundred fifty years ago when the logging industry was still strong, but on its way out. He was under the impression his great-grandfather, or great-great-grandfather, whichever it was, had been some sort of mechanic, taking care of the logging machinery, which would explain why the house was located at the end of the road, right near where the woods became dense. While now it seemed to be as far away from civilization as possible, back in the day it would have been as close as possible to the work.

Of course, there was over-logging and by the turn of the century the mountain was nearly stripped and the industry began moving west. The trees came back over time, thanks to a program of re-planting, and the state made sure deforestation didn't happen again. Aaron didn't know what his family did with the place after the logging was over, it was no landscape for farming, but someone in the family always lived there. When he inherited it, everyone assumed he would sell the property. He considered it. When he heard talk of them building a casino on the other side of the mountain he held on to the place, assuming it would go way up in value. But he never got around to doing a deal.

"You like being the king of the mountain," a woman told him once. She didn't mean it as a compliment.

Between bites from the bagel, keeping an eye out for fully antlered deer and doddering flocks of wild turkeys, he roamed through the news feeds and social media posts for any items about murders in Norristown. It was coming up on two full days since when Matt claimed the murders took place, and if they hadn't turned up by now Aaron was prepared to write the entire thing off as bullshit from a desperate punk. How long can a couple of bodies lay around in a motel before someone stumbles across them, or at least smells them?

Up popped a little article from the Norristown Observer, the local paper down there that had gone all digital a few years earlier. "Man and woman found at Norristown motel believed dead two days," said the headline. The item was very short. "Police are investigating two deaths this weekend at a motel on Church Street in Norristown, according to police sources. The victims appear to have been stabbed. A weapon was found at the scene."

Well, well, well, thought Aaron, *what do you know?* There was little information in that early story, but it confirmed there were a couple of murders at the right time period in the right town. Not enough to substantiate the wild claims of young Matthew, but well on the way there.

Aaron pulled up Google maps and focused on Church Street in Norristown. He asked the app to show him motels. The best candidate was the Blue Blanket Inn at the corner of Church and Warren Streets. Future news reports would identify the motel—property owners hate that—but Aaron was confident he had the right one. Matt said he was visiting his father in a hospital. Searching the map, Aaron found Riverside Care a few blocks away from the motel, at the foot of Warren, by the river. It was some sort of combo facility, including an urgent care, rehabilitation center, long-term care, and hospice center. It was part of some corporate entity called Schuylkill Health System Medical Group. *Jesus*, thought Aaron, *everything was part of something larger these days, like a Russian doll.*

Again, it seemed to fit with Matt's story. Aaron was becoming excited.

Now what to do with the information? Probably nothing. Most likely, the only pleasure he would derive was to watch from a distance as the police closed in. He'd prefer to have a front row seat, but he would settle for what he could get.

Aaron Stoltzfus did not consider himself a vindictive man. He was, however, a straightforward and self-defined man with a strong sense of what was right and what was wrong, and that wrongdoers needed to face consequences. In this he and Matt were much more alike than either of them yet realized.

Such a strong moral center as his, Aaron felt, made him a good sponsor for those recovering from addictions. He told it like it was, as they say, and viewed his sponsees with clear vision. If they were rationalizing inappropriate behavior he called them on it. If they were kidding themselves about their commitment to recovery, he let them know. If they had trouble accepting the things they couldn't change, he reminded them the world was not under their control. If they resisted changing the things they could, he did his best to light a fire under their butts. And he applied this across the board, as part of his work in Alcoholics Anonymous, Gamblers Anonymous, and Narcotics Anonymous. He didn't dabble in the Sex & Love Addicts Anonymous world, their jargon was too insular and their organizational behavior too malleable for his tastes. Plus, sex addicts skeeved him out.

It wasn't that Aaron lacked empathy and caring. In his view, in fact, he thought he was especially supportive. In the rooms, there was a lot of talk about the concept of acceptance, about how someone on the road to recovery needed to accept reality. Much of the talk was about accepting and getting past the disappointments, the traumas, and the heartbreak that cause so many to pick up a drink, or a drug, or hit the gambling tables. But Aaron also harped on the importance of accepting the good things, too, since in his experience many addicts dwelt on the negative, and not enough on the positive. Addicts sometimes had trouble even recognizing the good things in their life, and that infringed on their ability to be grateful for what they had. And gratitude was a cornerstone of recovery, as Aaron often said.

Young Matthew Martinez was a good example. During all that time in the casino, when he was rambling on about luck and his skills and what he seemed to imagine was his manifest destiny to become a big winner at the poker table, Matthew said next to nothing about all the great things that formed the foundation of his life. That nice apartment in a lovely region of the state. An attractive and caring partner in Jesse. Experience and skill in the restaurant business. There were plenty of people who would be jealous of such riches, yet Matthew took them for granted. As Aaron had come to see it, part of his current mission was to make sure that young man understood what he had. One of the best ways to show people the value of what they have is to abruptly take it from them. Wield a robust stick to inspire appreciation of the carrot.

And on a personal note, developing a plan of action pleased Aaron, because after what he suffered in the Ventura Hotel Casino parking lot, he wouldn't be happy until Matthew Martinez got his.

EIGHTEEN

Matt spent Sunday morning in an Atlantic City diner, eating his first real meal in days and searching the internet on his phone for ways to cope with the emotional and psychological fallout from accidentally killing someone. According to Reddit threads and Facebook groups, many people had apparently been responsible for the death of others, and there was plenty of advice to be had. Most of it boiled down to the predictable trio of therapy, support groups, and not harming yourself out of self-loathing, which was not helpful. Matt had no interest in going on a journey of mindfulness and healing. He just wanted the guilt and fear to go away.

Then on one site he stumbled across a remarkable piece of history, the existence of Cities of Refuge. As described in the Old Testament, the kingdoms of Israel and Judah had half a dozen cities where someone who accidentally committed murder could find asylum, safe from the blood vengeance of their victim's family and friends. There would be a trial, and if the killing was found to be indeed accidental the person could stay in the refuge city. They had to remain there until the death of the high priest, at which time the person could leave the city and return home if they wished.

I need a City of Refuge, thought Matt. He didn't mean a literal city, but a metaphorical one. A place where he could be safe for a time, so he could heal, get his head back on straight. Ideally play a little poker. The concept oddly gave Matt hope. If a situation like his was in the bible, with explicit instructions for how to treat someone like him—who was in the wrong place at the wrong time and didn't intend to kill anyone—then maybe he wasn't the worst person in the world.

He went through something that could have happened to anyone. It was through luck that he got away unscathed and not arrested.

***

Jesse was chilly toward Matt when he finally dragged himself back to the apartment Sunday afternoon, which he didn't appreciate even though he should have expected it. He had a lot on his mind, and didn't need more conflict. Due to his distracted, careless play at the tables on Saturday he had lost nearly all the money left in his stash, the money he stole from Debra and Anthony after the murders, and the money he stole back from Aaron. He had slid in and out of contemplating suicide. He spent a good chunk of the weekend asleep or drunk. On top of all that, the bodies had been found in the Norristown motel.

He felt a little pinched by life.

Conversation was civil, at first. Jesse asked him how he was. Matt said he was tired. She asked him how he did in Atlantic City. He said he had better weekends. She asked him if he was hungry. He said he was, and she offered to make him a sandwich with some of the chicken salad she had put together the day before.

"I made it for you yesterday because I thought you'd be home," she said, "but you never made it."

"A sandwich would be good," he said, ignoring the rest of it.

So it went for a time: he was self-absorbed and inattentive; she was aloof. Eventually she couldn't out-wait him any longer and needed to talk.

"I have to ask you," she started. "Are you going to pull more money from your inheritance so you can continue to gamble?"

He winced. "Babe, I don't know.."

"We agreed you wouldn't."

"It's my money."

"You promised."

"Things change."

"Things didn't change, Matt, you did. You went back on your word. This is not some new circumstance or anything like that. This is you becoming someone I can't trust."

He resisted the urge to storm out of the apartment. "I need to find a way out of this trap."

"What trap? Me? This apartment? Our life together?"

"No, not you. My life. I'm stuck in place. I feel like I'm chained to a stake in the yard and I can roam around in a small circle, and that's it. I'm moving but not going anywhere."

He had a moment when he thought he could still smell the motel room, on him, on his clothes, in his hair, and feared Jesse could smell it too.

She gave no sign of it. Instead, she closed her eyes in exasperation, like she was dealing with a problem child. "You're nearly thirty, you have a life in front of you," she said. "I mean, what the hell are you talking about?"

"I don't know."

"What about me?"

"You're the best thing in my life, you know that."

"No, I don't know that. I know nothing about us anymore." She shoved the sandwich in front of him. She said, "I was happy yesterday for a little while. After your sponsor told me you wanted to stop the gambling, I thought the old Matt might come through the door."

"My what?"

"I thought we could talk about the future again. Sure, we'll have some money challenges, but so does everyone our age. We can make choices together, and it would be like it used to. That's what I hoped. But here you are, the same old crap, hung over and, I assume, broke."

Matt stared at her, frowning. He again asked, "My what?"

"What do you mean, your what?"

"You said my sponsor?"

"Yeah. Your Gamblers Anonymous sponsor stopped by. I should have realized you were still in your bullshit when you blew off your meeting, without having the decency to tell him you wouldn't be here.

We waited for like two hours. I called and called, and you never picked up. You were right back at it, throwing your money down the drain."

"Gamblers Anonymous sponsor!?"

"He was nice, and he told me about how you wanted to quit. I asked him, why wouldn't Matt tell me he was going to meetings? He said you were embarrassed. I was thinking how I was going to make you feel okay about it, tell you how proud I was you were taking this big step. I feel like a fool now."

"What's this guy's name?"

"He's your sponsor, you don't know his name?"

"What did he tell you his name was?"

"Aaron something German."

The apartment felt tiny for Matt at that moment, the air too thick to breathe.

He said, "He's not my sponsor." His voice was hoarse, muted.

"I thought he said he was your sponsor, maybe I misunderstood, I don't know the terminology, my parents never made it into any program. But even if he's a friend, he seems like a good guy who could help you. He's got your best interests in mind, I think."

Matt subdued the panic enough so he could control his breathing. "I don't want you talking to him, telling him things about me."

"I didn't tell him anything about you." She waved the idea away. "He was telling me. I learned a lot about things you were keeping from me."

Matt apologized and said he needed to take a walk, he needed air, he needed to think. How did Aaron get his address? What was he up to, what did he want? He strolled around the apartment complex, but that wasn't enough, he needed to be somewhere, to think, to get away from Jesse's relentless gaze, her judgement. He trekked the mile and a quarter to the tavern, got a spot at the far end of the bar, had a lager, and endeavored to calm down. He paced his breathing. He closed his eyes and imagined himself sitting on a beach. When none of those worked, he got a shot of rye. That helped a little.

Aaron coming to the apartment was too strange an incident, he couldn't deal with it yet.

He considered ways he could siphon additional money from his inheritance without harming his relationship with Jesse, The devil on his shoulder reminded him he could break up with her, then he wouldn't have to answer to her about his money, but where would he live? How well would he do on his own? He hadn't been doing so great at being single before he met Jesse, and the prognosis of him doing it better in the future was not good.

It occurred to him he might have to flee anyway, if the investigation into the Norristown killings turned its attention to him.

Jesse liked him, perhaps loved him, and he, in his own limited way, loved her. But were they truly, metaphysically linked, or merely physically coupled? How does one tell? How does a person differentiate the quality of one romantic relationship versus another, if the motions and patterns are the same? If he didn't have answers for those questions, then how could he prioritize his relationship over his burgeoning poker career? Thinking about it hurt his head.

And what the hell was he going to do about Aaron?

He checked his phone for news of the motel murders. Coverage had picked up.

"Norristown police are investigating the stabbing deaths of two Montgomery County residents at the Blue Blanket Inn on Church Street," said the most complete story on the Norristown Observer site. "The bodies were discovered by an overnight clerk in search of a missing room key. Officers responded at approximately 4:30 a.m. Sunday morning, and found the bodies of a man and a woman on the floor of the room. The victims were unresponsive, and pronounced dead at the scene. Drugs were present in the room, as well as signs of a struggle."

Still not much. Matt didn't know how this sort of thing worked. Did police withhold a lot of information, like they often do on cop shows on television? If that was the case, there was no way for Matt to learn, with confidence, what they did or did not know. On the other hand, if they were bumblers like on a lot of those shows, they didn't have much information to share, and they would be motivated to close the case out in the quickest and easiest way. Round up the usual suspects.

Further down in the search results Matt saw the Observer updated the story a little after one thirty Sunday afternoon. "Because of the presence of a weapon, and stab wounds on the bodies, police are treating the deaths as homicides," it read.

Matt imagined the cops would be less motivated if they thought it was a couple of druggies killing each other in a fight, with an overdose or two. But talking about homicide made it seem like they were being more serious about it.

"Names of the victims have not yet been released," the story continued. "The bodies were not removed from the motel until late Sunday morning. Police are awaiting the medical examiner's report and toxicology results to determine the final causes of death. Janice Duma, who has lived at the motel for two and a half years, said it was a shock to see all the police cars and emergency vehicles in the parking lot on a Sunday morning. 'They kept coming and going for hours,' Duma said. 'No one expects something like this, especially on a day when I should be in church, but I stayed to see what was happening. The cops were everywhere.' A police spokesperson said this appears to be an isolated incident, and there is no danger to the general community. The investigation is ongoing."

Well, yeah, it's ongoing, thought Matt. He considered the name of the witness. He was pretty sure Janice was the name of the old woman who spoke to him in the bar at the motel. That was not good; she had a solid view of him that day. Thank goodness he didn't tell her his real name.

The story ended in a request for anyone having information to call a number for the "Norristown Police Crime Stoppers." *What a corny name*. It was unlikely anyone from that motel, and that bar, would be eager to have a heart-to-heart chat with the police. That much was in his favor, at least.

Matt was a sack of anxiety. He had another rye. He thought about all the details, any mistake he might have made. Details, details, details.

As he saw it, he had two big challenges.

One was dealing with the murders and their aftermath. Making sure he continued to leave no trail, give the police no reason to turn their attention his way. To do that he needed to get his act together, stop wallowing in his trauma. He'd have to work on that. He may, in the near future, be required to indulge in some misdirection, plant some false leads, to shift the attention of the investigation elsewhere. In a worst-case scenario he might have to flee. He would need to stay on top of news reports and be alert for any activities at the perimeter of his life that might suggest he was coming under scrutiny. Constant vigilance, as they say. He could do that.

The other big challenge was Jesse. If he had to flee, he couldn't take her with him. But if he ran, she'd see it as abandonment. Would she become angry and help the police? It was difficult to analyze likely possible outcomes. There were too many variables, or perhaps he was too distracted to parse things out.

He felt he was treading into a darkened, unfamiliar landscape where there might be hidden cliffs and venomous animals. Or there might be a convenient path. No way to tell from where he sat. He needed more time to think things through. Maybe create a risk/reward comparison chart.

The challenges could dictate the timeline, outside of his control. Jesse could give him an ultimatum. The police could identify him from facial recognition on security footage captured by a camera he didn't realize had been there. Jeez, things would start accelerating then. He'd feel his back against the wall, and then what would he do?

Did he also need to worry about Aaron Stoltzfus? Was he a wild card in this game? Or would he take himself out of it?

Matt thought of his card reading the day before and took some comfort from it. His finances would undergo a change, it said, which was likely good news since there was nowhere to go but up in that department. Then it told him he would transition to a new path, on into the future. Therefore, despite all the potential dangers, he believed it would end well for him. It always did.

When he returned to the apartment, Jesse wouldn't talk to him. He watched some television while she stayed in the bedroom reading. He waited until she was asleep before he crept in and got into bed with her, hoping that she would be a little more civil, a little more understanding, in the morning.

Lying there, viewing his phone, he checked the news feeds for an update. What he saw allowed him a huge sigh of relief. Sure enough, as he anticipated, at least one challenge was already resolved. Another illustration of how the universe protected him, another example of the good luck that followed him around like a puppy.

A man with a history of sex crimes who was a resident at the Blue Blanket Inn had been arrested for the murders. Here was the City of Refuge he sought, where he could hide for a while, maybe forever, and recover.

NINETEEN

I t was a good day for an early morning walk.

Aaron was in his early sixties, not the athletic scrapper of his youth when he was a college baseball player and a boxer, but still healthy and energetic, and he still liked his exercise. He kept weights in a corner of the barn across the road from the house, and a stationary bike in the living room that gave him a view of the television. What he most liked to do was walk. Walking is a person's finest medicine, many people have said, and Aaron believed it. He had his best ideas during these excursions, and if he had a problem with a work project, or a woman, or a sponsee from the rooms, by the time he finished he had at least the beginnings of a solution.

His favorite route was simply to take the road that sliced his property in two and continued on into the woods. It was built on the old right of way used to service the loggers. There were a few homes lower down the road, scattered on either side as it rose from the outskirts of Larnersville, but his house stood alone, a quarter mile from his nearest neighbor, the last line of civilization. As he understood it, when logging stopped, there were a series of owners of what is now the heavily wooded land beyond his house, none of whom had a vision for what to do with the ragged terrain. A large church organization eventually purchased a tract for cheap and built a camp in an area with a creek and a small pond and enough flat ground to erect a few cabins and a food hall. The camp sat behind a dense grove of white oaks, sycamores, and beeches, along with rhododendrons and azaleas at the border. To provide access they extended the road to the thick wooden gates of the camp, and for reasons lost to time kept going along the base of the crest, a stretch of nothing but trees and scrub. Perhaps there were plans to build that were never followed through. The road wrapped around until, on the other side, it caught up to another road with its own smattering of homes and small businesses that eventually reconnected with the main road, completing a long U shape. This configuration was ideal for Aaron. He had a finished road to walk on. In the off-season, when the camp was closed, which was ten months of the year, the road was always empty of cars and people, since there was no reason to take it through the woods: nothing was on it, and it had no value as a shortcut.

Aaron had a pleasant amble down the road, past the entrance to the camp, through the trees. It was still so early in the morning dew clung to everything, and he wore a fleece against the chill. He stayed on the alert for wildlife, always eager to say hello to the deer and foxes and groundhogs and rabbits and squirrels and chipmunks and turkeys that shared the mountain with him. On rare occasions he might see a bear further down the road, and he carried a mini air horn for moments like that, but fortunately he never had to use it; bears wanted to mind their own business.

He came around to an abandoned house of brick and stucco, then a car repair shop that had been closed for a few years, and beyond that a driveway leading deeper into the woods to some rich person's getaway cabin. He turned toward the mountain and entered a path across the road from the car shop, so disguised by shrubbery and a thicket of grasses that it was unnoticeable to someone who wasn't on the lookout for it.

He didn't know why the path was there. It was old, a shallow groove cut into the ground. It was regularly used when the logging industry was operating in the area, and was presumably created by native peoples long before that. To the best of his knowledge, he was the one person still alive who was aware it existed. He took that path up and over the downward slope of the mountain crest's tail end, a more direct route back to his house, where it dropped him behind the old storage and machine shed at the rear of his property.

After his walk he checked his supply of wood, walked across to the barn to put some food down for the cluster of feral cats that had adopted him, then went back into his house where he put on coffee and made a simple breakfast. He sat at his laptop to see what was happening in the world, and out of curiosity checked to see if there were any new developments in the two murders possibly committed by that annoying Matthew Martinez. He found a short article on the Norristown Observer site. It stunned him.

"A man was arrested after two bodies were found in a Norristown motel over the weekend," said the article. "The deceased have been identified as 29-year-old Debra Maines and 32-year-old Anthony Ciccone, both of Norristown. They were found in a room at the Blue Blanket Inn on Church Street, along with a variety of drugs. Both victims showed stab wounds, and a knife was found at the scene. Investigators are treating the deaths as homicide, pending final coroner reports. Christopher Roberts, 54, was arrested early this morning. Roberts, also known to acquaintances as Cooter, is a resident of the motel, and was known to spend time with both of the deceased, though police did not explain the nature of their relationship. He was detained yesterday as a person of interest, and a police spokesperson said Roberts made various self-incriminating statements during questioning, declining to provide details. Roberts is listed on the Pennsylvania Sex Offender Registry for past crimes in Montgomery County."

There were a few more details about the possibility of bond for the suspect, and a recap of the discovery of the bodies. Also, the little bit of interview with motel resident Janice Duma, talking about all the police cars and emergency vehicles. Aaron scanned a few more articles and found an Observer update focused on an interview with the Duma woman.

"The Observer spoke with Janice Duma, a resident of the motel and neighbor to Roberts, who she referred to as Cooter. She said she did not know his real name was Christopher until informed of this by the police. She had been talking with Roberts right up to when police arrived, she said, and never suspected there were bodies in the nearby room or that Roberts might have been responsible. 'No way,' said Duma. 'I've known him for more than a year, I've seen him every day, nearly every day, and he's never done anything like that.'"

So we have a talker, thought Aaron. He sensed Miss Janice liked the attention and her moment in the limelight; he was familiar with the type. She no doubt made herself available to the press. He would need to follow up. He had become invested in the idea of Matthew's world being upended, and the thought of him being hounded by police was delicious. Now, however, that vision was derailed by the arrest of this Roberts fellow. If Matthew had committed the murders as he claimed, poor Christopher Roberts had the misfortune of being in the wrong spot at the wrong moment with the wrong background. Aaron might have to fix that.

Aaron checked the time. He had a deadline that day, brochure copy for a consumer products client. If he focused, he might be able to get it finished and off to the client for review in an hour. Then drive down to Norristown, to take a gander at the Blue Blanket Inn and seek out chatty Ms. Janice Duma. Perhaps, if things worked out, he could even visit Matt's father.

TWENTY

Aaron parked down the block from the Blue Blanket Inn, on Warren Street, and walked up to the motel. It was much as he expected from images online. Two stories, external stairs and walkways, surrounded by parking, like a million other places scattered across the country, operating under different names but indistinguishable from each other. The Blue Blanket was sufficiently comfortable and safe, the little bar & grill a bonus. It was good and cheap enough for someone on a tight budget in town for a couple of days, someone passing through.

The motel's location would also attract the working poor who needed to live close to their job and public transportation, but didn't have the down payment or credit history for a genuine apartment. Aaron had traveled across the country multiple times, and had often witnessed the reality of people forced to stay in budget motels, many of them a lot more run-down than the Blue Blanket. A refuge for people scraping by. Some were addicts or prostitutes or ex-cons, of course, but there were plenty of families with small children, especially single parents hovering just beneath the poverty line. People who barely avoided inclusion in the homelessness statistics.

He walked into the bar & grill and quickly scanned the handful of patrons. There were a few laborer types, finished their shift, spending their pay in a bit of afternoon drinking. There were two older women, and Aaron was confident that one of them would be Janice Duma. A woman like her, living in the motel, would already be a regular customer, but with all the current hubbub from the murders, and the possibility of news reporters, she would be there every day, almost all day. Horses couldn't drag her away, he imagined, since she wouldn't want to miss any of the drama, or the chance to be quoted. He picked a seat at the bar between the two women, an empty stool between him and each of them, still close enough to have a conversation.

He ordered a shot of house bourbon with a draft beer back. Barflies warm up to those they perceive as part of their tribe, and dislike dilettante drinkers or those they see as slumming, so he kept it simple. They also shun those they see as nosy, so he stayed quiet and watched the afternoon talk show on the television, with its family drama and shopping tips.

He waited. If Janice Duma was who he thought she was, she couldn't resist the temptation to talk to him.

"Hi, honey," a female voice said to his right. "Never seen you in here before."

There she is, thought Aaron. *My Janice.*

He nodded in greeting and said, "No, never been."

When he didn't give her any more than that, she asked, "At the hospital down the way?"

"No, here seeing a guy. Thought I'd have a drink before I went back up to Scranton."

They both watched a commercial for a memory enhancement pill. "I could use one of those," she said.

He smiled. "Not me. There's a lot I'd rather forget."

She laughed at that, a stifled cackle that was oddly charming on her. "I'm Janice," she said. "Glad to meet you."

She wasn't exactly what he expected. There was none of the dissolution or brassiness he had often seen on older women in other bars, in other places. She was in her seventies but still vibrant and put together, despite her inexpensive, outdated clothing. She had a kind of style, her own brand of charisma. There was a unique story with this one, he was willing to bet.

"I'm Roy DeSoto," he said, reaching out his hand.

"Like on 'Emergency!'?" she asked, shaking it.

That's my girl, thought Aaron. Old enough to remember a television show from the seventies, sharp enough to recognize a character's name.

"Yeah, that's me," he said. "I used to get made fun of about it all the time. These days it's people our age catch that, and then only sometimes."

"You know," she said, leaning forward, "when I was younger people said I resembled Julie London."

"No doubt! I can still see it."

The cackle again. He got the bartender's attention and ordered another round for both of them.

"I thought maybe you were here because of the murders," she said, saying the final three words as a whisper.

"There were murders? Here?"

She nodded. "Two. I knew them. They came in here a lot. Young people. I think they were a couple, but I wasn't sure. They'd be together, then they wouldn't be."

"Young people these days don't know how to be together."

Janice nodded. "They were in the room dead two days. The clerk noticed a key missing and went to check it out. Found them on the floor, all cut up." She reveled in the lurid details.

"Do they know what happened?"

"Arrested this man who lives here. His name's Cooter, but the police and the news people don't call him that. I mean, wow, he's a buddy. A friendly guy, quiet. Not anyone you would suspect of anything."

"You think he did it?"

"Turns out there was some sex crime things in his past," she said, in a conspiratorial tone, leaning toward him. "But that's often a lot of muddy water, isn't it? You don't know how old the girl said she was, or maybe they both was drunk. I hope it wasn't children, that would be wrong."

"Yeah," Aaron agreed. "That would be wrong."

"Yeah. He spent time with the dead girl, though, a red head with a smart mouth, named Debbie. She turned some tricks on the side here, I know that, but I don't think she was a full-time hooker or anything.

When she needed a little pocket money. I know a lot of girls done that, when they were young."

"Cops though," said Aaron, his tone implying fundamental distrust of them.

"My daddy was black and my momma was white, I seen the way cops treated them all their life," said Janice. "You don't have to tell me about cops."

He nodded in solidarity. "I wonder if they have any evidence it was him, or was he convenient?"

"That's a cop thing, isn't it? Arrest the obvious person." They both nodded, a couple of old people who had seen it all and learned a few things about authority along the way. She said, "It was like a 'Law & Order' show or something here, when they came. And it was somebody we know! I was talking to Cooter, and then he was walking away, down the block, going somewhere. The cops come roaring up and knock on his door. They see me, I'm standing right in front of them, they ask me if I know the man lives there? I say, you mean Cooter? He left a minute ago. So they go after him."

"Police talked to you a lot that day, I'll bet."

"Don't you know it! Wanted to know if there was any strangers here. Any fights. That sort of thing."

"Were there any strangers?"

"We always get a few, it's a motel, right? That day there was a little Mexican guy I remember, but I've seen him here before. There was a young man with curly hair who talked with Debbie a little, he said his name was Alan. Sat right there on the same stool you're on. Seemed nice, but he left while she was still here."

"You told the police all that, I guess?"

"Oh sure! Later I went back to my room to take a nap and I seen her boyfriend Anthony, the one that got killed? I seen him leaving the room, so he must have gone, come back." She pronounced his name as two syllables, "Antnee."

"Hey now! You were a genuine witness!"

"Oh yeah." She sipped her drink, a little sip, lady-like. "The cops asked me, how did I know it was him?"

"What, they didn't believe you?"

"I don't know, but this detective woman who talked with me, she frowned when I told her. He has this gold sweatshirt with a big eagle on the back, wears it all the time, wearing it when I seen him. Cops were interested in that part."

"They tell you why?"

"The detective didn't, she wouldn't tell me anything. But later I heard cops talking to each other about the sweatshirt not being in the room with the bodies. Seemed important to them. I said, excuse me, I already told you I seen Anthony leave, wearing the sweatshirt, so of course it isn't in the room. He must of come back, he wasn't wearing it."

"What did they say to that?"

"Gave me those cop stares, you know? I asked the lady detective if I have to solve all their crimes for them, or just this one. I thought it was funny, but she didn't, got mad at me."

"It's a little funny," said Aaron.

"Said I had an attitude."

"You saw him come back?"

"Who, that fellow Anthony? No, I was taking a nap."

She finished her drink. The two of them sat, watching the television.

"They say drugs were there," said Janice. "I'm not surprised. I always thought Anthony was dealing drugs, but he never did it in here, in front of us. But I suspected. I know the kind. Football player in high school, it was the best years of his life, then he gets out, nobody cares if he scored some touchdown in some game. Not smart enough for college. Who wants to slave away in construction? But dealing meth or weed, make good money, intimidate people, that sounds good to guys like that."

Janice may be a lonely old drunk, but she was no fool, thought Aaron. "So you think maybe a deal went bad?"

"Drug people are bad news. I don't like them around."

"Yeah, they're bad. You want another vodka and cranberry?"

Janice did an exaggerated pout. "Why, you leaving, hon?"

"I'm afraid so. Lots of things still to do today."

"Then sure, a vodka and cran will do."

"I hope your friend Cooter doesn't get railroaded," said Aaron, getting one more for Janice and settling up with the bartender.

"Me too. Something happened between him and Debbie a couple weeks ago, the boyfriend told Cooter to never talk to her again. Then Anthony and Cooter had another argument about something else, that one was worse, a bunch of yelling. I don't know what it was about, Cooter wouldn't tell me. I can't imagine the three of them being in the same room together after that. Cooter's a skinny guy, too. Anthony would have broken him in half, knife or no knife."

Twenty-one

Aaron walked down to the Riverside Care facility at the base of Warren Street, by the murky waters of the Schuylkill. A sign with teal and cobalt blue splashes behind bold block serif type assured him they offered "Expert care, every step of the way." The lobby was clean, impersonal, and drenched in corporate values. It had been easy enough to find the name of Matt's father online, and he told the reception desk he was there to visit Enrique Martinez. He was surprised to learn the man was in hospice care, second floor in the south wing. This did not bode well. The old man could be seriously ill, at death's doorstep. Aaron hoped the man would be able to handle at least a bit of conversation.

Aaron went through the large wooden doors, leaving the sterility of the rest of the facility for the quiet, comforting ambience of the hospice facility. The young woman at the desk pointed the way to the old man's room. Aaron stepped in and stood there. Not what he hoped. It would have been a grand conversation, swapping humorous tales of Matthews's adventures and mistakes, with maybe a few secrets divulged. Unfortunately, the man in front of him was in a coma, as far as Aaron could tell. He was hooked up to unfamiliar devices. He wasn't going to talk to anyone.

Aaron wondered what the point was. If the man was brain-dead, why keep his body functioning? Why submit him to this indignity? He wondered if Matthew was behind it. Aaron had heard stories about how hospital staff gave terminally ill patients a gentle push into the next phase, through an increase in meds and such, as long as the responsible next of kin or guardian was on board. Was Matthew not on board?

"Hello," said a woman's voice behind him. "Who are you?"

Aaron turned, expecting to see a nurse. But this was no nurse. She was a lean woman in her early forties. Sharp cheekbones and gray eyes. Nicely dressed, and an aura of sexiness that comes from knowing who and what you are. He was immediately interested.

"Hello, I'm Aaron," he said, flashing a broad smile. "I'm a friend of Mr. Martinez's son Matthew."

"Ah, you're the sponsor," said Sofia. "Jesse told me about you."

Life is full of surprises, thought Aaron, *and here's one now.*

"Yes, Jesse and I met one morning when Matthew stood me up on a breakfast date." Giving her his warmest smile, he reached out his hand. "I came by to pay respects to his father."

She took it. "I'm the sister," she said. "Sofia."

"Delighted to meet you. I didn't realize Matthew had a sister. He doesn't talk about family much."

"I'm sure he doesn't. We're halfies. Different mothers. We're friend-ly, not close."

"That's too bad."

"It is what it is. These days, I think I'm closer with his girlfriend than with him."

Aaron nodded. "When people become addicted, they often change their social circle, and their behaviors," he explained in his comfort-ing mentor voice. "Later, when they go through recovery, they often change again. Never know what that will be like until it happens."

She held his gaze a little too long. When he turned away toward the man in the bed, he felt her eyes on him, evaluating him. *One door closes, another opens*, thought Aaron. If the father was a dead end, here was the sister standing right in front of him, decidedly not shy. She seemed... frisky, even in her father's hospice room.

"I'm starving," he said. "Could I interest you in a bite to eat? My treat."

A pretty good diner was over near the train station, Sofia said, and so they went, walking the three blocks along the river path. They sat in a booth. She said they had good matzah ball soup, and ordered it, then made the point she wasn't Jewish, but liked the soup. Aaron had a Greek omelet, and pointed out he wasn't Greek, but liked feta and spinach. He smiled. She laughed, lightly, but her eyes betrayed doubt about whether Aaron was teasing her in a flirting way, or just being snarky.

"Breakfast at this time of day?" she asked.

"One of life's fundamental pleasures," said Aaron, "is having an omelet in a good diner any damn time you please."

She smiled. "I applaud your point of view."

They talked. He asked about her life. When he chose to, Aaron had a way of making people feel they were, at that moment, the most important people in the world. Especially people he liked. People he liked were, most of the time, women. He liked talking to them, along with everything else that came with it. This was in contrast to his interactions with men, which tended to be brief and superficial. Aaron understood this about himself, and thought of it in rather simplistic terms: his relationships with men were transactional, while his relationships with women were deeper, more spiritual. He was also aware, however, that a number of those women would add a footnote: things got less spiritual when Aaron tired of them, and afterwards they felt as if the relationship was actually transactional all along. He understood the complaint but did nothing to resolve it.

Sofia opened right up to his charm. She talked about how she was older than Matt by more than a decade. That she had a better bond with their father than Matt did. She mentioned the conflicts between Matt and his father, and admitted she blamed Matt for a lot of it.

"Matty can be clueless and self-centered at times," she said. "While a lot of their fights happened after I was out and living my own life, dealing with my own problems, I paid enough attention to not be all that impressed with Matty's *jueguitos*, as Apá used to say. His little games."

"He likes his games," agreed Aaron. "I've seen that."

"That's not to say I don't feel badly for some of the stuff Matty went through. But it's all over, pretty much. The guy is almost thirty now and should be a grownup."

"Shouldn't we all. I'm still working on it."

She laughed. "Me too! But I'm doing my best!"

Aaron registered how readily Sofia was critical of her brother, how quick to be disappointed in him and talk about it with others. This was a crack he could shove a screwdriver into, and begin to apply pressure.

"Well, I'm impressed with you," said Aaron, his voice sincere, his eyes steady as he locked with hers. "Matthew's a fool if he doesn't recognize the two remarkable women he has in his life."

She blushed.

"There is one thing I want to warn you about Matthew," he said, his volume low. "I'm telling you this in strict confidence, because you're family."

"Oh boy," she said. "Okay."

"His gambling has not gone well over the last year, he tells me. He's lost a lot of money. I already talked with his girlfriend about his scheme to take money from their savings. What I didn't tell her—because I didn't want to upset her more than she already was—is that Matthew confided that he's close to committing crimes to get the money he feels he needs. I saw him become upset when he lost at the casino, and he threatened someone."

"Are you serious?"

"Oh yes. He's also bragged about ripping off hookers and small-time drug dealers."

"What? Where is he doing that?"

"Atlantic City, supposedly. The casinos are glitzy but the rest of the town can be dodgy. Though I have to say I suspect he was exaggerating. When they're in a weak position and their backs are to the wall, some addicts, young men in particular, try to impress others with how tough they are."

"Matty wouldn't do that kind of thing."

"He doesn't seem like the type, I agree. But you never know. You hear things at Narcotics Anonymous meetings, in particular, that can shock you. Stories about how the nicest young men and women from the nicest suburban families will lie, cheat, steal, and degrade themselves to get a fix. Horror stories."

"But that's drug addicts."

"In my world, you learn an addict is an addict."

Aaron watched Sofia consider how one can never know another person.

"And what about you?" she asked, hoping to change the vibe. "Where did you come from?"

"Rural New York. Some kind of Amish or Mennonite background on my dad's side that was abandoned long before I was born. We moved down to Stroudsburg when I was a kid which is where my mother was from. Job opportunities were better I think. I went to college out west, stayed there until a marriage fell apart, then moved back to Stroudsburg until another marriage fell apart. Then I inherited a house with land on a mountain, and that's where I've been for a while."

"House on a mountain. And I thought I lived in the middle of nowhere."

"And where is that?"

"Cressmanton."

"I never heard of it."

"Nor should you," said Sofia. "Out past Pottstown, a blip on the map, you're in and out before you realize there was a town. But I have this charming old stone farmhouse that someone renovated before my ex-husband and I bought it. I like it a lot. I'm a social media influencer and a mature dating coach, I should live in the city for what I do, but I can't give the place up."

"I don't blame you. Buildings like that, the ones with character and a history, can get hold of you."

"Would you like to see it some time?"

"Very much so."

"You come down here much?"

"No." He paused, then added, "But I have time today, for an adventure like that."

"Oh my," she said. "And what do we tell Matty?"

"I'm not sure. He might get upset. Also, it's considered inappropriate for a sponsor to have contact with a sponsee's family or friends."

"I never heard that rule!" She laughed as if the rule was funny, a foolish indulgence. "I know people in AA, they never mentioned that."

With good reason, thought Aaron, since it was something he made up. "Do they talk about their sponsors?"

"Well, no. Not usually."

"There you go."

"Should I keep it a secret, then?"

"That's up to you. You'll recognize the best time to share it with him, when that moment comes."

***

Hours later, lying under the blanket in the stone-walled bedroom, sharing a joint, glasses of wine on the bedside cabinets, Sofia said, "I don't think there's a rule about not talking to family and friends."

"Well, maybe it's my personal rule," he said. "Which I've broken, obviously."

"What's your greatest strength," she asked, "and your greatest weakness?"

"Wow, you light a joint and out come the job interview questions."

"I'm serious! You can tell a lot about a person by how they answer."

"Okay. My strength is that I'm calm, pretty much all the time. Even when things get hairy."

That was true. Aaron was normally even-tempered.

"Have you always been like that?"

"Absolutely not. A side benefit of getting older, I believe. May I say two strengths?"

"You may."

"The other is that I'm good by myself. I have to be, out there on the mountain, isolated. It's super quiet, and super dark at night when there's cloud cover. But I rather like it. I need to come down to places like Philadelphia and Atlantic City periodically, of course, if I want to see a big concert or major sports thing. There's a restaurant or two in Allentown I'll drive the fifty minutes for, on a whim even, to be around people in a bigger town. But for much of the time I'm happy to keep my own company."

That was somewhat true. He didn't tell her that, in his heart, he believed he was alone because he had alienated everyone over the course of his adult life, and that he feared he would die single and friendless. He didn't tell her that his loneliness was his own fault, due to his choices and his behavior—behavior he found himself unable to change.

"That's nice," she said. "How about your deepest flaw?"

"I have trouble walking away from a wrong that needs to be righted. An error that needs correcting. I don't like letting go of something like that."

"Ah! A white knight complex. I like that. Would you rescue me if I needed it?"

"Sure."

"When you talked about being old," she said, "I thought, he's not that old."

"I am old-ish. It happens to us all, if we're fortunate. Tell me what it takes to be a successful influencer, if you're not a nineteen-year-old in a swimsuit?"

"There's tons of influencers who aren't like that, in all sorts of areas."

"It seems like a lot of work."

"It can be a grind if you're not careful," she agreed. "There are days when it feels too much, but I tell myself I can't afford to stop."

"Because of your followers?"

"The audience for dating advice is huge, especially for women of a certain age, as they used to say. Over half of people in their sixties are sexually active, did you know that?"

"I did not." He grunted. "This here is research, is it?"

She laughed. "Your turn. Being a sponsor: what's it like to be the wise old man giving advice?"

He propped himself up to have a sip of wine. "A lot of pressure to be seen as the smartest guy in the room. Most addicts are intelligent, above average IQs. If they don't see you as at least as smart as them, a lot won't pay attention to what you have to say. They'll listen, but in their head they're thinking, 'That's your opinion, man.' They need to feel your advice is as reliable as what they'd get from a top doctor or lawyer, but more real, because you're one of them."

"I hope Matty is paying attention to what you say to him. He could learn a lot from you. I see in you a future version of him, if he could get over himself and start living like a responsible adult."

"I'm the future version of Matthew?" Aaron assumed she meant it as a compliment. He didn't take it that way.

"One version, anyway. The good version. I wish he understood the value of helping others, the way you do."

"Helping others is my mission in life," said Aaron, taking a sip of wine.

Twenty-Two

The following morning Aaron and Sofia had breakfast and kissed goodbye, both of them quite pleased with themselves and with how things went, although for different reasons. Aaron drove off, heading northeast. One of the online directories listing still-functioning pay phones told him there were several in Bethlehem, off of Route 78 out near the big distribution centers. He didn't know what kind of call tracing technology the police had, and whether it was possible to track a call after the fact, but he was taking no chances.

He called the Crime Stoppers number that was published in the Norristown Observer article about the murders. He expected a robotic voice telling him to leave his message, but to his surprise an actual human answered, a woman with a nervous, breathy voice. He told her he had information about the Blue Blanket Inn murders on Church Street, and he could sense the immediate change in her demeanor. She thanked him for calling. There was a brief pause. *Was she activating a recording device?* He would think calls were automatically recorded; if so, what was she doing? Whatever it was, he was grateful he had the foresight to drive so far out of his way. Should he have disguised his voice, somehow?

The woman came back and asked what his information was.

"I was down in Atlantic City on Friday and met a young man at the Ventura Hotel Casino," said Aaron. "He seemed drunk or high, and he was talking about killing a couple of people that day. Bragging about it, which was creepy. Scary too. I think he was the one who did the murders in Norristown."

"Why do you think that, sir?"

"He didn't say the name of the town, but it was the way he was talking about it, mentioned a motel room, some kind of argument. When I saw the news story about the murders in Norristown, I said to myself, hey, this could be what that guy was talking about."

"Did you get his name, sir?"

"He said his name was Matthew, didn't say his last name. Could be an alias, though, right? They do that, I'll bet."

"Can you describe the man, sir?"

"He was wearing a sweatshirt that didn't fit him right. He said it was a souvenir."

"A souvenir? Can you describe the sweatshirt?"

"Gold, with a big eagle on the back of it."

The operator paused; he thought he heard the tiniest sudden intake of breath. *Bingo!* thought Aaron. He was having a terrific time.

"Thank you for using Norristown Crime Stoppers to report this. Please provide as much detail as you can."

"That's it. That's all he said. But it was enough to get my attention."

"I understand. Can you describe him, more than the sweatshirt?"

"Late twenties or early thirties. Tall, a little stocky, with curly light brown hair. Wearing that sweatshirt."

"Young Caucasian man? He was white?"

"Yes."

"Anything else about him? Anything unusual?"

"No. He did say it happened right after a difficult visit with his father in hospice, so maybe there's a hospital near the motel? I don't know if that helps you."

"It all helps us, sir. May I ask, why didn't you report this right away?"

"You know what it's like in a casino—maybe you don't, sorry. I mean, you meet a lot of braggers and assholes, pardon my French, you don't want to waste your time talking with them, and you don't want to believe half of what they say. But I read about those murders. I put two and two together."

"Understood, sir. You said his name was Matthew, correct?"

"Yes. Seemed like a nice guy but you never know, do you?"

"No sir, you never do. Where is the man now?"

"I have no idea, but I think he said he lived in Toe-something, and he talked about it like it was in Pennsylvania. Could be New Jersey."

"Nothing more than that?"

Aaron made a point of being quiet, thinking. "He might have mentioned Bucks County."

The woman took a moment, perhaps referring to a map, then asked, "Could it have been Tohickon?"

"Maybe. That a Lenape word?"

"I don't know sir."

"Sounds right."

"Is there any additional information you can provide?"

"No. I mean, we were chatting, having a drink, it was cool, until he started talking murders, you know, and I got out of there quick. Even if he was bullshitting, that's still crazy, right? There's no reason to hang around crazy people like that."

That should do it, thought Aaron after the call ended. He didn't do all the work for them, the police would still need to cross-reference the patients in hospice at the medical place by the river, still need to determine Matthew's last name, cross reference it with Tohickon residents. It will mean more to them if they put a little elbow grease of their own into it. But they'll get there. And then they'll realize his details align with the ones provided by that woman Janice at the bar—except for the name, but that's a bonus, because the police will wonder why the young man would use a false name. And the sweatshirt! Aaron took a bit of a chance with that one, if they had found the sweatshirt in a bin a block away from the motel they would know Aaron was lying. Barring that, based on what Janice told him, it seemed like a tease the police wouldn't be able to resist. The dead man wore that sweatshirt, was seen wearing it that day, but it wasn't in the room with the bodies, so where was it? That would drive the cops crazy. It was the kind of detail they hold back from the media as insider knowledge, so it being mentioned in a tip is like sending up a firework. They would be obligated to make a visit to young Mr. Matthew Martinez and have a serious, in-depth conversation with him. The kid will shit himself. Aaron's regret was that he couldn't witness it.

TWENTY-THREE

The passage of time had done wonders for Matt's ability to rationalize his behavior on that catastrophic Friday, which began with two accidental killings in a budget motel and ended with a physical assault and robbery of an old man in a casino parking garage. There had been bad days, featuring flashbacks, anxiety attacks, and restless nights of little sleep. His feelings of guilt and shame had risen and receded like a psychic tide, making it impossible for him to concentrate on anything for long. He couldn't even sustain attention to watch a complete movie on television. There were occasional, fleeting moments of hallucination, sometimes seeing the bodies on the floor out of the corner of his eye, more often the phantom acrid smells of blood and the dying. It had been days of a walking nightmare.

But the arrest of the motel resident lifted the huge weight of fear off his shoulders and that inevitably led to repairing the other parts of him. Not actually healing, perhaps, true healing would take a long time. But enough for him to turn the page on the event, to focus on moving ahead with his life.

That arrest also had the benefit of reminding him of what a lucky guy he truly was. Of all the motels in the state, the incident had occurred in one where a convicted sex offender lived, one who had a prior relationship with the victims. It couldn't have gone better if he had planned it.

***

Both Matt and Jesse were home, in the living room, when the call came in from the Norristown Police Department. A polite and deferential woman who identified herself as Detective Evelyn Wisler explained she was investigating a pair of murders in her town, and believed Matt might have been a witness who could help their case. She wanted to interview him. Matt noticed the way she said it: on paper her invitation to talk would appear benign; her delivery, however, made it seem like a demand, one that could not be refused.

"Interview me?" Matt fought panic. He needed to keep his voice level. "About what?"

"We believe you spoke to one of the victims prior to their death, and we hope you might have heard or seen something that can help us."

"What...," was all he could get out before his voice faltered and his vision fuzzed. He thought he was ready for a conversation like this, but he obviously wasn't. Truth was, he didn't expect this, didn't think they could connect him to the murders. He had no plan, did not rehearse prepared answers to likely questions. He was drifting in space, alone, and his mind was a blank. He had enough sense to realize the best approach was to appear confused and ignorant of the entire subject... but he had to be careful, because they knew he had been there and spoken with Debra. He started over. "What, uhm, murders, what day?"

"Last Friday, at the Blue Blanket Inn, in Norristown."

"I don't know... I don't have any information about that." *How could they connect him to the motel? And so fast?*

"You were there close to noon, and we believe you spoke with a young woman named Debra Maines."

Oh man, he thought, *they're on top of me.* "Am I a suspect?" he asked, waving off Jesse who was crowding him, trying to hear the conversation.

"No, Mr. Martinez. A witness."

"I know nothing."

Jesse reached over and pushed the speaker button on his phone. She paced across the room as she listened.

"We realize that may well be true, but it often happens a witness will hear or see something that has no significance to them but can be a valuable part of solving the puzzle for us."

"Do I have to talk to you?"

"We're asking you to voluntarily meet with us. It's an interview as part of the investigation. If you refuse to be interviewed that's your right. But we have reason to believe, based on witness accounts, you were at the Blue Blanket Inn on the day of the murders and spoke with Ms. Maines, one of the victims. We think you can help us firm up the timeline and understand what was happening with the victim that morning, her state of mind and such. We hope you'll see it as your civic duty to help us track down the murderer."

"That's awful news about her," said Matt, "I didn't know." He thought it through, as quickly as he could. He had the right to refuse to talk to them, but he *was* at the bar, in fact, and he *did* talk to Debra. He imagined an innocent person would be horrified by the crime and eager to help solve it. If he refused the interview, it would be suspicious. It might bring a lot of attention on him. Which would be foolish, especially since the news stories said they already had a suspect in custody.

"If you try to make me talk with you I could get a lawyer, right? Should I get a lawyer?"

"You are free to have an attorney whether you consent to the interview or not. If you believe the nature of your relationship with Ms. Maines was such that you *need* an attorney, that is your right." *Oooh,* thought Matt, *Detective Wisler is sharp.* Her voice was smooth, and calm; the threats were in the words, and the way she emphasized *need.*

"I don't have a relationship with her!"

"I imagine that could well be true."

"We went to high school together."

"Yes, we know."

"It was a coincidence."

"A chance meeting would explain your conversation, Mr. Martinez. I understand that. We're interested in what she talked about. As I said, you could be a big help to the investigation."

Matt hesitated. He didn't know what the smart response was. Maybe what the detective said was true, that they hoped he could shed light on Debra's frame of mind, and on what she was doing there that day.

If he shut down, it could prompt them to pay extra attention. They could start taking apart what he was doing that day... *Oh no...* He had a horrible thought: were security cameras watching him when he stopped along the Atlantic City Parkway to dump the bags? Cops on TV have all sorts of facial recognition software, they could run the video through that. The bag filled with bloody stuff was probably still in that dumpster behind the Reebok store.

He heard you should never talk to the police, ever, even as a witness. He could be walking into some sort of trap, where they get his story all twisted. He could get a lawyer, but where would he do that? How could he afford it? And wouldn't that be a way of saying he had something to hide?

Jesse glared at him from across the room. She shook her head, though he couldn't tell if it was to advise him to tell the detective he wouldn't be interviewed, or in dismay at what she was hearing. She pointed to the phone and waved her other hand to hurry up his answer.

He impulsively said, "Where do we do this?"

"A location where you feel comfortable is fine. We can come out to interview you in your home, if you like."

Jesse leaned forward. "Not here! I don't want you in my house."

"I'm sorry, that was my girlfriend," said Matt, covering his eyes, still trying to sort things. "She's a little upset about a call from the police, I think."

"I understand. Our conversation would need to be private, of course, your girlfriend couldn't be present, which might be inconvenient for her if it is in your home. You can also come down to Norristown to talk with us here."

"I don't know..."

"We can also meet in the police offices out in Tohickon."

Jesse gestured but he couldn't understand what she was trying to say. She rolled her eyes and left the room.

He said, "You caught us at an awkward time. Can you call back in a little bit, or maybe I can call you in an hour or so?"

"Are you agreeing to meet with us for an interview, then?"

He hesitated, then said, "Yes, of course, I have nothing to hide. I want to help."

When Matt hung up he walked down the hallway to the bedroom, where he found Jesse already on the phone with his sister Sofia.

"Put her on speaker," he said.

"What did you do?" demanded Sofia.

"Me?" Matt was offended. "I didn't do anything!"

"Cops investigating a murder don't show up, out of the blue, without a reason."

"They said you were at this motel," said Jesse, tears in her eyes. "What were you doing there?"

"I wasn't at the motel. I was in the café there, getting a coffee after I saw my dad on Friday." It wasn't a café, and it wasn't a coffee, but he thought it close enough to the truth, for the moment.

"Then why do they want to interview you?"

"They think I talked to one of the people that were killed later that day."

"Did you?"

"I guess! I talked to a few people, you know, saying hi and what was on TV, that sort of thing. I talked to this girl that I went to high school with, for like a minute or two, that the policewoman said was killed later. We weren't friends or anything. There's nothing about it I remember."

"That was it?" asked Sofia, sounding like she didn't believe him.

"Yeah, that was it."

"I can't have police coming in my home interrogating my boyfriend," said Jesse. "It will ruin the apartment for me."

"The woman detective said it doesn't have to be at our place," he said. "I have to let her know where."

"So you're going to talk to them?" asked Sofia.

"Why shouldn't I? She said I'm not a suspect."

Sofia laughed. "Yeah, dumbass, you're a suspect even if they aren't calling you one."

"What makes you the expert here?" said Matt, rolling his eyes.

"Because I am the expert, at least out of the three of us," said Sofia. "Remember when I had to talk to the police about vandalism to my ex's car? My attorney friend prepped me on how to handle it, what the police were doing, all that. How they try to trick you and twist the facts around so they can pin things on you."

"But you did vandalize that car!" said Matt. "And that attorney was your new boyfriend helping you get away with it."

"It doesn't matter what I did or did not do, that's in the past, what matters is the advice he gave me," said Sofia. "Which you could use, if you would stop being judgmental and shut up for a minute and listen."

"You need to listen to her," agreed Jesse.

"If you had anything to do with those murders you need to get an attorney right now," said Sofia, "and refuse to talk to that detective. To begin with."

"I know nothing about those murders!"

There was a tense moment in the room as both women considered the situation, and whether Matt could be trusted.

"If this is an interview then you talking with them is okay, I guess," said Sofia. "If all they do is ask you what you saw and heard, fine, maybe they're gathering info. You're a witness."

"That's all I am."

"But if you have a reason, any reason at all, to think they might arrest you now or in the future, despite whatever you're telling us now, then you should treat the conversation as an interrogation."

"What are you saying? That you don't believe me?"

"What I'm saying is, in the unlikely scenario that you aren't telling us the absolute, entire truth about this, then you should probably clam up and get an attorney."

Great, thought Matt. By putting it that way, Sofia has now set it up that getting an attorney, even as a precaution, would be seen by his own family as an admission of guilt.

"What are you talking about?" said Jesse. She was crying again, about the disruption of the police, the threat to her orderly life, the possibility of her boyfriend involved in a crime.

"The way my lawyer friend explained it," said Sofia, "an *interview* is a conversation where the detective is trying to learn more about a situation, not about the person they're interviewing. An *interrogation* is all about the person they're talking to, and where the detective is trying to get an admission from a suspect."

"How is Matt supposed to know the difference?" asked Jesse.

"In an interrogation, if they're trying to get you to admit something, they need to advise you of your Miranda rights," said Sofia. "In a real witness interview they don't need to."

"What do you mean, 'real interview'?"

"Cops lie about this sort of thing all the time, making you think everything is cool, but they're out to nail you. If at any point that detective says you have a right to remain silent and to have an attorney present and all that, even if they're being all casual and friendly about it, you'll know you're a suspect and you're in the middle of an interrogation."

"No way I'm a suspect," said Matt. "I have nothing to worry about."

"I hope that's true," said Sofia.

Jesse sat on the bed and wept.

twenty-four

Matthew spent half an hour selecting the right wardrobe. What do you wear to a police interview? What's the right tone, the right vibe? He assumed he should appear deferential, but also confident. A suit and tie would be too much, trying too hard, like he was there for a job. Casual was the way to go, but it was such a broad category. Can't be so casual as if you were working in the garden, that would be disrespectful. Shabby clothes might make you appear poor and harmless, but that's not how the police would see it, they might interpret it as someone desperate for money and capable of murder in the course of a robbery. Expensive items might irritate the police; if you show up in Tom Ford or Brioni they'll resent you, not that Matt had anything like that in his closet. Where was the sweet spot? He settled on nice jeans and an untucked button-down, under a light topcoat, like he was stopping by to chat with the authorities on his way to have coffee with a friend.

The interview room in the Tohickon Police Department building was eight feet by ten feet. Matt sat at a rectangular wood-topped table, his sunglasses on against the bright overhead lighting, hands folded in front of him. The table was attached to the wall and the floor. Matt sat in one of the two plastic chairs on the rear side facing the door. Across the table were two identical chairs. In one of them sat Detective Evelyn Wisler, who turned out to be a Black woman in her forties with nice eyes, wearing a gray jacket over a high-necked cream-colored knit blouse.

As Wisler consulted her notes, Matt observed there were no windows, in either the wall or the door. The door appeared secure. *Prob-*

ably solid core metal, thought Matt. The floor was a medium gray, not linoleum tiles *(poured epoxy maybe?)* and smooth so it could be cleaned; there was a floor drain placed in one corner. Matt didn't want to think about the stuff that ended up on the floor needing to be hosed off. The walls were slate blue paint up to about waist high, then covered in a tan fabric the rest of the way, to a ceiling covered in acoustic tile. There was an abstract painting in muted colors of the type you might find in an office building, but flush against the wall behind Matt, not hung, maybe bolted in so it couldn't be used as a weapon by an agitated guest.

No clock. Matt had a list of places with no clocks, like casinos and restaurants. Now he could add police interview rooms.

Mounted near the ceiling were two small cameras, one pointed at Matt, the other capturing the table and chairs from the side. He would be recorded but couldn't see any microphone, and the video and recording must go to a digital set-up in a separate room since it wasn't there with him.

"Thank you for coming into town to speak with me today," said Wisler. Matt was struck by the even tone of her voice, more like a therapist than the detectives he saw on television.

"Anything I can do to help." Matt immediately regretted saying such a cliche. He tapped his fingers on his thigh. "I'm surprised you can use a room in a different police station," he said, trying to make something resembling small talk.

"Letting another town's department use an interview space is a courtesy we provide each other. More convenient for our witnesses. How are you feeling today?"

He wasn't paying attention, he was staring at the paperwork on the desk, there seemed to be a lot of it. What did she say? Was he supposed to answer? Maybe say something generic, and hope it's appropriate. Or should he admit he wasn't listening? She might get angry... Or...

"Mr. Martinez," she said, "I asked you, how are you feeling today?"

"I'm good."

"Would you like water? Need to go to the restroom?"

"No, I'm fine."

She considered the sunglasses, how his fingers drummed his leg, how he struggled to focus on their conversation.

"I noticed you wore your sunglasses into the building, then took them off" she said. "Then put them back on when you came in here. Do the lights bother you?"

"Yes, ma'am, they're a little bright. And I'm nervous."

She nodded. "I'll need you to take them off for our talk. Give me a minute..." She rose out of her chair, opened the door so she could reach the light controls in the hallway. She turned off the harsh overhead lighting and turned on four sconces embedded high up into the side walls so unobtrusively Matt hadn't noticed them. The room took on a warmer tone; with the diffuse lighting, the fabric-covered walls, and the painting, it was now more like a business office.

Detective Wisler asked, "Is that better?"

"Yes."

"I have a younger brother who's sensitive to light. And to noise; are you sensitive to noise, Mr. Martinez?"

"Sometimes. It distracts me." Her kind gesture built a little trust in him. *Was it kind, though,* he wondered, *or was something else going on?* His sister warned him the police were manipulative.

"I thought you might be. Quiet in this room, at least, can't hear all the noises out there." She gestured to the door with a toss of her head, then gazed carefully at him. She had a watchful stare that made Matt uncomfortable. He looked away, but wondered if he should, or should not, make eye contact with a police detective. *Even a female one? Would that be confrontational?* He'd rather avoid her eyes, but would it appear evasive?

"Let's get to it then, shall we?" Detective Wisler opened a notebook and grasped a pen. "Tell me about what you heard and saw at the Blue Blanket Inn last Friday."

Matt was confused. "Everything?"

"Your impressions, in general. We'll start there."

"Not much to tell. I stopped in for a beer, chatted with a few people, watched the television, then left."

"Why were you there?"

"I was visiting my father in hospice a couple blocks away."

"Riverside Care?"

"Yeah. He's in a coma."

"I'm sorry to hear it."

"Thank you." It occurred to Matt that Detective Wisler almost certainly was aware of his father's situation, and probably already had the answers to most of the questions she would ask. She was searching for what he lied about. Which was smart, now that he thought about it. He had to be careful.

He realized Wisler was waiting for more from him.

"It was sad and I was a little shaken up," continued Matt, remembering she wanted to know how he ended up at the motel. "I took a walk, to get some air. I stopped by the bar & grill there by the motel, before I headed down to Atlantic City."

"For a beer, you said?"

"Yeah."

"Going to the casinos, were you?"

"Yeah." He became aware that tension had pulled his facial muscles taut and he was afraid it would seem like he was smiling inappropriately. *Then what's the right expression?*

"Who did you talk to while you had your beer?"

"Other than ordering from the bartender, there was an older woman."

"Do you remember her name?"

"I think her name was Janice."

"What did you and Janice talk about?"

"Nothing. She was nice enough, maybe lonely, sort of chatting with whoever came in, you know?"

"Anyone else?"

This was the tricky part. The police knew he was there, and that he talked with Debra. What else did they know? How did they know it? He couldn't lie, they might catch him out, but he shouldn't volunteer anything either. He didn't think he left any fingerprints in the room, but he could have overlooked something... though Detective Wisler hadn't asked to fingerprint him... yet. He kept in mind the advice from Sofia, that once things started to change in Wisler's conversation and activities, when they stopped focusing on the events and started focusing on him, it meant they were eyeing him as a suspect, and he needed to lawyer up.

"I ran into someone I went to high school with, like I told you on the phone."

"Was this Ms. Maines?"

"Yes. She was sitting at the bar." He thought, *Janice would have told them Debra came over to me.* "I didn't recognize her at first, it's been years, but she came over to sit next to me. We talked for a few minutes, then I left."

"What did you two talk about?"

He wasn't sure what to say. What was safest? He answered, "Norristown, mostly. What stayed the same, what didn't."

"About the town... Not about high school days? About what was happening with some old friends?"

"No. She, uhm, she didn't know who I was."

Detective Wisler seemed surprised by this. "Didn't know who you were, but came over anyway?"

Matt cleared his throat. "She was lonely, maybe. Wanted someone to talk with."

"She didn't recognize you?"

"No."

"Have you changed that much?"

"No. More like I was invisible to her and her friends back then. I was some boy in the hallway to ignore."

The detective's tongue pushed against the inside of her cheek as she considered that. "You seem a little bitter about it."

Damn, I'm talking too much. He needed to be more careful. "No, not bitter," he said. "That's the way it was."

"How did she seem?"

"Fine. A little tipsy, maybe, which I thought was not good for that early in the day. She might have been high, too. I felt bad for her, I guess."

"You didn't feel bitter, but you felt pity?"

Why was the detective putting those two things together, when he didn't say it that way? He said, "It seemed like her life hadn't been working out great, if she was spending her day in a bar like that."

"You mean the same bar you were spending your day in?"

He had no answer to that one. Detective Wisler was sharp. She seemed so reassuring when they first met; now she seemed dangerous.

Wisler consulted her notes. It took a long time. Matt tried to stop his fingers from tapping on his leg, or, worse, on the table. She'd think he was nervous, and probably take it as a sign he was lying. But, of course, he *was* nervous, because he *was* lying.

"Who started the conversation?"

"She did."

"Even though she didn't recognize you."

"I mean she thought she recognized me, but didn't know from where."

"I see. A familiar face she couldn't place?"

"Something like that, I guess."

"Did she say that?"

"No, it was how it seemed."

"Did she say anything about her plans for the day?" asked Wisler.

"No, not that I remember."

"Mention anyone she was going to meet?"

"No."

"To clarify, you weren't close friends with her in school?"

Back to that again? Matt was getting whiplash, trying to follow the jumps in this interview. "No. I wouldn't even say we were friends. We knew of each other, the way you do at school. It's a big place, a lot of kids."

"I'm aware," said Wisler. "Went there myself."

"I had my classes, my circle of friends, she had hers, we didn't overlap much except when we might be at the same party or something like that. We never talked."

"So, big school or not, you did know of each other?" She was repeating what he said, but in a different way. It made his answers sound suspicious.

"I would say so, yes. But not to talk to."

"Understood. It seems ironic. When she knew who you were, she didn't talk with you. Now, when she doesn't know who you are, she does talk with you."

Matt noted that wasn't a question, though Wisler seemed to be waiting for a response. It was a strange thing to say, like the detective was linking ideas that had nothing to do with each other, but making it appear that way by how she said it. This was feeling like it was crossing the line Sofia warned him about, where the conversation wasn't so much about the events but about him. Where it slid into an interrogation. Sofia said, in an *interview* the questions from the police will be short and his answers will be a lot longer, because they're gathering information. When it becomes an *interrogation*, she said, the questions from the police will be longer, because they're manipulating you, putting you on the defensive, and that's what seemed to be happening. The ground felt shaky beneath him.

Wisler folded her hands on the table in front of her. "She recognized you well enough to come over to talk, though she couldn't place you," looping back to that point. It seemed to matter to her. "You could have reminded her who you were."

"Yeah, I guess. It might have been awkward though."

"Perhaps. You were overheard introducing yourself to her as 'Alan.' Why would you have done that?"

He saw this coming but was unable to stop it. So yes, this was the shift Sofia warned him about. If he asked for a lawyer now, it would be like holding a sign over his head that he was guilty, or at least had things to hide. He should have refused the interview right in the beginning, at least brought an attorney. Now the only thing he could do was stay as close as possible to the truth without incriminating himself and hope it didn't get any worse.

"I didn't mean any harm by it," he said. "She didn't know who I was. There was something about the situation I didn't like. Maybe because I thought she might be drunk, or high."

"You don't like talking to people when they're drunk or high?"

"It occurred to me she might be a hooker or something. And, to tell the truth, I didn't want to spend an hour talking old times with some stuck-up, drunk, mean girl from high school, I wanted to get down to the shore. So I made up a name." He thought, *Jesus the stuff spilling out of my mouth!*

"A mean girl?"

"Even if she was a reformed mean girl, she wasn't an investment of time I was willing to make." He liked the sound of that. It was a good line. It made him feel a little more confident. But he still felt he was talking too much and giving too much away.

"Did you go to a room with Ms. Maines?"

An important moment. Such a simple question, but everything could balance on it. If they somehow already had him in that room, it was game over for him no matter what he said next. There was only one option.

"No, I left after one beer—I was driving. She was still sitting there. You could ask that older woman."

"Which older woman?"

"The one I mentioned, Janice. The one who told you I introduced myself as Alan. I knew she was eavesdropping."

"One beer, you just said. The bartender told us you had two."

The room felt a lot warmer. "Yeah, sure, I guess. Does that matter?"

Detective Wisler ignored the question, referred to her notes again, which even Matt recognized as a theatrical pause. He thought he saw the slightest of smiles on her.

"Debra talked to several people," he said compulsively, even as he told himself to stay quiet. "Why are you so interested in me?"

"We're talking with everyone who was there, I assure you," said Wisler. "We had to seek you out special, though. Everyone else there that morning was a regular, more or less. But no one recognized you. You were a stranger."

"I happened to be in the neighborhood."

"So you said. Too bad you didn't contact us, once you heard about the murder of someone you knew and had just spoken with."

"I didn't know what happened. I don't follow the news."

"The news is mostly depressing anyway, especially on TV, you're not missing much." She looked into his eyes, and he looked away. She said, "We might have found you sooner, if you hadn't used a false name."

Matt felt an oddness around them. Something about the energy in the room was off, but he couldn't tell what it was. Could it just be the false name? "I wasn't trying to hide," he said, clarifying, words tumbling. "I didn't feel like giving Debra my real name. When she came over, I thought she remembered me, wanted to catch up. But I realized she didn't recognize me at all, which made me wonder why she was all friendly. It made me uncomfortable. I thought it was a good idea to use a fake name."

"I understand; you've explained that already."

"She came over first, though, I want to make sure you know that." *I'm talking too fast.* "You said there were witnesses, I know that old lady would tell you Debra came over to me."

"As I said, we did speak with all the witnesses."

"So how did you find me? I mean, I wasn't hiding, like I said. But I was a stranger, just there for a few minutes. Nobody was aware I was there."

"Not true, Mr. Martinez. Someone knew you, and knew you were there. We received an anonymous tip. Which we then confirmed by speaking again with the witnesses and cross-checking with the Riverside Care visitor log. Which gave us your real name, and your father's name. And that led us to the connection between you and Ms. Maines, and also your address up here. It's difficult to erase your tracks these days."

"I wasn't erasing my tracks." Matt's voice was strained. *I had been so careful.* "Who would have done that?"

"Done what?"

"The anonymous tip."

"We don't know. That's what the word 'anonymous' means."

"Why would someone go to the trouble to lie about me?"

"The information was not a lie, though, was it, Mr. Martinez? You were, in fact, at the bar talking with Debra Maines."

Two realizations jolted Matt. The first was that the tip had to have come from that old guy Aaron, he was mean enough and motivated enough to cause this kind of trouble. The second realization was that Matt had given Aaron the ammunition when, drunk and furious, he confronted Aaron in the parking garage and blurted out about killing two people. Now Matt had a serious problem: what did Aaron tell the police, and how much of it could they prove?

Detective Wisler asked, "What did you do with the gold sweatshirt?"

That stung in the back of his head, like he had been slapped. He realized the entire interview was leading up to this moment. *How could Aaron know about the sweatshirt?* Matt's psyche was lost in the dark. His armpits were damp. He had to think. The one person who saw him was that old lady, Janice, but he had his hood up and his face turned and she wouldn't have recognized him, she would have thought he was Anthony. That was how to play this. Deny, deny, deny. *It wasn't me.*

"What gold sweatshirt?"

"A gold sweatshirt that belonged to the young man who was murdered along with your high school friend Debra. His name was Anthony Ciccone. I understand you went to high school with him, too."

"Maybe. If that's who I think it is, he was a couple of years older. Doubt I'd know him if I bumped into him on the street."

"So, what did you do with the sweatshirt?"

"I don't understand what you're talking about. I don't have a gold sweatshirt. I didn't see it on Debra, and she was by herself so if it belonged to that other guy I know nothing about it."

"A witness said you were in Atlantic City bragging about the killings, and that you were wearing the sweatshirt as a souvenir."

Now that was interesting, albeit terrifying, information. Aaron had been passing along lies mixed with truths. No way to sort out the true stuff from the false without giving up too much information to the police. It felt like being caught in a fishing net, the more he'd struggle the more tangled he'd be. Matt had another moment of panic. He took a breath, considered the right balance of indignation and sincerity, and leaned in a little to show how absolutely innocent and serious he was.

"That's outrageous," he said. He had watched politicians accused of corruption handle interviews, and he mimicked them. "Completely not true. Have you considered the possibility that your anonymous caller is the killer, or an associate of the killer?" Matt internally winced; *an associate of the killer* sounded like something from a TV series, which, of course, it was. "Seems like a thing to send you down the wrong path, by feeding you bullshit."

Wisler nodded, slowly, in agreement. "Of course, that did occur to us."

Matt made a show of thinking, as if he were pulling out a memory half-forgotten. "I won some money off an older guy down in AC, he was upset about it. Maybe this is some sort of swatting thing he's pulling on me."

"The thing is, Mr. Martinez..."

"That's the word, right? Swatting?"

"Yes, that's the word. The thing is, according to witnesses, you are the only person who had anything like a conversation with Ms. Maines that morning. Otherwise, she stayed to herself. That's why we're talking here."

"But I left. Which you know from those witnesses."

"Yes, that's what they said."

"Whenever the murders happened, there must have been enough time for her to meet someone else, maybe someone already in the room waiting for her."

"It could have happened."

"There's a lot of possibilities."

"We aren't saying you're a suspect, Mr. Martinez. We have questions, is all."

"I read you arrested someone."

"A man is a person of interest, true. I still need to explore all the leads that I come across."

"From anonymous tips, people with a grudge. The swatting thing."

"As I explained, this is an informational interview, Mr. Martinez. We need to clear up a few things, and then you can go home."

"This is no longer an interview, this is an interrogation. You're trying to get me to give up incriminating information about myself. And you didn't read me my rights. As I understand it, you were supposed to read me my rights about the time you brought up that gold sweatshirt. I'm disappointed in you, Detective. I expected more professionalism."

"I'm sorry you're disappointed."

"I'm going to go home now," he said. "I know you're not allowed to keep me here. This interview is over."

THE FUNERAL

TWENTY-FIVE

Aaron's cell phone chirped. He was reading a historical novel set in eighteenth-century Scandinavia and was in no mood to talk to anyone. Normally he would not have answered; he was a man who disliked interruptions, especially over the phone, and especially from an unrecognized number. But it could be a sponsee, and if it was his purpose in this stage of his life to help others through the gifts of his experience and hard-earned wisdom, then he was obligated to pick up a call once in a while.

"I can't believe you did that to me, you vindictive motherfucker," said the furious voice on the other end.

"Master Matthew," said Aaron. "How are you?"

"I've been spending quality time with the police because of you."

"Because of me? I don't think so."

"You called in an anonymous tip. I know it was you."

"No, not me."

"That was a shitty thing to do."

Aaron chuckled. "Killing those people was a shitty thing to do. Although I confess you don't seem the type. You're big enough, and lose control of your emotions, but you don't seem competent enough. Unless you were lucky, as you like to think of yourself."

Matt was quiet for a moment. He asked, "How did you know about the gold sweatshirt?"

"What gold sweatshirt?"

"The detective was up in my face about it, but it wasn't in any of the news reports."

"I don't know what you're talking about, but based on what you're telling me it's one of those details the police don't release to the general public? Something like that gets their attention when it pops up again somewhere."

"How could you know about it?"

"How could you?"

"I didn't, until they asked about it."

Aaron grunted. He said, "Police interviews are fun, aren't they?"

"You went to the bar at the motel, didn't you? Talked to people there."

"That would be a bold move."

"I could check, you know," said Matt. "I could go down, talk to the bartender, to the old lady that's always around, find out if you were there asking questions."

"You could. But do you have any idea of how many bald men with gray beards there are in this world? A description like that could be anyone. Besides, I think they would be far more interested in why you returned to the bar at all. I'm sure everyone told the police about the big young stranger with curly hair. You'd be the center of attention if you showed your face there again. A stranger no more."

"They have nothing on me."

"And what purpose would going back there serve? If you were able to convince yourself, and then someone on the police force, that I had visited, so what? I've broken no laws. You could tell them we had met, you could claim I harbored a resentment toward you. Then I could explain why that was the case, about the assault in the parking garage and theft of my money. There might even be video of the incident, if the casino had cameras up there, and if they didn't erase it already. There might even have been witnesses. Honestly, I'm at a loss to understand what you think you're doing right now, making threats that you couldn't follow up on. I'm busy. I need to go."

Aaron hung up.

***

Matt roamed the gambling floor of the Ventura Hotel Casino. He was confident luck would be on his side, that he would locate them. They seemed like regulars. If he didn't find them that day he was prepared to stay overnight and search tomorrow. Or return next week.

There was no sign of Ruby at the blackjack tables.

He strolled up and down the aisles of slots, sunglasses on, earbuds playing music too loud, braving the anxiety from the casino noise and lights. The players had their backs to him, however, and while there were at least a dozen older, thin Asian men, none were Jon.

But of course, his luck delivered. Walking around the perimeter of the room, checking the bars and eateries, he found them having sandwiches in the café. He walked up to their table and smiled.

"Hello," he said with a small, awkward wave. "Remember me? Matt? We met at the restaurant?"

They recognized him, he saw it in their eyes. But they didn't seem happy about it.

"Yes, we remember you," said Ruby, not warmly. "You're the lucky poker guy who got drunk and lost a lot of money playing a numbers game."

Jon nodded and made a gesture with his hands, like he was interacting with a phone.

Without receiving an invitation, Matt sat down. "Yeah, that was me. Remember that man I was playing with? Older, bald, silver beard. Smug attitude. Named Aaron."

Ruby and Jon made eye contact with each other. "Yes," said Ruby with the hint of a question mark after it.

"He's harassing me," said Matt, earnest, leaning forward on his elbows. "He called the police on me and told them lies. Now I have that distraction, when I need to figure a bunch of things out."

Ruby made a pouty shape with her mouth. "Sounds difficult for you."

"I want to give the police your number, you can tell them he stole money from me, he cheated me, and now he's lying to the police about things to get me in trouble before I can try to get my money back. Say you know he's making me appear bad to the cops."

"He's telling the police lies?" Ruby gave him side-eye.

"Aaron's not a liar," said Jon. "Not the man to lie."

"But you saw him cheat me with that app on his phone. You said so yourself."

"I made an observation, that the game was on his phone," said Jon. "Didn't say he cheated. Said you'd never know if he did. Different."

Matt glanced from one to the other. Why were they so wary, stand-offish? "You were a lot friendlier to me that night."

"We saw Aaron last week, down here," said Ruby.

"Playing poker," said Jon.

Matt rolled his eyes. "I thought he quit poker years ago."

Ruby shrugged.

"That was the point of the long, bullshit story he told us about San Francisco," said Matt.

Ruby said, "He bought us a drink and we talked and he told us about you."

"Told you what?"

"Warned us," added Jon.

"Told us you attacked him in the parking lot and stole money from him," said Ruby. "You hit him. He's old, older than us, and you're big and young, and you hit him."

"He cheated me!"

"You don't know that," she said. "Maybe you should have been more careful."

"Maybe not get so drunk next time," said Jon.

"You a little crazy maybe, is what Aaron said." Ruby pointed a finger at him, then toward the exit. "We're not comfortable with you. You should go."

"You're comfortable with him?" Matt's voice rose. Other diners noticed.

"He's nice," said Ruby. "He doesn't get drunk."

Jon nodded. "Doesn't hit people and steal their money."

"So that's it? You're not going to help me? You'll let him have the police on me?"

Ruby was surprised that Matt wouldn't take no for the answer. "You're young, get excited easily. But if you don't leave I call security."

TWENTY-SIX

Aaron lived in Larnersville, in the Poconos, or at least the address on his business card was a post office box there. From what Matt could tell on the map Larnersville proper was about as big as a tennis court, not much more than a couple of gas stations, a restaurant, a post office, a church, a fireworks store, and a handful of other random small businesses serving a population of a couple thousand scattered across the mountains on either side of Route 80.

Matt had given it some thought. Aaron was a self-fashioned recovery guru, the kind that wanted to be respected, to hold the upper hand with people in recovery who, in their desperation to get their life back, hung onto his advice and approval. Such a man would need new meat to feed his desire for admiration, and it would be his Achilles heel. Aaron told Jesse he was Matt's addiction sponsor, and Matt bet the man actually was a sponsor, or had been—what better way to easily acquire weakened people to lord it over? A quick search online showed an Alcoholics Anonymous chapter active in Larnersville, meeting twice weekly in a church there. Not surprising, since what else is there to do every night in the middle of a sparsely populated mountain other than drink? Matt's best chance to come across Aaron, or find someone who knew him, was to attend a meeting.

He had no plan for what he was going to do if the two men did bump into each other. He would deal with that later. Improvise. Let the moment dictate. This went against Matt's instincts to plan and prepare, but since he had no idea what he would find, what the people would be like, how loyal they would be to Aaron if there was a confrontation, he thought it best to avoid a script and keep his options open.

Not having a script didn't work too well for the interactions with that police detective, but maybe it would be different in this situation. If he was going to embrace life, and all it held in store for him, he needed to be able to wing it once in a while.

The ride north was pleasant enough. Pulling off the main road into what passed for the center of Larnersville he saw the restaurant was more of a glorified diner. The fireworks store was down a bit, to the southeast, with a pizza place next to it. A road turned off at the pizza place and rose up the hill, dotted with a few small, old houses before disappearing into the trees. In the other direction, up a little from the restaurant to the northwest, was another road going up the hill, this one with side streets. What passed as the residential part of town. Matt headed that way.

The church was a small structure of weathered brick, with a round stained-glass rose window above a trio of peaked arches, and a bell tower. It was a quarter hour before the start of the Alcoholics Anonymous meeting. If Aaron was driving the Toyota he had in Atlantic City, Matt didn't see it in the parking lot. A small sign announced that the meeting was downstairs in the basement, via the outside steps.

Two dozen people were in the all-purpose room. Some sat on folding chairs, the others milled about with coffee, chatting. Most were over forty. A cluster of old-timers, men and women in their sixties and seventies, sat together to the side. Matt examined their faces, their clothes, and wondered who they were. What were their lives like before they became sober? What were the worst, most shameful moments of those lives, the things they never told anyone?

After what he had been through recently, it was a question he thought about often.

He knew about AA. His father was in and out for years, never putting together much sober time. Apá was the guy who would go to a meeting, then stop at a bar on the way home. There was one thing his father admired about AA, however: it was the only place where he met anyone who had genuinely transformed their lives.

"Most people," his father explained, "they don't change, they stay the same asshole forever, disguising it differently for different people." He could have been talking about himself.

No sign of Aaron among the faces. Matt positioned himself so he could monitor the entrance, in case the man was late. The meeting started with some housekeeping notes, something about a retreat somewhere, then a discussion about a donation to the church. The leader invited anyone new to the program, or visiting from out of town, to introduce themselves. Throughout the room eyes shifted to Matt. He wasn't expecting this, and he felt deeply uncomfortable and anxious from the attention. It was overwhelming. He shook his head, trying for a polite refusal, but it all felt threatening. He pinched his thigh, hard, to distract himself from the rising panic.

"I'd like to introduce myself," said a voice behind him. A nervous woman stood up. She had all the signs of an exhausted young mother. She gave her first name, and said she had her last drink the weekend prior, when she blacked out while watching her baby. That was the last straw for her husband, she said, and she needed to get help, for her baby, her marriage, and herself. Everyone welcomed her, and an older woman leaned over to squeeze the newcomer's hand. The room seemed to have forgotten about Matt, and he relaxed. He got lucky.

There was a reading from the Big Book before things opened for discussion. It didn't seem like Aaron was going to show. Matt considered his options. After the meeting he could ask one of the men where Aaron lived, but that would raise their suspicions. At best they might offer to take his name and number and promise to pass them along to Aaron when they see him, and that wouldn't work. He needed someone who wasn't a grizzled old-timer with a strong belief in anonymity.

Matt suspected Aaron was one of those older men in recovery programs who practiced what's known as the thirteenth step. Men that targeted women recent to the program, especially those single or separated. These women were also sometimes alienated from their families and friends as a result of their behavior. They were the ones most alone and vulnerable as they struggled toward sobriety, so would cling to a kind, knowledgeable older man offering to guide and mentor them. They would see him as a life ring in an open stormy sea, not realizing such men were actually sharks circling prey.

Matt scanned the room for a woman in her late thirties to middle fifties, attractive but without confidence. Someone who still seemed a little nervous being there, maybe concerned someone they know will see them. Not the young mother who introduced herself, she wasn't the right age and babies complicate things for men like Aaron. Not the ones in their sixties and seventies, nor the angry and bitter ones.

Then there she was, across the room, second row back. She raised her hand to speak, introduced herself as Cynthia, and talked about some party or something she had been to the weekend before where everyone else was drinking and she was uncomfortable. Cynthia was pretty but almost certain not to see herself that way. She would be self-conscious about her weight, not realizing her plush, fragile manner was sexy, in its way. He could sense her neediness from where he sat. He would have to approach her with care. If he led with questions about Aaron she might react as the men would. If he seemed to be flirting, she would retreat—she was at least a decade and a half older and, if she had any sense, would distrust him as a possible predator.

As the meeting ended and everyone stacked the folding chairs into the far corner of the room, he placed himself next to her and turned, surprise on his face.

"I thought I recognized your name and your voice," he said. "I'm Matt, we met at a meeting in Stroudsburg, I think."

Matt rarely lied outright, he was more of a liar by omission. He had heard the advice, however, that when you need to lie it's best to stick as close to the truth as possible, and keep it simple. But in a situation like this one, where there were no shards of truth to hang the lie onto, the best one could do was run with something plausible and lean into it.

"I don't go to meetings in Stroudsburg," she said, though she took his hand and shook it.

"I could be mistaken about the location, but not about you!" He needed to keep up momentum. "You look great. Did you cut your hair?"

"It's a little longer now, than it used to be," she said, her fingers reaching up.

"I knew there was something different." Man, he wasn't guessing anything right. Still, he had to sell the story and keep the pressure on. "It's my first time at this meeting. I'm searching for a friend of mine, Aaron Stoltzfus. He's my sponsor."

"I know Aaron," she said, a little more softly than she was speaking before.

All thirteen steppers break off the relationships: reel one in, throw it back, drop your line into the water once again, repeat. Matt wondered where Cynthia was in that lifecycle. If she was still sharing Aaron's bed, she might be more protective of his privacy than if she had already been discarded.

"Wow!" said Matt, with perhaps a little too much enthusiasm. "I need to chat with you then. I'm a little hungry, I haven't eaten all day. Can I buy you lunch at that diner I saw coming in?"

She hesitated, checked the room around her. He wasn't sure if she was shy, or cautious, or something else. She nodded her head.

TWEnTY-SEVEn

He had a club sandwich, she had a grilled cheese, and they sat in a booth by the window.

"You can call me Cindy, by the way," she said. "I use Cynthia in the rooms because it seems more formal, people respect me a little more, know what I mean? But everyone calls me Cindy."

"Okay, I'll call you Cindy, too." He gestured with his chin toward her sweatshirt. "You went to DeSales University?"

"No, my husband did. Ex-husband I guess now, sort of. The process isn't done but we're separated."

"Sorry to hear that."

"I'm living with my sister temporarily. It's okay. She gets on my nerves sometimes, though." She took a fork full of greens. "Guess I get on hers too, living in her house. I'm working and trying to save some money so I can move out."

"That's good. Where do you work?"

"Here," she said, looking around the restaurant.

"Oh. That's why the waitress waved when we walked in."

"Yeah. I didn't finish college, my husband was the smart one, then the drinking, and you know how that goes."

Matt wasn't sure exactly what she thought he should know. He asked, "You see Aaron a lot, do you?"

"Not so much anymore. We were kind of together, then we broke up."

"Oh. I thought maybe he was your sponsor."

"Started that way. I'm willing to forgive him if he takes me back, I'm not too proud to admit. It's lonely out here, nobody to talk to, nowhere to go."

The woman had no filter, thought Matt, letting everything out between bites. "But you're sober now, so that's good," he said.

She grimaced. "I'm sober-ish. It's not easy."

"No, I imagine not."

"You would know, though, right? You're in the program."

"Uhm, yeah, true. I meant, the whole thing you're going through."

"Yeah, right?" She took him in with a tilt of her head, like a spaniel. "So where did you meet Aaron?" she asked.

"Atlantic City," he said, without thinking it through.

"You mean, like at a casino?"

"Yeah."

"Huh." She thought about that for a moment. "Not the big casino in Bethlehem? He goes there, I know. Didn't realize he went to Atlantic City, too."

"Maybe he does that once in a while. Plus Bethlehem doesn't have everything. I live closer to it than the shore places, but their poker room was kind of crappy. Though I hear they remodeled."

"I don't know, maybe. I don't play cards." She thought again. "I thought you said you met him at a meeting in Stroudsburg?"

He coughed. "I said I thought you and I had met in Stroudsburg."

"Which we didn't because I don't go to meetings in Stroudsburg. Or casinos, for that matter."

They were quiet for a bit. It wasn't a bad place, clean and bright, and the sandwich was good. The other customers were a smattering of retirees, a few farmer types, and two well-dressed people who looked like they were driving through on the interstate and pulled off for some lunch.

She said, "You know that Bethlehem casino, it's owned by Indians who live like half the country away!"

"I didn't know that."

"Every person in the tribe gets like a million dollars a year from the gambling business." She shook her head in wonder at it all. "Is that crazy or what?"

"Another thing I missed out on, through the accident of where I was born."

"Tell me about it." She scratched the back of her hand. "Aaron is your sponsor, you said."

"Yeah."

"But you don't know how to get hold of him?"

"Uhm, no."

"Not even by phone?"

"Oh yeah, I have his number. But I prefer face to face."

"How do you do that if you don't know where he lives?"

It wasn't her husband who was the smart one after all. She was pretty clever, under the strawberry blonde hair. *She's worse than that detective*, thought Matt. "We connect closer to where I live," he said, hoping she would buy it.

She nodded. "Okay, cool."

He could tell she wasn't buying it. They again fell into silence. He considered how he would get the location to Aaron's house out of her, when she said, "You're not his sponsee."

"I'm not?"

"No."

"Why would you think that?"

"I can tell. You get things wrong you should get right without thinking. What's up with you two?"

He shoved a fry in his mouth, buying time to think. Eventually he said, "I am his sponsee, that much is true. But ... in addition ... I had a small beef with Aaron about money... that I borrowed. I owe him some. Gotta return it soon."

"I'll say you do. He's a vindictive guy when he thinks he's been stepped on. Aren't you worried he'll come after you?"

"Is that the thing he would do?"

"That's the thing he would do."

"You mean with a gun, or a tire iron? He's some kind of thug?"

She let out a noise that sounded half grunt, half laugh. "Sometimes, but not normally. He'd figure out some way to fuck you up, though. He's devious."

"Then it's good I'm returning the money, I guess! I want to put it in an envelope and stuff it in his door, without seeing him or anything, which would be awkward."

"Okay. He'll still want to thank you in person, he's also like that."

"He wouldn't find me, though."

"If he wants to, he'll find you."

She wasn't chatting, Matt recognized, she was dropping warnings.

She pointed southeast, along the road that passed by the restaurant. "Go down this street here, about a mile or so, then turn right on River Road right after the little bridge. The sign should be up, but if not there's another sign says it's County Road 204 but no one calls it that. Take River another mile at least, you'll climb up, until at the crest of a hill you'll see an old farmhouse falling apart, no roof, overgrown, and across from that is his road. No sign, I'm not sure it even has a name but I guess it must. Turn right and take that for a while. You'll pass houses, then the houses will stop, there will be trees, then the woods open up and there will be a small house, with a garden, and across the road is a big barn. That's his place."

"Okay. It all sounds rustic."

"Everything up here is rustic, including the people." She stole a few fries from his plate. "Well, I told you where he lives because you bought me lunch. I'd say leave him alone, though. In my opinion he's a little dangerous."

"How dangerous?"

"I know he was arrested for assault once or twice," she added. "Never convicted though."

Matt was surprised by that. He was learning so much. Aaron was more complex than he anticipated. "You had a thing with him even though you thought he was dangerous?"

Cindy shrugged. "Part of the appeal, I guess. He's a reformed bad boy." She smiled, and her eyes lit up. Matt could understand, at that moment, why Aaron pursued her. Beneath her insecurities and middle-aged frumpiness was a headstrong, barely disguised minx.

She said she had to leave to feed her sister's dog. She mentioned, in passing, that she had to walk up the hill because her sister had the car.

Even Matt, never one to pick up the subtle hints of women, recognized that one. "Let me drop you off," he said, and she accepted. Halfway up the hill she told him to pull over to a small blue bungalow with a porch and a large rhododendron bush at the front corner. She left the car without a thank you for either the lift or the lunch.

He drove back down to the restaurant and followed the road past it for a little more than a mile until he crossed the little bridge. He nearly missed River Road, tree branches obscured the sign. He headed up the hill, passing an odd mix of houses. Some were ancient wood frames, close to the road, while a few were recent construction, spacious ranches set back behind wood fencing. There was a small, abandoned machine shop of some kind, standing by a two-story house badly in need of painting and roof repair that nonetheless seemed inhabited. Then a small farm, then a shuttered, lone shed offering firewood. He came to the roofless farmhouse she told him about, its walls dark gray and decaying. He turned onto the road opposite and went further up the mountain.

He asked himself why he was doing this. Yes, he was angry about the cheating in that numbers game, the anonymous tip to the police, and the visit to his house. But driving up and surprising Aaron, provoking a confrontation that would lead to shouting and posturing and threats and what all... he realized that was neither sane nor effective. It was cathartic, though, and catharsis has its role to play.

Furthermore, he told himself, catharsis was called for because he understood he hated Aaron, which he couldn't easily admit to himself, let alone anyone else. Because it was juvenile, based primarily on how smooth Aaron was. The old man was good with what people called the soft skills, that invisible currency of getting ahead in the world. Reading the room, small talk, and adapting to unspoken rules is the stuff comprising the world's secret handshake. It's how people build relationships, find respect, acquire friends and lovers and mentors, attract business partners and clients, land jobs and get promotions. They were the skills that convinced people to like you, and being liked wasn't a nice perk, it was essential to doing well in the world.

Matt was never smooth like that, could never be. People like Aaron were born with a kind of Rosetta Stone in their brain that enabled them to interpret other people and their actions. Matt had no such device; understanding situations was a constant challenge. And he often got it wrong. Matt would tell himself, *Who cares?* But he cared. Once in a while he came across somebody who rubbed him the wrong way, simply because they had been given the things he never had. A few, like Aaron, also made him feel insulted by it, even harmed, and it festered. The situation needed to be resolved.

Matt passed a few small, isolated homes, one a wooden structure no bigger than a single car garage with a front door and dirty curtains on the windows. Soon the buildings disappeared and woods took over, an abrupt density of trees and brush full of furtive creatures watching him. A slight turn, a little rise, and the woods abruptly receded. He was at Aaron's place, the road cutting through the center of the property, as Cindy said. Matt wasn't prepared for how close everything would be. The large barn, old and in need of paint, was a few yards off the road to his left. On the other side there wasn't much more distance to the front step of the small house on the right. He was driving through the man's front lawn.

The house sat slightly askew, as if the first and second floors had settled in different directions. A cracked, indifferently maintained macadam drive entered between a shed and a vegetable garden, and in the rear of the side yard was a full firewood lean-to. Aaron stood by a half cord of wood, axe in hand, splitting the larger pieces.

At the sound of the car Aaron turned. Matt pulled his cap down and his collar up and kept going. He allowed himself a quick sideways glance, through the sunglasses, and caught Aaron staring right at him.

In that moment Matt realized he didn't want a confrontation, he didn't even want Aaron to know he had been there, though it was too late for that. He wanted to know where Aaron lived. Though what he would do with that information he had no idea. This improvisation, moving forward without a detailed plan, was disorienting for him. Probably doomed to fail, every time. And, yet, a little exciting, truth be told.

As Matt drove on, pretending to be someone who had somewhere to go, he saw nothing but woods in front of him and he feared the road would come to a dead end and he would be trapped on Aaron's home turf. He had seen movies like that; they never ended well.

He came to the entrance of some kind of camp, closed up in the off season. The road wrapped around the steep rise that served as a backdrop to Aaron's house, and eventually civilization came again in the form of an old auto service shop, then the odd house, then more, until he dropped back again on River Road. It was a long, lonely loop. Matt assumed the road by Aaron's house was rarely used, except when the camp was open, since it led nowhere. Should Matt ever have reason to come back, he needed to remember that. It meant no witnesses, for one. But also, with that kind of isolation and limited access, Aaron would be hard to surprise.

TWENTY-EIGHT

Aaron stepped into the restaurant and eyed the room. Mid-afternoon, with a few older couples starting an early dinner, and a table of four road crew workers finishing a late lunch. Cindy came out of the kitchen with two salads for a pair of young women by the window. He nodded to her, and she nodded back. He took off his watch cap, stuffed it in the pocket of his brushed leather barn coat, and put the coat on the empty chair.

"Hey," said Cindy when she came over.

"Hey," answered Aaron.

"This isn't my table. You wanna chat it's okay, we're not busy. But you need to sit over there." She gestured with her chin at a table twelve feet away, near the entrance to the restrooms. Aaron got up, moved his coat over, and sat so he had a good view of the room. He ordered a chicken salad wrap with sweet potato fries, and a cup of coffee, with a glass of water.

"How you been?" he asked.

"Okay. Been better. My knee's bothering me. Is that why you're here, to ask me about that?'

"Uh, no, I was wondering..."

"Hold that thought," said Cindy, acknowledging one of her customers gesturing for the check. She walked off. When she returned she was carrying his water and a cup of coffee.

She bumped him with her hip when she placed the coffee in front of him. "You were going to ask me something?"

"Yeah," he said. "Did anyone come by for me in the last few days?"

She raised her eyebrows, declining to commit to an answer. "Something going on?"

"A guy drove by my house yesterday, I thought I recognized him from another place and time. Not many people know where I live, or how to find it. Somebody must have told him."

"Why would you think it was me?"

"I don't. I have a list of possibles. You're number three."

She gave a little shrug with one shoulder. "There was a young guy, came to the meeting at the church looking for you. Said he was a friend, a sponsee."

"Big kid, curly hair?"

"Yeah. Said his name was Matt. That his real name?"

"As far as I know. Why ask that?"

She shrugged again. "I had a feeling he was lying about stuff. I'll be back." She talked to the four crew workers, then disappeared into the kitchen. When she came out she had Aaron's wrap.

"Lying about what?" asked Aaron, analyzing her face as he sipped coffee.

"I don't know. Everything, maybe. He said there was some money beef between the two of you."

Aaron shook his head. "No beef. Whatever money issue there was got dealt with a while ago."

"He said he owed you money. I asked, wasn't he concerned you'd be mad? He seemed like he didn't care."

"He doesn't care. So, you told him where I lived?"

"Yeah. He wanted to give you your money back. Did he?"

"Did he what?"

"Give your money back?"

"No. He drove by. Maybe he's shy about it."

"Or nervous. I'm off at five, you wanna get together. Watch a movie."

Aaron considered it. "How about a rain check on that? Sounds like a good idea but not tonight."

She went off to deal with other customers.

Aaron thought about it all. He assumed Matt drove up because of Aaron's visit with Jesse. Was he going to confront Aaron, then chickened out? Or was it to brag he had found where Aaron lived? Aaron wasn't sure how much he would like it if that curly-haired young pest was going to invade his mountain and be annoying.

Unfortunately, Aaron didn't have the option to end the game they were playing, there were too many psychological and emotional sunk costs. He had poisoned the well with Matthew's girl Jesse, and that needed tending. He had secretly started up with the sister, Sofia, which was occasional but worth the drive down, and he still wasn't sure how to best leverage that. Of course there were the police, breathing down Matt's neck, a delight just to think about. Aaron was too invested to quit. By cruising the mountain house and adding another dimension to the feud, Matt showed he wasn't likely to stop playing either.

What was more, by weaseling the location of Aaron's house out of Cindy, and doing that drive-by, Matt had committed yet another provocation that required a response. Moderate escalation was called for.

He took out his phone. He now had Matt's phone number, thanks to that threatening phone call about the police.

"These dark, empty woods can be dangerous for newbies," he texted. "Be cautious!" He added a little smiley face icon to the text and pushed send. It was an acknowledgement that he had seen Matt drive by. A little bit of a dare, a little bit of a threat.

Then he dug into his chicken salad wrap.

twenty-nine

Matt bolted up in bed. Something was on the roof above him, walking around. He checked the time, it was after two thirty in the morning. He went to the window, twisted his neck so he could see the edge of the roof, though the eave blocked any view he might have. He searched the pavement and parking lot below, even though that's not where the sound came from. As he crawled back into bed he disturbed Jesse.

"Stop pulling on the covers," she said.

"I'm getting back in."

"What were you doing?"

"There's something walking around on the roof."

"Yeah, squirrels. They do that all the time."

"In the middle of the night?"

"I don't know, maybe their boyfriend woke them up."

"It didn't sound like squirrels."

"Goodnight Matt."

He lay there, listening to the sounds above. To him they sounded more like footsteps than the skittering of rodents. He wondered if a bear could get up there; they were good climbers. The steps were moving to the other end of the apartment, toward the kitchen.

Something thumped on the balcony off the living room, as if it jumped off the roof and landed there. Matt got out of bed again to inspect. He walked down the hallway, asking himself if he had checked the sliding door was locked before he went to bed. He peeked around the wall and saw there was nothing, and nobody, on the balcony. Between the two chairs out there, the small table had been knocked over onto its side. He approached, checked the lock, and squinting through the dark across the parking lot he thought he saw someone running into the woods.

He ran down the stairs and out into the cold night air. There were no sounds other than the slapping of his bare feet on the pavement as he raced to the other side of the apartment complex. He slowed as he neared the spot where he saw the person, or animal, enter the woods. As he stepped off the pavement and onto the grass, a security light on the back of the building nearby was triggered, flooding the area with a pale light. Matt thought he saw a face in the trees, a face nearly—but not quite—human, with eyes that glistened with the reflected light. The face looked more like his father, than Aaron. It turned and was gone.

***

The next morning Jesse pulled the covers off his head and shook him.

"Get up, Matt," she said.

"A little more," he mumbled.

"You know how you hate it when you stay in bed too long, you say it makes it hard for you to get to sleep that night." She sat on the edge of the bed, putting on her shoes.

"Aaron was here last night."

She stopped what she was doing and turned. "What?"

"Yeah. He was on the roof, and he jumped off onto the balcony, then I chased him across the parking lot into the woods."

"On the roof?" she asked. "And into the woods? How could he get up on the roof?"

"I'm not sure he's human."

"Seriously?" She continued dressing. "You ran out of the house in your pajamas? Wasn't it cold?"

"A little."

"If you saw something run into those woods then it was probably a deer. Or it was a dream."

She was most likely right, it was a dream. Fueled by his anxiety about Aaron's harassment. But were dreams something to ignore? Didn't they carry warnings, and insights? In any case, that night, and for several nights after, he triple checked the front door, and the sliding door to the balcony, to make sure they were secure.

THIRTY

A week went by before Aaron received any kind of response to his text. It was a rainy evening, and he settled in to watch a British police procedural on Netflix. He had made himself a hot cup of lemon and ginger herbal tea, to which he added honey, and it sat on the side table next to him. There was also a small piece of spice cake made for him by a woman friend, one of the various he met through the recovery rooms. Women like Cindy. Women of a certain age, trying to stop drinking or taking pills or gambling away the family accounts, in order to get their life back together. Some of them were in the rooms because they couldn't stand what they saw in the mirror one day. Some were sat down by their kids and told they had to quit killing themselves. Some were getting sober because their partner threatened to leave if they didn't. Some were required to go by a judge.

Most of them, however they got there, were raw and vulnerable and feeling hollowed out. Many of those responded to Aaron's performance as a kind, warm older man, generous with his time, who built up their self-esteem. He gave them the human connection that had often been missing in their lives. A wise, patient man who became, for a time, their lover. He liked to think he was a good lover, one who could please them and make them feel seen and appreciated. Small gifts like spice cake, or a book, or a new watch, were the least they could do to show their gratitude. To him there was something fundamental about that ritual, something primitive at the animal level, like how crows and dolphins and cats bring you gifts if you feed them.

Things would go south, of course. They always went south. He became bored with these women, or they returned to their husbands, or they figured out he was more mercenary than kind. The periodic emotional turmoil was the cost of doing business.

A call came in. This time Aaron recognized the number.

"Master Matthew. Calling to threaten me again?"

"Threats? You threatened me with that text last week."

Aaron chuckled. "That was no threat. You were driving around on the mountain and I wanted to make sure you were safe about it. This isn't like a shopping plaza up here, it's dense with trees and distant from everything, and it's easy to become lost. It's possible to hurt yourself and not be found for months, even longer."

"You want me to stay away, I get that."

"I should have mentioned there are a lot of wild animals, not all of them friendly."

"Problem is, old man, I can go where I want, do what I want."

"Yes, as a general principle that's true... Is that why you called? To warn me you'll be coming back? A little dramatic, isn't it?"

"My dad passed away, and I want you to leave me alone. I can't deal with you right now. I got my mind on other things."

"I'm sorry to hear that."

"Don't pull that polite thing. I am so tired of your bullshit, messing with my life."

They were both silent.

Eventually Aaron said, "You're like the man in the boat."

"You're babbling."

"It's an old story. A man is riding his boat on the river, and another boat drifts into his path and bumps into him. The man inspects the other boat. If it is empty, the man maneuvers around it and continues on his way. He might even be concerned about why there was a drifting boat. But if there is someone in the other boat, lying on the floor drunk or asleep, the man becomes angry and curses the other one for the delay, demanding he pay for the inconvenience. Yet what is the difference? Same situation, same remedy to go around the other boat."

"What the hell are you talking about?"

"You're the man in the boat. Things are in your way. Many of them are a result of your own actions, some of them due to circumstances, but they are what they are, and you need to deal with them. But right now you don't see that. You see me, and you're placing your anger on me for all of these things."

"You sent the police after me, I know it."

"It shouldn't matter whether I did or not. The police talking to you about those murders is completely appropriate. You were there, you talked to the victim. That is what you need to face. You bitching at me is a diversion, and irrelevant."

"The cops aren't interested in me now anyway. I had two long interviews with them, and it's over. I'm not a suspect."

Aaron hoped that wasn't true. He wanted to get a lot more mileage out of it. "You should also consider the impact of it on your girlfriend, and your sister."

"What about my sister?"

"Phoning me at night, interrupting my program, disturbing my peace and quiet—I had a nice cup of tea that has now grown cold—is not going to help you resolve any of that. You need to find the courage to change those things that you can. As for me, I'm something you can't do anything about, so you need to let that go."

"Fuck you." Matt hung up.

Aaron smiled. He didn't feel like getting up to reheat his tea, so drank it tepid. He was aware of the death of Matthew's father, of course, Sofia had told him about it, and he consoled her as she grappled with her sadness. She told him the funeral plans and he would be sure to attend. It would be an excellent opportunity to assess the dynamics between Matthew and his sister and girlfriend, and to prod the boy further.

Aaron hoped the funeral might serve as a signpost. He had been unsure how to respond to Matthew casing his house. He didn't want to let it drop, but neither was he certain of the right approach, the level of severity; it was a matter of craftsmanship, in a way. He sent that text as a trial balloon, to see if Matt responded and how, so he could take cues from it. The phone call was a help. He now understood Matt was, in addition to being agitated by the police, rocked on his heels a little by his father's death. Aaron showing up at the funeral should stir the pot. He was still having a grand time toying with Matthew Martinez. He leaned back and put the television show back on.

THIrTY-ONE

The morning of the funeral was overcast and cool, which suited Matt's mood. As he struggled with his tie Jesse shouted from the kitchen, reminding him they promised Sofia they would be there early to help set up.

"I'm working on it," he said. Then, after a pause, "I'm glad the old man's gone, you know."

"I know you think that, this morning," she said, walking back into the bedroom.

"He killed my mother."

"He had flaws, and your life with him after she passed was difficult," said Jesse as she adjusted the knot in his tie. "But he didn't kill her. She had a heart attack."

"His behavior was so bad she left. She didn't fight to stay alive. She wanted out."

"Your mother would not have abandoned you."

"But she did."

"You're still grieving her, I know. You might take some peace in knowing a lot of your father's bad behavior in those final years was because he was still grieving her, too."

"How would that give me peace?"

"It can help you understand him better. Maybe even find a way to forgive him."

"Why would I want to forgive him?"

Jesse brushed some lint off Matt's jacket. She said, "Haven't you ever heard that advice, that holding on to resentment doesn't harm the other person, it harms you? Holding a grudge is bad for your well-being, for your soul."

Yes, he had heard it. He also was familiar with the one that said resentment is like taking poison hoping for the other person to die. Which was bullshit, as far as he was concerned. He was going to hold onto his grudges, nourish them, and keep them in a ventilated box in the closet of his mind where he could retrieve them any time he wished.

***

The service was held in a funeral home in the northeast part of Norristown, next to an auto supplies store and across the street from the big bowling alley. Sofia, who organized it, expected a few pointed questions about why it wasn't held in a church, but she would pay no attention. Her father hadn't stepped inside a church in decades. She had renounced Catholicism when she was in her early twenties, and her current beliefs fell into whatever gray area existed between evangelical smugness and new age hipsterism. She did not know what her brother's beliefs were, other than his jibber-jabber about luck, nor did she ask.

Matt and Jesse arrived offering to help Sofia, who didn't need any help. There were two reception rooms on either side of a wide hallway, and theirs was the smaller one. Chairs were arranged, all pointing forward to where the casket sat, opened. The three of them took up a position near the entrance so visitors could say hello and express awkward words of sympathy.

"Is this a viewing or a funeral service?" asked Jesse, confused.

"Both," said Sofia. "We didn't have a separate viewing, but some people would like to see him one more time."

Matt said, "I didn't realize it would be open casket."

"I told you that," said his sister.

He sniffed. "At least this way we can make sure he's dead, so we can sleep without fear at night."

Jesse grimaced and turned away. Sofia said, "Jesus, Matty."

"It would take a stake through his heart for me to be confident he wasn't a danger anymore," he said.

"This is why I didn't confer with you about the funeral plans."

"I'm glad we're getting him cremated," said Matt, getting the last word in.

To the side of the entrance was a sign-in book, and a memories board full of photographs. Their father with both his wives, and his children. Posing in front of a series of restaurants. Holding some kind of trophy. Standing in a tourist trap off a highway. Smoking a cigarette near an ocean.

"Those are what our lives are reduced to," said Matt, nodding toward the images. "Photos of how we wanted to be seen, but no photos of how we were."

"They do seem mocked up for a movie," agreed Sofia. "That's what you do at funerals."

Matt walked up to the casket and considered the body. He wasn't mourning the loss, in his mind he had said goodbye to his father years ago. He had done it when he made the break, knowing Enrique could never again be the man Matt wanted him to be because he never was to begin with.

The night he tossed Matt out, Apá was drunk early, in a foul mood. He brought up the sorest possible topic, what he called his "family plan," which was for Matt to attend a couple of years of community college to learn business and accounting, then work full-time in the restaurant. He was angry Matt wouldn't agree to it. Matt said it wasn't personal, he just wanted to cut his own path. This was a lie, however, as there was no way he would work for his father, not with the behavior Matt had been witnessing. Matt saw the pressure as an attempt to control him, to get him to do most of the work running the restaurant while his father strutted around, playing the boss, everyone calling him Apá. Matt was to be the dutiful son who didn't have an opinion, didn't ask questions, had no life of his own. They both dug in, words were exchanged, and then the slap.

And yet there were good times, since even the worst lives have their moments. His father had taught him how to play poker, for example, and for that he should be grateful. Matt had been a young teenager, and men—they were all men—would come over and sit around the dining room table, some sipping beer, the others iced tea. A couple of guys from work, a meat supplier who lived not that far away, a neighbor, and a golfing buddy. Apá would stake Matt a pile of coins from his large jar full of them, and they played penny-ante games, with liberal betting rules to drive the pots up. Dealers called the games, which were often junky seven-card stud variations that were a lot of fun for Matt, even if he sometimes became confused because play moved so fast. There was "roll your own" where all the cards were dealt face down and the player chose what to show. There was "queens follow" where all queens were wild, and any card dealt following a queen was also wild, which could get out of hand. A saner, if more frustrating, variation was "aces change" when the card following an ace was wild, but the next time a card followed an ace that one was now wild and the first one—the one you had been betting on—no longer was. There was "baseball" where threes and nines were wild, its variation "sixty nine" (the naughtiness of which went over Matt's head when he first started playing), and "acey ducey" where aces and twos were wild. There was even a version where the worst hand, rather than the best, won the pot, but they didn't play that one much. The guys from the restaurant would curse and bitch in Spanish, the others in English, and everyone treated Matt with kindness even as they cleaned him out. He felt like one of the guys, back then, secure that his father loved him and would take care of him and not turn on him like a psychopath.

You never know about people.

"I know it was rough for you, too, when mom died," said Matt, quietly, as if to be heard only by the corpse in front of him. "But you had your business, and your booze, and your staffers you were sleeping with. I had nothing to distract me. It was a time in my life when I could have used a father, someone to share my grief, give advice, help me over the rough spots. And man, there were a lot of rough spots. I needed someone I could trust and lean on. Instead, there was you."

Mourners trickled in; relatives, a few neighbors, men and women who had worked in Apá's restaurants. Many stopped and signed the book and reviewed the photos. They all paid proper condolences to Matt and Sofia, speaking in hushed tones about what a good man their father was and how he would be missed. Neither sibling believed a word of it. Most of the visitors then drifted toward the open casket at the front of the room, standing by the large flower arrangements. Some said a prayer, or a goodbye, or a curse, then found a seat.

A man in an ill-fitting gray suit stumbled down the hall, nodded to Matt and Sofia, then entered the room without signing the book.

Sofia leaned toward her brother. She asked, "Is that…?"

"Yes," said Matt. He turned to Jesse. "Man's name is Bernardino. Left dad's restaurant on bad terms. Surprising he's here."

"One of the people Matty was talking about, who needs to make sure dad passed on," said Sofia.

"What were the bad terms about?" asked Jess.

"Bern said dad kept money from him," said Matt. "Cheated him on his paychecks, didn't give him his tips."

"Is that true?"

"Knowing my father, pretty likely."

"His tie was askew," said Sofia. "Seemed a little tipsy."

A cluster of barely remembered distant relatives came in, and Matt introduced them to Jesse. "I'm not good talking to so many people," he whispered to her when the cluster moved on. "I don't know how long I can do this without running away."

"No one likes these things," said Jesse. "We're all uncomfortable. You'll get through it. Don't hold your wrist so tight, you'll wrinkle the sleeve."

A short man in a checked suit came up with a big smile and shook all of their hands with an energy more suitable to a wedding than a funeral. The man leaned forward and said, "I hope the old man left you two plenty in the will!"

The three of them watched him walk away.

"Wow, that was inappropriate," said Jesse, turning to go down the hall to the bathroom.

"One of our cousins," said Sofia. "That was on brand for him."

"He's not wrong, though, about the will," said Matt, making sure no one else was around. "I'm curious to see what he left us."

"I told you there won't be much money, if any," said Sofia. "It all went toward his health care."

"There's the house, though."

"I have to sort that out." She lowered her voice to a whisper. "What do you need the money for anyway? You'll just use it to fuel your gambling."

"None of your business what I use it for."

"Tell your girlfriend that when she gets back. Tell her you're going to use money from dad's house for buy-ins at the poker tables rather than a down payment on your own place."

He flushed, but didn't respond. Instead, he said, "Remember I want those elephant bookends. The only things out of the whole house I want to keep."

"I told you already, they aren't there," said Sofia. "After the last time we talked, I went over to the house and double-checked. Nowhere to be found."

"They were there the last time I visited him."

"What, years ago?"

"Oh, did he redecorate since then?"

"What's the big deal? They aren't valuable, we talked about this."

"They're valuable to me, they have meaning to me. Why isn't that enough?"

"It's enough, I don't know why they would be."

"They're the memento of my childhood that remains happy," said Matt, who gave Jesse's hand a quick squeeze when she returned. "As a little kid I thought they were special, like expensive and rare sculptures. Like see, we have a little culture in our house, a little sophistication."

"They were bookends, Matty."

A clean-cut man in his thirties entered the funeral home. He wore jeans with a navy sport coat over a pale gray dress shirt, and carried a guitar case. On his head he wore a dark gray fedora with a feather in the band. He came right up to them and gave Sofia a kiss on the lips as Matt and Jesse stared in surprise. The man whispered into Sofia's ear, she nodded, whispered something back.

"This is Pastor Steve," said Sofia. "He's giving the eulogy."

"Oh." Matt shook his hand. "I'm Matt, Sofia's brother, who didn't know anything about you coming today, and this is my girlfriend Jesse."

Pastor Steve nodded, mumbled something, then headed to the rear of the building in search of the rest room, following Jesse's instructions on how to find it.

"Who the hell is he?" asked Matt.

"Pastor Steve leads the Estuary Chapel in Eagleville," said Sofia.

"Our Lady of the Brackish Water?"

"Non-denominational."

"I don't doubt it. Does he know there isn't any estuary around here?"

"It's metaphorical. He's terrific, a good preacher. He talks in layman's terms, so anybody can understand the message. A wonderful inspiration to people."

"Uh huh. No priest, then?"

"No way I'm letting a priest in here," said Sofia, "and Pastor Steve was willing to do it. We're lucky to have him."

Matt nodded. "That was a super-friendly kiss. Especially for a preacher. You going out with him?"

Sofia shrugged one shoulder. "Not currently."

A commotion came from the front of the room. Bernardino, the drunk ex-employee in the gray suit and askew tie, was shouting at the casket in Spanish.

"What's he going on about?" asked Matt.

"He's calling dad a *puerco* and a *rata*," said Sofia. "Basically, a gluttonous pig and a dishonest rat. Also something about dad fucking burritos, but I might have gotten that wrong."

"Nice."

An older woman stepped up and started arguing with Bernardino.

"Oh my god," said Jesse. "What's happening?"

"Hard to tell," said Sofia. "This is fast, slangy Spanish. I can make out *borracha*, though, so now I think dad wasn't fucking burritos, but drunk women."

"Thank goodness for small favors," said Matt. "Taking advantage of them, probably."

Bernardino waved the woman away, turned to the corpse, and punched it in the chest.

THIRTY-TWO

A yell went up in unison throughout the room, and half the people in the event across the hall turned to see what was going on. Several men rushed up and moved Bernardino to the rear of the room where they sat him in a chair near the corner. One of the men stood nearby to monitor him, but Bernardino appeared spent, no more anger and fight in him.

"I better check to make sure everything is okay and try to calm people down," said Matt as he stepped away.

"That was interesting," said Sofia.

"Exceedingly," agreed Jesse.

Matt went first to the casket and checked his father's suit, shook a few hands thanking the men for moving Bernardino to a safe space, then stood listening as the angry woman, backed up by her friends, continued her tirade.

"How's Matt handling this?" asked Sofia, watching that play out.

"The usual," said Jesse. "Sometimes it seems like his dad's death isn't affecting him at all, but he'll get upset about something stupid in a way that's inappropriate. It gets weird when he does that in front of other people. He doesn't like me pointing out he's delaying his emotional response."

Sofia nodded. "It took him months before he reacted to his mother. Maybe even a couple years to deal with it."

They watched the activity at the front of the room. "So what's up with Pastor Steve?" asked Jesse. "You're still interested in him, right?"

"Sure. We went out for a while, but he's another guy who doesn't want to be talked about on social media, so he backed out. Said his congregation wouldn't approve of their preacher meeting strange women on Hinge."

"Where's he supposed to meet them?"

"Church, I guess. It comes down to not wanting the documentation to be public, and I get that. But he still wants me, I know. We have to negotiate the posting thing. But I have an influencer career to think about. I can't change how I do things, no matter how cute he is."

"Good luck. I have to admit I don't know how comfortable I would be, feeling like someone's content."

"That train has left the station, Jess. It's the modern world. We're all each other's content whether we like it or not."

"Jesus that was bizarre," said Matt as he rejoined them. "I guess Bernardino was angrier than I thought."

"And more drunk," added Sofia.

"The gang from the restaurant wanted to throw him out, but I said let him stay, if he calms down."

"Oh, that's not cool," said Jesse, and the other two followed her gaze. The woman who had argued with Bernardino, along with two of her female friends, were taking selfies with the corpse.

"Hey, stop that!" yelled Sofia. She eyed the women until they sat down.

"What is wrong with people?" asked Jesse.

"One of those things that happens these days, speaking of being each other's content," said Sofia. "They're supposedly called 'corpsies' but I don't know if that's true since I've never heard anyone use that word."

"I don't want to learn that's a real word," said Jesse.

"Someone on TikTok was talking about it," said Sofia. "If that makes it a real word."

Aaron Stoltzfus walked into the building and proceeded to the three of them. He gave them a restrained smile, with practiced kindness and understanding in his eyes. He greeted each of them by name.

"I was so sorry to hear about your loss," said Aaron. "I know there were tensions over the years, but what family is free of them? The important thing is we do our best to understand each other, and apply our life lessons as we move forward."

"Thank you, Aaron," said Jesse. "It's kind of you to come."

Matt stared at him, astonished the man had the gall to show up there. "How did you find this place?"

"Funerals are public notices, Matty," said Sofia.

Matt turned to his sister and girlfriend, and asked them both, "Did you invite him?"

"You've talked often enough about your father being ill," Aaron said to Matt, his voice calm and understanding, as Matt fumed. "When I heard he passed I wanted to pay my respects. It's hard losing a parent, I know from my own experience. We may expect it, yet, somehow, we're never prepared."

Matt caught his sister mouthing "thank you" to Aaron while holding his hands in hers.

"I'll leave you to greet others," Aaron offered.

Matt wanted to punch him in his smug face right then and there. "The nerve of him," he said, watching Aaron take a seat near the rear.

"He's being supportive," said Jesse. "He's a nice man with your best interests in mind."

"He's your sponsor for goodness sakes," whispered Sofia. "I don't know why you're all bent out of shape by him."

"He's not my sponsor," hissed Matt.

"Then he should be, he's good at what he does," said Sofia. Then blushing, added, "I'll bet."

"Ahh, fuck this," said Matt, walking into the main room.

"I better check on what's going on with Pastor Steve," said Sofia, walking down the hall toward the back.

Matt strode up to where Aaron sat, stood a few feet away, arms crossed, and said, "You're not wanted here. Go away. Or I'll make you go away."

"I don't think you could do that."

"I could do it." Matt lowered his voice. "Remember the parking garage? You want more of the same?"

"I'm an elderly man in my sixties. Is that the behavior you want to exhibit here, in a public place like this, in front of all these people?"

"Screw this place and these people."

Tensions were running high. Matt was a moment from lunging for Aaron's throat. Aaron, meanwhile, had moved his feet under him and shifted his weight forward, in anticipation of leaping out of his seat and defending himself. The tension was broken, however, by shouting on the other side of the room. The angry woman who had argued with Bernardino, and consoled herself by taking corpsies, had grabbed a fistful of flowers from the arrangements and was using them to whack Bernardino about his head. One of her friends joined in, slapping the man. Bernardino, drunk and sleepy, remained in his seat and weakly blocked the attacks. Insults and threats in Spanish filled the room as several men moved to break it up, pulling the two women away and making sure Bernardino didn't get up from his chair to retaliate.

Matt cursed under his breath, told Aaron he would deal with him later, and walked over to where a cluster of mourners formed a loose circle, the explosion of flower petals landing on their shoulders and the floor.

"Everyone, please calm down!" Matt screamed. "Please! Can you all put a lid on it for a little while till we get through the service? After that you can go outside and beat each other up as much as you like. Okay?"

Everyone returned to their seat. Matt checked his watch. Scheduled start time for the service was still a few minutes away. He stomped back to the entrance.

"What was the yelling about?" asked Jesse.

"I'm not sure, they were slipping in and out of English. What I could understand had something to do with being a liar and stealing food," he said. "That was all I caught. The rest of it was in that angry Spanish and I can't understand a word of it. Maybe Sofia can figure it out."

"She went to check on Pastor Steve."

Matt clenched and unclenched his hands. "Let's hope everyone can hold it together long enough to get this thing done."

"You're the one who can't hold it together," said Jesse. "I saw you back there with Aaron. You were as bad as the others. Are you over it now? Prepared to act like an adult at your father's funeral?"

He opened his mouth to say something, thought better of it. "I hope this starts before some other crap happens."

The associate director of the funeral home stepped in from the hall and stood in front of the crowd, his back to the casket. He was a gaunt man in his mid-fifties with an obvious toupee, and quite looked the part of a funeral home associate director. He called for attention and made a side remark about the need for everyone's best behavior. The service would start in a few minutes, he announced.

"I'm getting Sofia and the preacher," said Matt as he walked down the hall. There was a small reception room in the back. Pastor Steve's guitar case was open with his guitar sitting inside. His navy jacket was draped on it, with his fedora resting at the top. There was no sign of either Sofia or Pastor Steve.

"Sofia, where are you?" called Matt. "We're starting in a minute."

The door to the bathroom opened on the side of the room and out came Sofia, adjusting her clothes, followed by Pastor Steve.

"Dammit, Fifi, this is dad's funeral," said Matt, horrified. She said nothing as she walked by him, her face flush. Pastor Steve gave Matt a quick nod and picked up his guitar. Matt shook his head in dismay and walked quickly out of the room, followed slowly by Pastor Steve.

The room had quieted down by the time Pastor Steve entered. He had located a tall stool in the back of the funeral home somewhere and placed it in front of the casket. He propped the guitar against the bier holding up the casket and sat on the stool.

"My name is Pastor Steve," he announced. "I lead the Estuary Chapel in Eagleville, about six miles up the road. I encourage you to visit us. I like to say the Estuary Chapel is where the unhealthy salt water of a sinful world mixes with the clean, refreshing water of God's love."

"Jesus H Christ," Matt whispered to Jesse, who shushed him.

"We are here to honor the life of Enrique Martinez, father of two, husband of two, restauranteur, bowler, golfer, friend of the community. Being born into a Catholic family, Enrique did not embrace the message of John 3:3, in which Jesus tells Nicodemus he must be born again if he is to see the Kingdom of God. And so it is the message to all of us. Enrique, upon death, is transported to hell, as accepting Jesus is the single way to avoid this fate, and he did not undergo the spiritual transformation of becoming born again. This is his legacy to us, his warning to the living, so we may avoid this fate."

Matt leaned close to Jesse. "Did he say that my father is in hell because he didn't get reborn?"

"I'm pretty sure he said we were all going to hell, because we don't belong to his church," she answered.

Pastor Steve picked up his guitar. "I will now play a song of forgiveness and hope," he said.

Matt growled deep in his throat.

***

After the service, as mourners filed out, not sure what they witnessed, Pastor Steve drifted over to Sofia and appeared quite pleased with himself. Matt walked over and put his face a few inches from Pastor Steve's.

"I want to be clear about what I heard," said Matt. "We're all going to hell because we were raised Catholic?"

"If you are not born again, then upon death, you will go to hell, yes," said Pastor Steve, "in that you will suffer the hell of spiritual death through separation from God." His half smile told of his patience and tolerance. "Accepting Jesus is the way to avoid that dire fate."

"I wasn't asking you about that. I was asking about being raised Catholic."

Pastor Steve sighed with the exasperation of the wise, when engaged with the naïve. "As a Catholic, the doctrines in which you believe and the rituals in which you participate are false and against God's teaching."

"Are you kidding me?"

"For example, when alone, Catholics refer to the Pope as 'God,' rather than as the Vicar of Christ."

"They do nothing of the kind!"

Sofia, her cheeks red, turned her eyes down toward the floor. Jesse put her face in her hands. This was about to become unpleasant.

A voice came from behind Matt. "And what about gambling, Reverend?" asked Aaron. "What does the good book say about it?"

THIRTY-THREE

Everyone turned to Aaron, who stood nearby with his hands clasped behind his back and a smile on his face.

"Gambling is a sin," said Pastor Steve. "The Bible warns us to not succumb to the love of money. We are also discouraged from attempting to become rich. Instead, we are taught financial stewardship."

"But if I put ten dollars in the plate on Sunday and pray that I get a promotion at work, is that not a form of gambling?" Aaron surveyed everyone's faces. "Is ten bucks enough to get in the game? How much does it cost for God to hear my prayer?"

"He hears all our prayers."

"Then what are the gamblers' odds that he'll answer mine?"

Pastor Steve and Aaron glared at each other.

"And who are you,?" asked Pastor Steve.

"Aaron Stoltzfus," Aaron said. "Friend of the family."

"Ah. I've heard." He glanced at Sofia, who glanced at him, then at Aaron. Matt followed all of it, moving his eyes from one to the other. Jesse was watching the last few attendees trickle out, embarrassed by all of it.

Aaron sighed, and said, "I need to get back upstate. My condolences again. Hope to see each other soon." He walked down the hall and out of the building.

"May the precious blood of Jesus wash away your sins," Pastor Steve called out to Aaron's back. He turned, gave Sofia a nod, and said, "I think today went well." Sofia responded with something between a smile and a grimace. Pastor Steve took her hand in his, patted it, and said, "I left my cards on the table there, by the sign-in book, with the address of our church and our prayer number for twenty-four hour recorded ministry messages during your times of need. I look forward to seeing you at the Estuary Chapel."

Matt, Sofia, and Jesse watched him go.

"What a fucking asshole," said Matt.

"At least he's not bringing the police here," said Sofia.

"Not helpful Sofia," said Jesse.

"For your information they're not talking to me any longer," said Matt. "A couple of informational interviews, and it's over. I was never a suspect."

"How do you know that?" asked Sofia, unconvinced.

"They told me."

"They did," said Jesse in support. "I think they assumed there might be something, but once they talked with him a couple times, and understood he stopped by after seeing his father, they moved on. Plus they have a suspect in custody."

"Yeah," agreed Matt. "My luck held out. They lost interest. No big deal. I don't even know what it was all about."

"It was about you chatting with a woman who turned up dead," said Sofia. "Which seems like a big deal to me."

"What is your problem, sis?" demanded Matt.

"I got no problem. I'm a little annoyed that you would attack a preacher. The man was trying to provide spiritual comfort, giving of his time and energy, as a favor to me. Meanwhile you measure success by what you can get away with, and how much you win at cards."

"Get away with?"

Sofia was agitated and it was coming out toward her brother. "You were up to something in that motel bar, talking to that woman."

"I'm out of here," said Matt, upset by his sister. "I'll meet you in the car, Jesse." He stormed off.

Jesse and Sofia both sighed.

"I went overboard," said Sofia.

Jesse raised her brow. "You think?"

"I know Pastor Steve comes on a little strong, but that's his faith, right? Matt didn't need to be so aggressive and condescending."

"I don't know if Aaron helped or hurt."

"He helped! Didn't you see what he did? He stepped in and defused the situation. Kind of steered it to another track, put the spotlight on him. I thought it was clever."

Jesse shrugged. "Maybe you're right."

The room was empty, the casket lonely at the front surrounded by flowers.

"I'm at the point where I need a break from all of this," said Jesse. "From the stress of his gambling, and worrying about money, and the fights. There's been so much happening, people showing up at my door, like Aaron, and the police... who knows what's next."

"Okay. Then he'll come live with me for a little while. Not long. Super short term."

Jesse nodded, sadly. "It'll be up to him where he goes."

***

Outside the funeral home Pastor Steve walked across the parking lot, guitar case in hand. He didn't see Aaron leaning against the Toyota, hands in pockets, until he was a few feet away. He stopped, startled.

"I thought you left," said Pastor Steve.

"I left the building. Haven't left the parking lot yet."

Pastor Steve took a step closer. "I do know who you are, you're Sofia's elderly side piece. I'd appreciate it if you leave her alone. She's beyond your territory."

"You're a smug prig, you know that?"

"You're going to leave her alone. Do we understand each other?"

Aaron smiled, cleared his throat, and gave Pastor Steve a once-over. "My understanding is that you're not going out with her. Which means you have no jurisdiction, spiritual or otherwise."

"We're working through things."

"Are you?? If so, good for you. That's got nothing to do with me."

"What's that supposed to mean?"

"What Sofia and I have going is not exclusive," said Aaron, wagging an index finger. "Room for you to take your best shot."

"What's that supposed to mean?" Pastor Steve said again, with more emphasis. "The more the merrier? You're not going to fight for her? What kind of jerk says stuff like that?"

"What I'm saying is go for it, if that's what you want."

They were interrupted by Matt storming out of the building, talking to himself as he headed toward his car. They watched him cross the lot, stub his toe on something, curse, stand with clenched fists and emit what sounded like a bark, then keep going.

"That boy has a lot of anger," said Pastor Steve.

"Yes, he does," agreed Aaron. "I think he has a bunch of things going on, in that head of his."

"He also seems a little off to me, not wired right."

"We all have our quirks."

Pastor Steve turned back to Aaron. "I know you sponsor people in recovery. Sofia told me about it. I recognize you, my friend. I see you. You take advantage of people."

"It takes one to know one. You like to operate in the shadows, on the downlow. Like you want to do with Sofia."

"Why, because I'm cautious with her?"

"You want her to think it's something about the privacy of clergy. But I know your kind; you don't want to be on display as an older woman's Instagram boyfriend, it would cramp your style."

"Oh?"

"You prefer to advertise yourself as available. I've read about your church on Reddit, it seems a little freewheeling for a house of worship. More socializing than praying. Plenty of opportunities to meet young impressionable types."

Pastor Steve's eyes flared, and he pointed at Aaron. "Do not let the festive atmosphere and collegial nature of the Estuary Chapel blind you to the truth. We're a living, progressing congregation of imperfect Christ followers, and I have responsibilities. I cannot be a subject of gossip and titillation. I hope Sofia will be a part of the chapel as a serious congregant. Until then yes, I'm cautious."

"You talk weird. And you're not convincing."

A voice carried over from across the lot. "What are you two losers doing together?" Matt ambled over, a pocket flask in his hand.

"Ah, no," said Pastor Steve. "I'm not feeling it right now. You're his sponsor, I hear, he's your problem." He walked off.

"Where's he going?" asked Matt as he watched Pastor Steve toss the guitar case into the passenger seat of his large pickup truck, climb in, and rev the engine before pulling out.

"What is that, a 2016 Ford F-150?" asked Aaron.

"Maybe," said Matt. "Maybe a little more recent. What's a preacher doing with a big ass truck like that?"

"Carrying potato salad to church picnics."

"Needs a wash," sneered Matt. He offered Aaron a hit from the flask. "Bourbon. I know you like it."

Aaron drank a little, winced, and handed it back. He asked, "What's on your mind?"

"You wanna call a truce?"

Aaron wondered if it was a sincere proposal or another ploy. "Could be time. Why you bringing that up now?"

"Well, my dad's dead, which puts me in a better mood. Seems like a milestone reached, a corner turned. You did your best to set the cops onto me, but that petered out."

"Wasn't me, I told you that."

"Uh huh."

They both took another slug of bourbon.

"But you did it," said Aaron. "You told me you did it."

"What does that matter, either way?" asked Matt. "You're guilty of the things someone catches you doing. Otherwise it never happened. You like stories, so here's one for you. I once got mad at Apá and shoved a potato into the tailpipe of his car, because I read it would make it stall. He blamed it on these two brothers who lived around the corner and were always in trouble. He complained to the parents, but those poor parents were always hearing about what their brats got up to, from the neighbors and the teachers and even the cops. Their attitude was, if a neighbor had a complaint about those punks, then get in line, buddy. That was the end of it. He fixed his car, the blame was placed on those brothers, but no one paid any consequences, and I walked away squeaky clean. Everyone was fine, except my dad, which was the goal to begin with. Those motel deaths are sort of like that."

Aaron considered the younger man. He said, "I wonder if you aren't a psychopath."

"Sure, whatever that means exactly," said Matt, already a little woozy. "Point is, without the police thing you got nothing left in the arsenal, old man. I don't know, I feel like we're even somehow. Not a direct matchup, not a tit for tat situation that some outside observer could follow, but bottom line I think we're even now."

Aaron thought about it. The game wouldn't be any fun if he was the only one playing it. "You stole money from me."

"You stole it from me first. You cheated me. But I got it back, so that's a wash."

"I didn't cheat you."

"That app was rigged. If you didn't get me drunk I would've seen what you were doing."

"You hit me."

"Yeah, my bad. I can see you're still sore about it. I was drunk and a little crazy-angry, is all I can say. The way I see it, the police thing sort of evens out me hitting you, which I apologize for by the way. And the police, that's over, they have no interest in me."

"You sure about that?"

"They said so. They have a suspect who fits the bill a lot better. So yeah, it's over." Matt presented the flask again. "There's a little left. Finish it, and we'll consider the deal closed."

Aaron drank the last of the bourbon. The truce was in place.

***

"I saw you talking with Aaron when I walked out," said Jesse as they drove home. She was at the wheel, given Matt's condition. "What was that about?"

"I felt bad about how I behaved and went over to apologize," said Matt.

"Well, I'm glad." She was quiet. Then she said, "He's not the only one you should apologize to, you know."

There followed a long period of awkward silence. Matt waited for Jesse to explain who he should be apologizing to, and for what. Jesse, meanwhile, waited for Matt to agree with her and admit he needs to make amends. They stopped at a light.

"I don't remember them putting a Wawa here," Matt said, gaping at the gas pumps and market.

"It's been about a year," said Jesse.

"Used to be a hot dog and ice cream place, right?"

She didn't answer. The light changed and they moved on.

She turned to him and said, "I think you need to move out."

THIRTY-FOUR

The change wasn't immediate. Matt and Jesse talked about it for a week. The details of the conversations shifted a little, priorities moved around, some anecdotes were brought to the foreground while others receded. But in the main, the focus was consistent: Jesse felt she needed time away from Matt because of his behavior, and his attitude. Also, perhaps most important, she was afraid she couldn't trust him any longer. The matter with the police was the final straw.

"They're done with me," Matt said, again, during the final argument on the final day he was living there. Jesse pointed out, also not for the first time, that while that was true it was not relevant to Jesse's fundamental position, that over the past year if it wasn't one thing it was another. Lately, she said, there was always a glowing ball of stress hovering over their lives.

"You're always up to something," Jesse said. "Always a scheme, an evasion, a rationalization. You're never sitting around being the innocent bystander. You're always the one stirring things up, for your own purposes."

"I don't mean to."

"Maybe sometimes you don't. But it happens anyway, because you tend to be selfish, and to not think about other people, to not consider the impact your actions will have on them. On me, for one important example."

"I can learn to do better," he said.

"Can you? This is not the first time we've had this conversation."

Matt sat in his chair, pouting, peering out through the sliding doors onto the balcony and the parking lot beyond.

"As for the police," Jesse added, "I can't shake the feeling that you got away with something."

Matt's response was on the fringe of theatrical.

"Murder?!?" He made it clear how astonished he was by opening his eyes wide, and waving his arms about. "You think I murdered two people?!?"

That exact question had been said multiple times by Matt since the first call from Detective Wisler. He said it to Sofia, and to Jesse, and once or twice to the detective. The more he said it, the more it sounded implausible, then silly, and finally outrageous. Who, in all seriousness, could suggest such a thing?

Jesse didn't answer him. She had doubts and held on to them.

When they both were calm, she said, "I want a normal life, with stability."

He nodded, and on impulse asked, "It's the gambling, isn't it?"

"Of course, the gambling is part of it, what have I been saying all along?" she said, exasperated. "I want you to stop and get a normal job."

"I'm not good with people in the ways that matter for those jobs..."

"You're always going on about that..."

"I can do it, but it's exhausting."

"Whatever. Not every workplace is like that. Most don't have all the people and noise of a restaurant. There are places that would value what you have to offer."

"And how am I going to do that? I'm unqualified. How am I supposed to jump into a career in research or technology or something?"

"I don't know, one step at a time? You don't have to turn your life over to playing cards, that's not your one option."

"Playing cards is the best option for me to do what I'm good at."

"Matt," she sighed. "Face it. You're not good at it."

They were at an impasse and needed to return to their corner, get some water, and prepare for the next round, whatever form that might take. They both understood Matt had to leave, at least temporarily. It was Jesse's name on the lease, and the apartment was close to her job, so she would remain. Matt would crash at his sister's.

"I thought you couldn't afford the place on your salary alone," Matt said, in a last-ditch effort to delay the inevitable.

"When I said that, it was with our monthly budget in mind," she said. "If you leave, that budget changes. It's a whole lot less food. Less alcohol. I can get rid of most of the streaming services, and cancel the video gaming account. The amounts on the gas station cards will drop way down now that your trips to Atlantic City aren't included, and ditto on your hotel stays, and dining out when you're there. I've done the math. You'd be shocked to learn how affordable this life will be for me, without having to carry you."

Part V

THE MOUNTAIN

THIRTY-FIVE

They say a truce is only as good as the character of the people agreeing to it. This being the case, the truce between Matt and Aaron began unraveling almost immediately after it was established. Of course, on both sides, there were performative attempts to maintain separation, move on with their lives, put the conflict behind them. But enmity has its appeal. Especially for those motivated by resentment over an injustice and a desire for retribution. Both men were of that type, an unfortunate coincidence, and neither could let go, however much they pretended they would. The seeds of trouble were easily sewn.

When it was established that Matt would move in with her, Sofia called Aaron and told him. She was apologetic that they needed to curtail their meetings.

"We can still get together for a little play time," she explained, "just not at my house. Matt has issues with you, for whatever reason, and it would make him uncomfortable."

"Wouldn't be great for us either, him breathing down our necks," said Aaron.

"What is it with you two, anyway?"

He ignored her and asked, "What about Reverend Boy-toy? Curtailing that too?"

"Are you jealous?"

"Do I seem like the type?"

"You seem like the type who doesn't like the things he doesn't like."

Aaron was okay with the new arrangement at first; one had to go with the flow, after all, and he wasn't invested in Sofia. Seeing her on the sly had been, for him, a way to continue tormenting Matt from a distance, even though Matt didn't know about it (which provided its own esoteric pleasure). But as the days came and went his loneliness felt more pronounced. For the first time in years he had no small rotation of needy girlfriends. With merely his freelance work, collection of teas, and streaming television services to keep him company, he was unsatisfied. He sensed his mojo draining. His life had become limited to the view from his mountain retreat: snow in the winter, pest insects in the summer, and the disorderly sounds of the woods. It all now seemed inadequate. He missed the absurd, pointless, destructive, and yet somehow amusing competition with Matthew Martinez.

It was time to resurrect it.

While he had, sort of, agreed to a truce in the parking lot of the funeral home, Aaron had no intention of honoring that. Abandoning their little competition was the worst possible outcome, in his view; they had something special going, so letting it dissipate was an offense. He wanted to continue it indefinitely, for his amusement. If that wasn't possible, second best was to arrange a final crash into a wall, to end it with style; the human psyche cries out for closure.

What gave the feud an extra frisson of pleasure, as Aaron thought of it, was Matt almost certainly being a murderer. That kind of opponent didn't come with the mail. Aaron had met a few murderers in his life, one in jail, and two others in recovery rooms. In each case they were losers who killed someone out of stupidity. One panicked during a robbery of a convenience store and shot the clerk. Another drove too fast and ran over a pedestrian. The third slugged someone in the middle of a pointless argument about baseball in a bar and they fell, hitting their head. Sad cases, nitwits making bad decisions.

From Aaron's perspective Matt was different, because that young man did something extraordinary: he punched way above his station in a knife fight and prevailed. Aaron could speculate about what happened in that motel, though he would never know for sure. He was confident, however, that the two victims were trouble by any standard. A couple of drug dealers, no doubt, and likely a hooker and her pimp boyfriend. Lowlifes who would know how to take care of themselves.

Yet somehow this soft, suburban kid, seemingly not the kind to rob and kill anyone, took them down.

Was it his temper? Aaron had seen a glimpse of that in the Ventura parking lot. Whatever the explanation, it made Matt dangerous. In some unknown way, this normally reserved young man was capable of anything under extreme circumstances. It became a question of how much could he provoke Matt, and for how long, before the boy snapped? And, of course, what would happen then? It was a lot more excitement than Aaron had seen in a while.

To keep the embers glowing, Aaron had repeatedly phoned the Norristown police hotline, offering tidbits of additional information about Matt and demanding to know why he hadn't been arrested for the motel murders. He would remind the police officer on the other end that he was a citizen who wanted his streets to be safe, and claimed he had trouble sleeping knowing there was a killer roaming the Pennsylvania countryside, and so forth. He always made sure to add a new teaspoonful of inculpatory information about Matt that was plausible if not actually true.

None of this effort seemed to impact the murder investigation, unfortunately, and the police messaging via the news outlets remained that they had a suspect behind bars. Aaron viewed that man as a poor, homeless, friendless drifter, a lost soul who thought life inside, with its regular meals and healthcare, was a safer option than trying to make a go of it on the outside.

One day Aaron determined to stir the pot again, to try and get something going with one final call to the police. He had to drive into New Jersey for a client anyway, so he swung over to Easton and crossed the Delaware into Phillipsburg. He was still concerned with police call-tracing software. There was a taco shop on Main Street south of the railroad tracks, near the Baptist Church, where there was a pay phone.

The newspaper reports said the detective in charge of the Blue Blanket Inn murder investigation was a Detective Evelyn Wisler, who Aaron assumed was a woman since the barfly Janice had mentioned a female detective, and no American boy had been named that since

Evelyn Waugh died in the sixties. This time, when he called the Norristown Police hot line, he asked specifically for her. The person who answered was reluctant and asked what it pertained to. He told her, and she asked him to hold on. There was silence for a long time. He was close to hanging up when the line reconnected and a woman's voice announced herself, "Detective Wisler speaking. What can I do for you?"

"Hello detective," Aaron said, making his voice a little higher in a feeble attempt to disguise it. "I've called your tip line with information about a man, Matthew Martinez, who confessed to me that he had committed those murders at the Blue Blanket Inn. But I haven't seen anything about it in the news and I'm worried that it never reached you."

"You're worried?" asked Detective Wisler.

"Yes. If there's a killer roaming freely, we should all be worried."

"I got the information," she said. "Every tip that comes through the hot line is treated seriously."

"Good, good. I'm calling today to say you arrested the wrong man."

"I'm sorry, what are you saying?"

"The man you arrested, the articles say his name is Christopher Roberts. He's innocent."

"He confessed."

"Hah! A poor, mentally ill man confessed to something he didn't do. As if that's the first time."

"Do you have information that exonerates Mr. Roberts?"

"It's the Great Fire of London all over again!" Aaron was overdoing it, but it was too much fun. He was amusing himself.

"It's the what now?"

Aaron made a disapproving tsk sound. "In the middle of the seventeenth century there was a horrific fire that started in a bakery and destroyed most of London. A man confessed that he threw a fire grenade through the front window of the bakery, and they hung him. It was all nice and neat. The anti-foreigners were happy because he was French. The anti-Catholics were happy because he claimed to be an agent of the Pope. Problem was, the bakery didn't have a front window, the man was a cripple who couldn't have tossed that firebomb, and he hadn't even arrived in England until after fire broke out."

There was silence on the other end.

Eventually Detective Wisler asked, "What was your name again?"

"I'm a concerned citizen."

"Uh huh. I could find out who you are, you know."

"This is an anonymous tip line!"

"Anonymous means you don't have to leave a name. Doesn't mean I can't work out who you are. I'm a detective. I got skills."

He liked this woman, she had spunk. He asked, "Is that a threat? I've done nothing wrong!"

"Uh huh. Well mister citizen, you know filing a false police report is illegal?"

"You don't believe me?"

"Falsely incriminating another person is a second-degree misdemeanor and you can get two years in prison, plus thousands in fines. You in the market for that?"

"But I'm telling the truth!"

"The reason I took this call is that I thought it might be you, and I want to tell you to stop. I don't know what your beef is with Martinez, but I'm not running around on your tips any longer to give him a hard time."

"But I..."

"I'm going to give you the benefit of the doubt. Let's say you're not lying to me, that for some reason you think he did it. I investigated, based on your tips. He was at the bar, that much is true. Several people remember him. He was visiting his sick father at the medical center a few blocks away and walked up to get a midday beer. Maybe not the best idea before a long drive down to Atlantic City, but the timeline works out. He talked with the female victim, but it turns out they went to high school together, hadn't seen each other in over a decade, so it was one of those things that happen when you go back to your hometown. The witnesses all say he left the bar before she did and went on his way. We know when he checked into his hotel in Atlantic City, and with the window we have for the estimated times of death, he was likely way down the Expressway when they were killed, maybe even in his room eighty-something miles away."

Wisler delivered her explanation in a voice both calm and authoritative, like a librarian explaining the Dewey Decimal System. Aaron had to admit Detective Wisler was thorough and professional. And generous, considering the time she was spending with him. He was impressed. Too bad about having to screw with her.

"Plus, I met with him," she added. "I've been in the room with criminals of all types, including murderers, and he doesn't seem capable of what happened in that motel. I have a brother similar to Mr. Martinez in size, in temperament, and in his sensitivities and interpersonal social challenges..."

"Interpersonal social...?"

"... Both of those young men would be incapable of such a crime. They don't have the skills or the training."

"That sounds like unprofessional bias."

"Think of it as experienced gut instinct."

"He's a big guy," protested Aaron.

"I can tell you the crime scene was brutal. Martinez isn't big enough to do all that without help. The male victim was a beefy gym rat, and a known hothead thug, it would take a couple of strong men to take him down."

"What about the gold sweatshirt I saw him wearing? Isn't that important?"

He heard her sigh on the other end. He was fascinated with how this was going.

"That sweatshirt was one of the main reasons we followed up on your tip, and why I'm talking with you right now," she said. "Since we hadn't mentioned it in the press, it was significant when you brought it up in your first call. But after we spoke with Martinez, established his alibi, and cleared him, we realized you were bullshitting. Which annoyed us, to be honest."

"But if it was unreleased info then how could I know about it?"

"That was our question, and it concerned us for a while. Our first assumption was that you were the killer. But that didn't add up. Except for the sweatshirt, your info was all about Martinez, not the crime scene. Then we realized the sweatshirt was known to everyone at that bar. The deceased, Mr. Ciccone, wore it regularly, and everyone agrees it was ugly as sin. It was not some secret piece of evidence known to the police and the killer. Anyone going into that bar, buying a drink for the regulars, would have gotten an earful of stories about the incident and the investigation, that sweatshirt included. A few of those barflies would tell you everyone's dirty secrets, including their own, for the price of a beer and a hotdog. I assume that's what you did, went down there and learned what you could. Which means if I wanted to, I could follow your steps, talk to the same people you did, ask them about a man who sounds like he spends too much time on Wikipedia, find out what you look like, cross reference that with Martinez if indeed you know him, and I could learn who you are. Which is tempting, since following up on your tips, interviewing Martinez, and trying to determine if you might be the killer, ate up a lot of department person-hours and delayed this investigation. I find out who you are, then on a day when I'm in a bad mood I can have a couple of uniforms arrest you so I can ask you why you're wasting my time by illegally filing false reports."

"You're threatening me!"

"Mr. Martinez has no motive, and according to the timeline, no opportunity. He's one of over a dozen people who had contact with one or both of the victims that morning. Not to mention we have a suspect who has confessed. Even if I've misjudged you, mister citizen, and you aren't trolling me for some purpose of your own, then my advice is the same as if you are: drop it before you get us angry."

Aaron wasn't certain he wanted to let it go. "But what if I'm right? What if the guy who confessed is some sad case who wants back in because he can't make a go of it outside?"

Detective Wisler said nothing.

"What if I went to the press as an anonymous source," continued Aaron, "told them what I know, that I heard Martinez confess to the killings and you ignored that, so you could arrest the easy suspect? It would make a good run of news stories, wouldn't it? Philly would pick it up. A lot of reporters at the station, asking a lot of questions."

"Now who's threatening whom?" asked Wisler.

"I'm trying to protect a man from being mistreated by the system."

Wisler was quiet for a long time. Finally, she said, "You're forgetting the knife."

That surprised Aaron. He hadn't considered the murder weapon, for even a second.

She asked, "Remember the news reports about a knife in the room with the bodies?" When Aaron didn't answer, she continued, "It was the murder weapon. And information about the knife we kept to ourselves. I'm not going to tell you anything about it other than it was an uncommon item, and valuable."

"How valuable?"

"Retailing for more than seven hundred dollars, imported."

Aaron saw where this was headed. "You couldn't connect it to Martinez."

"We didn't need to. It was so unusual we could trace it from the website where it was bought. By Anthony Ciccone, the deceased."

Aaron was rocked back a little by this news. It was not what he expected. "Maybe this Ciccone guy pulled it and Martinez took it off of him."

"Oh, so this soft, card-playing kid is Jason Bourne now?"

"Well, maybe..."

"The suspect in custody admitted he stole the knife. We found his fingerprints on the sheath, under the bed. He and the deceased had a pretty big argument about it, where Ciccone accused him of taking it, which the suspect denied. But he did take it, it turned out, and hid it in that room on a day when all three of them were in and out of there getting high. Pretty solid case now, don't you think?"

Aaron was quiet. As a last-ditch effort, he suggested, "Maybe Martinez found the knife under the bed, and used it in the fight."

"That's your best suggestion?" Wisler laughed. "That Martinez happened to stop in at the bar, happened to run into an old schoolmate, happened to go to a room with her that happened to have a seven-hundred-dollar rare knife under the bed, which he happened to find at the right time when he had a fight with the schoolmate and her boyfriend? That would be an absurdly phenomenal piece of luck, wouldn't it?"

Yes, it would, thought Aaron.

"We're professionals in my office, and we're handling this. I don't want to hear from you again."

THIrTY-SIX

Sofia was not thrilled by the arrangement with her brother. She resented the disruption to her routine, her personal space, her privacy. Her dating life took a serious hit since she was not going to bring anyone back to the house for her brother's review and critique. The thing with Aaron was put on hold. She allowed Pastor Steve to come by and pick her up for dates, but never allowed him to stay over. Meanwhile, Pastor Steve was his own kind of handful, less understanding of her lifestyle than Aaron, but Sofia forgave him because he was a good-looking younger man. She saw his petulant little fits as his desire to fight for her. She was flattered by that, even if she also found it irritating.

Meanwhile, Matt was unhappy and lonely. He missed Jesse, even though he had felt she was penning him in. He liked her smile and the care she applied to their surroundings. He liked her cooking. He liked her, plain and simple. But he felt helpless to do anything about getting them back together. She was dissatisfied with him and his behavior, and didn't trust him. That last point was a big hurdle to overcome.

The biggest wedge between him and his sister was the police attention. More than once she asked him what the full story was. Matt routinely dithered and obfuscated in response.

"You sure do keep secrets, Matty," said Sofia one evening, after dinner, when they sat in the kitchen with cups of tea. And it was true. Matt was good with secrets, and always had been. He kept many secrets, some of them about things he had done, some of them about things he planned to do. The majority of his secrets, however, were about his thoughts. He assumed other people had secret thoughts, but it seemed to him he had a lot more than might be considered normal.

"I don't have secrets," he said.

"And you hold grudges. I'll bet you have a list of people you hold grudges against."

Matt had no answer because Sofia was correct, he had such a list, and he was a little astonished she guessed it. Was he that open a book? The truth was, he held grudges against everyone who had ever wronged him, no matter how small or unimportant that wrong might have been, or how distant in the past. He had a mental grudge list of names, and that list was long. In some cases the details of the relevant incident were forgotten, but the name remained. It imprisoned him in many ways, as he couldn't heal; at best he could lock the list away.

"Am I on that list?" she asked.

"No." This was true. He had no unresolved issues with his sister. Their relationship was what it was.

"Is Aaron on it?"

Aaron was at the top of the list, truce or no truce. Matt was not about to admit that. "I don't know if I would put him on any grudge list," said Matt. "I'm not happy with him, though."

"Do you ever forgive someone on the list?" she asked.

"I never actually said I have a list..."

"If you did..."

"I try to forgive people," he said. This was not true. People said forgiveness was a virtue, but in his view people who said that never experienced the joy of getting even.

"What would it take to cross off a name?" she asked as she cut two thin pieces of pound cake. "If there was a list?"

Matt believed most people were like him, that given the chance to push a button causing grievous harm to someone who had done them wrong, they would do it in a heartbeat. Anonymous revenge at a distance was an attractive concept, and he imagined most everyone else would agree.

"A sufficient level of damage," he said, without thinking.

"Sufficient? For what?"

"Sufficient to match the level of harm to me that put them on the list in the first place."

"Jesus, Matty, that's not a healthy attitude." She placed the pound cake in front of him. "I've read that when someone gets stuck in resentment, that's called 'anger rumination.' Which is a cool phrase about an uncool thing."

"Is that what you think I do?"

"Uh, yeah. I think you do it a lot."

"How would you know?"

"I worry that it made you do whatever it was got you into trouble with the police."

"I'm not in trouble with the police."

"Not right now, maybe, but they're still thinking about you, baby brother. Those fuckers get you in their sights they don't like to let go."

"I was a witness. They didn't have me in their sights."

"Sure, keep telling yourself that. About Aaron, I'd like you to forgive him for whatever it was you think he did."

"I don't know if I can. We agreed to a truce, though."

"Hardly the same," she said with a mouthful of pound cake. "But okay, fair enough for now. I hope it holds."

Three days later Jesse called and told Matt she was willing to give things another chance, if he promised to be more honest with her about what he was doing and why.

"Communication is so, so important," said Sofia when he told her about it.

"I understand," said Matt. "I'm learning."

THIRTY-SEVEN

Aaron rang the bell at the apartment in Tohickon. He wanted to find Jesse alone, and had that day to do it. Jesse opened the door with surprise on her face.

"Hi!" said Aaron, with a smile. "I was driving south and thought I would stop by. Things were a little tense at that funeral, I was hoping if I brought a peace offering Matthew and I could sit down and talk it through." He held up a bottle of pinot grigio.

"Oh!" said Jesse, uncomfortable. "I guess you didn't hear. Matt and I, we're taking a little break I'm afraid. That funeral was hard on all of us."

"I'm sorry to hear that." He frowned in concern, as if this was news to him. "Can I still leave this with you? It's imported."

She smiled. "I do like a good pinot grigio." Which he knew; there were several bottles on the kitchen counter when he visited the first time.

"Matt told me about the police investigation," he said. "That must have been stressful, too." She nodded, her eyes tearing a little. He checked his watch. "This wine is from near Milan, where it's already well into the evening, so I think we're allowed to crack it open. You seem like you could use it."

They sat in her living room with their glasses of wine. He asked her what the police investigation was like, for her. She talked about her worries. About her concern Matt was getting involved in things she didn't know about.

"You're his sponsor," she began, when she was two glasses in. "I know your relationship is complicated..."

"Not as complicated as some," he interrupted.

"Has he been telling you things, what he's been up to?"

"You mean has he been gambling? Yes, he has, that much I know, but I don't know where the stake is coming from."

"Does he talk about me at all?"

He chose to be kind. "Of course. He's said he loves you and is sorry for the pain he's caused."

She snorted. "He doesn't act like it."

"Dealing with addiction often brings with it a lot of shame, denial, and resentment. Many people, men especially, struggle to talk about that stuff."

"He could still tell me how he feels."

"He might not know how."

"I hear that." She topped off her glass. His was still full. "Sometimes I feel like he sees other people on the side. During his gambling trips."

"I'm sorry to hear that."

"He ever say anything about it?"

Here we go, thought Aaron. He focused, wanting to walk the line between assertion and insinuation. "You mean cheating on you?"

"Harsh way to put it, but yeah."

His face contorted into expressions of internal conflict, to be seen as a man wanting to tell the truth, but not wanting to offend. "He's never said he's done it. He has implied he's thought about it. Though not in so many words."

She nodded sadly, took in a healthy amount from her glass.

"Though it doesn't seem like something he would do," he said, pulling it back a bit.

"I'm beginning to think it actually is something he would do."

And so it went. Aaron was kind and understanding and empathetic, while carefully moving her toward doubts about Matt and his honesty. It didn't take long for a second bottle of wine to be opened. They drifted from Matt—at a certain point what more is there to say?—to talking about recent films, favorite concerts, and the pros and cons of vacationing in Florida.

Jesse excused herself and went to the bathroom. As soon as the door closed Aaron quickly moved down the hall into the bedroom. There were two dressers, and he identified Matt's by the usual stuff littering the surface: a dust-covered cologne bottle, a crumpled baseball cap, two souvenir key chains, and a small basket with coins. He opened the top drawer where some of Matt's socks and underwear remained. He lifted the top layer, slipped in a matchbook, closed the drawer and returned to the living room before Jesse left the bathroom.

She flopped back onto the couch.

"You're not trying to make a move on me, are you?" There was an ambivalence in her delivery. Aaron chalked it up to the wine.

"I am not making a move on you."

"That's good, because I know you have a thing going with Sofia."

He raised his eyebrows at that. "She told you."

"Yeah. She didn't tell Matt, though, and I'm sworn to secrecy about it. I'm not even supposed to tell you that I know."

He nodded, and declined to point out she had already betrayed her promises.

She rotated her glass in her hand, and asked, "What am I supposed to do?"

He leaned forward and gazed into her face as she kept her eyes on the wine glass. "Acknowledge reality," he said. "When you accept how things are, it enables you to access peace. Even in the midst of difficult times, you can relax, as long as you are honest with yourself about the situation."

"How does that work?"

"No matter where you are or what is happening, there is always room for your unique presence, and your unique experience. That is what you focus on, not the external pressures."

She was perplexed. She laughed, then stopped, not wishing to offend him. "I'm sorry. I don't understand. How do I do that?"

He took her glass and placed it on the table, then held the fingers on both of her hands in his own. "Take notice of what is happening in your body. Ask yourself, what are my feelings at this moment? Not your thoughts, your feelings. Our thoughts can be complicated and motivated by fear and worry, and they can be an unreliable measure of our current state. Focus instead on internal sensations. Where are the areas of stress in your body? Can you try to relax them?"

She giggled again.

"You're worried about bad things you're afraid might happen," he said. "But they haven't happened yet."

"They might. You don't appreciate how he is, he's not your boyfriend."

He squeezed her hand a tiny bit harder. "Let those bad things come, if they must. You have no control over them anyway. Then let them go. Like the tide at the ocean, or the passing of seasons. It is the normal order of things. Everything changes, including the bad times. Do you ever meditate?"

"Not usually."

"You should consider meditating. When you do, treat everything around you as impermanent, subject to change, something to release from your grasp. If it belongs to you, you won't need to clutch it so tightly."

"Let things go?" She seemed sincere in asking this.

"Release your hold on all of it, because it is all changeable. Release the regret and anxiety. Release the anticipation and excitement. Release the expectations and ambitions. Ignore the past and the possible futures. Focus on today."

"I'm closing my eyes. Is that right?"

"Sure."

"Do you do this with Matt?"

"I try to," he lied. "He fights me all the way, but I think I'm getting through to him."

They sat there for a while, as the sun set, until the wine ran out.

"I told you half the story," she said, sheepish. "I've asked Matt to move back."

Sofia, bless her, told him everything, including that. It was why he made it down to see Jesse as soon as he could, before Matt's return, in order to place the matchbook. He didn't blame Jesse for giving in and asking him back. It was difficult to break it off with someone who has been that strong a part of your life.

He said, "If you think that's the right thing to do."

"It's lonely," she said, explaining. "I need to make peace with the man he is, all the good and the bad."

"Keep an eye on the boy. He needs watching, that one, with his tendency to get into trouble. I've done my best to guide him on the right path, but he can be slippery."

He stood to leave. She put her hand on his arm to stop him.

"Before you go, there's one thing I need to ask," she said. "Do you know why the police were talking with him? I mean the real reason?"

***

Afterwards, when Aaron left, he reflected on the conversation. She seemed, to him, sad to see him go. She struck him as a woman with not enough friends, not enough people to confide in. He felt a little guilty for what he was putting her through. But perhaps she might find some spiritual guideposts in what he said that could help. In any case, he told himself as he drove out of the apartment complex, she was the one who moved in with a guy like Matt, so she deserved what she got.

THIRTY-EIGHT

Matt drove into the parking lot of the apartment complex in Tohickon and saw Jesse on the sidewalk talking to two young men dressed like they were on their way to the gym. She saw him park and said something to the men, who waved as they walked off. Matt nodded to her as he got out of the car.

"Friends of yours?" he asked.

"You know them, they're the couple who live at the end of the row over there," she said, pointing down the sidewalk. Matt shook his head, not placing them. "They're the ones with the standard poodle that passed away a few months ago."

"Oh, yeah," he said. "I know who they are."

He said his stuff was in the car, a box and a couple of suitcases. Well, let's get them inside then, she said. In the apartment Matt sat on the couch. The box rested on the dining table, the two suitcases on the floor. The apartment smelled like cookies; Jesse had been baking. He was forward on the cushion, hands clasped between his knees, and he launched into a string of promises about all the things he would change about himself. He would be more responsible. He would consult her on money matters as he now understood that their finances were intertwined. He would curb his poker playing. He would seek a new job, although he would do his best to avoid working in the restaurant business. He would be more present and sensitive to Jesse's needs.

Jesse, leaning against the dining table, watching him, her arms folded, wasn't sure how much to believe. "I applaud the thing about a job," she said. "I'm not asking you to give up poker entirely. But to live here, with me, you need to stop treating it as your career, because it isn't.

That was a dream you had—an unrealistic dream—and you need to move on."

"Understood. I've had two goals, like I told you. To keep our relationship alive and strong, and to find a way to play poker. You're giving me another chance at the first one, and I realize now how valuable that is. I can modify the second. Achieving half my goals is pretty good, right? A lot of people don't achieve any of theirs."

Matt still had every intention of finding the right way to fund his path to a lucrative gambling career, but he wasn't about to tell her that.

"I do want you back here," she said. "It's conditional on you keeping your promises, you know that right?"

He nodded.

"And how about the police?" she asked. "Were you telling me the truth about that? Or should I expect additional visits from them?"

"I explained all that before. I was in the wrong place at the wrong time. Them talking with me was due diligence. It's over now."

"Are you sure?"

"Yeah." He wasn't comfortable with her body language, nor with what she was saying. "What do you mean am I sure?" He felt like he had stepped into something.

"Aaron told me why things are so strange between the two of you. He said someone called the police and claimed you killed those two people in Norristown, after you talked to that woman."

Matt blinked, three times. "When did he tell..."

"That's why the police interviewed you, because someone called them and gave your name. And you blamed him."

"He..." Matt had to regroup. He was having trouble thinking fast enough for the situation. "He did it. He made that call."

"Can you prove that?"

"No, but..."

"Why on earth would Aaron do that to you? He's your sponsor."

"He's not my..."

"He's not even allowed to do something like that, right? Isn't there some kind of privileged communication thing?"

"I don't think that's..."

"And he's trying to help you. That's what sponsors do."

"He's not my sponsor."

"Maybe not anymore, but he was back then. With your behavior, you lost someone who could have helped you."

"He's lying, Jesse."

She gave him a long, assessing stare. "Okay. Let's play it out, if that's what you're telling me. If he's the one who called the police, does that mean you did tell him you killed those people?"

"No! Not at all!"

"So he made that up?"

"Yes!"

"How would he know you were even at the motel?"

"I don't know, maybe..."

"But you talked to that woman before she was killed. That much is true."

"Yeah, but I explained that..."

"So you're telling me Aaron made up the story about you killing people, but he told the truth about you having a drink with the woman?"

Matt finally saw the trap he had walked into. He should have seen it coming. It was the same trap he faced when he spoke to that detective. He had to give Aaron his due, the bastard came up with a way to put him in a nasty bind.

"How would he know you talked to that woman, if you didn't tell him?" She asked, pressing it.

She stared at him, as if trying to see inside his brain. Jesse couldn't believe he had murdered those two unfortunate people, Matt told himself, she just wanted to hear an answer that would resolve this. If he gave her one, and it wasn't too upsetting, she might be ready to move on. Otherwise, all bets were off.

Matt squeezed his hands together, dangling them between his knees, thinking. As rapidly as he could, he went through scenarios that would explain this.

She became impatient and said his name, with a hint of threat. Sounds came through the open balcony door: a barking dog, several people shouting a conversation across the parking lot, an airplane overhead. The cookies smelled delicious.

Try as he might, there was no plausible version that didn't include him telling Aaron something. He closed his eyes and put his fate in the hands of the universe. Would he remain lucky?

Jesse asked, "Did you tell Aaron you killed two people, or not?"

By his calculations, Matt had one option.

He said, "Yes, I told him that."

THirTy-nine

J esse flinched. "Did you kill them?"

"No, of course not. They arrested the man who did it."

She shook her head slowly, side to side. "Then why on earth would you say such a thing?"

"I was angry and wanted to intimidate him. I read about the murders and used it to make me sound scary."

As soon as the words came out of his mouth, Matt realized, with horror, that when he told Aaron that, the story hadn't made it to the news feeds; the bodies hadn't even been discovered. He had put his head in the noose. If Detective Wisler gathered everyone together in the drawing room and compared notes, like what happened in old-fashioned mystery stories, he was doomed. *I have to be more careful,* he warned himself.

"Oh." Jesse had tears in her eyes. "Well, you made the mature choice, obviously. A better option than, say, turning and walking away."

"I should have done that."

"Do you think? You owe him an apology. He believes you killed two people. He's torn up by the guilt of knowing that, and indecision about what to do."

"What do you mean?"

"He said he didn't phone the police. He isn't sure if he should have or not."

This was a curve ball Matt hadn't seen coming. Aaron was again mixing true and false information, making it difficult to pull the strands apart.

Matt found his voice again. "How do you know all that?"

"He told me."

"When did you have these conversations with him?"

"He stopped by, for you. He brought a peace offering and every-thing."

"What's the peace offering?"

"We drank it."

Matt sighed and put his head in his hands. He asked, "Do you believe me?"

She evaluated him for a minute. "I don't think you're capable of killing two people in cold blood, Matt. Unfortunately, I do think you're capable of telling someone you did, to achieve some kind of dramatic effect. You're a nitwit sometimes, not a butcher."

Matt nodded. "Have I passed the test? Can I move back in?"

"If you apologize to Aaron. And stop being a nitwit."

"That might be asking a lot, based on this conversation."

She agreed. He did his best to make himself appear smaller, more contrite and eager to please.

"Alright," she said. "Put your things away. I'll start dinner."

Matt wheeled one of the suitcases down the hall to the bedroom. He opened it on the bed and began the process of putting his clothes away. It was a relief to be back with her, though it perversely felt like a reversal. His leaving with a few belongings and moving in with his sister at times had the shape of an adventure: a little scary, not very comfortable, nonetheless an exciting step into the unknown. This return was like tossing out that adventure and going back to the previous story that had already been played out. He would need to work with Jesse to create a new story.

Perhaps that was how all relationships felt, even successful ones. Revisiting the same routes and activities, with their similar highs and lows, as the years pass by, adding a few variations along the way. There was comfort in that, he acknowledged, but also despair. He had styled himself as a professional poker player in the hopes of earning enough to break out of those patterns, to create a new path for himself and Jesse. Now, he feared that might never happen, that putting his clothes away was a form of surrender. He had promised to be a good boy, because it was the right thing to do at that moment, for him and for Jesse, and he was desperate to move on beyond that conversation before he said something else self-incriminating. He wished the likely future in front of them didn't promise so much boredom.

Creating a new story for us, he thought. *Stories.*

Ever since Aaron talked about dopamine and stories and poker, Matt had become hyperaware of the stories around him. How things that happened weren't stories until someone put them together and made them so. Yet, from another perspective, those stories could also be seen as always there, waiting to be named. Stories as evidence, as memory, as explanation, as training, as amusement. Creating life's borders.

He needed to think more about that. He'd do it later.

He took a short stack of underwear to his dresser. He opened the top drawer and moved things to the side to make room and he saw something odd. It was a matchbook from the Ventura Hotel Casino.

In his underwear drawer.

Matt turned and stormed down the hall.

"What the hell is this?" he squawked, holding up the matchbook.

Startled, Jesse turned, wooden spoon in hand. "What the hell is what? What is that?"

"A matchbook!"

"Do they even make matchbooks anymore?"

"From the Ventura Casino!" Matt was furious, indignant.

Jesse was perplexed. She asked, "So?"

"It was in my underwear drawer!"

"Okay... You go there all the time. What are you talking about?"

"But I don't smoke. I never took one of their matchbooks. So where did this come from?"

"I don't know. It's your underwear drawer." She turned back to what she was doing.

Matt said, "Aaron must have put it there."

"I don't think Aaron smokes, either."

"He put it there as a message!"

"What kind of message would that be?"

"What were you two doing when he was here?"

That got her attention. She turned back to him with narrowed eyes, holding the spoon like a club. "What are you saying?"

"Why was Aaron in our bedroom while I was gone?"

"Oh? That's where you're going with this? He wasn't here very long, and he most certainly wasn't in the bedroom."

"You were with him the whole time?"

"Yes! In the living room!"

"So this matchbook floated down the hallway and into my underwear drawer?"

"Are you out of your mind? I'm sure you brought it back with you from one of your trips."

"I would remember that," said Matt.

"You don't remember the names of half the people you used to work with every day." She put the spoon down, and her hand on her hips. "You don't remember to do the laundry when I ask you to. By the way I don't know what you get up to on those trips, without me, if that's the conversation we're having."

"Aaron left this as a message for me, and the message was that he was in my bedroom, going through my stuff, and that he was in there with you!"

"We never left the living room."

"You can do a lot in a living room," he said, lowering his voice.

She held up her arms in exasperation. "Are you accusing me of sleeping with a man old enough to be my father?"

"I wouldn't put it past him to try something like that."

"With me?"

"Yeah, with you."

"And you think I would go along??"

"He's a smooth guy."

Jesse cursed and shook her head in disbelief. "You'd need to talk to your sister about that, since she's the one he's been seeing."

That shut Matt up.

"Yeah," said Jesse. "Didn't know that, did you? You've been spending so much time gambling away our savings, and telling lies about being some kind of hit man, and giving me grief about trying to put a decent life together for us, that you can't even see the things that are right in front of you."

"How long has that been going on?"

"I don't know. It's none of my business. None of yours, either."

Matt was dumbfounded. Not yet angry—though that was right around the corner—mostly confused. "What about the matchbook?" he asked, somehow unable to let it go.

"Jesus Matt, you brought it back in your suitcase some trip and it ended up in your drawer. How the hell am I supposed to know? We got back together, and within half an hour you're ready to ruin our relationship all over again because of a stupid matchbook." She pressed her wrists to her temples in frustration. She said, "I'm already regretting that I let you back in."

Matt walked, a little dazed, to the couch and sat down. He had never held a Ventura Casino matchbook in his hands, he didn't even know they had them. There was no doubt in his mind that Aaron had placed it in his underwear drawer. He was confident Aaron hadn't seduced Jesse—that would be so out of character for Jesse as to be, well, at least nearly impossible. The purpose of the matchbook was to cause an argument, and he allowed himself to be sucked in. And the revelation about Sofia! Yet another time bomb Aaron had left for him. He wondered, *How many others were scattered across my life?*

FORTY

Matt tapped his left foot as he shuffled the deck. The house was quiet. Jesse was at work. The wind was aggressive outside the kitchen window, and it sent a plastic trash can percussively rolling across the middle of the parking lot.

Matt did a simple reading, selecting four cards from a face-down deck. He didn't need the universe explained to him, he wanted guidance on what to do next. This was a pivotal moment in his life, and he wanted to get it right.

The nine of hearts told him someone was desiring more in a relationship. The ace of spades pointed to a significant change, something coming to an end and making room for something new. The six of clubs was a promise of success if action was taken.

Matt got the message. It was time to take things to the next level with Jesse—get married, perhaps, have a baby, buy a house. Also, the feud with Aaron needed to end. Most of all, it validated what Matt had already decided to do: drive out to Aaron's house, confront him about breaking the truce, and put an end to this conflict however necessary. Matt didn't want to threaten Aaron but what choice did he have? The old man was vindictive, impulsive, unstable, and most of all untrustworthy. With people like that you can't appeal to their better nature. It was for Aaron's own good. He needed to move on, they both did.

At the final card Matt frowned. The eight of spades was a warning, telling him fate would soon disrupt his life, perhaps causing havoc. All he could do was be careful.

***

After the reading Matt drove to Sofia's house to have it out over her thing with Aaron. Her car was in the driveway, but the front door was locked and no one answered his knock. He went around the back. He found her on the enclosed patio having a coffee, reading a book, wrapped in a thick sweater against the chill.

She asked, "You're back already?"

He sat down and gestured at the flower garden at the rear of the yard. "Those flowers are pretty back there," he said. "Isn't it late in the season?"

"They're mums. They like this weather fine. Until a frost, anyway." She waited to see what the visit was about.

Eventually he said, "Jesse told me you're having an affair with Aaron."

She clucked her tongue. "She wasn't supposed to do that."

"We were arguing, things got heated, and it popped out."

"You moved back and you're arguing already?"

"Stuff needed to be dealt with."

Sofia sniffed. "I imagine so. Still does. I wouldn't call it an affair, by the way. That seems a little more ambitious than it deserves."

"Why didn't you tell me?"

"I assume you're kidding. Are you suggesting I submit my private life for your approval?"

"This is a little different, don't you think?"

"I don't see how."

"You kept it a secret so you must have known it was wrong."

"He said it was best to keep it quiet. That it's kind of a no-no, consorting with the family of a sponsee."

Matt snorted. "*Consorting* sounds like one of his words."

"He said it would complicate your emotional recovery. He has your back."

"And you believed him?"

"Of course. Why wouldn't I?"

"He was doing it to mess with me!"

"I don't see how, if you didn't know about it. Also, keep your voice down."

"He was finding things about me, about my life."

"Wouldn't you have already told him all that? He was your sponsor."

"He wasn't my sponsor!"

"If he wasn't your sponsor then why would he be spending so much time trying to help you overcome the gambling thing? You're not acting like yourself. And the murder investigation…"

"That was him! He called the police, left anonymous tips, telling them about me." He had already told Jesse, might as well tell Sofia.

"Why would he do that?

"Because he's evil!"

She glared at him, same as Jesse did. She looked at the ground, at him, at the sky, almost commented then thought better of it, finally said, "According to you, a nice older man, a professional man, who volunteers his time helping people like you recover from addiction—though not you, apparently, since you claim he wasn't your sponsor—for no reason whatsoever selected you to harass, to give your name to the police, to make your life miserable, even though he didn't know you from Adam. Do I have that right?"

Matt sat still, his face flushed, his mouth a tense, straight line. How many times was he going to find himself in the same trap, always burning his fingers on the same stove?

"This man then entered a pleasant relationship with me—and yes, Matty, it's fun and he's excellent company. He makes me feel good about myself. But you say it was to bug you, even though we kept it a secret and you had no idea, so I don't get that at all. What's more, he came to dad's funeral to support us—not me, both of us—yet somehow that's aggressive behavior designed to harm you? Is that right? That's your position? No point to any of it? No purpose? No goal, other than tormenting you by being a nice person? Who would do that, and why?"

She waited for an answer. When none came she shook her head, dismayed.

"This is disturbing behavior from you," she said. "It seems irrational. Or you're not telling me everything. So what are you going to do?"

"I'm going to go fuck him up."

Forty-one

Aaron was repairing his lawn mower before he put it away for the winter. He didn't have much lawn to cut, given how his property was dominated by the house, garden, woodshed and toolshed, as well as the marshy part at the edge of his property where water runoff from the mountain always wanted to pool. But what little there was needed to be kept in check so he didn't have patches of jungle where small mammals could hide and plan raids on his vegetables in the summer. He glanced at his phone when it chirped, saw who was calling, wiped off his hands, pushed the button to answer, and put it on speaker.

"Hello there," he said.

"I have good news, and I have bad news," said Sofia, her voice tinny in the comforting atmosphere of the mountain near end of day. "The good is Matty's already moved out and back in with Jesse, so we're free to see each other whenever and wherever we choose."

"That is good news. I'm getting a little bored up here."

"The bad news is some sort of confrontation occurred when Matty went back, and in the middle of the argument Jesse told him about us. Which she promised she wouldn't do."

"If I remember correctly, you promised you wouldn't tell Jesse." This was a *pro forma* response. In reality, he had every expectation she would blab it to Jesse, and that Jesse would blab it to Matthew. He was surprised it took so long.

"He didn't receive it well," said Sofia, ignoring the dig. "He drove over earlier. He was plenty mad at me and especially at you, out of proportion with the situation. I told him to pull up his big boy pants and move on, which he also didn't like."

"Did he complain about anything else?" he asked, thinking of the matchbook.

"No, not specifically. Mostly that you're an evil person, for reasons I don't understand. He seems hell-bent on revenge for whatever wrongs he thinks you've done."

"He'll get over it."

"I guess, but he has a hard time letting things go, especially when he believes he's in the right and some injustice has occurred. I think he means you harm."

"That's not good."

"No. This is how he is, which is why his relationship with Apá was so terrible. Dad often acted like a petty tyrant, and he was unfair, which he would never apologize for. So Matty had to carry increasing amounts of resentment forward. That mess was never going to get better. Might be the same with you."

"He's still like that, then?"

"Yeah, worse, in some ways, and also different. He's a grown man now after all. Sometimes I'm not sure I recognize who he's become. The thing about the police shook me."

Sofia paused, as if considering whether to say the next part.

She said, "He told me the police harassed him because someone called and left a tip that he killed those people. He's convinced it was you. That you were trying to ruin his life."

"He told you all that, did he?"

She paused again. Then asked, "Did you tell the police he killed those people?"

"He did kill them," said Aaron, admitting it but not admitting it. Sofia wouldn't be okay with a lot of what was going to follow but so be it. They were all entering a new phase in the game.

She gasped. She asked, "How could you know that?"

"He told me."

"When did he tell you this?"

"He attacked me in the parking lot of the casino. Hit me, knocked me down, stole money from me. He told me about the murders to scare me, bragging about them, to show what a tough guy he was. Hoped I'd be so scared I'd hand over cash. But I didn't, so he beat me."

"Why would he do that?"

"He was drunk, maybe high."

"No, I mean why would he attack you at all?"

"Because I won money from him in a betting game, and he didn't like it."

Silence on the other end. She said, "So you've been lying to me the whole time?"

"No," he said, lying. "I haven't lied to you. The thing we've had going has been totally legit, the entire time. It's meant a lot to me."

More silence. Then she said, "You claimed you were his Gamblers Anonymous sponsor."

"I am, he just doesn't want to admit it. All I've done is attempt to help him."

"By betting with him?"

"I was trying to teach him a lesson."

"Okay..." She sounded unconvinced. "Seriously, you did that?"

"Yes. Maybe not my best idea."

"It sounds mean. Did it work?"

"No. Not even a little bit."

"He lost money before and did nothing like that."

"It would have been the same day of the murders, so he was not in his right mind."

"Oh my god."

"He claimed I cheated him. I didn't, but that wasn't why he attacked me. He said it was all the money he had left for playing poker, and he wanted it back. He needed it to continue his big plan of being a professional gambler, and without that money he had no plan. Does that track, with your understanding of him?"

"Yes," she said softly.

"I didn't believe him, at first. I thought it was the booze and the wounded pride talking, shooting off his mouth. But I checked into the story down there. He did it, Sofia, I'm sorry to tell you."

"He's not capable."

"You wouldn't think so. But somehow, he outfought two drug dealers and killed them with a fancy dagger."

"That makes no sense."

"Not to me, either. Don't worry, though, the police aren't interested in him. Someone confessed, some broke, lonely loser who thinks life is too hard and scary, a guy who feels safer in prison than out of it."

"I would've thought prison was hard, and scary."

"Different kind of hard, different kind of scary."

She was quiet for a long time. She said, "Matty was never a violent person. But now... If what you're telling me is true then you need to be careful, because it would mean he's not only angry at you, but also motivated to keep you quiet."

"I don't know. He's been stewing about the police thing for a while, and hasn't gone berserk about it yet. He thinks he's in the clear now, so maybe the pressure is off."

"Or he thinks no one is watching him now." She groaned. "I can't believe I'm talking like this. Also, he said something about doing a reading that told him to take action."

"A reading? Like reading tea leaves?"

"I don't know what he meant, this is new behavior to me. He was saying a lot of crazy things."

"You think he's serious, about harming me?"

"He was at the time he said it, I think," she said. "By tomorrow, who knows? But stay on alert. Most of the time, he'll gnaw on things for a while, then get over it and calm down. Sometimes, though, he gets even more cranked up. I'm worried we won't know which it is until he's breaking into your house."

After the call Aaron sat down at his desk, with a view of the western part of his property, and beyond that down the road leading to the camp, where half a dozen deer walked across the road near the huge boulder, deposited there by a glacier eons ago. Early-season snowflakes drifted down from the cloud cover.

He pulled several sheets of stationery-quality paper and wrote a note by hand. It laid out everything about Matt, about the murders, about Matt's anger and erratic behavior. He admitted to some, but not all, of his part in the feud. He ended by noting how Sofia warned him Matt was coming, to confront and threaten him, perhaps to kill him, making it clear that if anything happened to him it was almost certainly the fault of Matthew Martinez.

He thought it was important to draft a document like that, in his handwriting, and sign and date it. Both Jesse and Sofia were aware of some of the story, but it was second-hand; he wasn't an attorney but assumed his first-hand account would carry at least some legal weight, along with any other evidence they could gather.

He slipped the sheets of the letter into an envelope and sealed it. On the envelope he wrote the name of his cousin, Jake Stoltzfus, who he had designated as executor of his estate, to make sure Jake got it. He placed the envelope in the fire-proof, water-proof safe that sat at the bottom of the utility closet off the kitchen, next to his .22 rifle. Already in the safe were other important papers, the few expensive pieces of jewelry of his mother's, and a large amount of cash. Aaron was a big believer in keeping cash on hand, for emergency use as well as financial privacy and, perhaps most important, tax avoidance.

FORTY-TWO

The wind died down overnight. The morning sun was bright but the air remained cold, and Jesse wore a thick scarf and a hat as she headed out for another day of work. She waved goodbye to Matt who stood on the balcony to watch her go, his bare feet freezing. Their spat resolved, they had agreed to work on things together. She was happy he promised to apply for jobs, and believed he would begin that day.

This was a foolish belief, as Matt had other plans.

He put on jeans and hiking shoes, a black fleece over a long-sleeved performance tee, and a gray down vest over that. He topped it with a forest green Carhartt beanie and he was ready. He liked the fit he saw in the mirror. Casual, masculine, ready for the mountain forest. When he looked the part, he felt the part.

It was a pleasant enough drive from Tohickon to Larnersville. He skirted Bethlehem and drove north through farmlands and golf courses, and into the Poconos, blasting tracks by My Chemical Romance, The White Stripes, Sleigh Bells, The Pixies, Incubus, and Greta Van Fleet. He wasn't in a hurry. When he turned on the road leading up to Aaron's house, the wind was starting to gust again. The weather people had warned a storm might be coming. Most of it was expected to remain further south, above Maryland, but it had a tail that could whip around across the Interstate 80 corridor bringing colder air and snow. He'd need to monitor that.

His plan was straightforward. He would knock on Aaron's door and ask to come in. He would apologize again for becoming violent that night at the casino, but assert that Aaron should not have cheated him out of the money. He would say it had reduced the two of them into a pointless tit for tat, and hope Aaron agreed. If Aaron brought up the murders in Norristown, Matt would stick to the same explanation that came out of the conversation with Jesse, that it was a foolish attempt to be threatening, a dumb thing to say, and it got out of hand. Ill-advised bragging from an angry drunk man. Aaron should buy that, if Matt was contrite enough, and if Aaron forgot Matt talked about the murders before anyone other than the killer knew about them. Even if he remembered, Matt would tell him he has the timeline wrong, and deny, deny, deny. If Aaron would get on board it would lead to a genuine truce and Matt could move on like the cards told him to.

Not that Matt wasn't still angry with Aaron; he was furious. He had a list in his head of all the wrongs that man had committed toward him, each one worse than the other from his point of view. So yes, Matt was still pissed off. Therefore, he had no intention of letting the feud end with a fizzle and a murmur. He would get Aaron to agree to terms. Then later, maybe months later—or even years later, how brilliant would that be?—Matt would find a way to totally screw over Aaron Stoltzfus, destroying what little life the old man had left. But first he needed to force Aaron's capitulation so there could be some breathing room, a break from the pettiness.

As Matt drove by Aaron's house, he was surprised to see Aaron's Toyota missing. Even though they met at the Jersey shore, one hundred and sixty miles away, Matt thought of Aaron as a house-bound recluse. The hermit who only came down from the mountain to torment him.

Matt was disappointed. How would he put his plan into mo-tion—and to be accurate, it was not much more than an outline of a plan—if Aaron wasn't there? He was riding on anger and adrenaline; both would dissipate soon enough, then things would settle right back to where they had been. He needed to act while his will was strong. It called for a change of tactics.

He slowed and observed the house. One thing he learned from that unfortunate incident in the motel was that he was more capable of improvisation than he thought. It was a new-found talent, like waking up and finding you can play the piano, and he wanted to celebrate it by putting it to good use in a challenging situation. This might be the moment, he realized, a growth opportunity. Maybe this was a bit of good luck.

He continued down the road past the camp, around to the other side of the mountain. He pulled in at the shuttered auto repair shop. He'd leave his car there, rather than have it announce his presence should Aaron return. Smiling to himself, he felt in control, and prepared. He started walking back along the road.

Matt was so caught up in his own thoughts he forgot to lock his car. He was so caught up in his own thoughts that earlier, he failed to notice the door of Aaron's barn was ajar, with Aaron standing in the shadows a step inside, watching Matt drive by.

Forty-Three

Half an hour earlier, Aaron had come outside, took stock of the wind speeds, and assessed the sky. The weather people had been flipping and flopping about snow, with the final consensus that there was a decent chance of it, and at his elevation it could accumulate. He had no plans to go anywhere that day, so he opened the barn and drove his car inside, where it would sit next to his motorcycles and stay out of the snow. It would be a lot easier to clear an empty driveway, should it come to that.

He was putting food out for the colony of feral cats that hung around the barn when he heard a car coming up the road. Hardly anyone came this far, and if they did it was someone lost. The car slowed as it neared his property, however, so Aaron stepped toward the door where he could see. He recognized the car, and saw Matt behind the wheel, looking the other way, checking out the house. Aaron assumed it was for a hostile purpose, and he was not in the mood to put up with something like that.

The car continued on and didn't return. Assuming Matt had come all that way to do him harm, rather than another pointless drive-by, Aaron concluded Matt was stowing his car somewhere in order to sneak up on Aaron's house. The likely place would be the old car shop around the bend.

Aaron trotted over to his house. He took the bolt-action single shot rifle out of the back of the kitchen utility closet. He put a watch cap on his head, stuffed a pair of gloves into one pocket of his coat, and slipped a box of .22 long rifle ammunition into the other. He left through the back door, went around the woodshed, and started up the path that cut across the lowest parts of the hill, over to the other side where the road wraps around.

When he reached the other side, he saw Matt's car parked in the tiny repair shop lot, as suspected. Matt intended to invade Aaron's peace on foot, unannounced. Safe to assume it wasn't to surprise him with pastries and a warm smile.

Aaron went to the car and found it unlocked. *Ha*, he thought, *stupid kid*. He reached in, pulled the hood lever, opened the hood, and yanked out the spark plug wires. He trotted back across the street and tossed the wires into the bushes. No one was driving that car anywhere. He continued up the path, heading back to intercept Matt.

When Aaron came over the crest behind his home he stopped and crouched. At that spot he had a view of his property and a little more than fifty yards up the road, but he saw no sign of Matt. He hoped the boy wasn't coming through the woods, since stumbling out of the trees and onto the path near him would be an unsafe surprise for both of them. He wondered whether Matt was armed.

Aaron waited, the wind chilling him. Snowflakes drifted down, enough to be called a flurry. He caught movement along the road, and Matt appeared, walking on the weeds and brush between the trees and the edge of the asphalt, checking his surroundings. For all his attempts at caution he was probably making plenty of noise, tromping through dead leaves and brittle sticks, though the wind carried the sound away before it reached Aaron. Matt seemed nervous, and Aaron wasn't sure if that made him more or less dangerous. He watched as Matt circled the house.

It occurred to Aaron he had left the back door unlocked, as dumb a thing as Matt leaving the car unlocked. *We're all human*, thought Aaron, as he watched Matt find his way to the back door, try the latch, and enter the house.

Forty-Four

Matt had been debating whether to break a window, and was surprised to find the back door open. When he told people he was a lucky guy, this is what he meant. It made him fleetingly concerned about whether he remembered to lock his car, however.

Matt acknowledged he was now guilty of breaking and entering. Not the worst crime he had committed during the year, obviously, and it amused him to see how easily he let himself indulge. It was as if the incident in the motel had reset his moral compass. As a kid he wouldn't dream of stealing a pen from a classmate but now see him go. A strange kind of personal development.

He'd have to think about the many possible variations and directions in personal evolution later. He had a house to explore.

It was a small building with intimate rooms. Kind of like the biggest, fanciest home in a Hobbit village. It boasted a living room with a fireplace, a dining area with a round table and four chairs. Shelves covered one wall and wrapped around to cover half of another, jammed with books and an impressive DVD collection. The books were a combination of novels, and nonfiction about business and communication and writing. Matt skimmed the movies; a lot of classic American and British stuff but also French and Japanese films, a few of which Matt thought maybe he had heard of. The art on the wall was a mix of paintings, drawings, prints, maps, framed magazine covers, and old photographs. It wasn't hung in the careful placement of his father's restaurants, or like in the homes of some of his wealthier friends, but tossed helter-skelter anywhere there was space, at different heights. The art was an undisciplined collection, not intentional décor.

All the cultural stuff made Matt a little jealous. Also, a little annoyed, truth be told, like Aaron was making a point about how he's better than regular people.

A water closet was crammed next to a pantry, and the kitchen had been remodeled with white subway tiles and high-end appliances. Good for Aaron, admitted Matt, at least the man must know how to cook and has his priorities straight when he isn't reading books and watching French thrillers from the 1960s.

Off the kitchen was a utility closet, with tools on shelves and hooks, and a home safe on the floor. In an antique cabinet, with bird's eye maple veneer, in a corner of the living room, he found a stocked liquor supply. There was vodka, gin, bourbon, rye, Aperol, Campari, sweet and dry vermouth, Grand Marnier, ouzo, and a small selection of wines. *Probably keeps this locked when his AA friends come over*, Matt thought. *Gotta protect the lie.*

A narrow staircase took a half-turn and Matt marveled at how any furniture could find its way upstairs, it didn't seem physically possible. There was only one genuine bedroom; the queen bed left little space for the bureau and armoire. The pieces were all wood and probably antique. Matt wondered whether Aaron inherited the furniture along with the house.

He found nothing valuable in the armoire or the bureau, and turned to the nightstand. There were pens and a notebook in the drawer, plus a couple of pill bottles. One was marked "vardenafil" which Matt had never heard of, and the other had an "R" written on it in permanent marker. He put them back, and opened the door to the large compartment of the nightstand. There were two shelves inside. On one sat three books. On the other was a wooden box. He opened the box and discovered it was full of cash.

"Jesus, you stupid old man, what are you doing?" said Matt, out loud.

The money was organized in bundles, wrapped in rubber bands, with sticky notes identifying how much was in each bundle. Matt did some quick calculations; there was about twelve thousand dollars in the box. Matt wondered if it was gambling winnings, or maybe getaway money... who could say what crafty old Aaron got up to? Without thinking too much about it Matt stuffed all the money into his coat pockets.

Suddenly he had a new poker stake. His relationship with Jesse was back on track, and now he could do the same with his poker career. *Checking off them goals!*

There was a section, past the bath, that wasn't quite another bedroom, as it was missing a fourth wall and a door, but wasn't quite anything else. It had been turned into an office area, with a desk up against a window providing Aaron with a view. The house was perfect for a man like Aaron living alone, but it was hard to imagine how a family could reside there comfortably.

Matt didn't see anything in the house that he could use against Aaron in any way, unfortunately. The guy seemed to live the life he claimed to lead, which was rather dull, all things considered.

Matt went back to the utility closet and the safe on the floor. *If Aaron's keeping all that cash in an unlocked wooden box,* thought Matt, *what does he have in the safe?* He was tempted to steal it. He could lift one side a little, but it was too heavy to pick up the entire thing.

Matt went out by the back door again, walked across the street as snow fell on his head and shoulders. The wind picked up the light coating on the road and sent it dancing. As he neared the large barn he saw a cat, then a second and third, then two more that ran around the corner of the barn when they saw him coming. He stepped inside. Daylight from behind him fell on several bowls of dry cat food and water. Two motorcycles sat to his right, a Harley and an old Indian that looked damn near an antique. A few feet away was a snowblower, a few pieces of gardening equipment, and a lawnmower against which were propped two flat carpet-covered wood dollies. There was a deep shelf with cans of paint, a canister of linseed oil, a jug marked "bug poison" in cursive handwriting, and several small plastic boxes. An SUV sat in the central area, and off to the left was an old Chevy Chevette in the process of being refurbished.

Now I know what Aaron does as a hobby, thought Matt. *He's a motorhead.*

Then he realized what was in front of him. The SUV was the Toyota he had seen Aaron driving. Unless he owned multiple cars, or was picked up by an Uber driver, Aaron hadn't left after all. A chill ran down Matt's spine as he understood that Aaron might still be around somewhere, close by. Maybe watching him.

Then Matt heard footfalls behind him.

Forty-Five

After he watched Matt enter through the back door, Aaron walked down from his perch on the hill above and positioned himself behind the woodshed, where he could poke his head around and have a good view of the house. Through the windows he saw Matt move around in the kitchen, then reappear in the bedroom upstairs. He wondered what Matt was doing in there; snooping, or something destructive?

Aaron lost sight of Matt for some time and imagined him rifling through papers on his desk and trying to break into his laptop. He considered going in and confronting him, weighed the pros and cons. He was still thinking it over when Matt came out of the house through the back door. Surprised, Aaron pulled back just in time before he was spotted. Matt crossed the street to the barn as snow swirled around him.

Aaron raced to the back door and moved quickly through his house, checking for damage, or anything missing. Everything on his desk seemed okay, but in his bedroom he saw the night table cabinet door open, and the wooden box sitting on his bed, empty. Downstairs he checked the utility closet and found the safe undisturbed.

In Aaron's view, out of everything he had watched Matt do, it was taking the money from the box that told him the most about Matt's character. Decent people can go through difficult experiences and come out better; they become kinder, more grateful for what they have, perhaps closer to their higher power. Unfortunately, the traumatic incident at the motel didn't transform Matt for the better, it turned him into a common thief.

Aaron went out the door, and across the road. As he came up to the barn doors he saw Matt standing a few feet in, staring at the Chevy Chevette. Matt heard him coming, and turned.

"It's a 1979," said Aaron as Matt stepped back in surprise. "Holley two-barrel carburetor, a flat hood, and a large chrome grille. Air-injection system to improve catalytic converter function. I'm zhooshing it up."

Matt's eyes took in the old man, then lingered over the rifle held in Aaron's right hand, pointed at an angle toward the ground in Matt's direction.

"Saw you go by, you dumb fuck," said Aaron. "I was standing about where you are now, watched you checking out the place, seeing if I was home. Saw you break into my house. Kept my eye on you the whole time."

"You have a gun." It was a statement, not a question. Matt's eyes kept darting to the rifle.

"Yeah. For hunting, and plinking."

Matt frowned. Fear and confusion passed across his face. In a hoarse voice he asked, "What do you hunt?"

"Self-protection from nature, more than hunting, to be honest. I'm out here in the middle of nowhere. This is black bear country. No mountain lions but the bobcats can get pretty big. Not that I would want to shoot either one of them, or that this rifle would stop them. Just make them mad, I imagine. I guess I'm hoping if I show a bear or a bobcat the gun, they'll get the hint and go away. The most dangerous animals we have around here are snakes, tell the truth. Copperheads and rattlers, but I'm not good enough to shoot one of them. Running away is more effective."

Aaron was pleased by the anxiety on Matt's face.

"Mostly, I go after groundhogs eating everything from my garden. The deer do more damage but there's not much I can do about them, they come by when I'm not around, and avoid the place when I am. They know I don't like them."

Aaron swallowed, his eyes darting around the barn. "You going to kill me?"

"Haven't decided yet. Why are you in my barn?"

"I was hoping to find you."

"Well, you found me. What are you after?"

"To talk. Try to sort things out between us."

"That's what phones are for."

"I don't like phones for important conversations."

Aaron nodded. "I know what you mean. Is that why you broke into my house?"

"The back door was open."

"Son, that is still burglary. If you're embarking on a new criminal career you should at least understand what the crimes are."

"Didn't mean any harm."

"How about all that money you stole from my nightstand? Didn't mean that, either?"

Matt moved his mouth like he was about to say something, thought differently about it, and stayed quiet.

"Now come out of the barn," said Aaron, with a toss of his head. "We'll go across the street, see if you did any more damage to my house, then we'll call the police, let you explain things to them. There's twenty or so officers in the township, one of them ought to be able to come by without making us wait too long."

Matt nodded. His pupils were dilated, his breathing rapid, and sweat lingered on his brow. He walked toward the cats watching from outside the barn, with Aaron holding the rifle pointed to within ten inches of Matt's heels. When Matt turned in the direction of the house he bolted, heading down the road toward the camp, betting he could outrun the much older man and reach the car on the other side of the mountain.

"Dammit," said Aaron. He walked to the center of the road, pulled the rifle up, and fired.

FORTY-SIX

The bullet missed Matt by centimeters as he fled down the road. Aaron saw the bottom edge of Matt's down vest flip up, spewing insulated filling into the air to mix with the drifting snowflakes. Matt looked terrified; he tried to stop as well as glance back over his shoulder at the same time, tripped over his own feet, and hit the ground hard. Aaron walked down the middle of the road, reloading the rifle. Limping, Matt hurried to the side of the road and behind the huge boulder.

"Dammit, dammit, dammit," said Aaron again, watching Matt scurry.

This was getting messy. Aaron had to follow up, though. He needed to learn why Matt was there and what he was planning, and he needed to get his money back. If he let Matt run off, he might never see that cash again, plus Matt might return the next day, or the next week, and they would be back in the same violent embrace. If what Sofia said was true, Aaron couldn't be sure that Matt wouldn't escalate things. Aaron would feel constantly endangered, not being able to sleep at night. No, he had to sort this out. His rifle loaded, he strolled up and stood on the road side of the boulder.

"I've rendered your car useless," said Aaron. He thought it might soften Matt up, to know his escape route was gone. "You can get it fixed, but it'll require calling a garage to come up on the mountain. Take a long while, they don't rush around here."

"No you didn't," yelled Matt from where he was sitting, in the weeds on the other side of the boulder. "You don't know where it is."

"You parked it there by Eddie's old repair shop. I told you I've been watching you."

"It was locked."

"No it wasn't. You're so nervous, so scared because you're in over your head, you're careless. If you want to get off this mountain you need to come out so we can chat."

"You shot at me!"

"You broke into my house, stole my money, and were running away. I wanted you to stop running."

"You missed my hip by a couple of inches!"

Yeah, that was close, thought Aaron. He fired in haste, and now, thinking back on it, he wasn't sure if he was aiming for Matt's back and missed, or tried to miss and got too close. If the distinction even mattered in the grand scheme of things. He walked closer to the boulder.

"I can hear you," said Matt. "I have a rock in each hand, I'll use them if you come around."

"And I have a rifle."

"So? You gonna shoot me? How will you explain that to the cops?"

"You're a thief."

"I want you to stay over there until we get this figured out," said Matt, his voice trembling.

Aaron shrugged and sat with his back to the boulder. The light snow was steady now, dusting everything. There was that beautiful silence of a snowfall. Two men, sitting quietly in the chill, like they were the last people left in the world.

"How did you find Cindy?" asked Aaron, eventually. "That was clever."

"You're the kind of man who will prey on women in AA. It's written all over you. My father was the same way, so I searched for the woman my father would have gone after."

"So you guessed?"

"You're forgetting the luck part."

"Oh, please drop that stuff!"

"I realize you thirteenth stepped me, but about the gambling. You get new pussy from AA, and you figure out how to get money from gambling addicts. I assume you run some version of this scam in other groups, too."

"You're being ungenerous," said Aaron, genuine hurt in his voice. "I help people get their lives back on track."

"It's going to catch up to you."

"I'll be fine."

"Is that story you told about the poker game in San Francisco real or bullshit?"

"It's true. Mostly."

"Because you talk about it changing who you were. My dad used to tell me people don't change. He said the only time he met people who genuinely changed was in AA. After you told that story, I thought you might be one of them."

"You think I'm not?"

"My dad also said in the end he still had to rely on their word they had changed, so maybe they were lying. People like you, manipulative pieces of shit."

"Again, not fair."

They sat. The snow was ebbing, and the wind less intense.

"You sound disappointed, that I wasn't one of those people like your dad talked about," said Aaron. "I think you might be doing some kind of transference thing, with me."

Matt didn't answer.

A dusting of snow clung to the grass and leaves. A red fox trotted down along the edge of the road, diving into the shrubs before it reached them.

"Do you want a last piece of advice?" asked Aaron.

"From you? No."

"I'll give it to you anyway, as a gift, then you can come out and we'll call the police. You've based so much of your self-image, and your interactions with the world, on this idea of luck. I think that's bizarre, and it's no way to play cards by the way. But here's the thing: luck doesn't exist, the way you talk about it."

"We already had this conversation, old man."

"I'm trying to help you."

"You're in denial."

"There's nothing you could say that would convince me luck is real."

"Say a stone falls from the top of a building," said Matt, trying to win the argument, wanting to have the final word. "The guy who walked past there, who's now half a block away, that's good luck for him. The guy who took a minute to pet a dog, he ends up walking right under when it falls, that's bad luck. In my life I'm the guy half a block away, all the time. That's how it is, for me."

"That's ridiculous. You don't understand what you're talking about."

"We're talking about luck."

"Nope. We're talking a sequence of events over time." Aaron pounded the rifle's shoulder stock a few times into the dirt next to him. "I'll tell you one last story."

"Jesus, old man, you like to hear yourself talk."

Aaron laughed. "You'll like this one. You'll even understand it."

"Not listening."

"This is a famous one from Taoism, you might know it."

"Yeah, sure." Matt couldn't remember what Taoism was.

"Alan Watts used to talk about it a lot."

"Who's Alan Watts?"

"Right, okay," said Aaron. He gazed up into the sky as he spoke, watching the snow drift down toward his face. "There was this farmer. His horse ran away one day. His neighbors came by to offer their condolences. 'What terrible luck to lose your horse like that,' they said. And in response the farmer said, 'Maybe.' The next day the horse returned, and along the way had picked up six wild horses that followed it home. All the same neighbors came back that evening to celebrate. 'What great good luck that was,' they said, 'you now have seven horses!' And in response the farmer said, 'Maybe.' The following day the farmer's son tried to tame one of the wild horses, but he fell off and broke his leg. 'What bad luck that was,' said the neighbors. And the farmer said, 'Maybe.' A few days later soldiers came to the farm to force the farmer's son into the army, but with his broken leg he couldn't march. 'Fighting in that war would be almost certain death,' said the neighbors, 'it is so lucky your son didn't have to go. It all worked out in the end!' And the old farmer again said, 'Maybe.'"

They sat in silence. After a while, Matt said, "Yeah?"

"Consider your own life. Your grandfather dies, seems like bad luck. But he leaves you money, so good luck. But you lose it all after a string of what you think is bad luck, but it's actually you being a lousy poker player. Then you break into my house and find cash, so good luck again..."

"That's a boring way to say if I wait long enough, luck will bend my way. Which is what I've been saying all the time."

"...which led to me sitting here with a rifle about to turn you over to the police, bad luck again. The point is that you never know the consequences of any action you or someone else takes. The world does what it does. Maybe that man hit by the falling stone in your story, he went to the hospital, where he met a nurse who became the love of his life, they married and had children, and he wouldn't have met her otherwise. That stone was the luckiest thing to happen. Everything affects everything else, in all kinds of ways. Whether you see it as good luck or bad luck is almost entirely a function of the moment you choose to make that judgement, who you are, and where you're standing. There's no luck, Matthew. It doesn't exist."

"You know what I can't figure out," said Matt, "is whether you're trying to give me good advice, or fucking with me to make my life miserable."

"I'm trying to give you good advice," said Aaron as he watched a fat groundhog waddle across the road. "But I'm also angry you stole my money and I'm going to turn you over to the cops. They can make your life miserable."

The groundhog bolted in panic as Matt burst from behind the boulder, large stones in each hand. Matt threw the stone in his left hand, with little force and accuracy, and it struck Aaron's wrist, knocking the rifle out of his hand. The stone in Matt's right hand, however, found the side of Aaron's head with force, drawing blood. Matt took off down the road.

Forty-seven

Matt neared the gate leading to the camp. He turned to see Aaron following. Aaron was dazed, and the side of his head where the stone had hit was dark with blood. Twice Aaron raised the rifle as if to shoot at Matt, but he never got as far as aiming, lowering the rifle again. There were a few more awkward steps, and Aaron stumbled off to the side, like a drunk on a dance floor. The rifle slipped from his hand as he collapsed into a bush by the edge of the road.

Matt stood for a full minute, trying to sort out the next thing to do.

He could run, get to his car, drive away. But then what?

Aaron was still alive, Matt could see him breathing, but he was concussed. Maybe there was brain damage. If left there, Aaron might die from exposure, then Matt could add second-degree murder to his list of crimes. The body would be discovered, police would investigate. They'd see Aaron's head was bashed with a rock, there would be signs of someone in the house, perhaps fingerprints, a box where money used to be. They would talk with Cindy who would tell them about Matt.

And if Aaron didn't die, if he came to and was able to walk back to his house, then he would call the police. Matt could try convincing them he was defending himself—he could show them the bullet hole in his down vest—but that story would be compromised by the break-in and the stolen money.

Matt wondered if police departments kept track of what happens in other jurisdictions. If his involvement with the cops up there in the Poconos was tracked in a database, that woman detective might recognize his name and connect him to the investigation of the motel murders. Hell, they wouldn't need to make the connection, if Aaron lived he would certainly tell the local cops about the Norristown incident. Then it would all become complicated, and hard to talk his way out of... maybe impossible.

He couldn't leave things the way they were, that much was clear.

He walked back, picked up the rifle, and stood by Aaron. He developed a scenario in which Aaron shot himself. An older man, living alone in the woods, no friends. Maybe money troubles? Gambling debts? Everyone had secrets, maybe Aaron's would come out and make suicide at least understandable if not inevitable. Would he kill himself out here, down the road from his house? Sure, why not?

It could work, if Matt's luck held out.

He pulled the still-unconscious Aaron deeper into the brush, like the man wanted some privacy in his final moments. There were a few exposed rocks that might cause a head injury if someone fell on them, and he made sure there was a little blood transfer. A lonely crank like Aaron, it would take a long time for anyone to miss him, and if Matt hid the body well enough it would take even longer to find him. He thought he read somewhere that evidence decays over time, and it gave him hope.

How would someone commit suicide with a .22 long rifle? Best way seemed to be putting the muzzle under their chin, pointing up toward the top rear of the skull, and reaching down to the trigger, if you're tall enough, and the rifle isn't too long.

Matt inspected the gun. A wood stock bolt action .22, as common as blue jays. He shot these rifles in the past, in his childhood, with a friend who inherited one from his uncle. He positioned the rifle, pointing through Aaron's head toward the top of his skull, hesitated, and fired. Aaron jolted, then went still again.

Matt sat on the ground, a little shocked at what he had done. He checked Aaron's pulse. That part of it was over. The old man was dead.

Matt inspected the body, he assumed blood from an exit wound would be different than blood from hitting a rock, and he wanted to mind the details. But there was no exit wound that he could find. Cell coverage up on the mountain was spotty, but he managed to find a couple of sources online that told him a .22 shot to the head sometimes won't leave an exit wound, especially if fired at close range, due to the small size and low velocity of the bullet. The skull can cause the bullet to shatter, sending fragments throughout the brain.

Well, then. This was an interesting situation.

What if this was another example of luck on his side, and he could turn it further to his advantage? For example, stage the suicide in a more suitable place. Like the house.

He couldn't drag Aaron's body all that distance. Even if he could, the damage to the clothes and the body, and whatever debris was picked up along the way, would put the lie to the staging. Then he remembered the two wooden dollies. He trotted to the barn, rifle slung over his shoulder. He retrieved the dollies, along with a couple dozen feet of nylon rope from a hook on the barn wall, and went back. For a moment Matt was afraid the body wouldn't be there, like in a horror movie. But there it was, waiting for him.

Matt put the empty cartridge in his pocket. In Aaron's jacket pocket he found the cartridge from that first shot near the barn, and a box of ammo. The wind had become negligible, thank goodness, and the snow flurries were over as he wheeled the body back. One of the dollies had a rope attached to it, so with Aaron's torso on one dolly and his thighs on the other, he pulled the body down the road to the house. The heels of Aaron's boots were dragging but there wasn't anything he could do about that.

He left the body at the back door and returned to the shooting site. He grabbed a fallen branch from an evergreen, and walked backwards to the house, waving the needles of the branch like a broom, obscuring the tracks in the thin layer of snow. It looked messy, but at least nothing was identifiable, and by the next day the sun would melt it, or more snow would cover it up.

He struggled getting the body through the door and into the living room. With considerable effort, he propped Aaron on the couch, assuming that would be the best location. He considered how to arrange the tableau. Maybe put a sad movie on the television, something from the DVD collection that touched on the loneliness of the elderly, or the long-term impact of a sad childhood, or the toll of substance abuse. He had done that sort of thing pretty well down in the motel, no reason he couldn't pull it off with Aaron.

Then he thought again of Cindy.

Cindy knew who he was, that he had a feud with Aaron, and that he was scouting Aaron's house. If there was any suspicion of foul play—any suspicion at all—they would talk with Aaron's friends and intimates, which would lead them to both the AA meetings in the area, and the restaurant where he no doubt ate occasionally, and both trails would lead them to Cindy. And Cindy, bless her little heart, would point them to Matt.

If they determined, with certainty, that it was suicide, alright then. But otherwise, Matt was in trouble. Thinking it through even further, he realized it was possible that after Matt's drive-by, Aaron could have brought Cindy up to speed, told her about that night in Atlantic City, the murders in Norristown, the threats and harassment. She might not wait to be asked by the police, once she hears what happened, but start volunteering info early and often. Jesus, Matt was cooked. The living room felt too small, too airless. He was dizzy. He tried to think, to ponder the angles.

The only way out was to eliminate Cindy.

Part VI

THE SAFE

FORTY-EIGHT

Matt had a long conversation with himself, and it wasn't pleasant. He tried to talk himself out of the next step and failed. Without Cindy, he had to admit, the cops would have a much harder time connecting him to Aaron. That's all there was to it.

After coming to that point, he felt calm. It was the same kind of calm that he experienced in the motel room, and, as with that incident, he assumed it would impact him later. But who knows, maybe not. With three killings he was now a seasoned pro, compared to most people. Maybe he was beyond a full emotional collapse. Maybe there will be a little anxiety, a few nights of difficult sleep, then he'll be over it.

If that turned out to be the case it probably raised serious questions about his mental health and moral compass. He'd have to think about that later.

He lifted Aaron under his arms and dragged him to the kitchen. He placed him in a corner, near the entrance to the basement, where the body couldn't be seen from the living room.

The keys to Aaron's SUV were on a wooden keyholder in the kitchen. The keyholder was an old souvenir board with a chipped painting of a woman in a bikini waterskiing on a lake, with "Greetings from the Poconos" beneath her, and six brass hooks below that. Matt wondered how old it was. He never understood the appeal of kitsch, other than it had to do with irony mixed with nostalgia, neither of which he understood, as well.

Matt backed Aaron's SUV out of the barn. It seemed a safer choice than taking his own, since he didn't want any potential witnesses getting a good look at his car. He also assumed Aaron's Toyota might make it easier with Cindy. He drove down the mountain, past the restaurant where he and Cindy had lunch, then up the hill to the small blue house.

This was the moment of greatest risk. If her sister answered, it would expose him and ruin his plan. If Cindy was working at the restaurant he couldn't go in to get her, because that, too, would expose him and ruin his plan. If she was out doing an errand he could wait for her to return, but he'd have limited time before neighbors became inquisitive. Even though Aaron said there was no such thing as luck, this moment was all about it.

It took three sets of knocks to get Cindy to answer the door. So, good luck. She was wearing black yoga pants and chunky gray New Balance sneakers, and an oversized sweatshirt with characters from the movie *Twilight* on it. He saw from her eyes and her swaying posture that she was drunk. Thank goodness, he thought. Good luck again. Screw that dead old man, what did he know?

"Aaron sent me down with his car," Matt said, jerking his thumb over his shoulder in the direction of the Toyota. "He's fixing a dead taillight on mine. He told me to ask you to come up, hang out."

She raised her eyebrows in a small show of attitude. "Him, me, and you?"

"No!" Matt laughed. "When he's done replacing the bulb on my car I'm heading home."

Her gaze slid past him, toward the street. "That is his car," she said, as if she were being crafty, not missing a trick.

"Yup."

"Why didn't he ask me up himself?"

"Cause he's, uhm, working on my car. The taillight. That's why I have his car."

"Are you the chauffeur, then?"

"Sort of."

"I thought you were frenemies," she said, though she mangled the last word, giving it five syllables.

"I guess we still are, in a way," he said, with a smile. "But we're cool, now."

There was stalemate, at least for a moment. Matt was prepared to keep at it for as long as it took to get her into the car, but ultimately, she had little resistance in her.

***

On their way up the mountain Matt felt compelled to chatter, to fill the space, to distract her from thinking about anything too much. "He talks about you sometimes," he said. "I think he's lonely, and regrets breaking it off with you. My gut feeling on that last part, though."

She raised her eyebrows at that. "He used to have dinner parties there," she said, "if you can believe that, a space that small."

"Right."

"Before I met him. He told me about them, though. Professors from East Stroudsburg, Kings's College, Moravian. Writers from Wilkes. Hippies from the mountains in New York. I think he misses those days."

"Sounds like a lot of snobby talk about a lot of lame ideas," he said, pretending to be unimpressed. "That's where he gets all those old stories, I'll bet."

"They call him The Professor in the rooms, because of the way he talks," she said. "But you would know that. It would have been interesting to go to those parties," she said, leaning back against the head rest. When Matt next stole a glance, her eyes were closed.

She perked up when they pulled into Aaron's driveway. "Where's your car?" she asked.

"In the barn," he said. He noted, again, how observant and curious she was. Which made her dangerous. Therefore, he made the right decision about her.

"He must be upstairs," said Matt when they stepped into the living room. "Probably showering."

Cindy nodded absently. "I keep telling him to move, a condo someplace, where there's a pool and a tennis court and, you know, other people."

"You and me both," said Matt. He pointed to the armchair. "Have a seat. Coffee, tea, or a whiskey?"

"A whiskey!?!" She waved him off. "You know I can't do that!!" As if she wasn't already drunk. Matt waited.

"Okay, a whiskey," she said, as if giving in to immense social pressure. "On ice. With a little water."

He smiled warmly. He found the remote and turned on the television and asked her if she liked the Food Network shows and she said yes, so he put one on. A woman with a midwestern accent was compiling some kind of casserole. He made Cindy's whiskey on ice and put it in front of her. She sipped it, said it was delicious, and wasn't it forever since she had one so good as this? She watched the woman on TV chop things and tell stories about family gatherings, as Matt put the muzzle of the rifle against Cindy's temple and shot her.

He dragged Aaron's body out of the kitchen and back onto the couch. Not perfect, the body was uncooperative, but as good as he could make it. Using a napkin, he took the poker from the fireplace, put it into Cindy's hands so her prints were on it, and then whacked Aaron on the arm with it, as hard as he could, then his head where the wound was from the rock, smearing blood on the poker and the couch. Matt wasn't sure if this was going to make sense as a story, or if the police forensic people were a lot more skillful than he assumed and would see right through his efforts. It would have to suffice.

Matt went upstairs and retrieved the pill bottles. He also found two joints in a drawer in the desk and grabbed them. Back downstairs he put the pills on the counter. He researched the vardenafil, found out it was an erection pill. He didn't know what the other one was. He thought cops always got excited when they found meds at a crime scene, it would give them something to talk about.

He took the gin and vodka out of the bird's eye maple cabinet and put them on the coffee table in the living room, between the body of Aaron on the couch and Cindy in the armchair. He spent a good amount of time placing the rifle in Aaron's hands, in what seemed like a believable position for suicide. He left the spent cartridge where it was and tossed another from his pocket onto the floor.

He examined the scene: an estranged couple got drunk, there was some kind of a fight, she whacked him with the poker, he shot her, then in a fit of remorse he killed himself. The average person never has a chance to stage a crime scene in their entire life, and here he was doing it for the second time that year. The surprising turns life takes!

He opened both the gin and vodka bottles. He knocked over the gin bottle, spilling the liquid over the coffee table and onto the floor. He poured vodka onto Cindy and Aaron. He took the whiskey bottle and threw it against the bookshelf, as if in anger, where it burst and scattered liquid over books and DVDs. He placed the joints on the table.

Can alcohol start a fire? He didn't know for sure, but alcohol was flammable. He Googled it. Alcohol will burn, he read, but oil was a lot better. Cooking oil was okay, but linseed oil would be even better. Duh. So he went into the kitchen where he found a container of canola oil. But then remembered where he had seen linseed oil. He trotted over to the barn and retrieved the canister.

Into the fireplace he placed crumpled paper from the short stack of old newspapers nearby, kindling, and some of the logs Aaron had piled. He made a sloppy job of it, like it was done by someone drunk, in the midst of an argument. He left the fire screen off to the side. He added the linseed oil to the wood and kindling. He pulled one of the logs half out of the firebox, let it rest right next to newspapers, and splashed oil around on all that, too. He put some oil on Cindy and Aaron, leaving about an inch in the bottom of the container, which he returned to the kitchen.

Wait, would an investigation discover traces of that oil on them, and assume a crime? Well, it's too late now.

The downstairs was filled with books. That stuff would go up easy, ideally, so the fire could jump to the wooden furniture and take the rest of the house. At least that was the idea. Man, he was making it up as he went along, not knowing what he was doing. He hoped it would be good enough.

He found long wooden matches on the mantel and lit the paper in the fireplace. It caught quick. He littered loose matches on the floor as if someone had been standing there and dropped them, making sure some of them were in the oil spots. He lit a match and touched it to the edge of the newspaper pile and dropped it onto a cluster of matches on the floor, igniting them. He tossed a lit match onto the coffee table where the flames caught the alcohol. The last, most distasteful act was to light the oil and alcohol on Cindy and on Aaron.

He left through the back door. This being his first foray into arson, he wasn't sure what to expect. Would the fire take the house, or only the first floor? He'd be happy with the living room, as long as Cindy and Aaron were consumed and took enough evidence with them to make an investigation difficult. He stood watching in the back yard and was surprised to see the fire blazing. The books were helping, apparently, as hoped.

As the glass in the first floor windows burst from the heat, Matt started down the road. Before he got to the big boulder, he turned to see the house overcome by flames. It was then he remembered the safe in the bottom of the utility closet, and wondered what was in it. He should have tried to get it out, maybe put it on one of the dollies and wheel it to the car, even though that thing was *heavy*. Too late now.

He listened for sirens as he rounded the hill, but there weren't any, not yet. He hoped the snow would have dampened the area enough that the fire didn't spread to the woods. He also hoped it didn't jump the road and set the barn on fire, those feral cats needed that home. He worried about the cats and wondered who would feed them.

He asked himself, *How am I doing?* Well, he answered, his primary goals were in good shape, he was on the verge of coming out of this smelling like roses. How about the secondary goals? Aaron was no longer a problem, and Matt was proud of himself for taking care of that. He felt bad about Cindy, it was nasty business. He was a little surprised he had the stomach to do it. It must be what people mean when they talk about reaching deep inside and doing what was necessary to succeed. Maybe he should be the influencer, not Sofia!

Oh no, Sofia… He stopped short of his car door, startled by the realization, thinking it through. She knew how angry he was, and that he was coming up to the mountain to provoke a confrontation. He may have openly threatened Aaron in her presence... This was not good. Sofia could be as dangerous to him as Cindy.

On the other hand, there was a chance she would never hear what happened. She'd assume Aaron lost interest in her, and wasn't he the type to do that? There would be a record of calls between them, he imagined, but a man like Aaron spoke on the phone with all kinds of people all the time, clients, sponsees, girlfriends. No reason for Sofia to stand out.

He got in his car.

God forbid, the police might follow a lead that brings them to Sofia. What were the chances she would turn on him? She had always protected him, in her way. Supported him when she could and if it wasn't inconvenient. Would she believe him a murderer, and hand him over to jackbooted thugs to rot in prison? When all he did was defend himself, and defend the life he and Jesse had waiting?

For that matter, could he do to Sofia what he did to Cindy? No, of course he couldn't, never in a million years. Besides, there was time for that question, a long time before events transpired to make the topic relevant. He'd think about it later.

He might have heard sirens in the distance, possibly. Had the flames grown so strong they reached above the trees, to be seen by Aaron's neighbors down the road? It was time to go. He'd drive away, head home, and go on with his life.

The car wouldn't start.

Forty-nine

Matt's car was dead. What could have happened? He had plenty of gas. Did the battery die? Oh, right. Aaron said he had disabled the car. Matt didn't believe him, but the fucker actually did it. Matt's understanding of cars was limited to how to drive them. He was parked at the top of the mountain, around the bend from a fire he started, and he was stranded. How long would it take to get a triple-A truck up there? Would the police be aware of him somehow, all the way on the other side of the mountain, and question his presence? If asked, what explanation would he offer for why he was there?

He needed to calm down. He had gotten out of that tight spot in the Blue Blanket Inn. He had talked his way through the interviews with Detective Wisler. He had managed the threat Aaron posed. He was able to think ahead about Cindy. He could deal with this.

He could walk. If he could get down to where the restaurant was he could grab an Uber and get home, come back later for his car. The walk would give him time to work things through, run different scenarios, be better prepared.

On the other hand, after the fire was out the police might investigate the area, what with the bodies and the rifle, and see an unfamiliar car at the shuttered repair shop, and question why it was there and where did the owner get to? Exactly what he didn't want. He needed to get the car fixed and out of the area as soon as possible.

He phoned for a repair truck.

It was agony, hearing the fire sirens approach Aaron's house on the other side of the crest, frightened that a police cruiser would pass any minute. But the repair truck arrived more quickly than Matt expected. The driver was a chubby kid about twenty-one or twenty-two, pink-cheeked and beardless, wearing a thick canvas barn coat and a dirty yellow Pittsburgh Pirates cap. When he hopped out of the cab of the tow truck, he gave Matt a nod, and said, "A fire truck passed me, going up the road on the wrap-around I think. Might be a house fire."

Not sure how to answer, Matt nodded.

"Name's Petey, how you holding up?" asked the kid. "What you doing up here on the mountain?"

Matt hadn't prepped enough, hesitated, and said, "Hoping for new hiking opportunities."

"The old Gregory trail?" Petey stepped back, surprised.

"Uhm, yeah."

"Hardly anyone knows about it anymore. Lot of it grown over. Someone told you about it, I guess?"

"Yeah." Matt was along for the ride, trying to hold on.

"I used to go along it myself, at least until the railroad trestle. You could walk almost all the way across it, but they closed it when a couple of drunk guys went too far and one of them fell off. People were saying they were gay as if that had anything to do with anything, but I said that's not the important part, the important part was they went up there drunk and that's what happens."

Petey tried to start the car. He unlatched and lifted the hood and inspected the engine. "Well now," he said, "no wonder you're not going nowhere, somebody ripped out your spark plug wires."

"Oh. Didn't take you long to figure that out."

"Usually I get a call and it's a real car like this one I can tell pretty quick what's going on. I was afraid coming up you might have one of them new electric sedans and there's not much I can do for you but tow it. This one should be easy."

"Easy?" Matt was afraid his car would be stuck there for days, waiting for a part.

"Depends on if you're lucky or not," said Petey, turning and starting across the road, followed closely by Matt. "Probably this group of boys live down the way done this. I call them boys but they're like a year younger than me, we went to school together. I got a good job, make a decent salary with tips and all, but none of them has a job and no prospects and don't have anything to do all day but get high and cause trouble. A couple of them live on the west side of the mountain down near the creek. It's a basin, their houses get flooded. Don't have enough money to move, but fixing a house after a flood is expensive, so their families are screwed either way. Makes them boys bitter and eager to cause pain to other people. My mom says to pray for them but I don't know what good that will do."

Petey checked the bushes along the side of the road. He made a noise of discovery, reached into a bush, and pulled out spark plug wires. "Here's two of them. Help me find the others." It didn't take long before Petey was putting them back in place.

"How did you know where to look?" asked Matt.

"It's the kind of thing them boys do," he said. "Vandalism, mostly, not stealing. I said to myself, if they didn't want to keep them, where would they throw them? Bushes seemed most likely. If not there I would've been staring into the trees."

Matt paid cash for Petey's services, and added a forty percent tip in gratitude.

When Matt came down off the mountain, he resisted the temptation to drive up Aaron's road far enough to rubberneck the fire, see how much of the house was left. He was careful to stay within the speed limit, and minded all traffic laws. He didn't want to get a ticket that placed him anywhere near Aaron's house.

***

When he arrived home he had time to do a little job research online, putting together a list of possibilities that made it seem like he had been productive that day. When she arrived home Jesse was a bit disappointed the list was so short, but pleased Matt had been putting in some effort to do the right thing.

That evening Sofia called him, to check up on how he was feeling, and whether he had calmed down.

"I'm better," said Matt. "I thought about what you said, and never went up to see Aaron. You're right, I need to let things go. Focus on my future with Jesse."

"Good," she said, laughing nervously. "I wanted to make sure you hadn't killed anyone since I saw you last!"

FIFTY

To the Sanford Township police department, which had jurisdiction over Aaron's house in Larnersville, it had all the signs of a murder-suicide after a bout of day drinking and squabbling turned violent. There had been a fire in the fireplace that went out of control once the two of them were dead, fed by all the books.

Aaron's computer and other electronics were still in the house, and his car was in the drive, so it didn't seem like robbery. Cindy's estranged husband was in Massachusetts at a sales meeting, nothing there either. Two people had seen Cindy that day and noticed she was already tipsy well before noon. Co-workers at the restaurant confirmed that Aaron and Cindy had a sometimes tense on-again, off-again relationship.

"I told her I didn't trust him," said Cindy's sister. "He seemed to be mostly out for himself."

Conversations with a few of Aaron's neighbors made it clear he maintained a rotation of girlfriends. They would see the procession of middle-aged women driving up and down in their cars, to and from his place, rarely the same one for very long. It was impressive for someone his age, said one sad-faced man sitting on his riding lawnmower. Several neighbors reported how some of those relationships ended with loud fights, they could hear the shouting in the middle of the night.

"One time I saw his girlfriend of the moment, a tall, skinny thing with a lot of dark hair, storming down the road in a blouse and underwear, holding her shoes and her skirt," said an elderly woman who lived a hundred yards down the hill. Her knitted eyebrows and curt nod of the head made it clear what she thought of such goings-on.

Monroe County did not have a medical examiner, it had an elected coroner. The coroner was not a doctor, he owned a funeral home in Mount Pocono. He determined that an autopsy was not necessary in this case, given the circumstances and the available evidence. He certified that cause of death for Cynthia (Cindy) Archer of Larnersville was a gunshot wound to the head, and that cause of death for Aaron Stoltzfus, also of Larnersville, was a self-inflicted gunshot wound to the head. The official conclusion, then, was murder-suicide.

It appeared to be a tragedy all around.

Since neither Aaron nor Cindy were famous, rich, or important to the citizens in the region, the story received little coverage. There was a brief, two-paragraph summary in the Pocono Times, a daily out of Stroudsburg. The free weekly Pocono Call, which claimed to be a newspaper but was mostly a collection of ads, didn't mention it at all, and neither did the Larnersville Vista, a monthly community event publication. Then everyone went about their business and forgot about it.

***

Matt fell into a depression in the days following the fire on the mountain, overwhelmed by what he had done. He watched television, barely ate, and made feeble attempts to talk with Jesse. He told her he was fighting a bug, and needed rest. Sitting there, doing next to nothing, he told himself a story about how he had no choice, that Aaron, through his various forms of secretive harassment, had forced him into drastic action. Over the course of a few days, the story became richer and more nuanced, with additional details illustrating Aaron's maliciousness in contrast to Matt's youthful naïveté. By the time he was done justifying and rationalizing, the killing of Cindy was nearly a matter of self-defense.

As he hoped, Matt shortly snapped out of his funk. He saw the brief obituaries online for Aaron and Cindy, published by the mortuary. He did not attend their funerals.

He settled back into his life. With Aaron's twelve thousand, he was able to play poker again without dipping into savings and battling Jesse about it. He did pull back on the gambling trips, however. He and Jesse agreed he would limit his full Atlantic City weekends to no more than once a month. Alternatively, he could indulge in no more than three day or evening visits to the poker room in the Bethlehem casino. But he couldn't do both Bethlehem and Atlantic City in the same month.

"These are guardrails, because you need them," said Jesse. Matt thought the comment uncharitable, but let it pass without response.

To his surprise, he took to heart a lot of what Aaron told him about luck, and it paid off. He began playing a smarter brand of poker, with a more conservative approach to betting. He wasn't winning more hands, necessarily, but he wasn't so reckless, and dropped earlier, so he wasn't losing as much as before, resulting in substantial savings in opportunity costs. Which meant he could extend his poker career, such as it was.

He also looked up Alan Watts, and took a couple of his books from the library. It all read like a rambling mish-mash of dreamy confusion to Matt, like being stuck in a room with Aaron babbling his stories that were supposed to open his mind and turn his life around. He wondered if you needed to be from Aaron's generation to get any meaning out of it. He returned the books early.

With Jesse's input, he started seriously exploring job possibilities. She convinced him his experience at the back and the front of restaurants gave him valuable skills he could use in other fields, many of them restaurant-adjacent but not within a restaurant setting. He could do food or beverage sales, she explained, or event planning. She said to consider restaurant consulting, helping new businesses get started, which would allow him to use all his knowledge but keep him far away from the chaos of day-to-day operations. The possibilities did begin to intrigue him. It was slow getting started—creating a good resume was a lot more work than he expected—but it was forward movement.

***

Jesse was at first alarmed by Matt's behavior, she saw it as depression, but reluctantly accepted his explanation that it was a virus. She didn't believe that, not in her gut, as she never fully believed his stories about the motel, or about that man Aaron, or about his trips to the New Jersey shore.

Nonetheless, she made peace with her version of trusting him. Because what option did she have? When you're in a relationship with someone, you're obligated to trust them, or at least take an official position that you do and convince yourself that you must. You can't have a real relationship always anticipating the worst of your partner. The illusions we sustain about the people we love.

She knew Matt wasn't like most people, his mind worked differently, and he felt things differently. But if she could redirect at least some of his energies toward a normal career, he could be more like the person she imagined he was when she first met him. That might be the best she could hope for.

Jesse turned to her own career, taking a course in project management her employer paid for. Work was heavily projectized at her company, and if she could get a certification it would be a path to promotion, not to mention more interesting activities.

***

Sofia struggled. After she made the phone call to warn him about Matt, she never heard from Aaron again. News of his death and the fire didn't reach her, so she was surprised and hurt by the sudden silence. Initially she hoped he was giving himself a little time to think about it. Then she became tired of waiting and phoned him. He didn't answer, over days of attempts. She blamed her brother for poisoning the relationship, and herself for intervening, even though she did so out of genuine concern for Aaron's safety. She assumed Aaron was exasperated with her family, that it was too much drama for his tastes. On her final attempt to reach him the message said the number was out of service.

"Are you sure you never went up to Aaron's after you found out about me and him? Or talk to him on the phone?" she asked Matt. They were sitting at her kitchen table, going over some paperwork related to a recently discovered pair of their father's savings accounts that had small balances and needed to be closed out.

"I told you, I never talked to him," said Matt. "I guess I got it out of my system, throwing a fit in your porch."

"He hasn't phoned, and he's not picking up when I call him."

Matt nodded sadly. "He's ghosting you, Fifi."

"That would be shitty," she said, waving the thought away.

"He's a jerk, like I said."

"Can you go up and check on him, see what's going on with him and me?"

"Uhm, I don't think so. I don't want to get involved."

"I'd go up but I don't even know where he lives."

"He seems like the kind of guy wouldn't appreciate a surprise like that, anyway."

She nodded. "Last time I tried calling him it said his number was out of service." The genuine concern on her face hurt him inside a little.

"I don't want to bruise your feelings," he said, "but I know he was seeing some waitress up there, he mentioned that to me." His eyes roamed the kitchen, anywhere other than looking at her. "Maybe they got married."

"That would be quick."

"Yeah, I guess it would. But he was old, probably figured he didn't have much time left."

"He was only in his sixties. Also, people don't change their cell phone numbers when they get married, Matty."

"He might. Maybe she made him do it, she didn't want other women calling him anymore. Like a fresh start."

"Stranger things have happened, I guess." She let it drop.

Believing Aaron ghosted her was the gateway to believing her brother did not commit any of the acts Aaron accused him of, but instead was the victim of a manipulative older man. Just as it appeared she was also a victim of the same man, someone not as trustworthy as he first appeared. As Matt said, Aaron was a smooth operator.

Sofia continued on with Pastor Steve until he delivered an ultimatum one evening, while they were having dinner at the Olive Garden near Collegeville. If they were to continue seeing each other, he said, she needed to become a member of the Estuary Chapel. It would require her to make a public profession of faith during a worship service, and also undergo a believer's baptism. They usually did the baptisms all at once in Skippack Creek, he explained, so that part of it would need to wait until warmer weather. She informed him there was no need to wait until warmer weather, she could tell him right then and there the answer was no, she wasn't doing some creepy ritual and joining a church.

The breakup gave her some good material for her dating blog, however. A couple of posts went more viral than normal.

It turned out that the coffee shop owner with the small dog in New Hope, who ended their relationship before it began due to his anxieties about her social media presence, had become a regular reader of her blog. He followed her tales of disappointment about being ignored by one man, and breaking up with another due to his religious fervor, and saw an opportunity to give it another go. He felt bad the way he left it that day, he explained to her when he phoned, and he would like another chance. Perhaps, he suggested, there's a way they could negotiate issues of privacy so that they both got what they needed. She said it was worth a try.

***

In New Ringgold, about an hour and a half southwest of Larnersville, Jake Stoltzfus stood in his garage, thinking about Aaron's floor safe that had been delivered and placed in the corner. It was one and a third cubic feet, approximately sixteen inches square on the outside, sixty-two pounds empty and a lot more than that now with whatever was inside, secured by a combination lock. It was obviously fireproof and waterproof, considering it made it to the other side of the fire and the hosing down from the pump trucks. He was told it was found in a utility closet, at the corner of the house furthest from the source of the fire, which helped it get through the blaze and, with luck, improved the chances of the contents surviving intact despite the heat.

Jake was Aaron's cousin, and executor of the estate. Jake didn't ask for this chore, but you don't always get to pick your own adventure.

Aaron had created three copies of his will that Jake was aware of. One had been sent to Jake, years earlier. Another was a digital copy in a secure account in the cloud. The third was, presumably, in the safe. Aaron's will was clear and thorough, explaining what should be done with the house, his books and art, and his financial accounts. The will also discussed in detail a few of the items to be found in the safe, such as the jewelry, while referring vaguely to cash and other valuable items and paperwork. The will said the combination to the safe could be found taped to the inside back cover of the book Aaron had "stolen from Jake," which referred to an old hardback copy of Joseph Heller's *Catch-22* that Aaron had borrowed when they were both in their twenties and never returned, which became a running joke between them. Unfortunately, that book, along with most of Aaron's library, had been destroyed in the fire.

Which was why Jake stood in his garage, waiting for the locksmith to show up.

FIFTY-ONE

J ake watched the locksmith, who sat on the ground as he inspected the safe. New Ringgold had a population of under three hundred, so Jake had to bring in a locksmith from Pottsville. It was a half-hour drive, with Jake paying for the man's travel time to and from. Opening the safe was going to be expensive, and Jake hoped the contents would be worth it.

"How do you open a safe like this without the combination?" he asked. "Cut it open with a saw? Or dynamite?"

The locksmith gave him a little side-eye. "Not dynamite."

"Heh heh, I was kidding," said Jake, who decided the man had no sense of humor. He should have come to that conclusion when the locksmith arrived. All business, the first thing the man did was demand to see the death certificate and proof that Jake was the executor of the estate. Maybe it was important to be careful in the man's profession.

"There's normally a few ways we can do this," said the locksmith. "We can cut it open with a metal saw, like you said, which is loud and messy, with the metal dust, filings, and so forth. Also sparks. Can damage the contents. So it should be our last resort."

"Yes. Sparks would be bad," said Jake, thinking of the junk that cluttered his garage, much of it flammable.

"This is a Donjon home model safe, which is bad and good news. Bad news, in that I'm not experienced enough with them to know how to manipulate the lock, even with specialized tools."

"You mean like a safecracker?"

"Kinda. The good news is we should be able to drill a small hole into the side of it, insert a scope, and deactivate the lock from the inside.

I've done that before, on models like this, lucky for you. It will damage the safe, though. You said you don't care about that, right?"

"Right."

"Otherwise you might have to go to the manufacturer for special service and that can take a long time, if they can help you at all."

"No. If you can drill in and get it open then please do it."

***

Jake and his wife Lena sat staring at the contents of the safe, spread across their dining room table.

"Did the locksmith see what was inside?" asked Lena. She was thin, like her husband, wearing a plaid flannel shirt several sizes too big over a thin turtleneck. Her eyes were wide as she surveyed the items.

"No," said Jake. "He was professional about it. Once he made sure the door was open he got up, took his fee, wished us luck, and left."

"Good. We wouldn't want him coming back in the middle of the night with his buddies."

The jewelry lay on a clean kitchen towel. It included a double-strand pearl necklace, with matching earrings, that Jake assumed was fake but Lena said no, these are the real thing, otherwise they wouldn't be in the safe. A platinum ring with a large solitary diamond accompanied by diamond baguettes on either side. Three brooches, one with an emerald in the center, the other two in gold plant patterns. Ruby earrings. Several gold necklaces.

"These seem like they're from the fifties or sixties," said Lena.

"The will says they belonged to Aaron's mom, so yeah."

There was a short pile of documents, mostly legal, related to ownership of the house, some additional property in southern New York State, and financial accounts. There was an original copy of Aaron's will, as well as his passport. On top was a sealed envelope, with Jake's name on it.

What had the full attention of Jake and Lena were the four stacks of fifties and hundreds, each over three inches tall. Jake hadn't counted the money yet, but he did a quick estimation and breathlessly announced it was probably around two hundred thousand dollars, maybe more.

"What was your cousin up to?" asked Lena.

"Knowing Aaron, I'd say tax evasion," said Jake, running his finger down the edge of a stack.

"I'll make tea," she said, going to the kitchen.

Jake reached for the envelope. Inside was a handwritten letter, dated before the fire. When Lena returned she found her husband in thought, deep lines in his brow and a slight tremor in his hands.

He met her eyes and said, "Babe, I think we need to call the police."

FIFTY-TWO

The Sanford Township Police Department didn't get a lot of mysteries, therefore this one intrigued them plenty. The letter written by Aaron Stoltzfus prior to his death described Matthew Martinez as young, somewhat naïve, and self-centered. Yet it suggested Martinez got away with staging a fake murder-suicide in Larnersville and, astonishingly, claimed he was responsible for an entirely separate double homicide in Norristown.

"The kid sounds like a doofus," said the police captain as they sat around the conference table in headquarters, shaking their head in amazement at the letter. "He'd have to be the luckiest young man in the country to get away with this sort of thing twice."

A digital copy of the letter was sent down to Detective Evelyn Wisler of the Norristown force, as Aaron directed the police to do in the letter. The subsequent Zoom call was notable for the unspoken embarrassment and regret both departments felt about the things they may have missed and the wrong choices they may have made. Internalized self-recrimination hung over the conversation like stale cigarette smoke.

"It would appear your victim Mr. Stoltzfus was the same man who repeatedly phoned our hotline pressuring us to arrest Matthew Martinez," said Detective Wisler.

"Just cause it's in the letter, doesn't mean it's true," pointed out the Sanford Township police captain.

"No, it doesn't. The evidence didn't point that way, and we already had a suspect who confessed. But we'll need to make sure."

"Maybe you'll be going back over your tracks," said the Sanford Township police captain.

"Yes, maybe I will."

"Meanwhile we'll see what we can find up here. According to the letter Martinez spent time on the mountain, at the Stoltzfus property, and meeting Cynthia Archer. Someone must have seen something."

***

Aaron's letter said Matt met Cindy at an Alcoholics Anonymous meeting in the church, and that seemed like a good place to start. Unfortunately, by definition membership in AA is anonymous. People know each other only by first names, a lot of them false for extra privacy, and members treat the confidentiality of the program as sacrosanct. It wasn't easy for the police to know who to speak with, who might have been at that one meeting Matt attended. They eventually identified three people who admitted they were there on the day mentioned in the letter. One didn't recall seeing Matt at all. The other two didn't remember much about the young stranger, other than he didn't speak up. Neither saw him talking with Cindy.

They didn't get much further at the restaurant. The waitress who worked that day was a gray-haired woman with a slight limp and a defiant attitude, and she was not enthusiastic about talking with the police. She knew Cindy was a member of AA, she said, and preferred giving people their privacy. She remembered Cindy coming in with someone, but couldn't recall anything helpful about it. When police showed her a picture of Matt, from his driver's license, she offered them a "maybe."

Cindy's sister didn't see her with Martinez, nor did any neighbors.

Aaron's house was mostly a charred hull, so there was no evidence. They found nothing in the barn.

They were getting nowhere.

Then one morning a chubby, pink-cheeked young man in his early twenties wearing a thick canvas barn coat and a dirty gold Pittsburgh

Pirates cap walked into the police station. He introduced himself as Petey, and said he drove a tow truck for his uncle's auto body and repair shop. The police sergeant said he was familiar with the auto shop.

"I heard you've been asking around about someone who might have been in town the same time as that house fire up there, where they found the two bodies," said Petey. "I had a call up there on the other side of the crest, where the road wraps around. A nervous guy, from out of town. Didn't think anything of it at the time, but now I'm wondering if I can you help you any."

The police sergeant eyed Petey up and down and said, "Son, you are the stroke of luck we've been hoping for."

***

"We've got an uncertain identification of Martinez having lunch with the female victim in a local restaurant," the Sanford Township police captain told Detective Wisler over Zoom. "But we've got a solid identification of him up on the mountain at the time of the fire, from a local boy who drives a tow truck and had to rescue Martinez when his car was incapacitated around the bend from the victim's house."

"Incapacitated?" asked Wisler. "What was wrong with his car?"

"The spark plug wires were pulled out and tossed in bushes across the road."

"That's weird."

"Ain't it though?" The captain nodded. "Our witness said he thought it might be a group of punks enjoy giving people trouble around here, doing petty nuisance stuff like that. Would make sense to me, except it's a big coincidence it happened when it did, and to who."

"I hear you," said Wisler.

"Him being up on the mountain at that time tells me he was involved in whatever went down, at least was there when it happened, but it's not much to go on. We could drive down and talk with him about it, see what he says, but that would tip our hand, spook him. I'd rather have more to press him with."

"I agree, we don't want him to see us coming too early."

"How are things going on your end?"

"There were three things that pretty much eliminated Martinez as a suspect," said Wisler. "One was him being in Atlantic City, or close to getting there, when the murders happened. But the bodies weren't discovered for nearly thirty-six hours, so time of death is a rough guess at best. Plus we don't have an exact time for when he left that bar, because goodness knows none of those drunks were watching the clock. They couldn't even agree what show was on the television. All of this means the time range is just loose enough to allow for Martinez to kill them and then be on his way to the shore."

"So he doesn't have a solid alibi. What are the other two?"

"I'll tell you when I'm done punching holes in them"

***

A steady, light rain had been coming down all day. Detective Wisler parked in the lot of the Blue Blanket Inn, and gingerly stepped around the puddles. Everyone turned to her as she paused inside the door of the bar & grill to pull off the hood and undo the buttons of her raincoat. She recognized most of them from previous interviews, and she quickly found Janice Duma in her usual spot, nursing her usual vodka and cranberry, watching a tall female weatherperson on the television talk about the storm. Wisler went directly to her and requested that they have a chat. Janice's eyes immediately betrayed her anxiety as the detective suggested they move to one of the three booths on the far wall, near the shuffleboard, for privacy.

"I told you everything I know," said Janice as she sat down.

"I know that," said Wisler. "No cause for you to be fearful. You told us what you could. I'm sorry to say I now realize we weren't listening well. Remember when you said you saw the male victim, Anthony Ciccone, leaving the motel in his gold sweatshirt?"

"Yeah...?"

"You said he was walking down the stairs. Which means he was facing toward the front of the motel, toward Church Street. You were near the rear, isn't that right?"

"Yes, ma'am. I was going to take a nap."

Wisler nodded. "You never saw his face, did you? You saw the sweatshirt, but he was walking away from you, so you never saw his face."

Janice thought about it. She clenched her drink tightly. "No, don't think I did. The fella I saw was big, Anthony was big, it was his sweatshirt. It was him, far as I could tell."

"Yes, that makes sense. But isn't it more accurate to say you assumed it was Anthony, given everything you said?"

Janice grimaced, and held the glass even tighter. Her eyes darted across the room, and back. "It was the honest truth, what I said... though I didn't think about seeing his face or not, until you brought it up now."

"Totally understandable. We should have clarified that point when we first spoke to you."

"If it wasn't Anthony, then who was it?" asked Janice. "Why would they steal such a god-awful sweatshirt?"

***

Christopher Roberts sat at the interview table in the Montgomery County Correctional Facility, where he awaited proceedings. He was a lean man in his fifties, average height, with a bulging belly like he was moderately pregnant. He sat a little stooped, like he thought he might hit his head on the ceiling. He had short, mostly gray hair, with streaky patches of dark brown. Blue eyes stared fearfully out of thin-framed glasses, and he hadn't had a shave in a few days. Periodically he pulled his lips back in a nervous grimace, revealing remarkably healthy teeth.

Across from him was Detective Wisler.

"I like your outfit," said Roberts. Wisler wore a dark brown suit over a pale blue button-down collared shirt open at the neck.

"Thank you, Mr. Roberts. Though with your history, complimenting a woman's appearance can be viewed as inappropriate."

"You can call me Cooter."

"I think we'll remain a little more formal, but I appreciate the gesture. How are you doing? They treating you okay?"

"Sure, I guess. They have a decent library; I'm in there a lot. I work in the kitchen, which is what I did when I was in before."

"You like that, do you?"

"What, kitchen work? It's okay. We all have to eat, and I like cooking and learning about cooking. But when I was at the motel I couldn't do any of that."

"Do you feel safer, more secure here? Than outside, I mean?"

"A little." His eyes rested on her, with an unhurried intensity, and he crumpled his brow. "Why did you ask me that?"

Wisler did a little throat clearing and moved a few inches forward in her chair. "What I want to know," she said, "is why you confessed to killing Debrah Maines and Anthony Ciccone even though you did not."

He sat staring at a spot above her right shoulder for a long time. She remained still, and quiet, as she waited. Muffled voices could be heard in the distance. A machine hummed in another room, somewhere close. The room smelled faintly of cleaner with a trace of fried chicken. She watched the gears move behind his eyes. His shoulders sank, not in despair, but in release: he had come to a conclusion, and he visibly relaxed.

He asked, "Why do you say that?"

"Because I know it's true. I'd like you to tell me about it.'

"I don't know what to say."

She nodded. "How about I ask you questions, or share some conclusions, and you respond. As best you can. How is that?"

"Okay."

"We know there were a couple of loud arguments between you and Anthony, prior to the murders. What were they about?"

"He told me to stay away from Debbie."

"Why?"

"I don't know. He didn't like the way I looked at her."

"Is that why you stole the knife?"

"Yeah. The second time, he was yelling at me, calling me names. Tony was a bully. We were waiting for Debbie to come up."

"To a motel room?"

"Yeah."

"The same one where the murders took place?"

"Yeah. We usually met there, when it was unoccupied."

"What did you do there?"

"Got high, mostly. Talked. He'd sometimes have stuff he needed to get rid of, and I had contacts. So we'd sit there and I'd call around and set up a meet for him, to go make a deal."

"Fencing stolen goods, you mean?"

"I made the calls. I wouldn't come with him. I wasn't involved in any transactions."

"Fair enough. So that second time, when he was calling you names. You were mad?"

"Yeah. He went to find Debbie, and I saw he left his backpack. The knife was in there, and I took it. You could tell it was expensive, I thought I could move it, get a little cash."

"And you hid it under the bed?"

"I heard him coming and I threw it under the bed, thinking I'd figure out a way to come back for it later. I never did."

"Then you had another argument about the knife, he accused you of stealing it?"

"I denied it. What else was I going to do? I didn't have it on me. He wasn't smart, he never thought to check under the bed."

"And there it stayed until the murders?"

"Somebody was lucky to find it when they needed it."

"Why the confession then, Mr. Roberts? Why say you did it?"

Roberts became silent again, before he spoke. "I'm not sure. I've done a lot of things I shouldn't have. I got away with most of them. They haven't made my life better, they've made it worse, taking everything into consideration. When the police came for me I thought, why not this?"

"What do you mean, why not this?"

"They were going to be putting me back in for something else, eventually, so it might as well be killing Tony."

"Why is that, Mr. Roberts?"

"Because he deserved it."

FIFTY-THREE

Matt Martinez sat in an interview room in police headquarters in Norristown, within Municipal Hall on Airy Street. Across the table was Detective Wisler. Off to the side, against the wall, leaned a uniformed cop in his thirties, watching but not talking. Wisler had made introductions, but Matt wasn't paying attention, though he got the idea the cop was from up in the Poconos and was there because of Aaron. Matt averted his eyes from the cop's stare, and looked over to Wisler. She was reviewing something in her notebook. Matt believed she had more, and deeper, lines in her face than last time.

"This is a bigger room than the other one," said Matt. "Not nearly as nice, though."

"Their station is a lot newer than ours," said Detective Wisler, without looking up. "This place is over fifty years old, and I'd be surprised if they've done anything to fix it up since I was in diapers."

"Why are we here?" asked the soft-voiced young man sitting next to Matt. His name was Kermit McKay, he was short with thinning sandy hair and a pale gray suit, and he was a lawyer. Sofia had made the connection, when Matt found out he was being called in for questioning. Kermit agreed to represent Matt during the initial interviews phase as part of the pro bono obligation placed upon him by his firm, but explained he would not be able to adequately represent Matt should he be arrested and charged with a crime.

Sitting in that room filled Matt with dread. The feeling had been building since the police contacted him again, demanding that he come into Norristown to answer questions. No doubt, this time it was going to be an interrogation, and they would be treating him as a suspect. He knew it from their attitude during the phone call. He knew it when both Sofia and Jesse reported the police detective had reached out requesting an interview, which both declined, thank goodness. He knew it from the hostile vibe in the room.

What had been keeping him awake at night was the question of evidence. Had he left fingerprints in the room or on the knife? Did they find security footage placing him in the wrong location at the wrong time, doing the wrong thing? What had changed?

"You're here because we now believe you were responsible for the deaths of Debra Maines and Anthony Ciccone in the Blue Blanket Inn, and also responsible for the deaths of Aaron Stoltzfus and Cynthia Archer in Larnersville."

Matt hadn't expected such an unadorned, unrestrained accusation. It was going to be all business, then.

"Those are extremely serious allegations," said Kermit the lawyer. "My client is an outstanding young man, a good citizen, a Norristown native and the son of a late, highly respected local businessman, restaurateur, and beloved member of the community. He's never been arrested nor had any past dealings with the police, not even a speeding ticket. Yet now you're painting him as an unhinged mass murderer. You better have plenty of convincing evidence, detective."

As Matt tightly clasped his hands and listened intently, Detective Wisler went over the range surrounding the time of death of Debra and Anthony, that it was broad enough to accommodate Matt killing them and then making it to Atlantic City. She told them the suspect originally arrested, Christopher Roberts, had made a false confession, and explained how Roberts had stolen the knife and hid it under the bed, where it could be found by Matt.

She even mentioned the man seen leaving the motel wearing the victim's gold sweatshirt, watching Matt's reaction, which never changed.

She acknowledged that neither Sofia nor Jesse would cooperate with a police interview. Digging into their lives in search of someone who might be able to provide information about Matt's activities, however, they came across the leader of an off-brand church, as Wisler put it, called the Estuary Chapel. Pastor Steve, still sore about being dumped by Sofia, was able to firmly connect Matt with Aaron, citing a specific moment in the parking lot after the funeral service for Matt's father. He also told of fears Sofia expressed to him about Matt's frame of mind toward Aaron, and her concern Matt might mean the older man harm.

As the cop against the wall nodded in agreement, Wisler told of the conversation with Petey the tow truck driver that placed Matt on the mountain at the same time as the death of Aaron and Cindy and the fire at Aaron's house. Finally, after a dramatic pause, she said that Aaron had left a handwritten, signed document that went over all of his dealings with Matt, Matt's confession of the murders, and Matt's threats toward Aaron.

So there it is, thought Matt. *No fingerprints, no security footage, just a poison pill Aaron created in case something happened to him. His last malicious gesture. Another one of his annoying stories.*

Kermit touched Matt's arm in a gesture for him to remain silent. "This is all speculation based on circumstantial evidence and the bitter rantings of an apparently deranged individual" said the attorney, folding his arms. "If you had anything of substance you would've just arrested him outright. This was a performance, running through an array of assumptions in an attempt to browbeat us. Perhaps to make us consider a plea deal."

"Circumstantial evidence puts people on death row," said Wisler.

"Pennsylvania hasn't executed anyone for over a quarter century."

"It's still on the books, Mr. McKay, pointing at a sizeable death row population."

As the lawyer and the detective bantered, Matt remained lost in thought. *They have nothing*, he realized. *They have absolutely nothing*. The one thing different from before was that the police now *believed* him to be guilty, rather than believing him innocent. This shift was based almost entirely on Aaron's say-so, and most of what Aaron had to say was second or third hand, all of it open to interpretation and dispute. Even better, what the police knew, and believed they knew, aligned well with the story Matt had been telling all along, especially the version he had recently told Sofia and Jesse. He needed to remain steadfast, and to trust the women to remain quiet.

"I want to make a statement," said Matt.

"No, you don't," said Kermit.

"But I do. Everything you went over, Detective Wisler, is in keeping with what we spoke about the last two times. Yes, I was in the bar at the motel, and talked to Debra for a minute or two, then left and drove to Atlantic City. Loose timeline or not, I was far away when the murders took place. I was never in that motel room, never saw Anthony, never saw a gold sweatshirt. Yes, I met Aaron in Atlantic City. He cheated me out of some money, we had words, he admitted he cheated and gave the money back. I thought that was the end of it. Unfortunately, I didn't realize how unstable he was, and how treacherous. He undertook an entire campaign to harass me and frame me for those murders, and even insinuated his way into a relationship with my sister so he could observe and manipulate. He came to my father's funeral, supposedly to pay his respects, and at his insistence we established a truce. I took him at his word on that. But he continued his harassment and defamation, now including that letter."

"You confronted him that day, didn't you?" asked Wisler.

"I went up there to talk to him about it, to understand why he was doing all that. But I didn't know exactly where he lived. I eventually realized I was lost, and never found his house. So no, I didn't confront him."

"You didn't see him that day at all?" She had the slightest smile. "Even though you were parked half a mile away?"

"I didn't know I was that close. The roads aren't marked well up there and I took the wrong one. I parked at the closed car repair shop and walked up a long driveway nearby, thinking it might be Aaron's house, but it wasn't. I walked a little further down the road, couldn't find it, and when I got back to my car it had been vandalized. The tow truck driver said it was local kids. He fixed it and I drove home. I didn't hear from Aaron again and assumed he lost interest in me. I didn't know he was dead until you informed me."

The four of them sat in silence for a minute. "Are you done?" asked Wisler.

Matt sighed, then started up again. "The only reason you think I had something to do with it is not because of any evidence, but because of his insane letter. Which means my attorney can't even bring him in and do a deposition. I have to defend myself against someone who can't be questioned about his false accusations because, from what you said, he was so unstable and dangerous that he committed murder-suicide. I feel victimized here."

Wisler made a small, derisive grunt. "Are you suggesting Mr. Stoltzfus killed Ms. Archer and himself just to blame it on you?"

"I would never be so vain as to think anyone would be capable of that. I just think, based on what I heard from you and what I witnessed myself, that he was fixated on me and just doing everything he could to create trouble and chaos. He was like the old story of the fisherman, when a boat drifts into his. If the boat is empty he just accepts it as a routine incident, shrugs his shoulders, and goes around. But if he finds someone asleep in the other boat he becomes pointlessly enraged, demanding revenge. Same problem, same solution, but now that man has someone to blame and it changes everything. That boat bumping into Aaron was all the things in his life that were going wrong, that disappointed him, that failed him. He wanted to put *me* in that other boat, to blame *me*, to take revenge on *me* for some reason, when he really just needed to get his life together. No one was there to help him see that, and it ended up with two people dead for no good reason other than too much alcohol and too many lonely, empty, sad days."

The uniformed officer leaning against the wall spoke for the first time. "A boat," he said. "The man thought you were in a boat?"

Matt glanced at his lawyer, who nodded his head. "I think we're done here," said Kermit. "You have no cause to arrest my client. You don't even have enough for a search warrant, or you would have done that already. So we'll be on our way."

***

Story against story, thought Matt as he and Kermit the attorney left the building. *And mine will win out in the end.*

Matt was confident that his story made sense and held up to scrutiny. He had no reason to kill any of those four people, did not own a weapon, and would have to be a supervillain to pull it off without being hurt himself and leaving a mountain of evidence. How could anyone believe a young, clean-cut suburban man like himself was capable of such crimes, especially since there was no motive?

Aaron's story, on the other hand, was clearly the ramblings of a vindictive old man driven off the edge by his isolation, and history of interpersonal conflicts.

Things were going to break Matt's way.

"That was a pretty good speech you gave in there," said Kermit. "But next time I tell you to be quiet, be quiet. Okay?"

Matt nearly responded, thought better of it, nodded.

"So you understand, handwritten documents are admissible, as long as they can verify authenticity," added the lawyer. "Doesn't mean a jury would believe it, necessarily. They could see it as an unstable man spouting off paranoid accusations. But they'll be allowed to read it. However, if you're lucky, that letter's all they have. I don't see how it makes a case against you. Have a good day." He shook Matt's hand.

Matt drove over to Eve's Lunch on Johnson Highway to get a zep, a particular kind of sandwich only available in Norristown, made with cooked salami, provolone, tomato, raw sweet onion, olive oil, and oregano. He had his with hot peppers.

He sat there eating and thought about what Aaron had said about stories. How poker players love them. How stories define us, the way we use them to construct our identities and to guide our behavior. Aaron, with an ability to influence others through his endless sack of bullshit, helped Matt to understand reality as a tale we create through the stories we tell ourselves and each other, and Matt was witnessing that unfold in front of him. Aaron weaponized a story against Matt, and Matt was going to do the same back. He would mold a truth he could live within, where he was safe from Detective Wisler and that cop leaning against the wall, where Sofia and Jesse had faith in him, and where he could be the truest version of himself that he was willing to put on display. The zep was a celebration meal, for having conquered Norristown's criminals and authorities both, and freed himself of the personal history he had with the town. He had been reborn.

As he watched the cars drive by, and the parade of customers dropping in for a sandwich, Matt also thought about the most important reason he would get away with everything. It was, of course, because he was a lucky guy.

AUTHOR'S NOTE

T hank you for reading *Lucky Guy*. Please consider leaving an honest review on the site where you purchased it, or on Amazon, Goodreads, or other platform of your choice. I'll be genuinely grateful, as your feedback helps other readers discover this story.

***

I had completed my debut novel, *Nina's Friends*, the initial entry of the Tajna Circle series. Before diving immediately into the second book (titled *Bent City)* I turned instead to *Lucky Guy*, for two compelling reasons. First, I was interested in exploring what philosophers call "moral luck," how our behavior is often judged based on circumstances beyond our control. Second, the two main characters, who first appeared in an unpublished short story set in a casino, noisily demanded attention and were telling me who they wanted to be in novel form. When that sort of thing happens, I tend to listen.

The character who became Matthew wanted to be an anti-hero protagonist with undiagnosed neurodivergence. The character who became Aaron wanted to be a conflicted Mephistopheles, à la Christopher Marlowe. I had my hands full with the two of them.

***

As the novel acquired shape, a couple of big influences took hold. I'm a long-time fan of Ridley Scott's first feature *The Duellists* from 1977, one of the best movies you've never seen. It's a beautifully crafted story of two French officers during the Napoleonic Wars who absurdly carry on a violent series of duels over twenty years, to the point where they can neither remember, nor explain, why they're still fighting. It is faithfully adapted from a 1908 Joseph Conrad novella *The Duel*, which itself is a fairly accurate account of an improbably real, decades-long rivalry at the turn of the 19th century. The literary critic Laurence Graver, in his 1969 work *Conrad's Short Fiction*, astutely said the conflict between the two men combined irreconcilable antagonism with irrational affection. That's how I feel about Matthew and Aaron in *Lucky Guy*: two odd, stubborn men locked in a love/hate relationship neither can give up on. It is part jealous competition, part patriarchal psychodrama. It was never going to end well (though the sources did share a happy-ish resolution).

I had also come under the spell, again, of Patricia Highsmith's 1955 novel *The Talented Mr. Ripley*, thanks to the 2024 miniseries *Ripley* with Andrew Scott. It is more faithful to Highsmith in both story and spirit than the 1999 Anthony Minghella version with Matt Damon, which is an entertaining movie but a poor adaptation. Ripley is an (ironically) untalented small-timer just trying to get by who falls into his European situation, wants to keep it going, but there are challenges and the stakes keep rising so what's a guy to do? The miniseries with Scott galvanized my desire to create a protagonist who ends up a criminal, whose character arc is towards becoming a worse person than when the story starts, rather than a better one.

***

One of the benefits of writing fiction when you are an older adult is that you have a lifetime of people and places and experiences to draw from, buffet style. *Lucky Guy* is a product of that. As is the case with most of my fiction, this book is chockablock with real things from my past. I'm originally from Norristown, and I resided in that motel during a horrific period of my life, though I didn't murder anyone there. I lived for a time in that upper Bucks County apartment, and I've visited that isolated house high up in the Poconos when it was owned by a friend. The San Francisco poker game story is essentially true. My father was in a hospice like the one described, and my last words to him as he lay in a coma were as full of disappointment as Matthew's. Many of the supporting characters are composites of real people I've known along the way. The lesson, obviously, is to pay attention since everything can become source.

When I was an undergraduate film student at New York University back in the seventies, one of our professors left mid-semester to pursue a good opportunity that came his way, and before he went he grabbed some paint and high on the wall opposite the equipment room he wrote, "Whatever happens, don't close your eyes." I've seen the same sentiment numerous times since, but that version, in that context, always stuck. Life is so rich and diverse and crazy and energetic, people are so weird and funny and exasperating, if you keep your eyes and ears and heart open you'll never be short of fantastic material to work with.

And yes, Matthew will be back.

James Irwin, northern New Jersey, October 2025

ACKNOWLEDGEMENTS

Many thanks to Jill Irwin who is the best beta reader, sounding board, sanity checker, travel partner, and loving supporter. If someone asks who my ideal target reader is I hold up a picture of her.

Thanks to Michael Ray for the early dialogue about the short story that eventually transformed into Part Two: The Casino. He asked detailed questions demanding answers, and thought the story could expand into something much longer (which it did: this novel). Also, we compared thoughts on Robert Bresson's *Notes on Cinematography* and I was delighted, it's not every day I get to do that.

Thanks to Nick Irwin for his perspectives, insights, and ongoing conversation about design.

Thanks to Tanya Anevski for being such a cheerleader and for harassing me to write more, and more quickly. I don't meet her expectations, I'm sure, but the cloud of urgency helps keep me motivated.

Finally, huge thanks to the readers of my first novel, *Nina's Friends*, for kindly giving me such positive feedback. It made all the difference.

ABOUT THE AUTHOR

James Irwin is the author of the novel *Nina's Friends*, as well as an array of short stories, essays, and creative non-fiction pieces. He used to be an award-winning media artist and university professor, and held leadership roles in national and international marketing communications. Originally from southeastern Pennsylvania, he now lives in northern New Jersey. He can be found at jrirwin.com